D1464222

# MANCH
## CITY COUNCIL

Please return / renew this item
by the last date shown.
Books may also be renewed by
phone or the Internet.

**Tel: 0161 254 7777**

**www.manchester.gov.uk/libraries**

By Kristen Callihan:

Firelight
Moonglow
Winterblaze
Shadowdance
Ember (ebook only)

# KRISTEN CALLIHAN

# WINTERBLAZE

## THE DARKEST LONDON

piatkus

PIATKUS

First published in the US in 2013 by Forever,
an imprint of Grand Central Publishing,
A division of Hachette Book Group, Inc.
First published in Great Britain in 2014 by Piatkus

A CIP catalogue record for this book
is available from the British Library.

ISBN 978-0-349-40604-6

Printed in Great Britain by Clays Ltd, St Ives, plc

Papers used by Piatkus are from well-managed forests
and other responsible sources.

MIX
Paper from
responsible sources
FSC® C104740

Piatkus
An imprint of
Little, Brown Book Group
100 Victoria Embankment
London EC4Y 0DY

An Hachette UK Company
www.hachette.co.uk

www.piatkus.co.uk

*I have always thought of this as Alex and Lauren's book. Without them, Winston Lane might have died in a dark alleyway after tangling with a werewolf.*

*And that simply wouldn't do.*

*Therefore, I thank you, and Winston most certainly thanks you!*

# *Acknowledgments*

As always, many thanks to my dedicated and wonderful agent Kristin Nelson. My hardworking and astute editor, Alex Logan. The awesome Grand Central/Forever team, Amy Pierpont, Lauren Plude, Jennifer Reese, Megha Parekh, and countless others—every day, I thank my lucky stars to be working with you.

To my family for their never-ending love and support, especially my husband and children who treat this job as though it was a team effort—and I suppose they're right!

Thank you, Amy Noble, for bidding on and winning the Darkest London package for the Brenda Novak Online Auction for Diabetes Research. I hope you enjoy your namesake.

Many thanks to Jenny Harlett and mixologist Krishna Ramsundar for the highly educational, if not slightly intoxicating lesson on absinthe. Any mistakes I made regarding the Green Fairy are solely my own.

And to the reviewers, bloggers, and readers who have spread the word about my books, given me support, and absolutely made my job worth it. I cannot say enough how much it means to me. You are my inspiration.

# WINTERBLAZE

WINTERBLAZE

# *Prologue*

*And now dear little children, who may this story read,*
*To idle, silly flattering words, I pray you ne'er give heed:*
*Unto an evil counsellor, close heart and ear and eye,*
*And take a lesson from this tale, of the*
*Spider and the Fly.*

"The Spider and the Fly"
Mary Howitt

*London, 1869, Victoria Station—An Auspicious*
*Beginning*

Winston Lane could never recall the impetus that prompted him to leave the confines of his first class railway compartment and step back onto the platform. The whistle had sounded, long and high, indicating that they would soon be off. And yet, he'd felt compelled. Was it for a quick draw upon his pipe? The need for a bit of air? His memory was muddled at best. Perhaps it was because the *whys* did not matter. From the moment he'd stepped off that train, his life changed completely. And it had been because of a woman.

Now *that* he remembered with the vividness of a fine oil painting. Great billows of hot, white steam clouded the cold air upon the platform, obscuring the shapes of the few railway workers attending to last minute duties, giving their movements a ghostlike subtlety. Idly he watched them, interested as always in the activities of the common man, when through the mists she emerged. It might have been lyrical had she been gliding along in peaceful repose, but no, this woman *strode*. A mannish, commanding walk as if she owned the very air about her. And though Winston had been raised to appreciate ladies who exuded utter femininity and eschew those who did not, he'd snapped to instant attention.

She was tall, nearly as tall as he, this assertive miss, and dressed in some dull frock that blended into the fading light. The only spot of color was her mass of vivid, carnelian red hair coiled at the back of her head like a crown. So very red, and glinting like a beacon. One look and he knew he had to have her. Which was rather extraordinary, for he wasn't the sort prone to impulse or rash feeling. And certainly not about women. They were interesting in the abstract, but one was much like any other. At nineteen, he was already set in his ways: orderly, bookish, and logical. Save there was nothing logical about the hot, hard pang that caught him in the gut as she walked by, her dark eyes flashing beneath the red slashes of her brows.

The pipe fell from Winston's hand, clattering upon the ground as he stood frozen, surely gaping like some slack-jawed idiot. She did not appear to notice him, but kept walking, her long legs eating up the ground, taking her away from him. This, he could not allow. In an instant, he was after her.

He nearly broke into a run to catch her. It was worth it.

The scent of book leather and lemons enveloped him, and his head went light. Books and clean woman. Had God ever divined a more perfect perfume? She was young. Perhaps younger than he was. Her pale skin was smooth, unlined, and unmarred, save for the tiny freckle just above her earlobe. He had the great urge to bite that little lobe.

She did not break her pace, but glanced at him sidelong as if to throw out a warning. He did not blame her; he was being unspeakably rude approaching this young lady without a proper introduction. Then again, they were the only ones on the platform, and he was not fool enough to let her out of his sight.

"Forgive me," he said, a bit breathless, for really this woman was fast on her feet, "I realize this is rather forward and usually I would never—"

"Never what?" she cut in, her voice crisp and smooth as fresh linen sheets. "Never proposition young ladies who have the temerity to walk unescorted in public areas?"

Well, now that he thought of it, she really ought to have a guardian with her. She did not appear to be from great wealth, so he wouldn't expect an abigail, but a sister or an aunt perhaps? Or a husband. A shudder went through him at the thought of her being married. He mentally shook himself, aware that he'd been staring at her, memorizing the sharp slope of her nose and the graceful curve of her jaw.

"I would never presume to proposition you, miss. Indeed, should any such scoundrel approach you, it would be my pleasure to set him to rights." And now he sounded like a prig, and a hypocrite.

She smirked. "Then let me guess. You are a member of the Society for the Protection of Young Ladies and Innocents and want to make certain I realize the perils of walking alone." Cool brown eyes glinted as she glanced at him, and Winston's already tight gut started to ache. "Or perhaps you merely seek a contribution?"

He could not help it; he grinned. "And if I were, would you listen to my testimony?"

Her soft, pink lips pursed. Whether in irritation or in amusement, he could not tell. Nor did he care. He wanted to run his tongue along them and ease them back to softness. The image made him twitch. He'd never had such importune thoughts. Yet speaking to her felt natural, as if he'd done so a thousand times before.

"I don't know, is your testimony any good?"

Like that, he was hard as iron. His voice came out rough. "While I am certainly capable of extolling the virtues of my testimony, there is only one way for you to truly find out."

When she blushed, it was a deep pink that clashed beautifully with her hair. "Well, you certainly talk a good talk," she murmured, and his smile grew.

They neared the end of the platform. Behind them the train gave one last, loud whistle.

His cheeky miss quirked one of her straight brows. "You'll miss your train, sir."

"Some things are worth missing, and some are not."

Coming to the stairway, she stopped and regarded him. When she spoke again, her voice was hard and uncompromising. "What do you want?"

*You.* "To know your name so that I might come to call upon you properly." He made a leg, the extravagant sort he'd done at court recently. "Winston Lane at your service, madam."

For the life of him, he did not know why he'd held back giving her his full name. The lie shamed him, and he moved to correct the blunder, but those pink lips twitched again and good intentions flew from his mind. What would it take to get her to truly smile? What would she look like flushed with passion? His skin went hot.

Her dark eyes looked over his shoulder. "Your train is leaving."

The platform beneath his feet trembled as the train groaned out of the station. He didn't even look. "I find," he said, keeping his eyes upon her gloriously stern visage, "that I no longer wish to leave London."

Unsurprisingly, she held his gaze without a blush or one of the coy looks the ladies in his sphere would have employed. "Do you always act the fool?"

*Never.* But he didn't have to say it. She read him well, and her eyes suddenly gleamed with acceptance. Slowly, she held her hand out so that he might take it. "Miss Poppy Ann Ellis."

Poppy. For her hair, he supposed. But to him, she was Boadicea, Athena, a goddess.

It was all he could do to keep himself from bridging the short distance between them and putting his mouth to hers. Instead, he took her hand with due formality. His gloved fingers curled around hers, and something within him settled. He shook only a little as he raised her hand to his lips. "Miss Ellis, I am your servant." *Always.*

Yet even as he spoke, fate was conspiring to make a liar of him.

# *Chapter One*

*The West End, August 28, 1883*

*A telegram, as sent to the SOS Home Office:*

> Daughter of the Elements STOP All of
> us must reap what we sow STOP Now it
> is your turn STOP I'll take not the
> heart of ice that resides in your
> sweet breast but the fragile one
> that beats in another and sail away
> with it on a ship of fire STOP When I
> tear it to shreds you will remember
> the agony of failing STOP Again STOP

The way to her parlor was along a winding stair, but down, not up. Down in the pit of the earth where sunlight and fresh air never reached. Yes, a proper English parlor with electric lights and air forced by means of an elaborate fan system—such strange modern devices that even the most jaded persons took a moment to stop and wonder.

Poppy had recently shown her sister Daisy the way in, a fact that she was beginning to regret as she settled back in her desk chair and surveyed the two women sitting in front of her. One of the women was Daisy, looking luminous as ever and trussed up in an extravagant frock which was no doubt highly fashionable, and equally uncomfortable. Having ferreted out Poppy's secrets with surprising speed, Daisy had earned the right to be here.

The other woman was the problem. Miss Mary Chase. Oh, she sat demure and quiet as Daisy prattled on in that way of hers, but the girl's glittering eyes took in every nook and cranny of Poppy's office. Learning and secreting away bits of information as only a GIM could do.

GIMs, or Ghosts in the Machines, were the best spies in the underworld. Blessed by a demon to have an immortal body with the ability to leave it in spirit form, they could drift into any room, listen in on any conversation. And now this GIM knew the way to Poppy's office. Bloody hell. Poppy had requested to speak with Daisy. She had not expected her sister to bring along a guest.

"Well?" Daisy prompted, breaking into Poppy's thoughts.

Poppy took a short breath and pulled herself together. Something that was getting harder and harder to do. Inside she was frozen and fairly certain that, one day, her outer skin would simply freeze over as well.

"You want me to bring this girl to Mother," Poppy repeated, her lips feeling numb. Mother was the head of The Society for the Suppression of Supernaturals, or SOS, an organization whose sole focus was to keep the world from learning the truth: that the monsters in their fairytales were real. Mother, whom no one, *no one*, ever met. Really, the nerve of Daisy sometimes. Poppy tapped her fingers to relieve the urge to wrap them about her sister's lovely neck.

Daisy too was a GIM. A decision she'd made in the face of a gruesome, prolonged death. She'd saved herself by making a devil's bargain. And now she would never die. Daisy would be here long after Poppy was dust in the ground. It made Poppy unaccountably sad, though she really couldn't say precisely why.

Daisy glanced at Poppy's thrumming fingers. Poppy instantly stopped. Daisy too tapped her fingers when she was agitated. A stupid slip to do in front of her sister. Damn it all.

When Daisy replied, it was with exaggerated patience. "Not precisely. I am here to make an introduction to Mother."

Poppy froze. Daisy could not possibly be implying what she thought she was. "Why did you not bring your request to Lena?" Poppy hedged.

Daisy's eyes gleamed bright for one sharp moment. "I had assumed my sister would be a little more accommodating. Perhaps I was wrong."

Poppy looked away first. It had been petty to bait Daisy. While Lena was Mother's official go-between and requests for Mother always went through her, she had also been Ian Ranulf's lover years ago. As Ian was now Daisy's husband, the women did not particularly find each other's presence comfortable.

"Look," Daisy leaned forward, her tone forgiving when Poppy knew she'd normally drag out her displeasure, "Mary is the best GIM we have."

"Then why do you want to lose her?"

Mary Chase stirred. "If I may speak for myself?" There was a bit of fire in her eyes, something Poppy had to admire, and so she nodded. Miss Chase settled her slim hands on her lap as she faced Poppy without blinking.

"My term of service with the GIMs is over." Her hands clenched for a moment. "Mrs. Lane, I want to be a Regulator. I have wanted this for some time."

Poppy managed not to wince upon hearing her name. Mrs. Lane. A farce, for her husband had left her. The pain that lived in her chest spread out to her arms and then down to her fingers. She didn't allow it to show but let her gaze wander over Miss Chase. The young woman appeared to be all of nineteen, but from Poppy's reports, she was closer to Poppy's own age, having lost her first life in 1873.

"I gather you know this," Poppy answered. "However, I feel compelled to remind you that being a Regulator is no easy task. They live a hard life, and it is often quite short." Regulators were the SOS's agents, men and women on the front lines of the supernatural world. They came face to face with things that gave monsters nightmares. Poppy leaned in a touch. "And believe me, many an immortal's head has rolled while on the job. Just because you cannot die, doesn't mean you cannot be killed, child."

Mary Chase's wide, brown eyes narrowed. "I am not a child. And I'm not afraid of death."

Poppy rose from her desk, no longer willing to sit still. "Everyone says that." She grabbed her thick cloak. "And then they discover that, in their heart, they have lied. I don't believe GIMs get a second chance should they lose their head, do they?"

"No," Mary said after a moment.

"Come."

The two women rose and followed her to the door. Poppy walked through it, not waiting to see if they kept up. Outside of the office, Mr. Smythe sat at his desk, his pasty skin blending with his grey hair. He faced a vast and dark corridor, and oftentimes Poppy wondered how he could stand looking into that abyss on a daily—sometimes nightly—basis. Mr. Smythe, however, never complained. He gave her a deferential nod as she passed. She had worked alongside Smythe for fourteen years, and yet he did not know about Winston or that she had a fondness for meat pies sold by street vendors. Not one person within the SOS truly knew her. People tended to stay away from Poppy as though they felt she was something alien and not like them. Which said quite a lot, given that most of her colleagues possessed gifts that were the epitome of unearthly. She did not precisely mind the isolation. She had Winston.... Poppy's step nearly halted. She did *not* have Win. He was gone. And she was alone.

"I had a good reason for this, you know," Daisy murmured just behind her as they slipped into the stone-lined corridor. Here and there electric torches glowed, turning Daisy's blond curls a harsh yellow. Mary Chase followed at an inconspicuous distance, her eyes lowered and subservient. *Ha.* Men might be fooled by the display but not Poppy.

"You better have," Poppy said, just as low. "You've come quite close to breaking my trust today, Dandelion."

Daisy made a noise of annoyance at the nickname, but she quickened her stride to catch up and then grabbed Poppy's elbow, forcing her to slow down. "Pop. Listen for a moment, will you?"

Every muscle in Poppy's body went heavy and cold. She knew that tone in Daisy's voice, as well as the soft, despicable pity that dimmed her eyes. "Well," Poppy said through her teeth, "out with it. And then explain what it has to do with Miss Chase here."

Daisy took a stabilizing breath. "She knows." Her voice dipped a bit. "Who you are."

The struggle not to break something, or *someone*, held Poppy in place, frozen with shock and outrage. Daisy took a half step back, her mouth opening and closing like a puppet's, her hand lifting as if in defense. Smart woman. Poppy couldn't fathom why her sister would break her trust in such a manner.

Poppy advanced. "Have you lost your nut? What on God's green earth gave you the right?"

Daisy's pointed silence gave her a moment's qualm, which Daisy pounced on. "I agree that it is bloody irritating to be managed by one's sister." Poppy scowled, and Daisy ignored it. "However, as you've been known to point out, I have only the best intentions." Daisy touched her arm. "You need a companion, Pop."

A harsh laugh burst from Poppy. "You think I'm that infirm, do you? I bid you to remember that I am thirty-two. Hardly ancient, despite what your society friends might think."

"I do not think that you are ancient, Pop," said Daisy quietly. "I think that you are in pain."

"Do not." Poppy took a sharp breath. "Do not ever pity me, Daisy."

Bad enough that her sisters knew Win had left her. It had been humiliating. But that was nothing compared to the emptiness and the dull, unwavering ache that his absence wrought upon her.

In the gloom, Daisy's eyes gleamed like star sapphires, the effect of her new GIM nature when emotions were roused within her. "Pity and empathy are not the same thing."

"You have brought a GIM to keep me company," Poppy snapped, "as if you fear I might do something drastic."

What nonsense. Poppy did not do drastic things. She

simply died a little more inside each day and wished the world to go away. That had not worked particularly well; the world was still here.

Daisy's gaze searched hers. "Mary is loyal and discreet. And she is entirely trustworthy. On my life, I swear that."

"Good thing to swear, as your life might very well be what I take." It was entirely too temping at the moment.

"I am shaking," Daisy said with an unladylike snort before becoming serious once more. "You need someone to keep you focused. And lord knows that bitch Lena will not do that for you. She's just as likely to stick her fangs into your neck when your back is turned."

"You really ought to get over your dislike of Lena."

"Pish," Daisy said with a wave of her hand, "that woman means nothing to me. And you know full well that I speak the truth in regard to her character."

Unfortunately, Daisy was right. Lena wasn't the helpful sort. She despised weakness even more than Poppy did.

Poppy sighed, then looked at Mary Chase who hovered just beyond the circle of light where Daisy and Poppy stood. The young GIM had drifted back, having correctly read Poppy's request for a modicum of privacy. Poppy turned back to Daisy. "I asked you here because I seek information, not a nanny."

"Then ask away," Daisy retorted. "Mary won't tell a soul, and as she is currently *my* right hand, I'd tell her anyway. So you can drop that repressive glare, Pop."

Just once, Poppy would love to wring her sister's neck. Hell, Daisy would easily recover so it wouldn't be outright murder. She studied the unflinching Mary Chase for a long moment. Sensible woman, crafty, discreet. It could all be a lie. Poppy's life depended on her choices. Which meant she had to use more than logic, but instinct as well, to survive.

"All right then, Miss Chase," she said to the woman. "You have your chance."

Miss Chase curtsied prettily. "Thank you, Mrs. Lane."

"Don't thank me just yet. A demon has escaped his prison," she said to them. "I received the report from Lena an hour ago. The only information we have of his current whereabouts is from a telegram, which may or may not have been sent by him. It makes mention of a ship of fire." Her hand rested upon the cold, stone wall. "It is imperative that the SOS locate him. Immediately."

Needing to move, Poppy turned away and strode up the cast-iron staircase that spiraled upward. Heels clanked upon the metal, then Poppy reached the top and turned the handle, which released several heavy bolts. The heavy door pushed open without a sound, and the familiar, comforting scent of books and wood polish greeted her as she stepped into her bookshop.

Daisy and Mary followed, and then she pushed the door shut and heard the sound of the bolts slipping back into place.

Daisy's pretty face was pale. She knew something. *Damn.* Instinct had Poppy's hackles rising before Daisy even spoke. "Winston is on holiday in Paris."

"Paris? Win hates Paris." Poppy had tried to get him to take her there on holiday years ago, and he'd outright refused, calling it a heathenish, boorish city, filled with wastrels and gadabouts. Poppy told him he'd overstated his case, but Win had made it up to her by keeping her in bed for their holiday, giving her an interesting demonstration of his own rather heathenish proclivities.

Thankfully, Daisy responded before Poppy could

dwell any further on that time. "All I know is that he went there after..." Daisy nibbled on her bottom lip.

"After what?" Poppy could not cull the worry from her voice. Win had left her, and still she was fretting over him like a bloody mother hen.

Daisy's nose wrinkled. "He beat a suspect to a pulp two weeks ago. The CID let him go, Poppy."

Poppy sagged against the counter. She could not fathom Win losing control of his temper. And the CID was his life. Winston Lane was an inspector, first and always.

What would he do now? How must he feel? Lost, she realized. Win had given up everything to become an inspector, including being cut off from his very powerful family. Daisy's voice broke through her musings.

"He is set to return aboard Archer's boat—"

"Ship. One does not call an ocean liner a boat."

"Ship," Daisy corrected with an eye roll. "At any rate, the *ship* is called *The Ignitus*." Daisy made a halfhearted attempt to smile. "Archer named it for Miranda."

Poppy's heart stopped. Ignitus, Latin for "set on fire."

Daisy's breath came out in visible puffs as the air about them chilled and ice began to crackle over the counter. Poppy couldn't rein in the reaction. Dear God, how had Isley known? She'd been so careful to keep this life separate from Win.

"When is the ship set to sail?" Poppy's body hummed with the urge to move, to run.

"I believe it's due to depart this Friday. That is two days from now." Daisy's smooth brow furrowed. "Poppy, you can't mean to meet it. The bloody thing is in Calais! We are in London," she added with unnecessary emphasis.

Rage pushed its way along Poppy's veins, making her see more clearly than she had in months. "Watch me."

* * *

*Port of Calais, August 30, 1883*

A man cannot run away from his life, no matter how far he goes. It was an uncomfortable truth Winston Lane had learned these past weeks when he'd forced himself to go on holiday. *A bit of rest and relaxation, Inspector, and you'll be right as rails.* Winston hadn't possessed the heart or the energy to correct Sheridan. It was "right as rain" and, no, he'd never be right again. Regardless, he'd taken himself far out of cold, dank London and straight to Paris, where he wouldn't be reminded of all he'd lost. But the holiday had been a dismal failure.

So he was going home. To London. And Poppy. Longing hit him so hard that he ached, the dissatisfied feeling within ebbing in favor of sharp, bright pain. He missed her. Missed her so much he could scarcely breathe. He didn't want to picture her but she came despite his will. Poppy, his Boadicea. She'd always been a warrior in his mind. Her flashing eyes and determined brows were enough to cow most men. As for Winston, her sharpness and strength inflamed him and made him want to slip beneath that hard outer shell she wore, find her softer bits, and do wicked things...

No, he would not think about her. She was an illusion. A liar. For the fourteen years of their marriage, she'd posed as a simple bookseller, while knowing all along about this other world, this supernatural London, filled with mythical beasts such as werewolves. And she'd kept it from him. Up until the day one such beast had ripped him to shreds.

But he'd avoided her for too long. It had been a cowardly and small act. He wanted an explanation, and he wanted to say his piece. And he'd have to face her as he was—a shell of a man.

"Now that's a bloody big boat," said Jack Talent at his side.

Stirred from his self-flagellation, Winston grunted. "Ship. One does not call an ocean liner a 'boat'."

Despite being thoroughly annoyed with his unwelcome and unexpected travel partner, Winston couldn't help but agree with the young man's assessment. However, "big" did not even begin to convey the magnitude of this hulking beast that would take them from the French port of Calais to Southampton, and eventually go on to New York. It was a giant, rising five stories above them, so high that they needed to crane their necks to see the topmast.

Taller than most London buildings, the craft was easily as long as two city blocks. It blotted out the sun. Standing by it, one felt as infinitesimal as a bug. And yet Winston could not help but be moved by this true feat of modern engineering. As was the six-story paddle wheel that gleamed in the morning light. One of two, the paddle wheels at full spin would take this leviathan and its four hundred passengers up to a speed of 15 knots.

"Leave it to Archer to purchase a ship such as this," he said.

Talent's mouth twitched. "Perhaps he felt the need to compensate for something."

Winston turned to Talent. "Perhaps you ought to tell him that yourself. It would save me the trouble of dispensing with you." He'd been trying to rid himself of the young man ever since he had entered Winston's railway car on the trip to Paris two weeks earlier.

"What are you doing here?" he'd asked as Talent plopped his carcass on the seat bench opposite him.

The young man who served as Ian Ranulf's valet looked back at him, unabashed even though Winston was certainly glaring a hole through his skull. "Ian sent me. I'm here to guard you."

As if the boy were a bloody nanny. Winston had wanted to be outraged. Except, after the attack, Ian and his other nosey brother-in-law Archer had given Winston the one thing he'd desperately needed, a sense of control after he'd been ripped apart and pieced back together. Not quite good as new. But alive.

Since the day he could move without biting pain, Ian and Archer had cajoled, hassled, and finally harassed him into coming to Ranulf House to train his body. They'd taught him how to fight, both with hand and sword, thrown medicine balls at him, and made him lift sacks of grain until his scarred and battered body screamed in protest. It had been a systematic torture of the flesh that had put nearly twenty pounds of muscle on his weakened frame and had made him capable of taking down a man twice his size with one punch. Unfortunately, that didn't help when the nightmares that haunted Winston were not of men, but of monsters.

So, having been unable to get rid of the pest, Winston was stuck with a pseudo-valet on a holiday that had made him more out of sorts than before. At the moment, Talent looked no less thrilled. His eyes scanned the sky, and a frown grew. "Something is off. Have you not noticed the sky?"

Indeed, for days now, the sky had been a boiling red sea shot through with streaks of black and vermilion. An ominous tapestry that sent a queer feeling through Winston's gut. "The color is a result of Krakatoa."

News reports had already come in that the far-away Pacific island volcano had erupted with cataclysmic devastation; half the island was gone in an instant. So great was the fallout that, even in Europe, volcanic ash filled the skies.

"See, now there is your first mistake, being a human and all." Talent's expression turned grim. "A volcano eruption is always cause for worry. For something *always* gets out."

Winston pushed the brim of his hat farther down on his forehead as a wind flew over the docks and sent bits of rubbish airborne. Around them, fellow travelers clutched their own hats and hurried toward the grand gangplank that led them up into the *Ignitus*. "Gets out?"

"As in gets out of hell. A volcano blows, and all sorts of nasty beings use that crack in the earth's crust to get to freedom."

Yet one more thing Winston would rather not know. He pulled in a lungful of briny air and then grabbed his valise. "Not to worry, Talent. Should a messenger from hell come calling, I will do my best to protect you."

Talent snorted. "And they say you don't have a sense of humor, Inspector."

*Chapter Two*

❦❦❦❦

Like all the other passengers, Winston and Talent stood on upper decks to see the *Ignitus* get underway. The ship's horn blew, long, low, and resonating with such strength that his flesh vibrated. As if awoken by the horn, the ship shuddered to life like a great beast coming out of hibernation. Far below, blue-green water began to froth and foam as the heavy paddle on their side of the boat started to spin. Most travelers were on the port side of the ship, wanting to see Calais fade away. Not Winston. He faced the sea, and where it would take him. Home.

He almost missed the subtle change in the air. At first, he thought the cold wind a sudden sea breeze, but the air had gone oddly still. The strangeness had him pausing. He glanced at Talent. The man's eyes narrowed as he peered out over the sea. He felt it too, then. In the next moment, distinct cold surrounded Winston. Colder and colder, until his breath came out in a puff.

Talent backed up a step. "What the bloody hell?"

Winston opened his mouth to answer when a faint

crackling sounded. Before their rather shocked eyes, a lacy ribbon of frost began to race over the rail. Winston snatched his hand back as white fingers of ice spread out in rapid fire, covering everything in its path. Around them came the sound of confused murmurs.

The crackling sound grew as the temperature dropped to frigid. And then the great ship groaned and shuddered. Winston and Talent both leaned over the rail and looked on with fascinated horror as the water about the ship turned to thick, unimaginable ice, and the bloody ship began to rise, trapped as it was within the ice's clutches.

Talent's mouth fell open. "Bugger me."

Winston was inclined to agree. "Come." He plucked Talent's sleeve to get the man's attention. "To the port side." Something was coming. He could feel it.

Stumbling and treading with care along the slick, icy deck, they made their way to the port side, shouldering past gawking passengers, most of whom milled about in a frightened and confused state. Crewmembers called for order, stumbling along much like Winston and Talent, as they tried to figure out what was happening.

"Look," said a young girl. "Someone is boarding the ship."

Several people shot to the rail and craned their necks to see.

Winston and Talent followed suit. The gangplank, which had been in the process of being removed, had been frozen in place. A woman strolled, pretty as you please, up it. Winston's heart flipped over in his chest. He drank her in, the steady clip of her legs beneath a fetching gown of black and white stripes, the determined set of her shoulders. A matching parasol obscured her face, but he'd know that walk anywhere. *Christ*. His body hardened painfully.

As if she felt his eyes upon her, the parasol tilted back, and she lifted her head. Even though he had to be a mere dot among the throng from her vantage point, she found him immediately. Those severe red brows, that dark, knowing gaze. A bolt of pure heat and lust shot through him, strong enough to make him suck in a draught of air. *Bloody. Buggering. Hell.*

An old gent beside him scowled beneath white, shaggy brows. "Who the deuce is that?" he asked no one in particular.

"Trouble," muttered Talent, his glare fixed on the young lady walking at Poppy's side. Winston recalled her as Mary Chase, assistant to Daisy Ranulf.

Winston did not know how Poppy had found him, or what the devil she was doing here. The only thing that he knew with absolute certainty at that moment was that Talent had been correct. Here came trouble.

Getting onboard had been a bit of a...spectacle. It could not be helped. Poppy wasn't about to watch the blasted ship sail away. Upon meeting a very harried looking first mate, who wanted to know what the devil was going on, she handed him Archer's card and letter of introduction, which simply told the captain that Poppy was to have carte blanche while aboard, bless her brother-in-law.

"Bring this to your captain and have someone see to my trunks. They are to be placed in Mr. Winston Lane's cabin directly."

Her little show had taken almost all of her energy. And she would need so much more of it before the day was out. The first mate's befuddled gaze went from her to the ice surrounding the boat and back. With an inward sigh, she addressed him once more. "Yes, it is rather strange weather we're having. Now," she nudged him with the tip of her parasol, "you're dawdling, sir. I suspect your captain will want an update."

Twitching as if coming out of a trance, the man finally glanced at the card. As it belonged to the owner of the ship, he started before giving her a curt nod. "Yes, madam. Of course. Welcome aboard."

He promptly left. As soon as he did, Poppy pulled in a long, deep breath and closed her eyes. The air about her warmed, and with a final pull of power, the ice that held the ship captive dissipated, causing the air to mist. The ship shuddered and swayed a bit, and a good many of the passengers shouted. Gods, but it hurt more to rein in her power than to set it free.

Miss Chase caught her elbow as she wavered. "Very well done, Mum."

"Child's play." Poppy straightened her spine. "Now to the real task. My husband."

Poppy found Winston as the ship left the harbor and the throngs of people dispersed, happy now to have gained something to speculate over for hours. He was by the rail of the first class deck where she'd initially spotted him. Waiting for her. The sight of him in the flesh was too much. He was the sun on a cloudless day, burning bright, making her vision blur. Would he speak to her? What would he say? Three months. Three months of not seeing him, not hearing his voice.

He stood, not in his usual straight-backed manner, but slouched against the railing in indolent repose. Watching. Like a leopard lazing in his perch.

The man she knew as Winston Lane had been lithe of form, his wheat blond hair swept back and neat, his mustache always trimmed and a point of pride. She remembered the day he started to grow one. It had been the same day he'd joined the CID. Most Yardmen wore mustaches, and thus, he announced, so would he. And while she'd missed the smooth feel of his upper lip, it had looked quite distinguished so she did not complain. But that elegant man was gone.

The man who faced her now had much broader shoulders and arms swelling with muscles evident even beneath his loose-fitting sack coat. His once short and orderly hair was a shaggy mess, hanging about his face, which she surmised had been in an attempt to hide his maiming. It hurt her to look at those four parallel scars that ran down the left side of his face. Archer had done a neat job of stitching, but the scars were still vivid red and taking up the whole of his cheek, the cruelest one tugging the corner of his upper lip into a permanent sneer. His beloved mustache was gone, the scar obviously making wearing one difficult now. Poppy wondered if he mourned the loss.

The wind shifted, and she caught his scent, a mix of clean wool, fragrant smoke, and *him*. For a moment, she was dizzy with it. His scent hadn't changed. She hadn't realized how very much she had missed it.

Their gazes clashed, and it was like a physical blow. She knew this man. She knew the texture of his skin, where it was silky smooth just above his collarbone and where it was rough along the length of his thighs. She knew the cadence of his breath, deep and even in sleep, and how it rasped in passion. She knew that a little furrow would form between his brows and he would bite his bottom lip just before he came. And he knew her. For a moment, the ghost of his voice was in her ear, whispering words designed to take her to the brink, "Spread your legs wider, sweeting. Show me how much you can take. Come for me."

It took a supreme act of will not to blush beet red.

Winston settled more comfortably against the railing as she came close.

"Poppy." His voice was a shadow of itself, smoky and faint. Her eyes went to the thick scar at his throat, just visible above his collar. Archer hadn't mentioned the possibility of permanent damage there, but the wound clearly affected him.

"Win."

The corners of his eyes tightened. She'd used her private nickname for him. A name that had never failed to soften him in the past. She clutched the handle of her parasol harder. Ye gods but this was awkward. The well-thought-out explanations she'd planned flew from her head, and she blurted out the first inane thing that came to mind. "You're here."

*Blast.*

The corner of his mouth twitched, and she might have thought him amused were it not for the hardness of his expression and the bunching of his shoulders. "Astute as always, my dear."

Heat washed over her cheeks, and the air about her turned a shade colder. The bloody obnoxious . . . At his side, Jack Talent made a coughing sound and wisely looked down at his feet.

Poppy decided to take the high road as it were. "May I introduce my assistant, Miss Mary Chase."

At that, Talent's head lifted, and his mouth flattened. Winston, however, sketched a graceful bow. "We've met before at Ranulf House. Miss Chase, a pleasure as always."

Poppy had expected him to say more, but her errant husband was uncharacteristically abrupt. Pressing her lips together, she gave a nod to Talent. "Good to see you, Mr. Talent. I trust you are well."

"As well as can be expected, madam." His dark green eyes cut to Winston. "Given my pleasant travel companion." He ignored Winston's raised brow and smiled unexpectedly. The action transformed his usually dour face and lit him from within. "You make a welcome addition, Mrs. Lane. Unfortunately, you must excuse me as I have trunks to unpack." The smile died. "Miss Chase."

"Mr. Talent." Mary all but gave the man the cut direct as she abruptly turned and touched Poppy's elbow. "Madam, I shall go see us settled as well."

Poppy waited until Mr. Talent was gone then leaned in close to Mary's ear. "I suspect you might want to take a promenade first or run the risk of meeting Mr. Talent once more." For they were sure to meet in the suite Poppy had taken over. Wisely, Mary nodded then drifted off, catching nearly every male eye in the vicinity as she went.

One pair of male eyes, however, remained fixed upon Poppy. She forced herself not to fume under Winston's stare. After he was attacked and realized that she was one of the SOS, he hadn't even waited for an explanation. That more than anything made her livid. To simply turn his back on fourteen years without a word. But on the heels of fury came a deep, writhing guilt. She'd lied to him all those years. Lying to a man who despised falsehoods and trusted her above all others was a recipe for disaster. Now they were worse than strangers, and she had no idea how to begin the conversation.

"You look well," he said, surprising her. His cold gaze traveled over her dress, and she felt the urge to fidget.

"Different. Did you always dress as such?" His jaw tightened. "When you weren't with me, that is?"

The accusation made her spine stiffen. "Of course not. I detest fancy gowns, as you well know. It is Miranda's gown. She and Daisy tossed a pile of her things together for my use. I am to appear a refined lady on holiday." "Refined" was so far from Poppy's true self that even she could not say the words without wincing. "Try to accept the farce."

"I've come to accept many farces where you are concerned. One more will do no further harm."

"You are determined to make this difficult."

"I am determined to speak the truth. If the truth proves difficult for you, that is no fault of mine."

A ribbon of ice crackled along the railing. Win glanced at it, and speculation crept over his features but, when he turned back to her, his expression was once again implacable and righteous.

With effort, she reeled in the need to freeze over the entire deck. "It shall be no difficulty. Indeed, I relish the opportunity to face the truth, not turn from it and hide away."

Oh, but that got him. His chin lifted so that the light fell directly on the ruined side of his face. Had she thought he was hiding behind his over-long hair? She'd been wrong on that count. His blue-grey eyes, so like deep ice on a winter lake, held hers. He was waiting. Waiting for her to remark upon his scars. And so she studied them ruthlessly.

He did not flinch, nor look away, but a slight tightening of his mouth betrayed his unease. Poppy ignored that mouth. She had to or she would want to touch it with her own. She had always admired Win's lips, the neat line of them and how they could be at one moment so very hard and unyielding, and in the next, utterly soft and beguiling. Instead, she looked at the scars.

The middle scar was slightly puffy, puckering his cheek, while the innermost one bisected his left eyebrow and the corner of his lip before ending at his chin. How it must have hurt. Her heart turned over at the memory of him ripped open and bloody. She had feared she would lose him then, never realizing that she already had.

The moment stretched. When his eyes narrowed in irritation, she shook herself out of maudlin thoughts and spoke. "You've healed well."

The scars pulled as his brow knotted. "Yes."

"Are you pained?" She didn't know what else to say.

Again came the slight twitch in his jaw and the tensing around the corners of his eyes as if he were perplexed. "At times. It is more discomfort than anything."

"I would expect as much." Gathering her parasol— ridiculous accessory as it was neither sunny nor raining— she moved to go.

"That is all?" His scowl was growing.

Poppy stopped. "What were you expecting? Pity? Scorn? Tears?"

He made a sound. "I never expect tears from you."

*How wrong you are on that count.*

"Nor do I want your pity."

"Good. Because you don't have it," she said.

The scars on his face whitened, and though she loathed admitting it to herself, this new Win, slightly wild and angry, stirred her blood. Her voice was not as steady as she would have liked when she spoke again. "Your face is ruined. And what of it? Those who judge you for it are fools. You are alive, which is more than most of the others who met your attacker can say. Why then should I have cause to pity?"

His expression closed down, giving her nothing of what he might be feeling. "Right, then," he said. "Enough about me. Have you come to do the pretty?"

"Do the pretty?" she repeated, aghast.

Win ignored the warning in her tone and smiled at her blandly. "Apologize? Grovel?" His smile grew, but it did not reach his eyes. No, they were full of anger. "Whatever you want to call it makes no difference to me. As long as you do what needs to be done."

*That bloody, smug...* Her blood began to boil as she glared at him. "If, for one moment, you believe that I am going to *grovel*, then you—"

"Belong in Bedlam?" he offered with a sharp bite in his voice.

Damn it, but the man always had a knack for finishing her sentences, and it was bloody annoying.

Cold humor was reflected in his expression, as if he knew he'd irritated her. "Believe me, sweeting, there are days when I wish it were that simple. But madness would be the easy way out, would it not?"

When she simply glared, he launched off the railing and stood before her. "And what is it that you wish for, Poppy? Deep down in that hidden heart of yours?"

He tapped the space between her breasts with one long finger. The gesture was so easily done, borne of years of constant physical contact, that she knew it had been an unplanned act. And yet she felt the touch with the whole of her body. Like a match strike, a flame flared to life within her, and she held her breath. Win felt it too, for he stilled, his gaze catching hers. She could see the shock there, that he hadn't meant to touch her, that he too felt that spark between them, as strong as it had always been. The moment pulled taut before anger filled his blue eyes once more. "Well? What do you wish, Poppy?"

What did she wish? The concept of thinking solely of herself was so utterly foreign that she couldn't begin to formulate a reply.

When Win spoke again, his voice was soft, almost benign, but his anger rang bone-deep. "Do you know what I suspect?"

"I am certain you will tell me, Inspector." Her mouth was too dry, the imprint of his fingertip still burning its way deeper into her flesh.

An ugly smile rose in the wake of her snappish retort. He bent forward, crowding her with his body and his words. "I think you wish I'd simply come home like a good lad and ignore the fact that my entire marriage was based on deception."

Pressure built behind her breastbone like a tide pushing against a dam. It was her turn to poke him, rather like provoking a sleeping bear, by the rumble building in his chest. She did so anyway. "What gives you the temerity to assume that I'd want you after the way you have treated me?"

Of all the looks Win had given her over the years, the one he employed now was something she'd never seen, as if he hated her just then. "You're not sorry you lied, are you? You're only sorry you were caught in the lie."

"Of course I am!" Like most deep truths, it was painful to say. But in the cruel hours she'd sat next to him while Archer put him back together, Poppy had vowed never to keep anything from Win again. No matter what the cost.

He was a fool. An arrogant one at that. Temerity indeed. Winston almost laughed. Of course Poppy hadn't come to beg for his return. Why do that onboard a ship headed to London? It was absurd, but he hadn't been thinking past the anger. Humiliation rode high on the list now, and he had to wonder, had he been waiting for her to find him this whole time? How disappointing to realize that she'd no intention of apologizing for anything. He looked away, squinting into the hazy sky. Any view was preferable to the sight of his wife just then.

They stood in awkward silence. He wanted to leave but was damned if he would do so now, like a dog with his tail between his legs.

A small tinge of hesitation softened Poppy's tone when she spoke. "You do not want to ask me why I am here?"

*Apparently, I was not even close to getting that right, sweeting.* He dragged in a breath, past the pained weight of disappointment. "Well now, let me guess." Lightly, he kicked the rail post, and the iron clanged as he muddled through the possibilities. "Ian has set Jack Talent on my tail. And now my dear wife, who works for the very organization designed to protect us weak humans from supernatural threats, has shown up on my ship." His teeth met with an audible click as he forced himself not to shout. "Which leads me to deduce that you too feel the need to protect my sorry hide." He tilted his head. "Tell me, am I far off?"

"No. I would say you covered the most pertinent points."

He took a hard step in her direction as blood rushed through his veins. "I don't know what is worse," he ground out through clenched teeth. "The fact that you all think I'm so weak that I need several nannies—including my wife—or the possibility that I am, in fact, so very weak."

"You are." Her lips flattened at his snarl but she continued on. "No human could properly defend himself against what's coming for you."

"And what in God's name would that be?" If the woman said a werewolf, he'd laugh. Let the bastard come; he was tired of running, tired of being afraid.

She hesitated, just the slightest hitch of breath. "It is a demon."

"A demon." Preposterous. "As in spawns of the devil and all that?" A bark of laughter left him, and he dragged a hand across the back of his aching neck. "It just keeps getting better and better, doesn't it?" When she didn't answer, he rounded on her. "And what next? A bloody vampire? Ghouls? A wee banshee?" He glared out over the sea. He did not want to know. "Enough already, Pop. Leave me be and let me fend for myself."

"I can't." She cleared her throat, and her voice returned with its usual strength. "He is a Primus of indeterminate power and is quite capable of dispatching you."

"Primus?" Winston really ought to stop asking questions altogether but curiosity was his downfall.

She made a soft sigh, the sort a beleaguered professor might use on a slow student. "When it comes to demons, there are the Primus and the Onus. Humans are born of mothers, but the Primus are the ancients, born of the collective thoughts, fears, and hopes of humanity when it was young. Religions told us there was a type of demon and, through our belief, we created them into existence." She smiled wanly. "You would be surprised what the power of mass thought can render."

"At the moment, I am surprised at a great number of things," Winston muttered.

Poppy nodded as if in sympathy. "Primus demons can have offspring. These are the lesser demons, human-demon hybrids, and shifters. They are called the Onus, as in a burden and responsibility the Primus do not want."

"And these demons live among us?"

"Many do, but it is always a struggle for them, for despite all of our apparent weakness and their superior strength, demons ultimately owe their existence to us. It chafes at their pride to know this, and some will take out that resentment by attacking humans."

Stifling another curse, Winston rubbed along the stiff line of scarring at his temple. It throbbed there, and he yearned just then for a strong drink. "Bugger all." His hand fell away, and he regarded his wife in the ensuing silence, wondering where to begin.

She was almost a stranger now, and yet the person who knew him better than anyone else. Hell, he needed to move. Like him, Poppy was a creature who could not stand being idle. Always moving, always in action, his Poppy. "Come and walk with me," he said.

# *Chapter Three*

❧❧❧

*London, 1869—Courting*

Winston was taking the object of his affection for a stroll in Hyde Park. Having never courted a woman, Winston did not know much about the business, but he knew that there ought to be a chaperone involved. However, Poppy Ellis had been the one to greet him in the parlor after he'd given his card to the footman. Indeed, she appeared to be the one responsible for her two younger sisters—a little one, no older than ten with golden-red hair and a curious stare, and a young lady nearing her fifteenth year with curling blond hair and an altogether too-knowing smile. That one had given him a saucy look beneath the fan of her golden lashes, as if she knew exactly what he was about and was glad of it. They'd been introduced as Miranda and Daisy before Poppy shooed them off with orders for Daisy to watch after "Panda."

The girls complied but not before he heard Miranda

whisper, quite loudly, "What does the man want with Poppy?"

Daisy answered *sotto voce*, "I suspect he wants to play with her."

"Like capture the pirate and such?"

Daisy had given him one last sidelong glance as he felt his face heat. "Something like that, dearest."

He needn't have looked at Poppy to know she was just as red-faced as he, and Winston ushered her out of the town home with haste.

Walking alongside her now, Winston did not feel discomfort so much as a stirring anticipation to know her better. He glanced at her strong, clean profile, and his heart beat faster. As if feeling his gaze, a small smile curved her soft lips, but she kept her eyes on the path before them.

"Daisy takes any chance she can to needle me."

"That is the way of siblings, I fear," he said.

"When my mother died a few years ago," she said, "the role of mothering went to me. Daisy had a hard time adjusting."

"I'm sorry for your loss."

She inclined her head. "It is hard. My father isn't the most attentive parent. But life goes on."

"I lost my mother five years ago. Influenza. I suspect it is not the same, as she treated me more as a..." He trailed off, his insides twisting.

"As?" Poppy prompted.

"As her pet, truth be told." He grimaced. What man wanted to admit being treated as a precious thing by his mother? "She doted on me, but whenever I opened my mouth to express an opinion, she closed her ears. The idea of me was far preferable to her than the actual man."

He'd never told a soul about his mother, but it hadn't occurred to him to keep it from Poppy. He knew her on some fundamental level that put him at ease and yet filled him with a gripping sense of anticipation.

They were silent for a few steps, and then she did something that had him nearly faltering. She laid her hand upon his arm. The gesture was what any young lady might do when being escorted, but he felt it as though she'd stroked her fingers along the whole of him. Pleasure rippled through him like a shockwave.

Aside from the brusque care of his nanny and occasional pats on the back from his brother, he'd never been touched. Not deliberately, not from someone seeking any meaningful connection. His mother might have bussed his cheek now and then, but she'd never laid a finger on him. As for his father? The very idea of a tender touch from him was laughable. Oddly, he hadn't realized this lack of touch until he'd received Poppy's. Now he wanted to purr, demand she touch his chest, anywhere and everywhere.

Poppy appeared oblivious to his struggle. "From the moment I was born, my mother had expectations of who I should be and how I should act."

Winston cleared his throat and focused on their conversation. "Did you object to those expectations?"

Her thin shoulders lifted. "How should I know? I've only now begun to live my own life. Nor were they necessarily bad expectations. They were simply..." She shrugged again. "Hers."

He needed to tell her everything. *Damn. Damn. Damn.*

Winston took a breath and pressed his arm closer to his side, trapping her hand there. Not very gentlemanly, but he didn't release her. "The other night, when we met, I did not give you my full name. I don't know why..." Her eyes were on him now, boring into him in that direct way of hers, and he forged on. "That isn't correct. I do know." *Damn.* "My father is the Duke of Marchland."

She walked on for a beat before speaking. "As in Marchland, cousin to the queen and one of the oldest titles in England?"

"Yes." His collar felt too tight. "I am his second son. Winston Hamon Belenus Lane, to be exact."

The hand at his arm gripped harder for one moment before slipping away. He felt the loss acutely.

"Mmm." She kept walking, not altering her pace, but not looking at him either. She glanced at the distant waters of the Serpentine where small canoes were out in droves as people took in the pleasant spring weather. Light danced off the water, and she squinted. "My father was born in the East End. Bethnal Green, to be exact." He winced at the way she mimicked his speech and the meaning behind it. "My mother was the seventh daughter of the Earl of Lister. But he disowned her when she chose to marry my father."

"Did she regret the decision?" A sinking feeling labored his steps.

"Yes." Again her eyes scanned the park, looking everywhere but at him. "Eventually, she realized that their worlds were too far apart."

"Perhaps it was not their worlds but their temperaments that were at odds." He was grasping at straws but he did not like the expression on her face nor the hard set of her shoulders.

Finally, she turned to him. "My lord—"

"Winston."

"*Lord* Winston. What is it you hope to accomplish by walking with me?"

Unable to take the cold way in which she spoke, he caught hold of her hand and tugged her beneath the canopy of a willow tree. Quiet surrounded them, and her bright hair turned bronze in the shadows. She glanced pointedly at his hand clutching hers, but he did not let go. "I want to get to know you."

Beneath her straight red brows, her brown eyes studied his face. "What is the point of getting to know someone whom you could never..." She sucked in a sharp breath, and her jaw went tight. "With whom you could never have a relationship?"

"Says who?"

Her brows snapped together. "Do not be obtuse. A duke's son and a merchant's daughter live in separate spheres. They do not commingle."

"To my knowledge, there is no law against it."

Her gaze was direct and snapped with impatience and intelligence. It made him hot and breathless. She glared. "There is a social law, and you well know it."

A gust of wind rushed over the grass and whipped about them, and a long strand of her vibrant hair broke free from her practical bun to tickle his nose. Gently, he tucked it back behind her ear, not quite touching her, but wanting to. "Social laws are broken all the time."

"To ill effect."

He smiled then. "It's always going to be like this, isn't it?"

She scowled. "What is?"

"You picking away at my logic, and me finding new ways to prove you wrong." And he could not wait.

She blushed beautifully. "You talk as if we're to have a future."

"Because we will."

She frowned. "It won't...I'm..."

"You're what?"

She huffed out a breath. Most unladylike. Most refreshing. "My life is complicated. I have responsibilities."

He moved just a bit closer. "I would not ask you to forgo them. I simply want..." So many things. He touched her cheek, a fleeting caress. "When I'm with you, I have no name," he whispered. "No title. It's just me. Just you. I want to keep that feeling, to keep you with me."

There. He'd said it. And her nose wrinkled. "I don't..." She paused, appearing utterly confounded by him. Confusion, he gathered, was a new thing for Poppy Ellis. And though the flush in her cheeks grew redder still, she spoke plainly. "Men don't usually fancy me."

He knew what it cost her to say it, and instinctively, he knew she was trying to scare him away by her admission. London society maintained a pack mentality; the undesirables were culled. What she did not know was that her brutal honesty made him admire her all the more.

He held her gaze with his. "This man does."

# *Chapter Four*

~~~~~~

Jack Talent was going to be a problem. Mary had known this as soon as she'd seen him sneering at her from the deck above when she had embarked with Mrs. Lane. He always looked at her as if he knew something about her that others did not. As if he saw inside of her soul and found her lacking. It rankled. Who was he to pass judgment upon her without so much as a by-your-leave? Or scowl at her when she knew he was guilty of his own crimes? Worse still, he was now at Inspector Lane's side. No doubt he would soon be whispering vitriol in his ear, much as he'd done with Ian Ranulf.

She would not let him. Not with so much at stake. Thus when she spied the arrogant tilt of Talent's dark head weaving through the crowd, she followed. It was an easy task; the man held little regard for those around him and simply cut through the slower-moving people like a scythe through dead grass. Mary moved just as quickly, but delicately, having long ago learned to slip and twist through a crowd without gaining any more notice than one would give a gentle breeze.

Talent turned a corner, headed, if she could believe it, toward the shuffleboard deck. Laughter and the sandy scratch of disks over wood lifted and faded in the wind. Talent touched the brim of his hat and nodded to a pretty young lady who looked quite fetching in a white polonaise with sea blue ribbons. The golden-haired girl smiled coyly back, and Mary almost rolled her eyes. *Yes, dear girl, engage with the devil. See how that works out for you.*

Coattails fluttering in the breeze, Talent moved on, circling a massive smokestack and heading to the windward side of the ship. On cautious feet, she followed, her senses alert—

He slammed into her without warning, taking her back against the wooden hull of a lifeboat. The craft creaked in protest, but then he was against her, stilling it. His big hand covered her mouth. As though she would scream. The fool.

His accusing eyes narrowed. "Following me, Miss Chase? Might want to be a little less obvious about it." He cocked his head. "Your scent is all over the wind." He leaned in for a sniff. "Cinnamon and spices. And here I thought you were supposed to be a proficient spy."

She merely stared back.

A smarmy snort left his lips. "What? Nothing to say?"

Oh, was she to talk with his brutish hand over her mouth?

Something in her expression must have conveyed this, for he let her go, stepping back two wide paces. She knew better than to believe the action was out of respect or even fear. No, he was simply giving himself enough space to fight should she attack. Mary almost laughed.

"Why are you here?" She wouldn't bother with indignation; it would only please him.

Talent crossed his arms over his chest. "Now that's my question, merrily."

"Do not call me that."

He laughed, if one could call the ugly sound a laugh. "What? Do you not flit through London, making certain everyone sees you as a merry bit of fluff?"

She hated him. Truly. Her spirit stretched along the walls of her flesh, yearning to escape and show this man how "frivolous" she could be. But she'd worked too hard to fail now.

"What I am is a Regulator in training." Satisfaction rose at the flash of shock that went through Talent's eyes. Mary moved closer to him. "While you are nothing more than The Ranulf's valet. A common lickspittle who never leaves his master's side. Until now. Which makes me wonder—"

He moved in a flash, crashing her back against the lifeboats with his body. His eyes shone a brilliant, violent green. "Do not..." He sucked in a breath through his bared teeth. "You will keep your sticky GIM fingers out of my business, Chase, or learn to regret it."

She could have him begging in an instant. And the funny thing was, he had no idea. None of the others knew what a GIM could truly do. Calmed by the thought, she held his gaze. "What are you doing here, bounder?" When he didn't move, she craned forward until their noses almost touched. "Whatever it is, think long and hard about getting in my way." She was not going back to her old life. No matter what she had to do.

Poppy did not take Winston's arm as they traversed the ship. In truth, he hadn't offered, but kept a steady, yet silent, clip down the first class deck, which was surprisingly wide and fitted with reclining chairs that were nestled against the ship walls. Varnished teak boards shone golden in the noon light. Archer had given Winston use of the owner's suite and all the trappings that went with it. It was a refined world that they had never been a part of as a couple. Poppy had lived it for a brief time and knew that Winston had too. But his family had cut him off because he'd insisted on being a detective. She wondered if he missed this life.

He set a brisk pace, knowing somehow it was what she craved. For a moment, she reveled in the simple feeling of walking with him. Often, when he had been on a particularly vexing case, they would take long walks through the city and talk his theories through. She'd loved those walks, loved being his sounding board. They were in the same business, after all, even if he never knew it. She too strove to weed out the dregs of society. And she felt the same stress and worry when she failed to hunt down the criminals of her world.

He had called her life a lie. And Poppy supposed it was true. To get through the day, she'd allowed herself to think of it more as a product of her trade than actual lying. In the darkest hours of the night, however, all those lies grew almost too heavy to bear.

When they reached a small space, unoccupied by others, Winston leaned back against the rail, crossing one long leg in front of the other, and the ends of his hair caught in the sea breeze. Dark gold strands whipped about his face, dancing along his mouth before he canted his head and the mass of it blew back. "Right then, vague warnings of my needing protection do me little good."

Out here, where he had the whistle of the wind to contend with, his voice was rougher, a gravelly rumble that made her skin shiver. She hid it by leaning back on the opposite wall, out of the wind, and tucking her hands into the wide pockets of her travel gown. "When I last knew this demon, he went under the false identity of Lord Isley, which I believe he subsumed from an earl he murdered. However that is just one of many names and identities he employs. His name doesn't matter, in any regard."

"Go on." Not taking his eyes from her, he reached into his coat and withdrew a battered pack of cigarettes.

Poppy frowned at it. Win enjoyed his pipe but she'd never seen him smoke a cigarette. "Archer believes those to bode ill for a person's health."

The corner of his mouth kicked up. God, that crooked smile of his. How many times had he used it right before he seduced the knickers off of her? She braced her shoulder blades against cold steel as he pulled out a pack of matches and lit one from the protected cup of his palm. The tiny, yellow flame reflected in his eyes before he bent his head to light his cigarette. The black tip flared red, and then a puff of smoke left his lips. "So I've heard. Never mind the fact that every other physician in London believes smoke helps clear the lungs."

The noxious cloud drifted over to tickle her nose. "I'd put my money on Archer."

He grunted, and she waved away a fresh cloud of smoke. "Not to mention that your pipe emits a much nicer scent."

Win's mouth quirked again. "The pipe pulls at my scars." His eyes grew heavily lidded. "You were telling me about the demon." He drew on his blasted cigarette again.

Poppy tried to relax her shoulders but she was too keyed up. "He can change appearance to suit his needs. Thus you cannot trust anyone. *Anyone.*"

Win grunted and, taking one last draw on his cigarette, tossed it down and crushed it with his boot. "Even you?"

She did not so much as flinch. "Even me. Should I suddenly feel hotter to the touch or avoid prolonged eye contact, then you may suspect me. His eyes will give him away eventually, for he cannot fully control the way they flash with inhuman light. No demon can."

"This demon," Win said, "do you know why he is after me?"

"He sent me a message saying…" Her jaw locked and then released. "Saying that he'd take my heart and destroy it."

She felt, rather than saw, Win tense. He grasped her elbow and guided her deeper into the shadows of the deck. "Go on," he said.

With great reluctance, she repeated the words of the telegram verbatim, aware that her cheeks were warm, despite the cool wind. His grip upon her elbow grew stronger as they walked for several lengths without talking. Then he stopped and turned to face her, his body blocking out the wind. "Why you, Poppy?"

She could not avoid his eyes, those canny eyes that always saw a bit too clearly for comfort. "Because I am SOS." She had to tell him the whole story, only years of keeping it inside made the words slow in coming. Frustration, anger, regret, and yes, self-pity pressed against her breastbone. It ought to be easier.

And then he touched her. The first deliberately intimate touch he'd given her in months. The rough pads of his fingertips caressed her cheek, lighting a slow path of sensation along her skin. She closed her eyes, letting herself sink into the feeling. Down he went, to her neck, where she was so sensitive that his touch made her shudder. He stood close. His warm breath blew over her lips as his fingers traced the tendons along her neck, and the shiver within her grew. It was almost painful the way she wanted to lean on him and feel his arms wrap about her. But she didn't know how to ask anymore. He'd left her. And she wasn't supposed to be weak.

A small puff of air left her lips as his fingers delved beneath her high collar. A dark whisper heated her ear. "Why you?" he repeated, more emphatic now.

She couldn't think when he stroked her neck, and the bastard knew it. Thus she didn't note the way his fingertip hooked over the thin gold chain she wore until it was too late. With a brisk flick of his hand, he pulled the hidden necklace out into the light. The little golden Isis pendant fluttered in the breeze as he held it aloft, hooked over his forefingers. His blue-grey eyes bore into her. "Is it because you are Mother?"

She couldn't speak. Outrage flooded her veins, bitter and hot, followed directly by admiration that he'd sussed her secret out.

Gently, he let the pendant drop, and it dangled awkwardly over her collar. She tucked it away, years of discipline demanding she do nothing less. "How?" She had planned to tell him. Of course she had. Hiding was no longer feasible.

Win angled his head, considering her, and still his eyes did not yield their careful study of her, as though she were a particularly confounding specimen under his scope. "That thing that saved me in the alley—"

"Augustus," Poppy supplied, suppressing a smile at the thought of how Augustus would react to hearing himself being referred to as a "thing." "He...well, he is a demon too. The very best sort." When Win raised a brow in speculation, she added, "Demons are not inherently evil. Every living being has a choice as to how it will live its life."

Winston's mouth flattened. "In any event, this Augustus said that he wouldn't want to lose Mother over me." Calculating eyes snapped back to her. "Later, when Ian told me about the SOS, he said it was led by an unknown woman named Mother." A small shrug. "I cannot fathom why this Mother would care if I died, unless she were you."

It had been a miracle that Win hadn't figured her out earlier. She studied the knot in his cravat. "Yes, well, you are correct. I am Mother." Even saying it aloud sent a skein of foreboding down her skin, and she caught his wrist. "Win, whatever you think of me..." She licked her lips. "Blast it.... Only a handful of people know. If it were to get out—"

"Do you honestly believe," he cut in, speaking through his teeth, "that I would endanger you out of a petty need for revenge?"

Beneath her fingertips, his pulse beat a hard tattoo as he glared down at her. "No," she said at last. "No. Save years of training are hard to deny."

He eased a bit, the tension in his jaw leaving, though his eyes were still distant and cold. He glanced down at her hand, clutching his wrist, and she let it drop. "My being Mother is not entirely the whole of the issue."

His lip curled. "What is the whole issue?"

Oh, but his attitude scathed, and she fought back her own irritation.

"I put him in his prison."

"How? When?"

Poppy put a hand to her brow and was not surprised to find it clammy. She was tired. So very tired. And hungry.

Her stomach growled with unseemly volume. Poppy spoke over it. "He killed my mother, Win."

Win lurched forward. "What?"

Poppy stared at the ocean. From the grand height of the deck, the water had the look of a stretched hide of dark blue leather. "Miranda and Daisy think she died shortly after giving birth to my brother. It was yet another lie. Designed to protect them. The truth is that Isley killed her." She clutched the rail hard. "He never would have bested her if she hadn't been mourning the death of my brother." Poppy had to believe that, for that loss had affected them all. Her brother had been so small, so innocent. And Mother had been devastated. Her grip tightened. "It took me two years to track Isley down and cage him."

"Cage him?"

"He cannot be destroyed." The very thought made her teeth gnash. "He is too powerful. He can only be sent back to the place we would call hell."

"How can you be sure?"

"Because I've bloody beheaded him twice!"

Win leaned back with a shocked huff. Awkward silence filled the space between them for a long minute until he spoke again. "When did you capture him?"

"One month after we married."

Win seemed to sag. "And what is your plan to lure him out now?"

"To wait."

"I'm sorry?" His smile was thin. "To wait? That is the whole of this grand production?"

Her lips pursed. "Believe me, Isley had his sick little game in place well before I arrived. He wants me here, and he has a reason for it. I've simply opened play. The next move will be his."

Win's nostrils flared as if scenting something off. "You know each other well."

"I hunted him for three years." She did not like the accusation in his tone nor the way it made her skin twitch. "This is the only way to draw him out. Besides, we are on a ship. His ilk can only be sent back to hell when standing upon the earth."

"So then," Win said, "this demon is after me because he believes that it will hurt you. I would counter that the solution might be a bit more simplistic." His expression grew implacable, but the scars on his face seemed to stand out more. "You only have to make it clear that you no longer care for me."

Her heart stopped painfully then promptly beat a wild rhythm. "He would see through that in an instant."

"Why?"

"Because it would be a lie!"

Pride had her turning because she could not look at him now. But she got all of five feet away before he caught her by the upper arm, his grip hard and biting as he wrenched her round. "Oh no, you don't." He let her go but boxed her in against the railing with his frame. "You do not get to walk away from me. Not yet."

"Why? You've walked away from me." Her nails dug into her palms. "Hell, you left me, Winston."

His eye twitched, a fleeting gesture, followed not by repentance but irritation. "And *you* followed *me* here." His long finger pointed in accusation. "Evading the situation now does you little credit."

"Why, you bloody hypocrite..."

"Call me all the names you like." His rough countenance hardened. "It will not put me off from having answers."

"You haven't asked a question."

He loomed, looking thoroughly capable of mayhem, before he leaned against the wall behind them with a grunt and gave her the gimlet eye. "Why did you keep it all from me?" he blurted out. "While I may understand why you were reticent to let me in, I cannot accept that you did not know me well enough to believe that I would ever have betrayed that trust." He slammed a fist against the wall. "By the love of God, I thought you knew me better. That you knew my heart entirely." His shoulders sank a little. "The way I thought I knew yours."

Deep inside her, the black, ugly feelings she'd kept bottled up boiled over, burning her lungs, choking her throat. She rounded on him, fisting her hands so hard her knuckles ached. "I took a vow, Win. An oath never to reveal what I was, or what I did, to anyone. *Anyone*. Not to you, not to my family. Have you any idea how difficult it was to keep it inside? Or the isolation I felt in doing so? Bloody hell, do you think I do not feel the depth of my betrayal to all of you? Miranda can barely meet my eyes anymore. Daisy looks at me as though she has one over on me. And you. I ached to tell you. I died a little each day I could not. But this is what I was born and bred to do. My word is my honor. Break it and I am nothing. Break it and everything I sacrificed is for nothing."

It wasn't until the words died on the air that Poppy realized they were nose to nose, shouting like common riffraff, while their fellow passengers hurried by with eyes averted and postures stiff in disapproval. Win's chest lifted and fell in a soft yet quick cadence as they glared at each other.

He was mere inches away, his eyes dark with close-kept emotion, yet he seemed utterly unreachable. She pulled in a breath and ended any possibility of bridging that gap.

"To speak with perfect honesty, had you not found out, I would never have told. Because I keep my word. No matter how painful it might be to do so."

He flinched, his broad shoulders tense beneath his coat. In the resounding silence, the wind howled, and she held back a shiver, waiting, and refusing to hide from his response. Slowly he nodded, his gaze on his feet. He stood like that for a moment.

"Well," he said at last, his voice a rasp. "Now I know." He moved as if he might touch her but stopped short. "I am sorry, you know. For not asking you sooner. It was wrong of me. You deserved to have your say." Then, moving with utter control despite his evident fury, he stalked away. Poppy watched him go, admiring the long lines of his body even as she contemplated throttling his stubborn hide. For the first time, she wondered if things were truly hopeless.

# *Chapter Five*

~~~~~~~~~~~~~~~~

Mary discovered that working with Mrs. Lane was a far different endeavor than being a cog in Lucien's machine. After years of double talk, decadence, and playing the part Lucien wrote for her, Mrs. Lane's forthright manner and decisive action was cool water on a summer's day.

Not one to sit about and have a servant handle things, Mrs. Lane went straight to unpacking. She did not speak a word about Inspector Lane, nor betray any emotion on her countenance, but her slim hands shook now and then when she did not keep them busy. Mary gathered that their discussion had not ended well. However, as they were not decamping, Mrs. Lane must have emerged victorious. Mary hadn't really doubted the outcome, not after spending the last few days in Mrs. Lane's company.

"Will you wear the pink for dinner tonight, mum?" Mary asked her, as she unpacked the gowns Lady Archer had provided. The pink satin evening gown was exquisite and a stroke of brilliance, as it would highlight Mrs. Lane's bold coloring in an unexpected way.

Mrs. Lane's keen gaze sought her out. "You realize that I do not truly mean to use you as my ladies maid."

"You might as well," Mary said without heat. "I'm quite good at it, and Lady Archer did not select evening wear that you can get into on your own."

"Humph. I cannot think of anything more banal than picking out dinner gowns. Or striving to impress others with my clothing." Mrs. Lane's red brows drew together in a slash. "Blasted Miranda and Daisy. I should have known better than to entrust my wardrobe to them. I do not see why I cannot wear my current outfit."

Mary bit the inside of her cheek. From what she knew of the Ellis sisters, there was a time when young Poppy Ellis had attended societal events. And she had been raised to be a lady, despite having lived the past decade among the middle class. Mrs. Lane turned back to her trunk, a massive blue leather one that, when she opened it, contained a veritable arsenal of weaponry. Some that Mary recognized and far more that she did not. She could not help but be awed by the efficiency and speed with which Mrs. Lane had prepared. Between Mrs. Lane assembling her weapons and her sisters selecting gowns, they had gathered everything needed for an ocean voyage in little over an hour.

"I suppose you could," Mary said, choosing to ignore her employer's fit of pique. "It would invoke plenty of conversation, at the very least."

One elegant red brow rose pointedly. Mary gathered her courage and met Mrs. Lane's piercing gaze.

Mrs. Lane's crisp voice broke the silence. "You remind me of Mr. Lane. He too believes his cheekiness is amusing." The small note of wistfulness in Mrs. Lane's voice was well concealed but Mary heard it.

Mary spoke carefully as she hung up the pink to air out. "The inspector is stubborn as well?"

For a moment, Mary feared she'd overstepped her bounds irrevocably. Then Mrs. Lane answered. "He is that. But at the moment, he is angry. Justifiably, I'm afraid."

A flurry of activity told Mary just how upset Mrs. Lane was. Mary kept her gaze averted. "Show him what he is missing." The words hung in the air, and she could feel Mrs. Lane's stare. Reluctantly, she turned to find that her employer appeared befuddled. Mary sighed inwardly. "When it comes to dealing with the female sex, men generally think with their smaller head. Inspector Lane has merely forgotten to listen to his."

Mrs. Lane's lips twitched spasmodically. "So you suggest," she asked in even tones, "that I remind him to think with his cock?"

Mary's cheeks heated. "Normally, I would suggest the reverse, but in a case of overabundant logical thinking, I believe a return to balance is in order."

A strangled noise left Mrs. Lane's throat but she maintained her poise. "You are a most unusual woman, Miss Chase."

Rather the pot calling the kettle but . . . "Yes."

Thankfully, Mrs. Lane turned back to her unpacking. "I shall take your suggestion under advisement."

They worked in silence with Mrs. Lane sorting through her box of horrors as Mary exalted in the rainbow of silken gowns her sisters had selected, far more than Mrs. Lane would be able to wear on such a short trip.

"Here." Mrs. Lane suddenly appeared by her side and handed her a slim box of polished ash wood. "These are for you."

Mary hesitated. Lucien often gave her gifts. Gifts of adornment. He did it to be kind, never understanding that she did not want to be dressed up like a doll. Mrs. Lane, however, wasn't the sort prone to frivolity.

"Me?"

"Of course. Did I not just say?" Mrs. Lane bustled back to her trunk and began rooting about in it once more, dropping a heavy scimitar knife on the dressing table with a thud.

Mary's fingers were careful as she set the box down and opened it. Nestled in black velvet were four gleaming metal stars. Japanese throwing stars shaped more like stylized suns. Their edges glinted, sharp and wicked.

"Happo shuriken," she murmured. "How lovely."

"Do you know how to use them?" Mrs. Lane asked from the depths of her trunk.

"A little. There aren't very many Japanese gentlemen about, even fewer willing to teach their weaponry." The GIM's knowledge was second-hand. *My, but they were beautiful.*

Mrs. Lane straightened. "I want you to practice every day. Do it in here or your rooms, where no one can see. The walls are as good a target as any."

That she had little care for the resulting state of said wall had Mary holding back a smile. "Yes, mum."

Mrs. Lane nodded. "They don't usually deliver a killing blow, but they'll slow down your enemy well enough. I've a gun and knife for you as well. A good Regulator must be proficient in all forms of combat. As much as I wish that you had received proper training beforehand, there is little use crying over it now. We'll get you set to rights later."

"I am not entirely without training." Although she

gathered that her notion of training was not in keeping with Mrs. Lane's exacting standards.

Mrs. Lane's expression was proof enough of that. "You'll do for now. Which is why I let you come along." She sighed and ran a hand along her hair, her straight nose wrinkling when she encountered her hat. She tugged it off, completely destroying her coiffure.

"If you'd like, mum, I could find a way to incorporate some weapons within your millinery and gowns."

Mrs. Lane's pale face lit up with almost girlish glee. "Most excellent idea, Miss Chase." With an idle flick of the wrist, she tossed her hat to Mary and then proceeded to attack her trunk once more. "Eventually, I'll have to inform Mr. Lane of our plans. Sooner rather than later, I'm afraid." Her voice lost its usual confidence, and though her face was hidden behind the lid of the trunk, Mary fancied she was frowning. Then her tone became brisk once more. "At the very least, we have Mr. Talent, which is a boon. He will watch over my husband while I confront the demon."

Mary was about to answer that she did not know how helpful Talent would be, as he usually pouted like a boy in short pants and then promptly did what he liked, when they heard a commotion coming from the hall. One word in particular cut through the rumble: *murder*.

"Blast it!" Mrs. Lane grabbed a hip holster from the trunk and strapped it on. The dark glint in her eyes was unnerving as she grabbed her knife. "God help that demon if he has harmed my husband."

"Bad discussion with the wife, Inspector?"

Winston did not bother acknowledging Talent as he strode down yet another endless corridor on this hulking beast of a ship. Bad discussion? It was the understatement of the year. Instead of getting anywhere with Poppy, she'd made him feel small and dishonorable, which was damned aggravating given that she was in the right; he had acted dishonorably in leaving her without asking for an explanation.

Worse was that, from the moment he'd seen her on the gangplank, his body and his soul had awakened, much like being jolted from a dream. No matter her betrayal, the anger he felt about it, or her present machinations, she made him alive. She excited him. And he wanted her still. *Perfect. Bloody perfect.*

Beside him, Talent nodded sagely as if he'd responded instead of remaining tight-lipped. "You look terrible at any rate. Pinched about the mouth. Remind me to add a bit of lavender to your shaving water. Soothes the nerves."

Winston halted. "I believe I made it clear that you are not my valet. Nor," he added, taking a step into Talent's space, "is it your business to speculate about my personal discourse. Good or bad. I'm not Ian Ranulf who you can goad into a temper with your insolence."

Talent did not so much as blink. "So this isn't you in a temper?"

Winston held that insouciant gaze. "Pray you never see me in one."

The man grinned. "I live among wolves. You wouldn't stand a chance against me—" Talent yelped as he was slammed to the floor, his legs flying out from under him.

With a grin of his own, Winston pressed the end of his walking stick into the man's chest as he bent over him. "You were saying?"

Talent eyed him, clearly considering brawling in the narrow passageway, but other passengers were approaching.

Waiting until the horrified couple scrambled away from the undignified spectacle of a man sprawled upon the floor, Talent knocked aside the stick and leapt neatly to his feet. "Thought you were more of a 'the pen is mightier than the sword' type, Inspector."

"Depends on the fight." Winston set his lapels back in order. "Rest assured, I can do battle with both."

They stepped out onto the promenade deck. Fresh sea air hit Winston, and he drew in a deep breath. They walked on a ways. "Mrs. Lane claims a demon is on the boat with the sole intent to bedevil me." It wasn't easy for Winston to say, much less think.

"Bloody demons." Talent's mouth twisted. "If you ask me, it's safer to slice their heads off and be done with them."

"I find your cavalier attitude toward murder somewhat disturbing, Mr. Talent."

"Oh do you? I suspect you'd be singing a different tune should one catch you," Talent said darkly. "They like to play with their prey, you know."

*Lovely.* "Are you saying there aren't any demons worthy of redemption?"

"Not one who'd have Mrs. Lane rushing out to save your hide."

It took a moment to find a calm tone. "This is all moot, as Mrs. Lane tells me this one cannot be beheaded."

"Every supernatural can be destroyed from beheading."

Winston did not like the speculation that resided in the younger man's eyes, nor the itching fury that was mounting in his chest. The railing made a dull clang as he punched it with the side of his fist. "She cannot have exaggerated to—"

"Bring you to heel?" Talent supplied with a dry snort.

"Who the bloody hell knows what a woman will say or do to get her way?" His expression darkened. "Look at Miss Chase. Suddenly she's a bleating Regulator in training. Sneaking little…" He pushed a hard breath through his nose.

Winston faced Talent, and the breeze sent his hair scattering across his ruined cheek. "Do you want to be a Regulator?"

Talent scowled at the sea. "Would do a lot better than Chase."

Fighting a smile, Winston kept his voice neutral. "I suspect you'd make a fine Regulator." He tilted his head, and the fluttering strands whipped back. "Why not apply?"

Hot color washed over Talent's broad cheeks. "You can't apply," he muttered. "You can only be invited. Doesn't matter, I've better things to do with my time."

Ah, there was the rub. Miss Chase had been invited, and Mr. Talent had not. Winston might have believed that was where their animosity stemmed, but he knew better. It was clearly older than that.

"Daisy works with the SOS now," Winston said. "Why not ask her to press your suit?"

Talent's gaze snapped back to him. "Oh, I well know it. Who do you think got Mary Chase in? It takes months, *months* to process a novice, and yet Chase is in, within, what, a week? Working with your wife?" He pointed an accusatory finger at Winston as his scowl grew. "I'd be asking yourself why, Lane. I know I am."

This time, Winston stepped near, letting the blunt tip of Talent's finger press into his chest. "If my wife has any secrets, they are hers to keep." *And mine to discover.*

Talent's mouth opened as if he would retort but then he froze, his nostrils flaring and his gaze growing flat. "I smell blood."

Carried on the wind came the scent of copper. And shit and piss. Win knew the smell too well. Not just blood. "That is death."

Moving as one, they stalked toward the scent. Winston's hand tightened on his walking stick. Above, seagulls squabbled in mid-air, diving and swooping around the massive smokestack.

"Attracted to the blood," murmured Talent.

Ahead, the deck narrowed as it curved toward the bow of the ship. Lifeboats creaked, and the paddle churned, but not a soul stirred.

They crept closer to the source of the scent. A grunt and a sound unnervingly like that of a man slurping soup came from the other side of the steam funnel. Winston's hand slipped to the gun hidden within his inner coat pocket. At CID, he wasn't allowed to carry one, as the populace of London had an aversion to police arming themselves. Even so, he'd used a gun before, when the danger was high. And only a fool would carry a weapon and not know how to wield it. He'd like to think himself not a fool, but a gun hadn't helped him when a werewolf attacked him. Winston swallowed down the rush of bitterness that filled his mouth.

"Have you a weapon?" he whispered.

Talent spared him a glance. "I'm a shifter."

Winston supposed that would have to do.

Together, they rushed around the corner, Winston's gun out and cocked.

"Hell," Talent said.

Winston stopped short as he spied the body. Male, young, wearing officer's whites. Torn and bloody throat, his pants gaping open, sightless eyes gazing up to the heavens. Winston took in the particulars, then a shadow flickered in the periphery of his vision. Winston took off after it, with Talent at his heels.

Their feet pounded on the deck as they raced along. The sound of an iron door wrenching open had Winston increasing his pace. He skidded around the corner and tore through the open hatch. A man paused on the stair, his eyes gleaming yellow as he grinned back at them.

Bloody hell. His appearance was identical to the man who lay dead on the deck.

"Demon," Talent said behind Winston. "Used his victim's blood to assume his appearance."

Winston launched forward. He couldn't shoot in this bloody iron box of a hall, but he could tackle the thing. Unfortunately, it leapt out of range and practically flew down the next flight of stairs. Winston and Talent pounded after it. The stairs rattled and shook with their effort. Sweat stung his eyes as he ran.

The demon slammed open a lower door and disappeared through it. Winston followed an instant later. Dimly lit and barren of any fripperies, the corridor stretched in four directions. The sound of the demon's retreating footsteps echoed throughout, coming at them from everywhere.

"Where are we?" he snapped to Talent.

"Cargo level, I'd say."

Winston tossed his hat aside. He'd left his walking stick somewhere on deck and had only the gun for protection. "Divide and conquer. There are two main cargo holds. You take the fore, and I'll take the aft."

"I'll take aft." Talent flashed a grin. "It's farther away and I'm faster, human."

They both knew the demon more likely had fled aft—being as it was farther away. Thus it was more dangerous. As Win hadn't the time to argue, he let it go.

"I'll give you that one." He nodded toward the dark stretch of hall. "Go then. We meet in the center."

Talent ran off without another word. Taking a deep breath, Winston did the same, going about twenty feet before he encountered the first cargo hold entrance. The door hung wide open. A sign of entry? Or a diversion?

Inside was a cavernous space, cool and slightly damp. Far above, iron beams, painted a dull red, ran along the ceiling like the ribs of Jonah's whale. Towers of crates, lashed down by thick hemp netting, made a tight maze ideal for hiding.

"Perfect," he muttered, keeping his back to the wall as he entered with his gun pointed down but at the ready.

Careful to keep his step light and silent, Winston moved to the first crate. Being deep in the bowels of the ship, the hum of the engines was immense and enough to vibrate his bones. Farther in he went, on a bloody wild goose chase, he feared. Something creaked and he tensed. Puddles of yellow electric light from the overhead lamps were far and few, leaving too many corners for darkness to dwell.

The heaviness of the gun in Winston's hand brought to mind another time. Of a foul alleyway, filled with fog and death. He'd nearly lost his life there.

*Don't think of it.* But his vision blurred as his mouth filled with saliva. Hands shaking, Winston pressed himself against the wall of the ship, and cold iron bore into his shoulder blades as he fought for control. The squeak of a door hinge had him freezing. From his vantage point, he could see nothing more than the crate in front of him and darkness beyond. *He cannot be destroyed.* What if Poppy had been telling the truth? And here Winston was, armed with only a gun. *Hell.* He ought to go back. But, if he stayed and fought, it could end here. Winston swallowed hard. He had to try.

Bugger, but he couldn't hear a thing over the roar of the blasted engines. His breath and heartbeat sounded overloud in his ears, an irritant that could get him killed. And something was coming. He could feel it by the dip in his guts.

Focusing on a spot before him, Winston let every muscle relax, going still and quiet. Exhale. Inhale. Softly. The pumping of his blood slowed too. And with this came an elevation of his senses. It was a trick he'd learned in his training days from his grizzled old partner, Nelson, when Win had come too close to getting his head knocked off by a suspect. He'd forgotten it in his recent fears. No more. Win exhaled again and concentrated on the air about him and the sounds of the engines thrumming, a steady beat that—

There! The scuff of a shoe from the left had him adjusting his grip on his pistol. Sweat trickled along his neck, tickling him. He stared at the edge of the crate until the wood grain blurred and the shadowed passage came into sharp focus. Another scrape, the shuffling of fabric. The bastard was coming closer.

Win's heartbeat thumped against the side of his throat. His thighs quivered, and his arms burned, aching with the need to move. *Steady.* And then he heard it, the lightest intake of breath.

With a burst of strength and speed, Winston whipped around the corner, slammed into the body standing there, and aimed for the head. His finger was already pressing down on the trigger when a flash of shining red hair and the scent of lemons stayed his hand. A second later, he registered the sharp point of a knife digging into the underside of his jaw. For a moment, he could only stare.

Bulging purple glass lenses stared back at him, giving the impression of coming nose to nose with a mechanical owl. But the delicate slope of her nose and the sharp angle of her jaw was pure Poppy.

Another moment more and he became aware of the fact that his gun was pressed hard against her temple.

"Shit!" He lurched away as if burned. "What in the bloody hell?"

Poppy wrenched the enormous brass goggles from her eyes and glared. "What are you doing here?"

Her smooth cheeks were flushed, and her red hair straggled from beneath the leather straps of the goggles, but she appeared collected and cool. Not so for him.

"What am I—" He scrubbed a damp hand over his face. "Infernal woman, you nearly gave me an apoplexy. They ought to count you among the ten plagues of Egypt!"

Her mouth puckered. Not from irritation, he realized, but from repressing a laugh. Obstinate, crazy...

"Oh, I'm much more effective than a plague. Well, more accurate at any rate."

"I almost blew your head off!"

With a deft twirl of her fingers, she tucked her knife back into the sheath strapped around her hips. "And I almost filleted you. Had I not such fine reflexes—" He snorted, and she spoke louder, "I'd be a widow right now."

"We'll have to thank God for small mercies." He grasped her elbow and towed her behind the crate. His voice lowered. "Why are you here?"

"There's a dead man up on deck. He's causing quite a commotion."

"Yes, I know. Talent and I almost caught the bastard who did it in the act. It was a demon. We followed him down here."

Damn it all, he'd almost killed her, and she talked as though they were at tea. Her sharp eyes took in their surroundings. "Where is Talent now?"

"Ferreting the demon out from the other end of the ship. Hopefully he won't run afoul of Miss Chase and nearly kill her as well."

"She's up inspecting the body, so that is doubtful." Poppy kept her profile to him. "I think he got away." Her gaze returned to him. "I came in through the east entrance. You?"

"West." His fingers twitched at his side.

"As I thought. Either we missed him or he's gone."

How could she be so calm? The thrill of the chase, even the fear, had transmuted into something earthier and basic. His blood was up, and to his horror, he had a cockstand one could hang a hat on. Winston wanted nothing more than to toss up Poppy's skirts and pound into her. Like a rutting animal. Worse, the blasted woman appeared completely unaffected and would most likely slap him should he try anything. He shook his head and took a breath.

"Go back to the cabin, and I'll search the rest of the area."

They'd been together long enough for him to know her "surely you jest" look quite well. He did not care a whit. The woman wasn't facing that *thing*. Nor could he think with her nearby. His hand curled around Poppy's arm, holding her secure lest she get any fanciful notions of leaving his side. "Either you go, or we both wait it out here."

Her breath was cool on his cheek. "Listen, I've more experience with these matters than—"

"Forgive me, but I was under the impression that your

role within your organization was of an administrative nature."

Moss brown eyes flashed darkly. "Are you suggesting that I cannot handle myself in the field?"

"I am suggesting that one of us has greater experience in the field and that person is not you."

"Of all the preposterous, pompous—"

Winston clamped a hand over her mouth and dropped to a crouch. The step of a boot had sounded beyond, and his blood froze. Poppy did not fight, and he let his hand slide free.

"Left corner about ten yards off." Poppy's voice was but a breath. Which rather amused him, given that they'd just been talking loud enough for anyone to hear them. Still, he simply nodded and held her tight against him. Christ but they'd been squabbling like infants, and now they were trapped. His muscles tensed as a deliberate step sounded just around the crate. Whoever it was wasn't bothering with stealth. Poppy stiffened as well. Their eyes met, and her hand slipped into his pocket and wrapped around his gun. *Bloody blasting hell.* He held her gaze, his heart wrenching in his chest for fear for her. It ought to be him protecting her. But he gave a slight nod. *Let her aim be true.*

Out of the corner of his eye, a shadow loomed. Everything slowed and yet sped up as he twisted to the side, and Poppy lifted the gun and fired. Her arm bobbled at the last second. A bad shot. Winston reached out for the gun, ready to take it from her and shoot the demon down. Smoke clogged his throat and ruined his vision. His ears rang from the report of the gun. But not enough to miss Talent's irate shout.

"What the bleeding devil?"

Gun smoke dissipated, and Talent stood, glaring pure murder down at them. "Are you trying to kill me?"

Poppy wrenched free of Winston and rose. "Had I been, you would be dead, Mr. Talent."

Getting to his feet was far harder, for visions of Poppy being cut down before him still swirled within Winston's head. But he straightened and adjusted his lapels if only to do something to calm himself. "You shot wide, didn't you?" And damn if pride didn't swell within him. Fancy that.

Poppy did not smile, but it lurked in her eyes. That, and a certain smugness that irked. "How good of you to notice, Mr. Lane."

"Well, I didn't," snapped Talent. "You scared ten years off my life."

"Mr. Lane and I were defending ourselves. You ought to have made your presence known."

Talent snorted. "Right. 'Excuse me, Mr. Demon, I'm walking toward you to ascertain whether or not you are my mates. Care to clarify for me?'"

Winston smothered a laugh with a cough. "Well then. All's well and all of that."

They both glared at him, so he simply led the way out.

"How did you track the thing down here?" Winston asked Poppy as they left the hold while scanning the area for lingering threats. His nerves were shot for the day and, short of drinking a restorative, he could only ask questions and hope the familiar practice would further calm him.

"Goggles." Poppy tapped a purple lens resting on the top of her head. "Demons are born in the Underworld and thus carry a trace of it on their flesh in the form of chemical rays. The violet lens picks up those rays." She gave a nod in the direction of the stairwell. "He left strong traces all the way down, but they trailed off here. I suspect because he calmed down once in his element."

She handed him the goggles. "The rays are strongest when they are afraid or exerting themselves."

They'd reached the stairwell. Torn between gaping at his wife—she of the demon hunting expertise—and the goggles, he took a moment to put them on. The world dimmed to a soft violet, not nearly light enough to see properly. Winston gnashed his teeth. Poppy had walked into that hold nearly blind.

"Here." Poppy leaned in and fiddled with something on the side of the lens. A click and a soft whirring sounded. Win started as a series of lights flickered around the rims of the lenses.

Beside him, Talent made a sound of pleasure. "Would you look at that. Brilliant."

Poppy's crisp voice was at Winston's ear. "Now you look."

He turned his head toward the iron stairs and sucked in a breath. Footsteps of eerie, glowing violet covered the treads, and a ghostly mist of the same glowing substance hovered in the air.

"Fluorescence," he said.

"Just so," said Poppy. "Special lenses, designed by the SOS, capture the refrangibility of the light within the demon's essence."

With a resigned sigh, he took off the device. "First werewolves, now this. As a man of logic, I cannot believe I'm saying this, but there are times I think I preferred my state of ignorance." Win handed Talent the goggles so that he might try them, then turned his attention upon Poppy. "Hell of a thing to discover that the crackpots raving in Piccadilly Circus about monsters among us aren't all mad."

Poppy flashed Winston a rare grin. "Don't go picking out your corner of Piccadilly just yet. There are far greater curiosities than mere demons and werewolves."

And wasn't that the truth? "Do not worry, sweet; if anything is to drive me mad, it will be you."

Mary hated death. Which was rather ironic considering that, as a GIM, she was exposed to as much death as the average grave digger. Though they had the fortune to work with death that was safely boxed up. Fresh death was a GIM's specialty, and the corpse upon the first class promenade deck was certainly fresh. She edged farther away from the crowd of officers that hovered over their fallen comrade. Mrs. Lane had sent her to watch the proceedings and guard over the corpse, but Mary could not fathom what she could guard it from. The poor man was dead. And beginning to smell.

Discreetly as possible, she pressed a lace kerchief to her nose. It would be intolerable for Mrs. Lane to find out that Mary had a weak stomach when it came to these matters. Somebody had placed a blanket over the man's upper half, but his legs peeked out from beneath it. Blood, blackening from exposure to the air, seeped around the white trousers of his uniform. Swallowing hard, she looked away and into the eyes of a young officer.

"Oh." She hadn't even heard him approaching.

His pleasant face broke into a kind smile. "You shouldn't be here, Miss. This isn't a sight for a lady."

Mary had no response. She was also instructed not to break her cover. Damn but she ought to have come in her ethereal form.

The officer's genial smile remained. "Besides, the gulls have begun to make a play for him."

Bile rose in Mary's throat.

"Don't worry, Miss. We'll keep them away."

She stumbled, bumping into the metal call box that jutted out from the wall. Instantly, the officer was there, grasping her arm. It wasn't until he touched her that she felt the sting. Gasping, she pulled away. Blood smeared her arm and stained his white glove red.

"I fear you've scratched yourself," he said with a frown at her arm and then to the call box.

"Bother." Mary cursed herself for being so affected. This could not continue. She had to master death. Yet even as resolve filled her, the breeze sent the stench of decay over her, and she blanched.

Thankfully, the officer was too busy inspecting her arm.

"We can't have our lovely guest bleeding, now can we?" His dark eyes gleamed with good humor as he stripped off his glove, and with gentle care, wiped the blood from her arm with his bare thumb.

His touch was a lovely warmth against her cold flesh, and she couldn't find it in herself to protest. He finished by pressing his glove to her arm.

"Shall I see you back to your rooms, Miss?"

And let Poppy discover her weakness? Or, heaven forbid, Jack Talent? She'd rather stop her heart for good. Mary slipped from the officer's grasp. "That is quite all right. I'm perfectly well, honestly."

She backed away. There was little she could do here now anyway.

"Good day then, Miss." The officer bowed politely before returning to the scene of the crime.

# *Chapter Six*

━━━━❦◦❧━━━━

The walk back to his stateroom was not enough time to calm Winston's thoughts. Demons and Poppy danced around in his head. He'd spent so much time these past months stubbornly maintaining his ire at being lied to that he hadn't given any thought to the danger Poppy actually placed herself in. The realization made him ill. Fighting demons? Of course she was. Why would he expect anything less from her? All these years of marriage, he'd felt a policeman's guilt, worrying that his wife would live in fear for him. Hell, she might as well have been patting him on the head and sending him off to school.

Poppy followed along beside him, blithely ignoring the baffled looks their fellow travelers gave to her goggles and mussed hair. Not to mention the blasted knife she still had strapped low on her hips. It was as if she were sending out a dare to all and sundry: Do not fuss with me. That Winston found the costume exceedingly alluring was simply one more irritant to his day.

Still gritting his teeth, he opened the door to his suite

and came face to face with a massive steamer trunk tossed open and spilling forth froths of lacy petticoats and silken gowns.

"Well, bugger me."

He would have expected books and sensible gowns for Poppy's travel kit, but then as his wife was nothing like the woman he thought he knew, why should fripperies be a surprise? Mindful of his shins, he picked his way around it as Poppy briskly closed the door and turned to confront him.

Poppy's face, while not an open book, was so familiar to him that he could read her well, and it was amusing to watch her mind work through possible things to say to him. He almost grinned because it was hard to best Poppy. It always had been. But the grin did not grow, for the anger within him was stronger. She expected to "save" him? He liked to think himself a modern man, open to new ideas and possibilities, but a man had his limits. Being nannied by his wife was one of them.

"You are traveling rather heavily these days, Poppy," he said to break their stalemate.

Poppy's steady brown eyes assessed him, looking for clues. God, he'd missed watching her think. He pushed the thought from his mind as she came closer. Her voice almost sounded husky when she spoke. "We'll be sharing a suite."

"Obviously." The notion had his cock's full attention, which made him want to punch something or turn the air blue with curses.

Those watchful eyes of hers narrowed. "You aren't going to kick up a fuss?"

"Would it change things if I did?"

"I daresay no." With quick tugs at the tips of her black

kid gloves, she removed them and tossed them aside, not bothering to see where they landed. "Though I admit, capitulation was not what I expected."

Had he not needed to keep an eye on her, capitulation wasn't what she would have received, either, but he couldn't very well say that. He had to say something, for she was staring at him again, calculating. Give her enough spare time, and she'd figure him out. "Come now, Poppy, you know how I enjoy rattling your chains." He allowed himself a small smile. "It is a rare sight to see you off balance." He shouldn't have said that. Now heat was creeping up his back and over his collar. A rattled Poppy stirred his blood. Always.

As if thinking much the same thing, pink tinged her cheeks. But she merely pursed her lips, and those straight brows of hers drew together. Time for a change of subject.

"What makes you immune from harm?" He had a good idea, but he wanted to hear her say it. "Why do you think you can fight this thing whereas I cannot?"

She blinked, nonplussed. "You don't know?"

Meaning she thought he'd asked one of her family members. "I'll be damned if I asked someone else to tell me my wife's secrets," he said. "It's bloody bad enough that you kept them from me."

He did not like the feeling that came over him upon seeing the hurt in her eyes. Bollocks to that. "One sister creates fire, the other moves the earth." Winston stared at Poppy. "And the eldest? What can she do?"

Poppy did not answer.

"You froze the boat in the water, didn't you?" Even as he said the words, part of him marveled at the notion. Such power living and breathing within his wife's body. Had he not seen it happen, he wouldn't have believed it.

Poppy's expression remained implacable. "Yes."

"Show me."

"Why? I've already admitted it." A hint of sarcasm laced her words. "I'm not a bloody parlor trick, you know."

His muscles tightened as he held himself still. "You are stalling. Rather badly at that."

She scowled. Winston began to speak when a blast of icy air hit him in the face and burned down his throat. Like before, the sound of ice crackling filled the room. A white web of frost covered the trunk nearest his wife. Ice crawled in a line over the floor toward his shoes.

Winston's heart leapt, a mixture of natural fear and outright wonder grabbing hold of him. In a blink of an eye, the deathly cold breeze stopped. Even so, his breath came out in visible puffs as he stared at her.

Demurely, Poppy clasped her hands before her and raised her eyes to his. "Will that do, husband?"

Impudent woman. He almost laughed. Until the thought came over him that she could freeze him where he stood. And she was on this boat to protect him from some threat. Hell. It did not matter if she could readily defend herself. She was his wife, which meant it was his duty to lay down his life to protect *her*. He'd say it was his right, but the uncomfortable truth that he'd walked out on her kept him from shouting that to the tops of the mainmast.

"How does it work? Your power."

She smiled a little, as if expecting the question. Then she well knew his curiosity was endless.

"I do not know, not the science of it at any rate. I can only tell you that I can freeze or unfreeze water. I need to be touching the object with my hand to freeze it."

"A sort of reverse conductivity." She was bloody marvelous.

"Yes. However, I do not feel heat or cold while I am set-ting the power free." Her gaze wandered to the porthole where the ocean canvassed behind him. "And if there is open water about, I am able to draw it to me and freeze it at will. Lastly, there is a cost for using my power." She let go of a tiny sigh. "The more power I draw, the more physi-cally drained I am afterward."

"Then don't use it."

When her gaze flew to his, he took a step closer to her and cupped her smooth cheek. "I mean it, Boadicea. Do not use it." He gentled his tone, when he'd rather shout, and ran a thumb along her soft bottom lip. "Do not think to fight this thing. Not for me."

Again came that little smile, an expression that held equal parts amusement and resignation. "You didn't really expect me to agree, did you?" She shook her head, as if to say *silly man*, and his world turned red. He could barely hear her next words past the rage rushing through his ears. "Perhaps in other instances I might fall for the seduction of that smoke and silk voice, Win. But not in this."

Poppy took herself off to the dressing room. Her dress was filthy and her hair a bedraggled mess. Never mind that her husband loomed before her with a preternatural calm that spoke of imminent disaster, for she did not trust that look in his eyes. Unfortunately, Win followed. Stub-born man.

His low, smoky voice disrupted her peace just as she was undoing her hair.

"That night Archer stitched me up," he said, "and you held me down when I screamed. How did it make you feel?"

Oh, but he played dirty. She looked up to find him propped against the doorjamb of the dressing room. He hadn't removed his suit coat or bowler, and the faint scent of sea air clung to him.

"It was the worst night of my life," she whispered. "I wanted to scream too. I wanted to kill the bastard who hurt you with my bare hands."

His gaze held hers. "And yet you dismiss me for feeling the same helpless rage over the idea of you being hurt."

Poppy had to swallow several times before she could speak. "I did not think you would—"

"Care?" His mouth tilted in that half-smile that could at once annoy and drive her to distraction. "Regardless of the disappointments that have arisen between us, sweeting, you should understand that I will always care."

His lids lowered a fraction, and he was retreating behind his usual mask of civility. It made her want to hit something. Her hands were clumsy as she moved to unpin the rest of her hair. It fell down in a curtain of deep red, cutting Win off from her view. A blessed relief.

"I care too, Win." And even if he no longer wanted her, she could not live in a world where Win did not exist. "If I do not fight, then who will?"

A second later, Win's bowler flew across the room, bouncing off the wall from the force of his throw. "Damn it! You are hunting a demon that you admit cannot be destroyed on this ship. Have you gone completely insane?"

She laughed, though she felt no joy. "I told you I have fought him many times before. This is my life. Did you not believe that as well?"

His nostrils flared on a sharply drawn breath, and he gripped the back of his neck with both hands, sending the muscles along his chest and arms bulging beneath his coat. His struggle to regain control played out over his features, and Poppy watched with fascination. Win never shouted at her when they argued. They simply did not engage in rousing fights of passion. However, Poppy was inclined to prefer this new method of discussion, for his anger did something to her insides and made her want to stir him up some more.

When he spoke, it was through clenched teeth. "Is it worth your health, your life?"

She winced then, for she knew more than he the fragile state of her health. But it could not be helped. "Yes."

He deflated at that. With a muttered curse, he paced the room as Poppy undid the buttons of her bodice and slid it off.

"At least promise me that you will not go chasing after him alone," Win said finally.

She did not look up but moved on to the hooks of her skirts. "I promise." It was an easy vow to make. But she could not help adding, "So long as he does not attack me."

Win gave a short nod. But she knew he would never truly give up on something once he was on the case. "Fine then... What are you doing?"

"Undressing." She let her skirts fall.

"Now?" His glare was back, a warning this time as she pulled at the ties of her drawers.

Poppy made a noise of annoyance. "It isn't as though you haven't seen me undress. Many times."

"That was before." He thrust his hands deep within his pockets as he retreated back to the doorway.

"Yes, well, I'm undressing now, and I don't see you attempting to leave." Her drawers landed in a heap of white around her ankles, leaving just the chemise hovering around mid-thigh and her corset.

After a visible swallow, Win's shoulders tensed. "I need to shave."

At home, they had shared a bath. Win would lean over the sink and shave as Poppy let down her hair. Hurt swelled within her breast. Whether he did not want to give in to that intimacy or didn't want her seeing him maneuver around his damaged face, she couldn't tell, nor did it matter. He did not trust her regardless.

"Then you'll have to wait." Holding his gaze, she reached to unravel the ties of her corset. It fell to the floor. He swallowed again, and a look of hot need filled his eyes before he dampened it. Despite her bravado, an answering lick of heat flickered between her thighs. *Make him remember.* Dear God, but she was going to take the advice of Mary Chase, an unmarried girl. Unmarried *woman* who was the protégée of Lucien Stone, notorious sinner and seducer. Poppy moved to the dressing table, aware of the sway of her breasts beneath her thin chemise. The silence was too thick, enough to hear the sound of the clock in the outer room ticking and Win's breath working a sharp, unsteady pace.

Her limbs did not quite work normally. She was too aware for that. Fingers cold, she took hold of her hairbrush. His eyes followed, and her body reacted, pulling tight, shivering, not from cold now but with heat. Thick bristles moved through her hair, the faint sound a symphony in the quiet room. And always his eyes upon her.

By the time she got to one hundred strokes, she hadn't the courage to look up at him and discover his expression. His immense calm had apparently returned, for he hadn't so much as moved from his spot by the door. She was a fool to play this game, a fool to think she could outlast his patience. Irritation prickled her neck at the thought, and she set down the brush with a distinct clatter. Well then. Perhaps she ought to do something less mundane than brush her hair.

Tossing the thick length of it over her shoulder, she propped her leg upon the bench and bent to undo her garters. That the position also thrust her backside out and highlighted the length of her legs was a boon. Reward came in the form of his breath drawn quick and sharp. When he spoke, it was almost a shock to her system, for he had been so silent.

"What game are you playing at, Poppy?"

"No game." She lifted the edge of her chemise just enough to expose her garter ties. "I take my duty in keeping you safe quite seriously."

"Enough of this madness. You are not my protector. You. Are. My. Wife."

"Is that what I am?" The garter wouldn't come loose. She bent over farther. Gods, but she was too aware of her exposure and the way the cool air touched her naked thighs like a caress. A wicked urge had her parting her legs farther. "You've done a fine job of making me feel like one lately."

She didn't see him move, didn't know to react, until a whisper of linen over wool just behind her back made her turn. Too late. He caught her elbow and spun her around. Angry and tired, she snapped. Poppy lifted her arm, throwing him off, then grabbed his wrist. One good shove and he was the one pinned against the wall, his cheek pressed to it, his arm behind his back—

His counter-attack was so fast that she felt it before she saw it. Her shoulder blades slammed against the wooden wardrobe doors. Hard, but not enough to hurt. And then he was there, his thigh pushing between hers so that she could not kick out, his grip firm as he held one of her wrists high above her head.

Well then.

Blood up and breathing quickened, her breasts rose and fell against the crush of his chest. She could move, but not much. He bent close until they were nose to nose. It was delicious. And maddening.

Win's eyes, glinting with dark humor, bore into hers. "Would you look at that. Poppy Lane ensnared."

She allowed a grin then and adjusted the grip of her free hand that was trapped between them. "Oh, I don't know."

She felt the exact moment he realized she held his cods in her hand, for they tightened as he huffed out a choked breath. And then he began to swell, his long length thickening and rising against the heel of her hand. She swallowed hard. "I believe it is you caught in a snare, Mr. Lane."

Challenge glimmered in his eyes, and he nudged against her palm, gently, teasing, patronizing. "Go on then. Here is my body. Guard it well, wife."

Bastard. Her knees buckled with the urge to sink down and draw him out of his trousers. "I do not find you amusing."

He leaned in a touch, his cock a hard press against her arm, his stones filling her hand. His lips canted with a little smile. Those expressive lips that she knew could be soft, or hard. So hard. She watched them move. "Not even a little?"

Slowly she lifted her eyes and then stroked, running a finger down the center of his tight sack. He grew tighter, a strangled sound gurgling in his throat as he pushed into her touch.

"Poppy." A dark warning. An invitation. "You take my cock in hand, you had better be ready to toss it off."

"Your rude behavior won't scare me away." But it made her inexplicably hot. Damn him.

His gaze grew shadowed. "Who said I wanted you scared?"

She tried to breathe, but he was too close, his cock throbbing now against her hand. "And how do you want me?"

His lips touched her temple, the merest caress before slipping away. "I want you safe. I want you gone from here."

She glared back at him, and their mouths brushed. Desire and frustration made his eyes go dark. She sympathized, but wouldn't let him go. "I am here to protect you, Win. Whether you like it or not."

The wrong thing to say, apparently. His nostrils flared, and his gaze frosted over. "So then," he murmured against her lips, "is this the full-service guarding that you usually provide?"

She wrenched him.

"Ah!" Win fell to the floor, cupping himself. "Christ!" He hissed again, then looked up at her through the wild strands of his hair as Poppy stepped around him. "Bad form, Poppy. Exceedingly."

"Come now, I did not do it that hard."

His even, white teeth snapped together with a click. "Had you balls, madam, I'd be happy to reciprocate. Then we'd see who was flippant."

"Idle threats, Win."

"Poppy Ann Lane," he snarled. "You get back here."

"You know," she tossed over her shoulder, "at the moment, I'm sorely considering going by Poppy Ellis once more."

"We are not finished with this."

Her heels clipped against the floor as she strode farther away. "Oh, I believe we are."

# *Chapter Seven*

~~~~~~❧~~~~~~

*London, 1869—A Kiss*

It had been one week since he'd last seen her. Propriety demanded that Winston wait that long to call on Poppy again. But he was beginning to think to hell with propriety. The way he thought of Poppy was far from proper. And waiting had nearly driven him mad. Her scent, from where she'd brushed up against him on the way back to her home, had faded from his coat, and he longed for it. He'd longed for everything about her—the sound of her voice, the quick flash of her eyes, and her touch.

But now she was with him again, walking at his side, her slim hand a light, yet profound weight upon his arm. They hadn't spoken for some moments, Poppy nibbling on her bottom lip as they strolled along, and he wondering what had caused her sudden and obvious case of nervousness. Her cheek held a faint blush, and her eyes would not fully meet his.

Unable to stand the suspense any longer, he cleared his throat. "Have I done something to offend you?" He refused to entertain the notion that she did not want to be with him.

Her smooth gait bobbled, but she corrected it quickly. Her flush, however, spread. "No." She made a small noise, and her fingers twitched on his arm. "I am...well, that is to say, I am simply glad to see you, Mr. Lane."

It was his turn to falter. He stopped and turned to face her. Pink-cheeked and flustered, she met his eyes with effort, and a grin spread over his face, one that he felt with his whole being. "I am very glad to see you too, Miss Ellis."

Watching him, she too began to grin, a slow, wide unfurling of a smile that had him leaning toward her. But then, with sudden and violent fury, the wind whipped about them and it started to rain, a spring downpour that had idle strollers scrambling to leave and the more prepared London folk pulling out their umbrellas.

"Come!" Grabbing her hand, he ran them along the path, toward the willow that they'd stopped under before.

Breathless and laughing, they huddled underneath its canopy, and Poppy smiled up at him. "I had no idea you could move so quickly, Mr. Lane."

He laughed a bit, but tried to pull it in. "Ought I have taken better care of your sensibilities, Miss Ellis?"

Poppy shook her head, her eyes still alight. "I would be extremely disappointed should you coddle me, Mr. Lane."

Beneath the willow, it remained relatively dry, but a drop broke through and landed on her high, curved cheek. It rolled down from the corner of her eye like a tear. He caught it with his thumb and rubbed it away from her smooth skin. Touching her sent a bolt of heat down his center, and he stepped closer, cupping her jaw, loving the way her breath audibly quickened.

Then he did what he'd been dying to do since he'd met her. His lips brushed hers, and his breath hitched. Soft. So utterly soft. Yet the contact made his lungs hurt. He pulled back just enough that their lips still touched when they breathed. "As I suspected. You are heaven." And then he had to do it again, caress her parted lips. He hadn't realized how a kiss could make him go utterly weak.

She stumbled into him, her hands clutching at his lapels as if she too had gone weak, and their lips mashed awkwardly. Poppy pulled back, turning a brilliant shade of magenta. Tenderness kicked into his heart.

"I'm sorry." She turned impossibly pinker. "I...I haven't kissed a man before."

He grinned. "Me either."

She hit his shoulder lightly. "You know what I mean."

"Mmm..." He wrapped an arm about her waist, drawing her nearer as he leaned against the willow, pleased to note that she did not protest. One thing he knew decidedly about Poppy Ellis was that she did not let anyone order her about. Sweet God, but her weight along his body felt good. "I do." He brushed another kiss over her lips; now that he'd started, he couldn't stop. "But it doesn't change the fact that I haven't kissed anyone either."

She studied him as though he were an exotic animal, or perhaps she merely thought him mad. "Why not?"

He stroked her cheek. "Because I hadn't wanted to until now." It was the truth. He was male, and thus he'd spent his fair share of time thinking of tupping, but his imaginings had been of faceless women. He wasn't the sort to seduce the busty chambermaid or pay for a whore's services.

When she opened her mouth to question, he slid his

hand into her hair to cup the back of her warm neck. "Shall we practice together?" he murmured before finding her lips again.

Her eyes fluttered closed as he sampled her mouth with small touches of his lips.

Her voice grew husky. "I am quite…"—another kiss—"a proponent of…"—he kissed her again—"thorough practicing."

"Good," he whispered against her mouth.

She sighed, and the need to taste her turned into a desperate thing. He kissed her harder, opening her lips with his, coming at her from different angles to learn the texture of her—the softness of her lips and the sweet moistness of her mouth. On impulse, he touched his tongue to hers, and his world went white hot. She tasted like rain and felt like heaven. He groaned and did it again, his hand clutching her satin hair to keep her in place. But she wasn't going anywhere. Her fingers tangled into his hair as she kissed him back, her slick tongue twining with his.

Rain fell in ice-cold drops against his cheeks. He wouldn't be surprised if they sizzled on contact; he was so hot. His breath came in bursts as his body started to shiver with need. When he could no longer breathe, he broke off the kiss, only far enough to look at her flushed cheeks and sparkling eyes. *Where have you been all my life? And what took you so long to find me?* He had the strangest feeling that only now, at this moment, had he truly become whole.

"I'm going to marry you," he whispered against her lips.

He felt her smile, and her slim arms pulled him closer. "Cheeky. One kiss and already you are so sure of yourself?"

In this? "Oh, yes."

# Chapter Eight

~~~✦~~~

Cool quiet greeted Jack as he entered the solace of his room. He loved that first moment of truly being alone in a secure space. It stripped a layer away from him, as if taking off his greatcoat. He'd never had a home that was solely his, not really. But thanks to Ian Ranulf, he'd had a room and a position as part of a pack. At the end of a long day, Jack liked nothing better than to shut his door, lie upon his bed, and read a good book. No one knew, of course. And he'd deny it if asked, but it was the truth. He craved his own personal space like he craved air.

It had hurt when Ian first urged him to go with Lane. Jack wasn't an idiot. He knew what Ian was doing. Throwing him out of the nest. Perhaps he had hidden behind the walls of Ian's home for too long. He was man enough to admit that at least.

Now he was tired. The damned demon had eluded him all day. Jack craved a stiff drink and a short nap before heading out once more. Shrugging out of his coat and tossing it aside, Jack had taken two steps when he stopped short. He wasn't alone. His knife was in his hand and he was whirling around to face his bed in an instant, knowing in the back of his mind that he'd have already been dead if it was a true attack. When he saw what greeted him, all available blood within his body surged south, and his heart pounded. Great, hot fuck. His knife hand shook before he clenched it tight.

His gaze sought the particulars first, the lithe length of her legs, a tiny peek of a tawny nipple through gauzy silk, the dark, seductive shadow at the apex of her thighs. Reclined upon his bed like some sort of modern day Salome, wrapped in swaths of diaphanous gold silk and smiling with coy promise. Mary Chase. In his room. Ruining the sanctity of it.

He swallowed twice before his mouth worked. "What the bloody hell are you doing?" Revenge, if he had to guess.

Her smile grew, and little dimples broke out on her cheeks. He wasn't aware that she had dimples. Jack mentally shook himself and tightened his grip on the knife. His blood pounded through his veins, straight to his cock, damn it all.

"I asked you a question," he said when she didn't answer.

With her usual grace, she rose to her knees, and that thin fabric shifted, lovingly caressing her slight curves. "I should think that obvious, Jack."

Jack? He wasn't aware that she even knew his first name. He didn't trust her an inch and would rather face a full-turned werewolf or a blood-starved demon before he touched her. But he could look. So he let himself, doing so with insolence, lingering on places that made him go hot. "I knew you'd have superior tits," he drawled, hoping she'd slap him and get out.

She only smiled and slithered out of the bed, heading toward him. His skin grew tighter, hotter. Piss and shit, she was going to touch him. He backed up a step but halted when she grinned at the movement.

Her low, caramel-thick voice drifted over him. "I am tired of fighting, aren't you?"

"Not particularly."

Her cinnamon spice perfume surrounded him before she did. "I do wonder, Jack, why you deny what is so plain to see." Slim, hot arms wrapped about his neck, and soft breasts pressed against his chest. He forced himself to look down into her eyes. Those wide, golden eyes could beguile a man in an instant. They gleamed now, not golden but her more human light brown. Petal soft lips touched his ear. "Why you don't take what you want."

"Because I don't want you." He didn't. His insides twisted from being this close to her, but his body didn't seem to care.

As close as she was, she felt the reaction, and a soft chuckle rumbled against his skin, making it twitch. "Liar."

It wasn't right. She wasn't right. She was too compliant. Too easy. A shiver of warning, touched with icy fear, lit down his spine an instant before her palm cupped his cheek, and she drew his mouth down to hers. Cold, dead. He reared back, a shout bubbling up, but iron-hard hands held him fast as a tongue snaked into his mouth and down his throat in a river of white-hot fire. Into his belly, tearing into his soul. And then he was screaming.

The heavy weight of silk satin settled upon Poppy's shoulders, and she resisted the urge to squirm. There were worse things than getting trussed up in a dinner gown, she was sure; she just could not think of them at the moment. The color of a pink rose in bloom, the gown Mary Chase laced her into was inarguably beautiful. Held up by sleeves that were thin enough to be called straps, the low squared-off bodice did surprising wonders to Poppy's meager bosom. And while the style of the day, according to Daisy and Miranda, was to adorn one's dress with as much frills and laces as possible—thus giving a woman the appearance of a flower, which really made Poppy want to roll her eyes—this bodice was utterly smooth and devoid of ornamentation. For which Poppy was thankful. The skirt, however, was another matter.

Mary gave the bodice a final tug, and Poppy expelled a pained breath as Mary moved on to fuss with the gown's more problematic area, namely the overskirt, with its numerous drapings, train, and whatnot. Bloody hell, but there were so many yards of undulating pale pink that Poppy could barely feel her own legs. They'd been smothered.

In an effort not to panic, she smoothed a hand over the tight waist of her bodice and glanced down at Mary, whose mouth had a decidedly unhappy pinch about the corners. "You are certain that you do not want to join us for dinner?" Poppy could not give an apple in Eden about the rules.

"No, mum." Mary fluffed the overskirt, her nimble fingers making certain the draping rested just so. "I believe it would be a good time to make another round of the ship."

"Good thinking." Poppy took a breath and, not getting nearly enough air in the blasted torture chamber of a dress, took another. "I wish I could go with you."

Her palm still held the memory of Win, the weight and feel of him. Admittedly, she had played rather dirty. But the man knew precisely how to drive her to madness.

Which both vexed her and secretly thrilled her. Regardless, she wasn't keen on coming face to face with him just now. He had to be ... smarting.

Hands hovering around her middle, she took a light breath and glanced back down at Mary. "You will be careful."

Mary rose in an effortless glide. "Of course. I intend to roam in the astral plane." Which meant her body would be tucked safely in her room as her spirit slipped into all sorts of places Poppy could not go. Mary reached for Poppy's evening fan, a confection of white lace, blush pink satin, and white painted cast iron supports that could crack a bone with one good whack. A clever little weapon, as most males viewed a lady's evening fan as frippery. Their mistake. Mary turned back, and the lamplight shone on her slim upper arm. A scratch marred her skin, not a gash, but deep enough to have drawn blood.

Poppy moved to touch it, but stopped when Mary flinched and averted her eyes. "What happened?"

Looking away, she fiddled with Poppy's evening gloves. "I lost my balance and had a run-in with a call box."

She looked so thoroughly disgruntled that Poppy almost smiled. "Yes, well, call boxes have been known to be a nuisance now and then."

Mary's cheek twitched as if she were fighting a smile, or a frown, as she stepped back and looked over Poppy with a critical eye. Poppy refused to squirm but stood like the proverbial wolf in sheep's clothing, hoping that she'd pass muster.

Mary smiled with satisfaction. "More than enough to make Mr. Lane remember."

Poppy expelled a nervous laugh. "I do not believe Mr. Lane has a faulty memory." No, it worked all too well.

Mary shook her head slowly. "He is suffering. Anyone can see it." Her grin was cheeky then. "I'd wager that he will suffer a bit more before the night is out."

Poppy might have answered but Winston walked in. How he always knew to appear the precise moment she was ready was a mystery. One that she put aside in favor of looking at her husband. Fitted out in crisp white-and-black evening kit that outlined his lean frame, he stood tall and just a bit defiant in the center of the room. His shaggy hair had been tamed and swept back from his strong face. And while she was sure there were those who would stare at his scars and not the man beneath, all she saw was a man who'd been to hell and back, and was tougher for it. Like steel wrought and forged, he'd transformed into something more than before.

Soulful eyes of blue-grey travelled over her, taking in her elaborate coiffure and evening gown with one glance. Not a glimmer of appreciation or emotion in that look. His voice was as crisp as his suit. "Shall we?"

Suffering, was he? Hardly. Poppy stiffened her spine. "Of course."

# Chapter Nine

❧ ❧

Pink. She was wearing blasted pink. Poppy never wore pink. Never wore much of any color other than brown or grey. He hadn't cared either way; he never really looked at her clothes, just her. But now. Now, she had to wear pink. Win stared down at his plate, at the pale slab of whiting fish swimming in cream sauce, and tried not to think of pink. He and Poppy had not exchanged more than a few words since their "chat" earlier, both of them clearly still angry, and his cods still egregiously sore. Which ought to have been enough to put him off lustful thoughts for a good while. But no, his baser self simply flew past that unpleasantness and went straight to the fact that Poppy had held him in her hand. *Stroked* him. And that it had been three months since he'd tupped his wife. Suddenly, it was imperative that he do so. Which was about when logic returned to tell him he hadn't a snowflake's chance in hell.

Poppy moved beside him, a slight adjustment of her seat, and he heard the rustle of that satin. Undulating yards and folds of shining, pale pink. Pink ought to have clashed horribly with her red hair. It did not. Instead it made him think of other places she was pink and red.

His fist curled around the cool, thick handle of his fork. The table and those around him faded in favor of another vision, of a nest of vibrant red curls and petal pink folds, glimmering and wet. Long, white legs spread in supplication, leading the way to that gorgeous pink and red offering. His cock rose hard and insistent against his trousers. He bit the inside of his cheek to keep from grunting, God help him. He stabbed at his food, making hash of the fish.

Poppy was saying something, her low erotic voice stroking his sensitized skin. Something about being pleased that parliament passed the Explosive Substances Act, which seemed a fitting subject to hold her interest, given her secret work. Personally, he didn't give a fig. The scent of books and lemons drifted across their small divide, and his lids fluttered closed.

"What say you, Lane?"

All eyes were on him. Win forced his head up. Mr. Babcock was looking directly at him, his bulbous and veiny nose quivering as if smelling Win's weakness. They didn't want him here. Every averted glance, the stiffness in which they held themselves around him, cried out that fact. English gentlemen did not have ruined faces, and if they did, they kept them politely out of sight, hidden away like Quasimodo within the bell tower. His words came out slow and as sluggish, it seemed, as his heated blood.

"I find I have no opinion." It was a rude and unconscionable response, but he did not care. He was tired of pretending. Tired of everything save forgetting himself in the hot silk of pink and red.

Poppy's gaze on him burned stronger than the rest. He

ignored it and took a bite of what was before him. Only after he began chewing did he register that the waiter had replaced his fish with a plate of beef and mushrooms. He bloody hated mushrooms. His throat closed but he forced the bite down, gagging on the slimy feel of it.

At the periphery of his vision, her arm moved, and her hand came an inch closer to his plate, as though she thought to touch him.

*Do not do it, sweet. Or I shall pull you down beneath this table and fuck you senseless.*

The violence of his own thoughts shocked him. And perhaps she felt his disquiet as well, for she made no further move toward him. Even so, he felt her gaze remain on him as the conversation started up again, stilted and confused. Good Englishmen did not respond as he did. It upset the balance. Now they all sought to cover his gaffe. That small bit of pity he heard beneath it all squelched the desire that ran amok in his veins. And thank God for that, as his cockstand mercifully subsided. He'd had concerns of being stuck at the table indefinitely.

Win laid down his fork and pushed back from the table, and all those pairs of eyes followed his every movement. "If you will excuse me." Carefully, he placed his linen next to his plate. "I fear I am not well at the moment."

He did not wait for a reply but quit the table.

Mrs. Babcock's voice chased after him as he went. "It's seasickness. Happens to the best of travelers at times."

Mrs. Babcock had no idea.

Poppy's knees wobbled as she walked back to her stateroom. It was a humiliating thing to acknowledge, but true. She feared what she would find when she finally tracked Win down. His behavior at dinner unnerved her.

Win always said the correct thing, always. And the way he sat, hunched over, his expression brooding, was almost frightening in its intensity. Jesus, the man had eaten a mushroom. Hated mushrooms. His throat closed...

Her stride lengthened and became more natural, or as natural as the blasted evening gown would allow. At the stateroom door, she found herself faltering. She could almost feel him within. Her cold hand curled around the door handle. Taking a deep breath, she entered.

He was pacing the floor, his powerful body eating up the space with quick, controlled movements. He glanced up at her entrance, but then went back to pacing, his shaggy hair hiding his eyes from her. Win in a temper was a display to which few were privy, for he had always held his in so brilliantly. Poppy found them fascinating, a small peek at the man behind the proper façade.

Madness must run in her veins because his ire made her so very hot. Her breath hitched before she could speak. "What is wrong?"

He thrust up a hand. "Do not engage me, Poppy. I am in no mood for a discussion right now."

She slammed the door shut behind her. Correction. He made her bloody furious. She ripped her gloves off and flung them on the side table. "Why is it that we must wait for your favor to engage in conversation?"

He stopped short, and his glare was a blaze of winter-blue anger. "Pardon, madam, but are you accusing me of being petulant?"

"Oh, don't be coy, Win. You know you are, and it's bloody annoying."

A slow wash of red crept up his neck. Poppy held his gaze as her heart pounded. Win would never hurt her, not physically. He'd been a gentleman, careful and considerate. But that was before. There was a wildness in his eyes that had her breath coming short.

The moment stretched until she fought the urge to fidget or look away. But then it snapped when he spoke.

"Your dress is pink."

She blinked. "Yes."

"I don't like it. Take it off."

The bloody, rude, arrogant bastard. *No one* ordered her about in such a manner. She was of a mind to tell him just that. Only she paused. Win was not *no one*. He was her husband. And beneath the flare of anger in his eyes and the mulish set of his jaw, she saw something that made her breath catch—interest, need. He wanted her dress off, did he?

"No," she said. Lust curled between her legs, and her pulse raced.

Win's eyes narrowed. Poppy stepped away from the door and closer to him. Closer to the bed. There was more than one way to communicate. And if he refused to do so with words, then perhaps actions would take them past this impasse. Behind the folds of her skirts, her hands were fists, trembling and cold. But her chin lifted.

"You want my dress off, then take it off yourself."

His mouth opened and shut. The line of his shoulders tensed. They regarded each other in silence until the mad rush of her blood filled her ears and drowned out all other sound.

"I have half a mind to call your bluff," he said in a low growl.

"That would imply I am bluffing."

His nostrils flared. Standing tall and tense, he was the most stirring man she'd ever seen. She'd loved mussing up his polish. Now he was all ragged edges, and she wanted to see it unleashed. Cold heat danced along her skin, lifted the tiny hairs along her arms, and tightened her nipples. His gaze went to her bodice, honing in on her reaction with stunning precision. His body stiffened further.

"Do it," she said. "Take the dress off me, Win."

His wintry eyes held hers for one more moment, and then he was stalking forward. With every step he took, the heat within her coiled tighter. He stopped before her, and a visible tremor ran through him. Then his hands were on her, the pads of his fingers rough as he grasped her shoulders and whirled her around in a brisk move. His knuckles grazed her back as he caught hold of her dress and undid the hooks with hard tugs. Poppy braced herself so she would not fall back onto him. Not yet.

"Pink," he muttered. "Have you any idea..."

The bodice loosened, gaping. "Idea?" Her voice was a breath, her legs trembling.

He didn't answer but continued to undo her bodice with angry hands. The satin slid over her arms, the bodice falling forward and down to her waist. Cool air hit her exposed skin and she trembled, waiting for the rest. It did not come. On a curse, he stepped away, leaving her wanting. Slowly, Poppy turned, not bothering to hold her bodice up.

But he did not look at her body or the deep pink corset she wore. His eyes held hers. "Are you trying to provoke me?"

Was he blind? The expanse of his chest lifted and fell with each labored breath he took. She let her gaze travel down the length of him, still properly kitted out in his fine evening clothes. Oh but there was one thing about him that was most improper. Her mouth went dry. His massive erection was straining to break free of his trousers.

One of them made a sound; she couldn't be sure

whether it was she or Win, but that magnificent cockstand seemed to grow. Poppy ached to take it in hand, stroke and squeeze, tease it to completion. She knew exactly how to do it, exactly how he liked to be worked. Her body swayed with wanting. She could practically feel that cock in her mouth, filling it up, and she licked her parched lips.

"Finish what you started, husband."

He uncoiled like a snake, his hand catching her on the shoulder. One deft push and she was falling back onto the bed. She went willingly, anticipation thrumming through her veins and making her heart pound. He loomed over her, still so very angry, his body tense and his eyes flashing. But she could see the cracks forming around the façade, and it thrilled her.

"What do you want, Poppy?" His voice was sandpaper against steel. Satin rustled as he yanked her skirts up around her hips. Fabric tore, the shining pink billowing about her waist.

"Do you want this?" He cupped her, his hand hot and rough against her silk drawers. She almost groaned, but held it back. He would have to work for some things. A shiver went through her as two long fingers delved between the slit in her drawers and stroked through her wetness. "Do you want me here?"

He leaned in, not touching her with his body, only his hand and his tormenting fingers. Anger flashed in his eyes as he fondled her, not with finesse but with base intent. It made her white hot, and her thighs parted for him.

Win's nostrils flared again as he looked down at what she offered. "Pink and red," he murmured. "Enough to drive a man mad."

She swallowed hard, and he glanced back at her. "Do you want me, Poppy?"

She held his gaze, willing herself not to plead, not to say a word, but his fingers suddenly plunged into her, and her body tensed. It was too good, too much. Her thighs quivered with the need to demand *more, and harder, damn you.*

Win's eyes blazed, his mouth parting as he breathed. "Answer me." His free hand went to the fall of his trousers. "It won't change a thing. Getting me to fuck you won't change a thing."

Everything had already changed. She wanted to shout at him, rail with her fists, but she lay compliant and simply stared back, waiting, letting him finger her as he opened his trousers.

His cock bobbed free, pulsing and dark and enormously erect. Win's cock. That her staid, serious husband had such a large and thick cock was a secret she took almost perverse pleasure in. Nobody had seen it but her. Only she knew what he hid beneath his unassuming suits and his elegant manners. Her breath left in a rush, anticipation drawing her so tight that she trembled.

Their gazes clashed, each waiting for the other to yield. His hips moved between her thighs, a brush of wool against silk drawers. The hot crown of his cock touched her, and she almost jumped.

"It won't change a thing," he said again, weaker yet insistent, almost as if he were willing it so.

Defiance surged through her, and she opened her legs wider. "Prove it."

He grabbed her hips and thrust. Poppy's entire body tensed, the invasion of his thick length almost painful, and so damn intense that she bit her lip to keep from crying out. And it wasn't even all of him. She knew he had more to give. He pulled back and plunged again, delving further, rendering her incapable of speech. Heat swirled and spread from where he plundered. He moved automatically, as if he was determined not to feel, only take her.

The bed ropes squeaked in a steady rhythm. In. Out. Push. Pull. His hips slammed into hers, each thrust shoving her farther up the bedding, only his hands on her thighs keeping her in position. *Harder. Make me feel it.*

His eyes held hers as his cock moved, filling and emptying her. Oh God, but when he invaded, she could scarcely bear the pleasure of it. Inside she quaked, her body so very hot that she longed to rip free of her clothing, longed to rip his off as well and feel his skin upon hers. But she did not move, barely breathed, for fear of breaking the spell.

*Win.* How could she tell him how much she missed this? How much she'd yearned for him. Even now, when he tupped her like a dockside whore. *Win. Feel me.* His gaze bore into her, so cold, detached. Poppy melted against his assault. Her breath turned to rough pants. She was soaking now. Her sex pulsing. The sound of their combined breathing, the wet slap of flesh against flesh, and the rocking bed filled the silence between them.

A small sigh escaped her. Poppy cursed her weakness, but he'd heard it. Win's lips parted. The pump of his hips did not stop but the rhythm changed, his strokes shifting from purposeful to lingering. And she felt it with the whole of her body, the way he slowly started to . . . *explore* her. The ice in his expression thawed, melting as his eyes stayed on hers. His body leaned into hers, closer, closer, almost touching. A shiver of heat caught hold of her, and she arched her back. Her nipples ached to be sucked, and the lack of the sensation only made them more sensitive. Fisting the sheets, she held on, letting him take her.

When that familiar crinkle between his brows formed and he bit his lower lip, she exploded, a keening cry breaking from her lips. Winston came with a hiss between his clenched teeth, his fingers biting into her hips. He stayed tense, grinding his length into her for one long, glorious moment. His chest brushed against hers as he panted, the soft bursts of breath warming her neck. Poppy licked her lips and stared up at the ceiling, too weak to do anything more and too afraid to wrap her arms about him as she wanted to do. Then he was up, pulling out in a move that made her cringe from the loss. Cool air filled the space between her legs that had once been scalding hot. She had barely lifted her head when she heard the door to the suite slam shut, leaving her alone once more.

# Chapter Ten

❧❧❧

*London, 1869—A Proposal*

Do you suppose," Poppy said, glancing down at him with her steady brown eyes, "that man walking along the path realizes the lady he's escorting is no older than fifteen?"

Winston stirred slightly, for he too had been watching the couple as he and Poppy reclined under their willow tree. For a week now, they'd taken a daily walk together, and always they ended up sitting beneath the willow where he'd kissed her for the first time. Today, however, she'd eased his head down onto her lap. The shocking intimacy of it, and that Poppy—his reserved and proper Poppy—had been the one to initiate liberties had almost unmanned him. But he was not so foolish as to protest. Besides, the comfort of her lap was utter heaven.

Poppy had felt him start at her question, for her cheeks pinked. "I like to people gaze. I can't seem to help myself."

He let his fingers touch hers where they rested lightly on his arm. "Neither can I." When she glanced down in surprise, he smiled. "Now then, you were saying about the strolling couple? Tell me your theory. You cannot see her face, as they are walking away from us. So then why do you assume she is a youth?"

Poppy's fingers pulled free from his and drifted up to his hair. He almost purred at the way she toyed with the ends as her gaze went back to the couple. "Her walk. She is not used to gowns of that length. Her skirts are tangling about her ankles because she hasn't yet learned to properly step."

"Mmm." He willed himself not to close his eyes but kept them upon the couple. He hadn't noticed that. "I do believe you are correct."

Poppy's brown eyes gleamed as she leaned in, the action bringing her rather pert bosom wonderfully close to his nose. "The question is, however, does he know?"

Winston cleared his throat, taking in a subtle breath of her intoxicating scent. *Soon.* Soon he would see those breasts. Anticipation simmered as he gave her a conspiratorial smile and paid attention to the subject at hand. "No, the question is, does she know he is cash poor?"

"Cash poor?" She nibbled on her bottom lip, but stopped quickly, as if correcting herself, and Winston wondered if she constantly self-governed her actions.

"I see nothing in his clothing to indicate poverty," Poppy said.

Because the sad truth was that clothing made the man, or woman. With a lift of his chin, Winston gestured toward the man. "Observe the soles of his shoes. There is a hole wearing on the left one. No man with proper means would allow that to happen. Unless," he nodded back at the man, "he saves his funds to address the more obvious items in his wardrobe."

He was rewarded with Poppy's grin, a full cheeky one that made her nose wrinkle.

"Very clever, Mr. Lane." She looked at him, and he grew a little dizzy basking under her admiration.

"I would like to be a detective." Winston blinked. Now that he hadn't meant to say. He hadn't even fully wanted to admit it to himself.

Poppy, however, did not see the strangeness of his desire. "Why not, then? I think you would be brilliant."

Had they been in private, he would have turned and nuzzled her belly before pulling her down atop of him. As it was, he ran a finger along the folds of her simple worsted gown. "My family would not condone it."

Her own blunt-tipped finger traced his ear, sending little shivers down his spine. "No, I suppose they wouldn't."

There it was again, that wall he could literally feel shooting up between them. The wall she erected whenever she remembered how disparate their families were. Annoyed, he plucked at her skirt, taking it out on her clothing, but she surprised him and rested her cool palm on the crown of his head.

"Why do you want to do it, Winston? When you could live a life of luxury and comfort?"

He rolled fully onto his back so that he could look at her without craning his neck. Behind the fiery nimbus of her hair, the lacy green branches swayed in the gentle breeze. "That is the first time you called me by my name."

She pursed her lips. "Shall I stop?"

He lifted a hand and cupped the back of her slim neck. "I want to hear it fall from your lips for all of my days."

Gorgeous, awkward pink flooded her cheeks. "Romantic drivel."

"Mmm." His thumb slid under the tight confines of her high collar and found her pulse. "I like a challenge." It was an answer to both her question and her statement.

Her laugh was short and a bit breathless. "Yes."

His fingers pushed through her silky hair. "I find the world a puzzle to be solved."

"You would." She leaned in just a touch closer.

Gods but he wanted to nibble at the perky tips of her breasts. He eased her even closer, wanting her to feel the heat of his breath. As if answering his prayers, hard little nipples appeared against her bodice. He smiled. "And I want to do some good in the world, not simply take from it."

"You would make a fine detective, Win."

Win. That did it.

It was an easy thing to pull her down and roll her alongside of him. She squeaked as she went. He barred her protest by resting his chest lightly upon hers while his legs tangled in her skirts.

"Winston Lane!" She laughed as he kissed her neck. "Unhand me. You are going to get us arrested for public indecency."

The light in her eyes and the way her breasts lifted and fell beneath her dress told a different story. One that had him grinning over the possibilities. He nuzzled the spot under her ear before kissing his way up her jaw. "All the better to fully acquaint myself with the law, my dear."

She laughed but stayed him with her hand, her eyes suddenly serious. "Why do you want to be with me?"

The soft confusion in her voice gave him pause, and he studied her before a tender smile tugged at his lips.

"Because you are honest and direct," he touched the curve of her cheek, "and, for whatever reason, I feel wholly myself when I am with you."

A shadow of something flickered in her eyes, and she frowned. "You believe me to be something better than I am, sir."

The sadness that dwelled in her eyes bothered him. His fingers trailed to the downy red hair at her temple. "And you give yourself too little credit." He cupped her face when she moved to protest, and he spoke first. "Why do you want to be with me?" No sooner were the words out than he wanted to take them back. Perhaps she did not have an answer. No one in his life ever really wanted to be around him. His studiousness made his brother edgy, and his father had always detested the sight of him. Winston swallowed hard. But Poppy merely smiled, and it was the dawn breaking over a winter sky. Her brown eyes traveled over his face.

"Strangely enough," she said, "for the very reasons you served to me."

He grinned wide. "As I thought. We were made for each other."

Her lips moved as he kissed them. *Trying to talk. Dear girl.* He deepened the kiss, sliding his tongue home. And she melted against him, her capable hands clutching at his biceps in a way that made him want to protect her, take on the world for her. "Marry me, Poppy." He kissed her again. Again. "Marry me. Marry me. Marry me." Soft kisses to underscore the seriousness of his need, and how he'd just laid his heart's desire bare beneath that tree.

"Win." Her fingers curled into his hair. She held him still and kissed him with a passion that had his heart racing. But she did not say yes.

# Chapter Eleven

"Bugger all." Winston pinched the bridge of his nose. God, tunneling into Poppy had been like coming home. She was the only woman he'd ever been with, had ever wanted. And he had swived her as if she were nothing more than a whore. He was a bastard to do it. He should not have touched her. Nothing was settled between them, and sex only complicated matters. He should have left the room the moment she'd entered it. Hell, there were so many things he should have done differently, he was losing track of them now. He had become, as Sheridan liked to say, a monumental cock-up.

Winston sank farther back into the corner of his booth in the Grand Salon and tapped a quick rhythm out on the marble tabletop. "Christ," he said to the tiny reflection of himself that floated along the surface of his coffee, "you have become quite the maudlin sop, haven't you?" Laughing softly, he rubbed a hand over his face. *Step one on the road back to sanity, stop talking to yourself.*

Beyond the lofty silence in the salon, he could hear

the muffled gaiety of his fellow travelers in the dining hall across the way, the occasional clink of china, and the ever-present hum of the engines. And then, over it all, came the sound of footsteps, steady and deliberate. For no accountable reason, the sound had the hairs along Winston's arms standing at attention and sent a shiver of warning down his spine. Slowly, like a man forced to face his executioner, Winston raised his head.

A man strolled directly down the center aisle of the salon, his reflection wavering in the polished marble floor. Attired in the precise lines of a black walking suit, his only nod to color was a scarlet ascot and the glint of gold from his watch chain. His features were lost beneath the brim of his top hat but a glimmer lit his eyes as they locked onto Winston. His stride was languid, as if he enjoyed having Winston watch him, and Winston's jaw locked, equal parts revulsion and irritation heating his blood. But years of instinct told him not to look away.

The man moved under a shaft of gaslight, and Winston's blood stilled. Perhaps it was a trick of the light but, for one sharp moment, the man appeared to have scars upon his cheek just as Winston did. His hair was the same wheat color and shaggy, a waving, rumpled mess that mirrored Winston's. Then the man came closer, and the illusion faded, revealing close-cut reddish brown hair and a face devoid of scars. He stopped directly in front of Winston's table.

"Hello, Winston Lane." The voice was smooth, soft even, and enough to send another tremor of foreboding down Winston's spine. Christ, was this the demon Poppy had warned him about? Only one way to find out.

"Do I know you?" Winston asked plainly. No chance in hell was he revealing his disquiet to this man.

The man's thin lips furled into a smile. "Now there's a question." Without waiting to be asked, he pulled out the chair across from Winston and sat. The scent of coal smoke and patchouli tickled Winston's nostrils. Crossing one leg over the other, the man sat back and regarded Winston with shadowed eyes. "*Do* you know me?"

The man was either mad, or he was the demon. Win didn't like his odds at the moment.

When Win didn't answer him, the man made a sound of amusement. "Since you have no memory of our earlier meeting, which," he pulled a thin, gold case from his coat pocket, "is in truth my fault entirely, you may call me Mr. Jones."

"Mr. Jones," Winston repeated dubiously. *My aunt Fanny.* Out of reflex, Win's hand moved to the place where he kept his gun, only to realize, rather belatedly, that he'd left his coat behind.

"I've gone by many names, Loki, Dolus. You might even call me the devil. Which would be missing the point. Who I am is not as important as what I do. I grant bargains in exchange for souls." With precise movements, the man took out an Egyptian cigarette and lit it, filling the space between them with an aromatic perfume. His thumb drew across his lower lip to catch an errant flake of tobacco before he spoke again. "Ask me next why I am here."

"How about this," Win snapped back, "what the bloody hell do you want?"

Abruptly, Jones sat forward, and his eyes were entirely colorless, like chips of ice in a glass. "I've come to collect my due." With that, he reached into his suit coat pocket once more and produced a rolled length of old foolscap. The roll of paper called to Winston in a way he did not understand, nor like. But he felt the familiarity of it with a soul deep shudder.

"Your due?" This was new. Poppy hadn't said a word about debts. His mouth went dry.

Jones drew on his cigarette again and exhaled slowly, sending interlocking rings of blue smoke drifting into the air. Quite a trick. The man tapped out a line of ash. "It is like this," Jones said. "On April the fifth, eighteen sixty-nine, you signed this contract."

"Bollocks! You're having me on." But he did not miss that the date was precisely fourteen years prior to the date that he'd been attacked by the werewolf in a dank London alley.

Taking one more draw on his cigarette before setting it down, Jones carefully unrolled the foolscap and pushed the paper forward. One long, polished nail tapped the document that lay between them. "Read it."

Nothing on Earth could induce Winston to touch that paper. "You're mad. I've never even seen you before." Shit. But the denial *felt* like a lie.

Jones took up his cigarette again and inhaled with almost indecent pleasure. "That is your signature, is it not?"

Winston's own, familiar signature was slashed across the bottom of the paper. Ignoring it, Winston leaned in, and the paper crinkled under his forearms. "I would have remembered *this*."

"Ah, now that was part of the agreement. You were to forget everything upon signing. After all, if my clients remembered their deals, they might try to find a way out of them before payment." Cigarette dangling between his pale lips, Jones bent over the table to peer at the contract. "See there. Paragraph 13?" Jones pointed to a particular paragraph. "Upon signature, the principal—that would be you—shall lose all memory of the agreement—"

"Why in the bloody hell would anyone in their right mind agree to forget what they've signed?" It was all too fantastic. He did not do such things. Christ, but his heart was pounding again. *This* was why the demon tracked him down? Did Poppy know of it? Nausea boiled within his stomach.

"Well, that is rather the point, isn't it?" Jones crossed one leg over the other. "You weren't in your right mind at the time. A fact of which I took advantage. This human notion of fairness and honor makes you weak." He blew out another chain of smoke rings. "I snare more 'gentlemen' this way than any other." With a snap of his fingers, a waiter appeared with tray in hand.

The waiter set down two double-tiered glasses and a small carafe of water. A clear colored liquid winked and swayed in the bottom of each glass. The ingenious little liquor glasses, with their top tiers filled with ice, were made for only one drink: absinthe. The waiter's movements were precise yet held a bit of theater, as if he knew well that his patrons expected it in this moment. He'd be correct, generally. Only Winston was in no mood. Such excitement had long dimmed for him. Even so, his eyes stayed on the waiter's hands as he lifted the water carafe and poured it into the top tier of the glass, which served as a filter. Slowly, the water filled up the tier before dripping down into the lower glass. The second the water hit the absinthe, everything transformed, the liquid turning a luminous and milky peridot color. No sugar was used; this was a high-quality brew. The warm scent of anise drifted up, and Winston's mouth watered even as his pulse quickened.

Too many days and nights had he lost to the Green Fairy. He'd almost succumbed to her long ago, drowning himself in the euphoric haze she provided. Because he had wanted a woman that he could not—A memory slammed into him, fragmented but strong.

Running a hand over his face, Winston fought for control as the waiter departed. His mind was a fog. Jones's white eyes bore into Winston. "No more games. You will remember it all. Now." Jones pushed a glass closer to Winston. "Drink and remember, Winston Lane."

"No." A cold sweat broke out over his brow. Winston would not drink. To do so would be his undoing. He knew it instinctively.

Jones's icy eyes went crimson. "Drink it, or I'll do it the hard way."

Winston considered the hard way, but his hand moved of its own accord, as if compelled to obey. Absinthe spilled over his lips, pouring down his throat in a river of fire. The glass teetered as he gasped. Images flashed before his eyes. Drunken laughter, a haze of smoke, Poppy's smiling eyes, his father's scowl. *You will not marry the daughter of a merchant. Win, I cannot marry you; your father will destroy my family.* Jones's long-fingered hand offering up a bone quill. *Sign it and start anew, Winston Lane.*

Winston's thighs banged against the table as he surged up, toppling his glass and sending absinthe across the marble. Jones's hand snatched up Winston's wrist and yanked him back down with bone-crushing force.

"Calm yourself." Jones's hand was warmer than human flesh, and though Winston wrenched at his arm, the man's grip was unbreakable. "Really, I detest this part. The next thing will be you begging, and that becomes quite tedious."

"I never beg," Winston said through his teeth.

"Well, good. I hate whiners." Apparently deciding that Winston wasn't going anywhere, Jones let him go. "Fourteen years ago, I gave you a new life. You wanted to dispose of the position given to you by birth and become a detective. You wanted a certain redheaded chit to be your wife. I gave you those things."

Gave him Poppy? No, not her. What they had was real. "You cannot manipulate a person's experiences," Winston ground out.

Jones selected a fresh cigarette and lit it. "What is a man but what he thinks himself to be? Moreover, what is a life but a collection of memories?" Jones exhaled. "And I, my ignorant fellow, manipulate memories. For a fee, that is."

"Jesus."

"No," Jones smiled, "I am not he." The smile left. "I altered the memories of you and those within your sphere. Thus it became your truth, their truth."

"My father did not disown me?" The memory of being disowned was still there, clear as day. *I no longer have a son named Winston. From this day forth.*

Jones laughed shortly. "Ra's balls, you are the son of a duke. The spare, yes, but do you honestly think he'd let you go? He was ready to crush all opposition to pull you to heel. No son of his was going to gad about playing at detective."

Jones was repeating his father's words. He could hear them play in his head now and felt the same suffocating anger. *You marry that chit and every door in London will shut in your face. I'll see you a beggar before a son of mine gads about playing at detective.*

"Until his dying day, he believed you'd gone to the grave before him," Jones said. "Your name is on the family tomb. Very impressive structure."

Christ, his father had thought him dead. He didn't know how he felt about that, seeing as he'd bargained his soul to get away from him. Had he really been so desperate? Yes, he realized, yes he had.

"This is why you are here?"

Jones grinned. "Poppy Ann warned you about me, did she?"

The way he spoke of Poppy, with such familiarity, sent a bolt of sheer rage through Winston's chest. "Did she know? Of this." He waved his hand in the direction of the paper.

Jones snorted in amusement. "You are wise to ask. That woman keeps secrets upon secrets. She's a bloody menace."

Winston wasn't about to dignify that with a remark. The silence grew taut until Jones exhaled with a long, suffering sigh. "She is entirely ignorant. Fooled by a lie as well." His smile was pure evil. "So much for your righteous indignation toward liars, Winston."

Winston's fists ached with the need to smash the man's face. He breathed through the anger and said nothing as Jones continued. "However, if you need to throw a bit of blame her way, you may be happy to know that your interest in Poppy aroused my curiosity enough to meet with you." He shrugged. "Enough of trifle talk. Let us move on to payment."

Though his stomach rolled, Winston pulled himself together and sat straight. Inside he might want to scream and run but he had made this mess, so he'd face his fate. "My soul, is it?"

Jones sucked on his cigarette then put it down and picked up the contract. "Yes, your soul. As the contract states, the deal was to expire when Death came for you."

Swallowing hard, Winston spoke. "You're going to take me now?" God, he hadn't even made his peace with Poppy. Right then, he wanted to hold her so badly the muscles along his arms clenched.

Jones's teeth were sharp and white as they flashed in the gaslight. "Not precisely. You created a bit of a dilemma when you met Death last April. You cheated him."

"Cheated *him*?" Winston snapped. "You mean that werewolf?"

"That wasn't a werewolf. Had that been the werewolf in question, you'd be rife with syphilis right now. Which you most certainly aren't."

Odd as it was, a feeling of relief coursed through Winton's body. Months ago, the fear he'd been infected had become the veritable white elephant in the room, and he'd forced Archer to do the tests. He'd proven clean but never knew why.

"No," continued Jones, "it was Death you faced that night, sent by me. He simply chose that disguise." Something dark passed over Jones's face before he pushed it away and looked at Winston with a near-pleasant expression. "You were supposed to die but that SOS bastard saved you. And now, dear boy, you are in breach of contract."

"Bollocks! It isn't any fault of mine that Death lost. I wasn't very aware at the time, you realize."

"Doesn't matter. You did not die when you were supposed to."

"So then what? What is it you want if not 'precisely' my soul?"

Again, Jones placed the contract before Winston, and his long nail tapped on a paragraph. "What I am owed."

Winston glanced down at the gleaming nail and the words before it. A bolt of sensation shot through Winston, as if he'd done this very thing before. It took a moment for his eyes to focus on the contract. Reading was a slow, laborious process as the words kept blurring before him. But the meaning of them started to sink in, and as it did, he turned ice cold and his body trembled.

*Should the principal fail to comply with the terms so listed, the grantor shall take as recompense the soul of the principal's first born.* All the blood drained from his face in a rush that made him sway. "No!" He leapt up and grabbed Jones by his lapels, hauling him close. "Not a chance in bloody hell, do you hear me? Not one damn chance!"

For a moment, Jones stared back, but then small licks of flame began to creep out from under his collar and dance over his face, and those strange eyes grew larger, less human looking. His voice went deep, hollow, as if he spoke from the depths of a black tunnel. "You think you can forfeit?"

"I would have never agreed to that." Winston jerked Jones closer, heedless of the heat biting at his knuckles. "Never."

"Agree you did. Because you, in the cocksure bloom of youth, believed yourself invincible. That when the time came, it would all go swimmingly. And because," he leaned with a low, rolling chuckle, "you failed to properly read the contract, dear boy."

Not wanting to touch him a second longer, Winston let Jones go with a shove. "It doesn't matter. I've left Poppy, and there is no chance of you getting what you want." Christ, but he'd just tupped her. If they had a child, only to…A shudder went through him, and he fell back into his seat.

Jones grinned. "How naive you are being, Winston Lane. How long has it been since you left her? Three months?" He darted forward in a move too quick to be human. "Are you so very sure of her then?"

Despite being seated, Winston's knees went weak. "She would have told me if she was with child." They'd tried for so many years. And failed.

"Poppy Lane divulge an inconvenient truth? Heaven forefend." Jones straightened his crooked lapels. "Come, man, I can alter lives. Did you really think I would waltz back into yours and demand what I cannot have? Ridiculous human. A child grows in her womb. I can feel it."

Surely fate could not be so cruel as to bless them now. But, God, what if she was with child? Horror washed over Winston in a cold wave. Swallowing down bile, he slumped into his chair. *Jesus.* Winston sank his head into his hands and tried to breathe.

"Ah, yes. A son is on the way, I believe." Jones sighed. "I shall raise it as my own."

"Like hell!" Tableware rattled as Win slammed his hand down upon the table.

Jones shrugged lightly. "It is the bargain you made. No use crying about it now."

Rage surged hot and thick along Winston's flesh. His fists twitched with the need to do violence. With supreme effort, he calmed himself and focused because everything he held dear depended on what he would say. "Right then. You're a bargain demon; let us bargain."

The demon's expression eased into one of childlike delight. "Shrewd Winston Lane. I knew you'd make a counter offer."

Perhaps this was why the demon was here after all. He wanted something else. Winston only had to draw it out and find the right angle of attack. "Go on then, Jones. Tell me what you will take instead."

Jones tapped his long nail against his chin, and the gold ring he wore caught the light. It was of a serpent coiled in on itself. Tiny ruby eyes seemed to stare back at Winston. "How about this? You do me a small service, and your child will be spared."

Winston rubbed his burning eyes. He'd lied to his wife, far worse than she'd done to him. Good God, but he'd bargained away his child's very existence. His chest felt as though it were bleeding out. "What is to say that you won't manipulate events to get your way? That this isn't an illusion as well?"

"You may find it hard to believe but I must operate under rules," Jones said. "I make bargains. I keep bargains. I cannot toy with what is not struck in a deal."

"You're right," Winston snapped. "I find it hard to believe."

"Fair enough," Jones answered with a short laugh. "Only it's true." He shrugged. "Should we strike a bargain, I will adhere to the terms." He held Winston's gaze. "I must."

"Rather charitable of you to admit to it," Winston grumbled.

"Also a must." Jones leaned in. "Now then, what say you? Have we an accord?"

"What is the service?"

Jones tutted. "That you cannot know until you agree."

Pinching the bridge of his nose, Winston regarded him. "First you must swear that, if I agree, Poppy will not be harmed in any manner. Ever."

Jones's right eye twitched. "You are in no position to throw in terms."

Winston relaxed against his seat. "I don't know. We both want something. Which means we both have something to lose."

The air about them trembled as Jones glared back, and Winston held his gaze.

Jones blinked first. "I will not harm Poppy Lane." His mouth tightened. "Unless she attacks me."

"I've heard that before," Win muttered.

Jones sniffed as though insulted. "One must be able to protect oneself."

"Fair enough." Nothing about this was fair, but as he was buggered, he'd take what he could. "We have an agreement. Now, tell me what you want."

Pure satisfaction flashed through Jones's eyes, and a new qualm of unease rocked within Winston. But what was done was done.

Jones picked up his cigarette and let it dangle in his mouth as he reached into his jacket and pulled a thin file folder from within. Winston blinked. The folder was too large for Jones to have been carrying it inside his coat. *Illusions*. He knew it, and if he interpreted Jones's indulgent look, Jones wanted him to know it. The file hit the marble tabletop with a little slap.

"I have a case for you, Lane."

Winston opened the file but there was only one page attached. Immediately, Winston lifted his head to gape at Jones. "You cannot be serious. A woman?"

Jones exhaled. "You think because I am not human that I'm incapable of love?"

Winston shrugged. He hadn't been speaking of love, but if Jones brought it up, she must be important to him.

"I don't know what to think, honestly." *Come on, you bastard, give me what I need.*

Jones's thin lips curled. "Let me add to your education. We are more than capable."

*Good.* Then he could be manipulated just as much as Winston could. "This is impossible." He tossed the file back onto the table. "Aside from the fact that the case is sixteen years cold, you've got no leads save for a name."

"Come now, it isn't all that bad. I've started a breadcrumb trail for you to follow. See here? Upon arrival in London, you are to visit the Komtesse Krogstad of Chelsea. Call it a gift, if you will."

Hardly. "And who is this Moira Darling you want me to find?"

"Many things. But above all, she is a woman who has stolen from me."

"You have not even listed what it is she stole from you."

"The man can read!" Jones tilted his head. "Are you certain you've done this before? I must say, my faith is wavering."

"Hmm. Perhaps you ought to go with another detective and leave me be." Winston crossed one leg over the other as he sat back. He itched for a meditative smoke and eyed the cigarette case between them with longing.

Jones tossed the gold case to Winston. "Have one. You are entirely too twitchy."

Winston didn't bother to thank him, but took a cigarette. He lit it, and something in him calmed. It wasn't his pipe but the ritual was nearly the same. "Let me see if I understand this. You have the power to irrevocably alter lives, take souls, and yet you cannot find this one woman on your own?"

Jones stilled, and something mad flared in his white

eyes. Win felt the force of the demon's rage deep in his gut. It took all he had not to cower beneath it. Jones's jaw twitched, then he spoke, his words oddly flat. "As I said, there are rules which govern me. Moira Darling is out of my reach."

It might have given Win some satisfaction to see Jones struggle with the confession, but Win was too sick at heart to feel anything other than fear and rage. Yet he affected professionalism, in part because he knew it would irritate Jones.

"Are you telling me this is all you know about the case?"

"No. I'm telling you this is all I'm willing to reveal about the case." When Winston stared at him, Jones smirked. "Perhaps I don't want you to succeed."

"Perhaps you simply like toying with me."

"That is a given." Jones laughed then leaned forward, bringing with him the scent of smoke and darkness. "I made you the detective you are today. Now use those skills. You have four days."

"Now wait just a moment! Four days is hardly enough—"

"Four days to find what Moira Darling stole from me and return it, or I will take your child."

# Chapter Twelve

━━━◦◦━━━

Poppy was wide awake and doing a horrible attempt at reading in bed when Winston finally returned. He walked on cat feet lately, thus she didn't hear him coming until the door was opening and he was facing her, his expression grim but careful, as though he expected a fight. But she didn't have it in her. It had been a mistake to push him. And humiliating to think that she'd believed if he just touched her again, had sex with her, that it would break down the wall between them. If anything, the wall was higher now. Watching him, she set down her book and remained silent.

Broad shoulders squared, he moved farther into the room. Red rimmed his blue-grey eyes, and water clung in crystalline drops to the ends of his hair, turning it the color of old brass. "I took a walk. It's raining."

"It usually is." Her voice was as rough as his in the awkward silence.

Win ducked his head and, frowning, began to pull off his sodden coat. His cravat, waistcoat, and boots followed, all of them carefully placed upon the back of a chair. When he got to his shirt, he stopped and looked back up at her. Poppy couldn't know what he was thinking. Before, she'd always known his moods and what to expect. Now, she felt unbalanced. Drawing her knees up to her chest, she covered her legs with the billowing folds of her nightgown.

"I think it best that you sleep in Talent's quarters tonight." She couldn't look at him.

Out of the corner of her eye, she saw him nod, but he came closer anyway. When he stopped before the bed, she forced herself to face him, only to find his expression solemn. "If you wish," he said in a low voice, then his hands went to his shirt.

"If you are thinking of getting in this bed with me, think again." If he did, she'd lose all sense of herself. Sometime between crying and curling up in a lonely ball upon the bed, she realized that if he could not accept who and what she was, then so be it.

He paused, and his brows lifted. A glint lit his eyes. She'd almost forgotten how Win loved a challenge. Proof, she supposed, of her exhaustion. But he'd have a fight on his hands. The glint in his eyes grew. "Do you suppose I've come to ravage you, Boadicea?" His finely shaped lips twitched, and her face heated.

"Again, you mean?"

His smile fell. "I dishonored you. And it shames me to my soul."

And like that, her ire left her. He spoke of honor. She had clearly forgotten hers as well. Blast it, but she shouldn't have let him wander the ship alone. No matter what personal strife had arisen between them, it was still her duty to protect Win. Even if he hated her for it. She could only be thankful that he'd returned in one piece. Damn it all.

He did not give her a chance to reply before he whipped his shirt over his head and tossed it away.

Her breath left her. Not since he'd first been attacked had she seen his torso. He hadn't allowed it. He stood stock-still and let her drink in her fill of him. Despite his sudden reveal, or perhaps because of it, she looked not at his chest, but at his face. His jaw was set and hard as he gazed at a spot on the wall.

"Go on," he said, "look at me."

Good God, but he'd changed. Gone was the lithe torso. In its place, a network of corded muscle reigned. He was still lean; his body would never run to pure bulk, but the definition and the strength had increased, and he'd added a good fifteen pounds to his frame. She'd known this before he'd taken his shirt off, but seeing the bare results was another matter. A part of her mourned the loss of his earlier self, though this newer Win intrigued her as well. He was a study of power tempered by grace. "You're bigger," she said inanely.

He made a sound halfway between a grunt and a snort. And she realized that she'd missed the point of this exercise entirely. Taking a breath, she looked over the scars that marred his fine, ivory skin. It had been bad, his attack. Thick, ropey scars covered his left pectoral muscle, shoulder, and forearm, while thinner, redder slashes crisscrossed over his rippling abdomen and the swell of his biceps. He'd been so close to death.

Unable to help herself, she rose onto her knees and reached out to trace the thick slash just over his heart. His warm skin twitched at the contact, but he held still.

"You've healed well, Win."

His eyes flicked to hers. "You keep saying that. Don't." His voice was a whip of censure.

"It is the truth," she snapped back.

He took a step forward, the action sending her palm against his chest. "Don't patronize me. Just look at *me*. Look at what I've become."

White lined the livid red scars on his face as he glared at her.

"I am looking," she said, feeling the rapid beat of his heart beneath her hand. "What would you have me say, Win?"

"That I am deformed. That I will never be the same again."

"No. *That* would be patronizing you. And what I cannot understand is why you want me to do so." His breath left in a hiss as he stepped even closer. So close that his nose almost bumped hers. Poppy did not back away. "Why do you want my pity, Win? Or is it that you want me to turn away in disgust?" Her eyes searched his, and it became a chore to speak. "Do you want me to be the one to end this so that you don't have to?"

They stared at each other, neither of them daring to move. And then he took a deep breath as his eyes closed. "I don't know." His head fell forward, and his forehead rested on hers. "I don't know what to think anymore."

Nothing could stop her then from wrapping her arms about him and pulling him closer. He fell into her, his arms twining about her waist in a hard grip, his fingers grabbing the loose folds at the back of her nightgown. Something within her sighed in relief at his hold and the feel of his body pressed against her. They'd always fit together so well. Hugging him made her feel safe, feel needed as well. So many people needed her, and yet never for this basic sort of comfort. They needed her to fix things. Only Win had needed her heart.

His lips pressed against her neck as they held each other up, and his breath warmed her. Poppy closed her eyes and let herself relax further into him. When he finally spoke, his words were muffled by her skin. "You were always my anchor, Poppy. Now I am adrift."

Gently, she touched the cool strands of his hair, still damp from the rain. But his body was so nice and warm. "I am unmoored as well, Win. And I don't know what to do. For it was you who cut the ties."

A deep, shuddering sigh left him, and his fingers dug deeper into her flesh. "I am not...I have spells, Poppy. I become unable to breathe; I fall ill." She felt him swallow against her shoulder. "I am not the man you knew. I am not—" He stopped abruptly and took another breath. "I was angry and embarrassed. I could not face you."

Anger stirred within her breast, and she tried to pull back. But he held tight and wouldn't let her go. "It isn't logical. Hell, it isn't fair, the way I feel." Only then did he move away enough to look her in the eyes. His were pained. "I am ashamed, Pop. And yet every time I try to govern my feelings, I fail."

Poppy broke free of his grip, realizing belatedly it was because he let her. With a sigh, she sank down onto the bed. "You hurt me, Win." She swallowed hard. "And I hurt you."

He moved as if to touch her cheek but let his hand fall. "Yes."

"How do we get past it?" Poppy's fingers clenched. "Do you want to, Win?"

His expression darkened, making his patchwork of scars appear twisted. "Move over."

She scuttled to the other side of the bed, and her back met with the pillows piled high behind her. To her surprise, he sank down and rested his head upon her lap. The warm weight of him seeped through her thin gown as he looked up at her, his winter eyes clear yet unreadable. Then he turned and curled in on her, his face pressing against the small swell of her lower belly. His breath left in a gust of warm air as he slowly lifted his hand. Everything in her stilled. The tips of his fingers stroked her, a violent shiver wracking his frame as he made contact.

Her chest tightened, and she blinked up at the ceiling, knowing that if she looked at his face just then she'd fall apart. His raspy voice drifted up through the thick silence. "Were you going to tell me?"

She swallowed several times. "Yes." She cleared her throat. "Of course."

Gentle fingers traced across the small rise of her belly. "When?"

A pained half-laugh escaped her, and she pressed her palm over her eyes. "I don't know. I'd only just realized it myself. It was such a-a..." Oh, God, she didn't want to speak. For years they had tried. Years of nothing but disappointment. It had ripped her heart open to discover that they'd finally achieved what they both wanted on the heels of his defection.

"You left me, Win." Her fingers dug into the throbbing points at her temple as she gritted her teeth. "Wouldn't talk to me."

He hugged her tighter, a sound of pain breaking from him, but he did not speak. What could he say in any event?

"And I thought..." She licked her lips. "I did not want you to come home out of obligation." She glanced down at him. "I still don't."

The ruined side of his face was to her. The paleness of his flesh made his scars vivid red. She wanted to touch them, lay her hand on his cheek, and send cool comfort into him. And her childish self wanted to yank him by his ungoverned locks and throw him from the room for causing her pain. His attention remained fixed on her belly, as his eyes began to water. Her fingers found their way into Win's hair. She stroked his head as if to calm them both.

With a harsh sound, he cleared his throat and blinked rapidly. "I failed us both, Boadicea." He fisted the loose folds of her gown and held on tight. "And will fail us more before the day is done."

"Win." Her voice broke, and she took a breath. "There is nothing so broken that cannot be mended."

A wobbling, pained smiled ghosted over his lips. "Oh," he said in a shaking voice, "I beg to differ." Slowly, he rolled away and sat up at the edge of the bed, giving his back to her. His hair fell about his face as he glared down at his clenched hands, and she ached to rub the broad expanse of his back. She might hurt, but he seemed utterly lost.

"I'm the veriest of hypocrites, Pop." As he turned back to her, the depth of regret and sorrow reflected in his eyes took her breath. "I left you for lying when I have done ten times worse."

Though they no longer touched, Winston could feel Poppy tense. He knew his wife so well in this regard. She was preparing herself, governing her emotions. Before he had left Poppy, they never had a true row. It was all very civilized, their arguments. Voices might become raised, tempers flare, but one of them would leave the room before there was any danger of getting out of hand. Staring at his clenched fists, Win wondered if their mutual civility had really been a disservice. For it had made it too easy to walk away when things grew sticky.

He had walked away. And it disgusted him. Slowly, he relaxed his fingers. Never again would he turn from a fight with Poppy. Christ, but that was an easy thing to say when he had less than a week to save both his and their child's soul.

Swallowing against the fear, he turned back to Poppy. Her pristine white nightgown covered her from neck to foot and made her appear all of twelve. The red silk of her hair ran over her shoulders and down to her waist. He pulled his gaze up to her eyes. Those eyes, dark and glinting beneath straight red brows. Those eyes never failed to draw him in.

"The demon found me."

Horror slashed across her features, and she lurched forward. "When? What did he want?"

He rested a hand on the bed between them. "Poppy... Hell. He wants our child."

Quite abruptly, the temperature in the room dropped, as if someone had walked in from an Arctic night. "Over my dead body."

"No, over mine." His voice came out stronger than he felt. "I made a bargain with him."

"What!" Poppy wrenched herself out of the bed, her long hair swinging.

Win rubbed the back of his neck. "Fourteen years ago, I loved a woman. I was the son of a duke who would not let me marry this woman, and I wanted to be a detective."

Poppy blanched. "You were cut off and I agreed— Oh-ho no..." Her fists bunched tight as if she might hit him. "Do not tell me..." Red swarmed up her cheeks, and the room grew icy. Currents of air swirled about them.

"Yes, Boadicea." He made a furtive gesture to touch her but dropped his hand when she bared her teeth like a feral thing. "He found me and gave me my heart's desire in exchange for my soul." The sound of his swallowing was overly loud in the silence. "It's all been a lie. Our life…"

"Do not!" She hissed through her teeth before going on. "Do not tell me this, Win."

"It is worse." On a breath, he told her the rest. With each word out of his mouth, each lie revealed, the room grew colder, until he shivered and icicles hung from the lamps and frost coated the portholes.

"Damn him to hell," Poppy shouted when he finished. She whirled about and slammed her palm against a chair, sending it flying. "Bloody fucking bastard!"

Icy air tore about the room, howling in the small space and blinding his eyes. Squinting, he braced himself, waiting for the explosion to turn his way. It did not come. The frost blew itself out, as quickly and deftly as if one had slammed the door shut on it. Standing in the center of the room, her back to him and her head bowed, she pressed a fist against her mouth for one silent moment. Then she took a quick breath, letting her hand fall, and looked up at the ceiling as if it might hold answers or a way out.

When she spoke, her voice cracked. "All right. The damage is done." She sucked in another shallow breath. "Now we need to contain it. So you've been charged to find this woman? And then we are free?" With shaking hands, she smoothed her gown. "Fine then, let us find her. Not that I bloody well trust Isley to deliver."

She wouldn't meet his eyes, but simply moved to pick up an overturned chair.

"Poppy, look at me."

She did not.

"Then shout at me...Blame me for my idiocy. Anything." He cursed and tried to come near, but she hissed between her teeth with such vehemence that he stopped. "I've done you a terrible wrong," he said. "Have a proper go at me. In truth, I would welcome it."

She made a sound that might have been amusement but had too much anger behind it. "I'm certain you would." She brushed back a stray wisp of hair with a steady hand, then straightened a pillow, looking anywhere but at him, and he wanted to punch something, wanted her to punch him, as he deserved. But her voice grew composed. "You were tricked by something far more devious than yourself. You hadn't a chance once Isley got his claws into you. What more is there to say?"

That he was a hypocrite? That he'd put their family in danger because of his selfishness? Winston had a dozen self-recriminations, and it irked him that she wouldn't address a one. Instead, she retreated behind that shell of hers, where no one could see her pain or rage. Just as she always did. No matter what occurred, Poppy was an entity unto herself, and he was the one on the outside.

# *Chapter Thirteen*

∿

**P**oppy slipped from the cabin and made her way below decks. Shortly after their argument, Win had left. God, she did not want to think of him now. She *refused* to think of him, or her child. For if she did, she would be screaming. Her life with Win had been manipulated? Her child's fate in Isley's grasp?

Blood filled her mouth from the force of biting her lip. She swallowed the metallic taste down with a curse. How dare Isley? She thought Win an exiled son of a duke. When really he'd given it all up for her. Her? At the cost of his soul, of their child's. Black hate filled her vision as she made her way to the ship's rear stairwell. Isley would pay.

She would search the ship, starting from the bottom. The demon had fled there, and Poppy had to believe that he was one of Isley's minions. The change from first class to second was subtle. The decor, while not as ornate, was still fine, lovely even. There was simply less open space and more people. They moved about, bustling to the large dining hall or to the game rooms, library, or second-class promenade. If anything, the feeling of excitement was somehow amplified here, for these people viewed this short voyage as an event, the holiday of a lifetime.

Unlike the shift from first to second class, descending into third class was like entering another world. Gone were the fine wood paneling, the wide halls, and plush carpeting. Her boot heels clicked against bare wood floors as she moved in and out of shadows, as the lights were spaced farther apart. It was noisier here too. The hum of the engines was more prevalent lower down, and the chatter of passengers echoed off of the bare walls. Someone was singing. An accordion wheezed and spat out a tune, and then a fiddle began to play along.

People moved through the tight spaces in droves, brushing her shoulders as they went about their business. Isley would relish this environment. Like most demons, he loved nothing better than to be around humanity. Their vitality gave him energy. Following the sound of the music, Poppy found herself in the dining hall, a Spartan place with whitewashed walls and wooden chairs pushed against them. Women chatted in groups of two or three, while the men gathered in larger clusters. Laughing children darted like minnows around the adults. Not a surprise to see them up and about. This was a holiday for them as well.

Lively music filled the air, and the floors shook with the beat of dancing feet. The men and women crowding the space had formed a circle around a group of dancers in the center of the room.

One dancer in particular garnered much attention. A spritely woman, no higher than Poppy's shoulder, twirled and leapt. Kicking up her feet to the fast rhythm, she held the men in thrall and made most women smile. It was hard not to when she carried such joy in her expression, her rounded cheeks pink with exertion and her eyes flashing. She had no partner; she did not need one. There was no question that her skill on the dance floor was unparalleled. Poppy edged closer, weaving through the crowd. The young lady tossed her head back and laughed as her heels slammed against the floor, faster and faster. The fiddler came closer, his bow flying over the strings with near inhuman speed. Faster, faster, the fiddle's notes growing wilder. Gypsy music. Lovely, erotic, enticing.

Calls of encouragement rang out. People clapped. The fiddler, a long and lanky gent, grinned with devilish glee from behind his black beard.

Heart pounding along with the beat of the wicked music, Poppy made it to the edge of the dance floor. Excitement rushed through her like potent wine. Here was her quarry, beguiling the crowd and drawing them closer. Indeed, it was all she could do not to jump in and dance along, twirl about too. Holding her fists at her sides, she stared down her prey, knowing that the demon would feel her—if he hadn't already. Sure enough, their gazes clashed, and the true devil flashed in those seemingly innocent eyes. Isley.

Poppy hardened her gaze, and Isley's rhythm lost a single beat. It was enough to have Poppy grinning in return. *Bastard. Hiding away with these people. How many had he tricked already? How many souls were gambled away with false dreams and promises of better tomorrows?*

The girl on the dance floor spun faster, her golden hair a blur as the music reached its crescendo and then, as if one, she and the fiddle stopped. Around Poppy, the crowd roared their appreciation, but her attention stayed on her prey. People surged forward to praise the girl who stood panting and grinning as the fiddler slipped off to drink his fill of the vodka offered to him.

As for Poppy, she eased back to the door, knowing Isley would follow. The air was cooler in the hall. She moved toward a door marked STAFF. It was a simple thing to pick the lock and slip inside. The first class cargo hold was a cavernous space. That it encroached upon the third class passengers' living space was no surprise. Poppy walked among crates lashed securely against the walls. The faint scent of coal smoke mixed with the wood of the crates. The vibration of the massive engines and the constant *thwump, thwump* of the paddle wheels that they powered was almost a living thing against her skin. Her bones hummed. But her mind and heart were calm. Behind her came the sound of the door opening once again and the click of a boot heel on the iron floor.

Poppy rested a palm against a crate. "You're quite the dancer."

A light, feminine voice echoed in the space. "I was lovely, was I not?"

Poppy turned to study the body that Isley had created for himself. Because it was a creation. Poppy did not know the specific mechanics of it, but Isley's bodies were as real as hers, yet they were created not by God, but by Isley's will. As far as she knew, he was the only demon able to do so. Other demons relied on possession or the stealing of a person's blood to shift their shape into something else.

Impish and young, the female Isley preened. Poppy bit the inside of her lower lip. "I daresay you accumulated many offers after that display."

Isley fluffed out his skirts. "Oh, plenty. Alas, they were all male, and I find I no longer enjoy pleasures with the male sex." Pretty pink cheeks plumped on a smile. "As there do not seem to be any Sapphos onboard, I do believe a change back to the male persuasion may be in order." His eyes flashed white as he looked Poppy over. "And how is dear Winston?"

Crossing her arms over her chest, Poppy leaned against the crate. Her muscles twitched with the need to lash out, and her jaw ached from keeping in the words she wanted to shout. He dared threaten her family. Her child. Her fists curled tight. "I must say, Isley, I am disappointed. Are you so afraid of facing me that you had to ensure our meeting was over open water where I cannot send you back to your prison?"

His white irises turned red. "Dumb luck will not be on your side this time, girl."

"Face me on solid ground and tell me that again." She itched to pull a blade free and slice his neck. If only to give him a pinch of pain.

Isley strolled closer, making the most of the girlish form he inhabited. Wide, working woman's skirts flounced with each step. "We shall see." He tossed a coy look over one shoulder. He was a mere ten feet away. Close enough that the scent of patchouli mixed with wood smoke touched her senses. His cold gaze slid over her once again. "Now that you have matured, you remind me of your mother. You have her enticing confidence and those severe, unforgiving eyes."

"And you haven't changed. Still a babbling bore."

His lip curled. "What makes you believe my interest is in you? Winston Lane is rife with mental anguish." His sharp teeth flashed. "Just the sort of snack I relish."

"Oh, yes, this absurd notion that you have the rights to my child's soul." Bitterness filled her mouth, but she wouldn't let it show.

"Not absurd. Your husband signed it away quite handily."

Poppy kept her eyes on Isley but made no further moves. "Do not pretend for a moment that your endgame isn't to bedevil me. Otherwise, you would not have sent that charming telegram."

"And here you are." Again, he grinned. "Running in to rescue another family member not worth saving."

It proved too hard to keep her voice neutral. "Leave Winston out of this, and let us settle this once and for all."

"No. He made the bargain. He has to work his way out of it."

"He made that bargain because of me!" *Don't fight him. Not yet.* But she could not stop from taking a step closer to him.

"Yes," snapped Isley. "He did. And you get to suffer in the knowledge that your acquaintance with the solid, upstanding Winston Lane wrought his downfall."

"Bastard."

"No! I am the past that has returned to haunt you," he said with sudden vigor. "I will watch you stumble, watch you fight, see you witness your man die and your happiness fade." In a flash, he was right before her, not as the young girl, but as Winston.

Hatred burned in those winter blue eyes that appeared just like Winston's. Not Win, she told herself. His scarred visage twisted with the violence of his anger. "You will feel what I felt as you hunted me those fourteen years ago. Feel the same fury as I did when forced underground by an ignorant girl in the midst of a tantrum."

He leaned closer, his chest almost touching hers. "I will see you pay. And then I will take your child."

Poppy struck, a hard punch to the windpipe. Isley

gagged, his forehead hitting her shoulder as he hunched forward from the hit. Poppy spun, grabbing his wrist and, in the same moment, slammed her elbow into the back of his. His arm hyper extended, and then the bone snapped at the joint. Isley screeched. His return hit caught her in the sternum. Poppy flew back, hitting the floor so hard that her brain seemed to slosh about in her skull as she slid several feet.

It was that jar to the body that set her thinking sanely once again. She could not afford such physicality. Not now. Isley stalked forward, rage igniting over his flesh in preternatural orange flames, his one arm flopping at his side, and looking so much like Winston that her heart turned over in her chest. She scrambled to her feet and grabbed one of the crowbars that hung on the wall.

Isley halted a step. His eyes gleamed as he laughed. "And what do you plan to do with that, Poppy Ann?" The grin grew evil, an abomination on Win's face. "Pray I don't get a hold of it and crack your arm the way you did mine."

Poppy adjusted her grip. "Hurts, does it? Good."

He was on her in the next breath. His fist caught her on the side of her head, and black spots burst over her vision. *Not Win, he's not Win.* Poppy swung at the face she'd loved for so long, but Isley caught her, slamming her to the iron floor, then pressing his weight against her so that she could not kick out. His knees crushed down on her arms, keeping her from truly touching him as he grabbed her throat and bore down on her windpipe. She convulsed against the cold floor. The black spots before her eyes grew larger.

"I could crush your throat with one squeeze," he whispered.

Win's face stared at her, so cold, so detached. It might be the last thing she'd see. That it was not truly Win but a sick facsimile had rage surging through her limbs. She glared up at him.

"Go on," she ground out. "Kill me as you did my mother."

Isley paused as if he hadn't expected her dare. His grip lessened a fraction. Poppy sucked in a draught of damp air. Isley frowned. "Why do you assume she was always in the right, girl?" Her teeth rattled as he gave her a shake. "What have her schemes brought you? Loneliness, a marriage of lies, your sisters' disappointment and distrust?"

"Enough!" She would not listen to him spin his web.

His weight crushed down on her. "No, my dear. Not nearly enough. You go through life with blinders on, prancing about on tenuous moral high ground, and damn my eyes if you didn't find a husband just the same."

"So you seek to teach us a lesson, do you?" She laughed, her throat aching from his grip. "I shall be ill."

Isley snarled, and he bent close enough to smell. "You could be like me. If you let go of these rules and truly lived, you could be like me." He moved to release her, easing back off her arms. It was enough.

She caught him by the hand that still held onto her neck, and then she set her power free. Ice lashed over his body, freezing him in place. He'd soon break free, but not until she was done. Power rippled along her skin as she fed it into his body, keeping him frozen. Only his eyes gave any indication that he heard every word she said. "Right now, you are very much like me in one fatal way."

Her free hand settled over the crowbar lying next to her. With a grunt, she swung the crowbar hard. His head shattered like fine crystal, shards of ice flying from the force. "Your body is comprised almost entirely of water." She let go, and the body toppled and broke into a thousand scattered pieces about her.

Dark smoke drifted up from the wreckage of Isley's body and an ear-ringing screech filled the space. The smoke gathered, growing darker, more substantial, until it took on the shape of a man. The black, writhing man-shape hovered over her as red glowing eyes formed where the face ought to be.

Poppy climbed to her feet and faced the thing head on. The black mass broke apart only to reform around her, a storm of unnatural wind that plucked at her clothes and scraped her skin. Isley's growl came at her from all directions. "Does Winston Lane know you cry for him? That you want him back so very desperately?"

He was grasping at straws, looking for her weakness. She held herself still within the storm. "Go back to hell where you belong, Isley."

The wind picked up, blinding her. "Only if you come with me, Poppy Ann." And then he was gone.

# *Chapter Fourteen*

❦⟶⟵

*London, 1869—In Bed, Finally*

It's so hot."

Winston choked out a laugh. "It most certainly is." Pleasure and the fact that Poppy Ellis had her slim, cool hand wrapped around his overheated cock made him shiver. He drew a finger along the length of her neck before kissing the sweet little spot where her pulse pounded. "Which is your fault entirely."

Lying on her bed, his shirt undone and his trousers unbuttoned, he marveled at how he'd arrived at this moment. Well, he knew *how.* He'd crept into her room like a thief. How it was that she'd managed to practically undress him while retaining her clothes was the mystery. One he was going to rectify. He undid another one of the hundred little pearl buttons marching up her nightgown as he kissed her softly.

She gave him an experimental stroke, and he groaned,

his lips clinging to hers. "Poppy. You are going to unman me." Another button popped free.

"I thought it would feel cool. Wriggly even."

"Wriggly?" His voice was strangled. "How on earth... oh, God..." He canted his hips, pushing into her grip. "Do that again...harder." His thighs trembled, and his cods ached. And he loved it. He licked his lips. "H-how did you come to such a conclusion?"

"Well," she kissed his neck, her strokes continuing at a maddening pace. "From the renderings I've seen, it appears to simply hang, dangling away from the body."

He laughed, the sound muffled against her damp skin. His fingers were somewhat frantic now, needing to get to their prize. The nightgown gapped, and the sweet curve of her small breast came into his view. Win's mind went blank, then dark with lust. His hand actually shook as he slipped it beneath the fine linen and cupped her smooth flesh. Gods, but it was too good. He'd never felt a breast before, but he was fairly certain no other breast would have felt as good to him as Poppy Ellis's breast.

Distracted by this touch, Poppy stopped her questing and made a little noise. Pleasure. He could tell by the way her lips parted on a breath. He leaned in, snatching a kiss before giving her breast an experimental squeeze. She made the sound again.

Beneath his palm, her silky nipple began to rise. Impatiently, he wrenched back the nightgown to get a better view. She was beautiful, gorgeous, and bloody perfect. The pink bud of her nipple was shrinking, growing tighter. He brushed his thumb over it, loving the way it moved against him, and how she squirmed at his ministrations. His mouth watered. He wanted to suck that nipple, bite it just enough to feel it give against his teeth. His cock swelled larger.

"Win." Her mouth found his and clung, her tongue tasting and teasing as her hand went back to playing with him. "Win."

"Present," he murmured. What if...He pinched her nipple, and she moaned. Heat washed over him so strong that he couldn't breathe through it. His cock thrust against her palm. He wanted inside of her. He had no notion of how it would feel, and suddenly it became imperative that he find out.

His free hand slid to her knee, pushing up her gown to get at her cool, smooth skin. Her legs were endless, and he wanted to explore them at his leisure. Some day but not now. They both sucked in a breath when his fingers touched her curls and then found her slick skin. Wet. That was how it would feel inside of her. Hot and wet. He stroked, exploring her in gentle touches that soon grew stronger. Then it was Poppy who canted her hips.

"Ah, God, Win." She panted and moved against his fingers. "Do that again."

He complied and came in contact with the hottest part of her. "How do you like it, Pop?"

Her throat moved when she swallowed. "Softly."

"Softly? Like this?" He swirled his thumb around her bud, gently, so very gently.

She groaned, and her long legs spread open like the pages of a book offering up their secrets. Win swallowed convulsively. He looked down.

"Lovely." Dark red curls, pink glistening lips. They caught the whole of his concentration, and he slowly discovered every inch as she writhed against him, tilting her hips, encouraging him lower. Unable to stop himself, he pushed a finger in. Hot, wet, and *tight*. He closed his eyes on a groan. She would be heaven. His cock agreed and ground itself against her now relaxed hand. As if hearing his plea, she gripped him hard. Her free hand grabbed onto his hair.

Determined brown eyes gazed up at him. "Win, come into me."

Winston considered himself intelligent. And though he panted, and his body literally shook with needful lust, he paused. "We aren't married."

She froze at his whisper. Her red tongue swept out to lick her lips, distracting him. He forced his gaze to her eyes. She blinked as though dazed. "No. But Win..." Her cheeks went scarlet. "I need you."

He kissed her hard, telling her with his kiss how much he needed her too. His finger sank deeper into her, earning a whimper, and his heart nearly pounded out of his chest. But he pulled back. "You know how much I want you," he said, willing himself not to stroke her. "But I will not dishonor you—"

"It is not a dishonor." She pulled him closer. "Not when it is what I want. What we want."

He almost moved then. Almost. His gaze caught hers. "Does that mean we will marry?"

Maybe later he would analyze how one could feel such intense lust while being felled by equally intense pain. Now, however, he slowly took his hand away from her as her expression closed down, giving him his answer long before she spoke. "I cannot."

He pushed himself up to sitting. "Poppy darling, I must ask.... Why the bloody hell not?" Cursing again, he pressed the heels of his hands against his eyes. "What are we doing here?"

"I thought that was obvious." The bed squeaked as she sat. He risked a look. She was buttoning up her gown.

On a sigh, he tucked himself back into his trousers and tried to bring himself to rights as well before getting off her too-tempting bed. Rising, he faced her. "Do not double talk me, Poppy. You invited me to your rooms in the middle of the night—"

"I did not hear you complain."

"Offered up your virginity," he said over her, "and yet you continue to refuse my suit." Which hurt, more than he wanted to admit. "Why? I confess, I do not understand you."

She sat, long legs crossed before her, with a mulish expression pulling at her features.

"Why?" he said again, for she would not answer.

Poppy's cheeks went pink, then red. "I did not expect this. I did not expect you. I did not think that someone would—" Her breath hitched on a hiccup. "That someone would—"

He took a step toward her. "Would what?"

She ducked her head. "Want me."

"Want you?" he repeated, stunned. He sank to his knees beside the bed and took her cold hand in his. "I don't simply want you, I love you!"

"I know," she whispered, her face so very pale. "Which makes it so much worse. To have your love is a miracle to me. And I cannot accept it."

For a moment, he could only stare at her. He'd never said those words in his life, never even felt them for another soul. And what did she say in return? Nothing. No reassurance. When he found his voice, it was weak and rusty. "For the love of God, Poppy, at least tell me why."

She blinked rapidly. "You are the son of a duke."

The numbness started in his face and then crawled along his arms, down to his fingers. From beyond the buzzing of his ears he heard himself ask. "Has my father contacted you?"

Her hand slipped away. "Not only me, but my father as well. We will be ruined if I continue my association with you."

"We cannot let him win!" He punched the side of her bed, and the frame rattled. "We marry, and he will let it go—"

"Not even you truly believe that, Win." Her brown eyes appeared so very old and tired then. "He will make us pay for defying him. I think you know that as well."

"Then we leave. We can go to America or—"

"Win." Poppy cupped his cheek with a hand that was remarkably steady. "I cannot leave London. My life is here. And it is complicated." Her hand drifted away. "I never meant for it to go so far. Only I could not help myself with you."

"You—" His breath hitched. Humiliating. And yet he could not stop his head from falling down into her lap. "Do not make me live without you, Boadicea. I cannot do it."

He heard her swallow, felt her hand come down to stroke his hair. He did not acknowledge the touch; he was too cold. Cold enough that his body shook and his throat convulsed. "You are my cornerstone."

"And you are my happiness. But we will both have to go on," she whispered, breaking his heart, tearing apart his soul. Her body curled over his as she kissed his cheek. "Can we not have this night to say good-bye?"

Win shot away from the bed on his next breath. His chest heaved as he stood. "If you thought I would play a part in this...farewell—" He scrubbed his palm across his cheek, wiping away the humiliating tear that trickled down. "Then you don't know me at all. Good-bye, Miss Ellis."

He left her then, knowing that his final words had been a lie. He'd never truly be able to say good-bye to her. She was already part of his soul. Whether he wanted her to be or not.

# Chapter Fifteen

Poppy needed to get off this bloody ship. How one could stand to be trapped on board a vessel for weeks on end, she didn't know. As it was, she had to fight the urge to punch the walls or scream at her fellow passengers, most of whom had the rather annoying habit of greeting her good morning when she'd really rather they stay away. Bloody polite society.

She quickened her stride when yet another couple turned into the corridor and began strolling her way. These two, at least, were smart enough to properly interpret her stony expression and lack of eye contact as a signal to "please bugger off." Poppy got past them and made it out into the main first class lobby. It was beautiful, with its mahogany paneling, stained-glass windows, and soaring height, giving one the feeling of walking into both a cathedral and a library all at once. She only noticed because it was something Win would have remarked upon. This did not alleviate her current mood, one that had descended on her as she'd dressed for the day.

Her boot heels clattered as she descended the center staircase at a swift pace, earning several censorious looks in the process. The stares of others only helped to shore up those lovely thick walls she'd developed to contain herself. She brushed by a loitering group of passengers who were complaining about the too-dry eggs at breakfast. Through a gateway of tall potted palms, she entered the cafe lounge.

He sat at the far corner table, where the massive skylight windows let in a dull, grey light. He had a way of sitting, so very straight and proper, his feet planted and his arms resting at his sides, that it ought to make him appear priggish. It did not. Whether it was the wide breadth of his shoulders, his knobby wrists peeking out from his cuffs, or the stern expression surrounded by that unkempt hair, she did not know, but he looked more a wild thing playing at being a gentleman, and she'd no doubt that if she lobbed the throwing knife she had hidden in her pocket, he'd react in an instant. Win's greatest talent was making the world believe him harmless. Like the spider to the fly, he drew people into his confidence before tapping into their secrets. It was what made him both maddening and thrilling to her in a way no other man had even come close to.

She drew near, knowing that he was aware of her. She fancied she could see the knowledge hardening over his fine, strong features. He let it go for a few steps more then rose gracefully to his feet and drew out a chair for her.

"Morning," he said in his raspy voice. "Have you eaten?"

She sat in her chair as he poured fresh coffee into his cup and pushed it toward her. "No." She took a grateful drink.

He frowned, which, with his scars, made him appear all the more disreputable. "You ought to take better care. The child needs nourishment."

The cup clinked as she set it down. "Which would be moot if I were to simply cast the food back up." She scowled down at her hands, aware that he was staring at her. "I feel slightly ill this morning."

Her chest ached where Isley had struck her, and her head throbbed. She wanted to nap, even though she'd just risen. She wanted someone else to carry her load for a moment or two. Hell, she just wanted off this great, rocking prison. As that would happen in a few hours, she refused to be churlish about it a moment longer and slowly lifted her gaze to his. Win's eyes gave her no indication of his feelings.

"You've a plan, I gather." She took another sip of coffee and felt a bit more restored. Perhaps a sweet bun was in order, after all.

"Yes." Win lifted a hand in the air, and a waiter started over. "Find this Moira Darling and solve the case for the bastard." He turned to the waiter. "My wife will have..."

"Sweet buns," she supplied. When he left, she turned back to Win. "You've always been able to do that? How?"

His gorgeously stern mouth quirked, and she was hit anew by the need to kiss those lips. "Because I know how to read you." The smile faded. "Or I used to think I did."

Her heart kicked in her chest. "You obviously still do it well enough to know I wanted food."

"There is that," he murmured, stealing a sip of coffee.

"Win?" Poppy ran a finger along the edge of the marble tabletop, studying her progress rather than face him.

"Did it... Would you have preferred it if I had expressed my anger more... vocally? Over the years, that is." Blast, but her cheeks were too hot.

He set his coffee cup on its saucer. "Would it have been so terrible? To let me in, let me share your burden?"

Her finger slid back and forth over the marble. She cleared her throat. "I thought you'd prefer your wife to exhibit at least some womanly virtue."

From the corner of her eye, she saw him lean back in his chair, and she made herself look up. His arms were folded, resting on his lean middle. A hint of wry amusement flickered in his eyes, but there was irritation dwelling there as well. "I see. So then you would rather I behaved the common husband, demanded you stay at home, darn my stockings, and so forth?!"

"That is hardly the same."

"Is it not?" His shoulders tightened. "I was under the impression that the things we were *not* brought us together as much as the things we were."

Typical Winston logic. Her face heated further. He moved then, in his quick, economical way, and sat up fully in the chair once more. "I've a lead to follow in London. The Komtesse Krogstad. I've never heard of her, but she apparently knew the demon as Lord Isley sixteen years ago."

"I know her," Poppy said with a lurch. "She lives in Chelsea."

His steady blue-grey eyes held hers. "How do you know her?" Which translated to: *When during our marriage were you consorting with komtesses? And why?*

She refused to apologize. "She's a demimondaine and a member of the Aesthetic movement, which means she interacts with a great deal of, shall we say, eccentrics. It puts her in a key position to notice certain supernatural activities." Poppy paused as the waiter returned and set down a basket of fresh baked bread and two plates. Her mouth actually watered at the scent, and she tucked into a sweet bun, chewing vigorously before swallowing it down with another sip of coffee. *Heaven*. "The Komtesse has been an SOS informant for years."

"Mmm." Win selected a roll and tore off a chunk before popping it in his mouth. Unlike her, his manners remained impeccable. Well, she thought irritably, he wasn't beset by sudden bouts of insatiable hunger. She took another large bite of the sweet bread.

"Questioning her," he said, "ought to go a bit more smoothly in that case."

Poppy forced herself to ignore the bread. "Win, I want to help you."

He stared back with those eyes that saw everything and gave nothing away unless he let them. "I want you to help me," he said softly, and her insides went warm.

"Good." She nodded and snuck just one more bite of the roll.

He looked like he might say more so she cut him off, not wanting to hear him discuss last night before she could. "We shall solve this case, eradicate this bloody bargain, capture Isley, and then..."

"And then," he prompted, his voice even, almost dull, his expression going hard once again. "What then, Poppy?"

Her heart pounded. Did he dare make *her* ask? Beg for them to be a family? Not like this. Her hand clenched the smooth curve of the coffee cup. "And then this business shall be over, of course."

Something snuffed in his eyes, like a flame blown

out, and again came the feeling of failing a test that he'd laid out for her. It made her want to throw the cup across the room, just to see it smash. She calmly returned his gaze.

"Right," he said. But when she made to rise, his hand snaked out and clamped around her wrist, holding her still. "Until then, let me correct certain misapprehensions. We may no longer live as husband and wife, but there is more than just you and me to consider. There is our child. We are in this together now." His grip tightened. "Together, Boadicea. If you fall, I *will* catch you. I do not expect you to trust me on that. Not yet." His eyes were hard, and he stared her down, but his touch suddenly became unbearably gentle and secure. "But I shall work at every moment to make you believe it."

Disembarking went smoothly. The train ride from Southampton to London was made in relative silence. It wasn't until they stood on the platform at Victoria Station and faced each other over their stacked travel trunks that the reality of returning home fell upon them. Win's deepset eyes watched her, letting the moment grow between them, and she saw his hesitation, as if he did not want to be the one to state the obvious—that he would now go back to whatever rooms he'd let.

Irritatingly, the backs of Poppy's eyes began to burn and prickle. She'd grown used to him again. When he'd left, it had taken weeks to finally get a full night's rest. A hard-earned struggle now destroyed by two days of being with him once again. Damn it all.

This man could hurt her. More than anyone on earth. For she had exposed her heart to him in all its pink, fleshy glory. He knew its pathways and its weaknesses. Where she would bleed the most if he chose to slice into her. In truth, he'd already made the first cut, leaving her blood to run not hot but ice cold down the walls of her chest. Wounded as she was, it would not take much for him to finish her. This man could do much worse than hurt her. This man could destroy her.

Behind them, Mary Chase and Jack Talent waited, both of them trying their best to blend into the scenery. Ye gods, would the ignominy of her situation ever end? She detested public spectacle, and now it was hers.

She straightened, refusing to hug herself or acknowledge the thickness in her throat. "Well then, I suppose we ought to go."

A rare break in the cloud cover sent a few rays of brilliant light down upon them, and Win's eyes fell into shadow under the brim of his bowler. "Yes," he said in his husky voice, then shifted his weight, sending more of his features into darkness.

She looked at him and set her jaw firm. *Do not make me ask it. Do not make me.*

The line of his shoulders became stiff and unyielding. "Look here, I do not think we should separate. It isn't safe."

Sternness tempered his tone, as if he thought she'd argue. It took her a moment to clear her throat. "If you think it best."

"I do." He gave her a sharp nod then turned to Talent. "Take our trunks to Ranulf House."

Talent frowned. "I ought to go with you."

Win gave a tight, quick smile. "I believe we can all agree that I am no longer in imminent danger of being attacked by the demon." Because of their loyalty, Poppy and Win had given both Talent and Mary a basic explanation of the situation.

Win, obviously seeing the disappointment etched on Talent's face, added, "Should further developments arise, I shall not hesitate to solicit your help, Mr. Talent."

Talent appeared somewhat mollified. "And where do I put Miss Chase here?" he asked with a bored flick of his thumb in Mary's direction.

Mary bristled. "You do not 'put' me anywhere, Mr. Talent."

Win cleared his throat. "Find Miss Chase proper accommodations in Ranulf House." His visage grew stern. "And behave."

Talent muttered under his breath but complied with a sweeping bow. Poppy bit back a smile as the pair began to bicker about who would hail a porter and who would find the cab.

Sighing, Win left them to it and his assessing gaze swept over her once more. "Have you a need to rest now?"

"No." She might go mad if she were to be cooped up in another room so soon, and the day promised to be fresh and bright for once. She fell in step beside Winston.

"Win, why Ranulf House?"

"It is where I've been staying."

"You've been staying with the lycans?" Shock colored her words. Lycans, while not werewolves, could turn into them, and they had the ability to unleash claws and fangs. They were more than capable of hurting Win in the exact fashion he'd been hurt before. And he'd set up house with them.

His expression turned wry. "A man might as well face his fears, or let them rule him."

She wanted to wrap her arms about him so badly that

her limbs twitched. She knew he did not think of himself as brave. But he was. More so than she.

Win shifted his weight as though uncomfortable with her silence. "The place is a veritable fortress."

"It is at that." No demon in its right mind would try to infiltrate a den of lycans.

# Chapter Sixteen

———— ❧ ————

Winston guided Poppy to the hack stands but she stopped short. He followed the direction of her gaze. A smart town coach painted glossy, ox-blood red and trimmed in gold stood at the curb. No crest graced the doors, but the coachman and two outriders were dressed in fine black livery. As if sensing her notice, one of the toms jumped down and bowed.

"A friend of yours?" Win asked.

"Yes." She appeared both pleased and yet put out. Before he could ask another question, Poppy started forward, and Win followed.

The coach's window curtains were drawn tight, and Win blinked in the dim interior as he climbed inside.

"Forgive the darkness, Mr. Lane," said a woman.

His sight adjusted and settled on a diminutive woman tucked up against the black velvet squabs. Raven hair surrounded the pale moon of her face. Her red lips lifted in a ghost of a smile. "I've a skin ailment which erupts upon exposure to sunlight." Her words came out clipped with a deep roll in the middle. Russian perhaps, but she'd been in England long enough for it to have faded.

Her gown, however, was purely Asiatic. Made of crimson silk and embroidered with silver dragons, it was exotic and strange, yet seemed to suit her in some way that he suspected proper English gowns would not.

He took the seat on the opposite bench next to Poppy, who appeared perfectly at ease. "I've heard of such ailments," he said. "Any small bit of sunlight exposure results in rapid skin burns."

The smile grew a shade more. "Precisely."

"Winston," Poppy said. "This is Lena. She is my lieutenant, for lack of a better word."

"Madam." Poppy hadn't offered a last name, but Win's upbringing protested against using the woman's given name.

Lena inclined her head, and the beaded hair sticks that speared her coiffure clattered. "Mr. Lane." She turned her dark eyes back to Poppy. "What news?"

Poppy informed Lena with clipped tones then leaned back with a small sigh, and for once, she appeared utterly exhausted. Win let his hand fall to the seat, and their pinkies touched.

"Do you know who this Moira Darling could be?" Poppy asked Lena. The tip of her pinky moved against his. The light touch sent a lightning bolt of lust down the pathways of his nerves. Crossing one leg over the other, he watched Lena carefully.

The woman's slim shoulders swayed gently with the rhythm of the coach as she stared back at Poppy. "No."

For the life of him, Win could not tell if she was lying. Quite the feat since he ferreted out the best of liars. Save one. Poppy studied Lena as well, but seemed to be satisfied with the answer.

Again Poppy's little finger stroked him. He stroked back, trailing his pinky along her slimmer one. A shiver of sensation lit over his heated skin. Win cleared his throat. "She stole something from him. We do not know what."

At this, Lena gave a brittle smile. "Sounds like Isley, having a fit of pique over losing some nonsensical object."

Win felt along the delicate edge of Poppy's nail but he paused. "How well do you know Isley?"

Lena did not blink, and in the shadows of the coach, her dark irises glittered like bits of jet. "Enough to know that he always wants something from someone." Her lashes swept down for a moment before she focused on Poppy. "I shall put out inquiries about this Darling woman."

Poppy's hand slipped away as she sat up straight. "Keep it quiet."

Lena's thin brows furrowed. "I always do." Her mouth opened but she hesitated before finally answering. "You well know the dangers of interacting with Isley. It would be my honor to take over this investigation, should you wish it."

Poppy scowled. "You think that because I am with child, I cannot defend myself?"

Lena shrugged. "Hardly. It was merely a suggestion."

The look on Poppy's face made it quite clear what she thought of that, but she answered calmly enough. "This fight is Win's and mine." Her hand fell back to the squabs and rested next to his thigh. Win did not take it, but showed his support by facing Lena's burning gaze unflinchingly.

Apparently satisfied, Lena nodded, then studied Poppy in the ensuing silence. A look passed between them, and Winston understood that Lena wanted to discuss business.

Poppy held the other woman's gaze. "Report."

"Isley's appearance is already stirring up trouble," Lena said. "We've had five murders in the last two days. Lower level demons cutting down humans for fun. They've been dealt with, but the Nex are using Isley to incite protests within the underground."

"The Nex?" Winston looked from Lena to Poppy. "As in the Latin term for slaughter?"

"To signify both the slaughter of ignorant humans and the metaphorical destruction of supernaturals' basic rights. Pithy, isn't it?" Poppy's mouth pinched. "They are a resistance group who seeks to expose supernaturals to the world and are a bloody thorn in the SOS's side."

Lena made a sound of annoyance. "They are using Isley as a figurehead because he has escaped from Hell. Not many have done so, and no demon wants to return." Black humor filled her eyes. "Hell is a most uncomfortable place to be."

"I gather," Win muttered. "But are not all demons from Hell?"

"No." Lena crossed one leg over the other, causing her silk gown to hiss. "Demons are born in another plane of existence. There are many names for this place: Duat, the underworld, the shadowlands," she lifted a shoulder as if to say names were meaningless, "but it is not hell. It is simply another place. Hell is a prison, designed for those who do evil and seek to bedevil this world."

Poppy's naturally ivory skin turned wan, and shadows dwelled beneath her eyes. "Send word to Michael Scott. Have him run the usual story."

Win jolted up. "Michael Scott, the bleeding shock journalist with *The Cryer*?" When Winston had been on the Ranulf case, that bloody man had run wild with sordid tales of werewolves and liver-eating madmen. Of course now Win knew they were true. At the time, it had been one more nuisance to drive him to distraction.

"The very one," Poppy said, unrepentant. "We constantly leak stories. You know tales of vampires, werewolves, ghosts that haunt St. Giles and such."

Win's mouth fell open before he snapped it shut. "You willingly let Londoners know about such things? Wouldn't it be safer to quash all evidence?" He wasn't for lying to the public but he understood working for the greater good.

"That would in actuality be harder to do." Poppy gave him a small, pained smile. "You understand better than anyone that people always know deep down when they're being lied to." It was bold of Poppy to say so, but he kept his expression neutral. Discomfort spread over her features but she pushed on. "So we give them an enticing version of the truth. Give them a bit of a thrill, then they are satisfied."

It was quite clever.

With a sweep of her straight lashes, Poppy dropped the subject and turned back to Lena. "Pull Regulators off of low priority cases and put them on patrol. Double shift until the situation dies down." Her red brows drew together. "They'll balk. We are sorely understaffed," she said to Win before addressing Lena again. "Tell them that a double shift means double pay."

Lena nodded then rested her hand upon her knee as if relaxing, but Win had the thought that this woman never truly relaxed. "We need to increase our recruiting efforts, that is clear." Her gaze turned speculative. "How goes it with the GIM?"

"Miss Chase," Poppy interjected Mary's name with enough emphasis to make clear that Lena ought to afford the lady some respect, "is doing well. She needs further combat training but that can be attained easily enough."

The coach hit a rut, and Lena's hair sticks clattered. "Rumor has it Lucien Stone suffers a fit of ennui and considers stepping down as head of the GIMs."

"I've heard so as well." Poppy settled more comfortably against the squabs, and Winston stared. His wife commanded the space around her like a duke with utter and total confidence in her place within this world. "If he does, Daisy will take over. Her connection to the Lycans as their queen would give them an iron-clad alliance."

Lena's red lips formed a brief smile. "It was wise of you to bring the lycans and GIMs together."

A jolt passed through Winston's middle. "What?" He looked between the two women, and noted Poppy's implacable expression. "You planned for Daisy to become a GIM?"

"Don't be ridiculous," Poppy said with a wave of her hand. "I had no idea Daisy suffered from syphilis." Something dark passed over Poppy's face before clearing. "I merely knew Conall Ranulf's character, and I knew Ian's. Ian would make a better leader of the Lycans than his brother. He had honor when his brother did not, and he believes in the SOS's cause. Ignoring Ian's desperate request for help pushed him to make an alliance with Lucien Stone and the GIMs." Her gaze held steady even as the coach swayed. "Lucien and Ian were old friends. It seemed the natural course of things."

This was his wife? This Machiavellian creature?

As if reading his shock, her expression turned wry. "It was a gamble that paid out."

"And the fact that your sister was in danger?" Daisy had been stalked by a mad werewolf. Disappointment colored Winston's tone.

Poppy closed down, going cold. "Ian Ranulf is one of the most powerful supernaturals I know. He vowed to keep Daisy safe, and I had to trust in that."

"It is an awful amount of trust to place, Poppy. You played with your sister's life."

Ice cold air filled the coach. "We were monitoring the situation."

Anger twisted like a knife in his gut. "How could I forget?"

The SOS had also been watching as he investigated the case and ended up being attacked by the werewolf, but it was a cheap shot, and he regretted it as soon as it left his mouth. Poppy was a creature of logic and control, just as he was. And perhaps that was the problem. Logic and control ought not to rule love and color decisions concerning family, yet it had. It had crept into their lives at some point when neither of them was looking. He hated that this was how their fate had unraveled.

The cold surrounding Winston had a bite to it now. Poppy glared at him from across the small divide between them. "I might have brought her to SOS headquarters. And if you know anything of Daisy, you'll know that she would have found a way out and back to Ian. The woman has the curiosity of a cat and was obviously attracted to Ranulf." Poppy's brown eyes bore into him. "Every morning we rise up from our beds and death is there, hanging over us, waiting for an opportunity. Life is a gamble, husband. The question is, will you play your hand when the risk is at its greatest?"

"What do you know of the Komtesse Krogstad?" Win asked Poppy, after Lena let them off at the Chelsea Embankment.

She almost started at the sound of his voice. Their

argument in the coach had left Poppy tender and bruised of heart. She had thought—hoped—he would understand her work and how there were times in which the only choice was between bad and worse. But he had looked at her with wounded and disillusioned eyes. Poppy braced herself and let the hurt slide over her. She would let it go for now. They had work to do.

"That she is not really a komtesse."

Afternoon sunlight bathed the wide walking park that fronted the Thames, casting everything in a golden glow. It was cooler here by the water, with a forgiving breeze carrying the scent of brine. Poppy smoothed back a strand of hair that had slipped free before taking a huge bite of the Chelsea bun they'd stopped to purchase a block over. Cinnamon and lemony sweetness filled her mouth. Gods, but it was delicious. She could eat two more, given the opportunity. Having never been the sort to go weak-kneed over sweets, she could only surmise it was due to the baby, which left her elated and terrified all at once.

She popped the last bite into her mouth then licked her sticky fingers. Win's gaze rested on the action, and something within her tightened. She let her hand fall. "She's a cobbler's daughter from Christiania. She had a knack for attracting extremely wealthy protectors. Apparently, she worked her way through Norway and down the Rhine before settling in London. Posing as a komtesse added cachet to both her and her paramours, so everyone was happy with her illicit title usage."

Win cleared his throat and turned his attention forward. "Was? Does she not have a protector now?"

"She doesn't need one. At the moment, the komtesse does what pleases her and nothing more." Poppy glanced at his stern profile. "She is quite lovely, actually."

He made a sound. "You've visited her before?"

She could see in his eyes that the possibility irritated him, as it was one more thing he did not know about his wife. To hell with him then. The bloody bastard had bargained away their child. Her voice grew as hard as the square pavers beneath her feet. "On occasion. The komtesse is one of our best informants. And she's very fond of the occult."

He tilted his head down, away from the sun's harsh glare, leaving only the smooth sweep of his unmarred jaw visible. "She believes in it, but does she know the full truth?"

"Her belief only goes so far. She'll turn a blind eye toward anything that would frighten her. The occasional séance to call ghosts of lovers past, however, is quite entertaining."

Directly in front of them, a piano grinder had set his pushcart down. Discordant clanking filled the air as he turned the crank. A horrid noise, yet lively enough to entice a group of girls to dance. Two little ones, no older than seven, and two young ladies around fifteen danced a quick jig to the music as their older sisters looked on with their arms linked in easy companionship. Like a few others, Poppy slowed to watch them, her heart warming as she thought of her own sisters at that age.

Win stood by her side, close enough to feel the heat of his body but not quite touching. "Remember the day Miranda and Daisy taught me the polka?"

She felt herself smile. "They were so proud to teach you something you did not know." It was a lifetime ago; that day Poppy had played the piano as the girls danced Win about the parlor until the three of them fell down laughing. It had been the first time Miranda had truly laughed since their mother had died, and Poppy had nearly wept in gratitude that Win had been able to coax it out of her.

He leaned in a touch, his voice at her ear, and she could hear the smile in his tone. "I was happy to learn from them. And proud to teach them the waltz."

How graceful he had been and careful to lead the girls through the steps, quietly correcting them yet taking no notice of their furious blushes when they made a mistake. He'd waltzed with her as well. Later that night, just the two of them in the darkened parlor. They hadn't needed music then; their bodies had their own rhythm. Her cheeks heated, and she knew that if she turned her head, she'd find him watching her. Would she see the ghost of those days haunting his gaze? Poppy did not think she could bear it.

"I should not have spoken to you the way I did," he said in a low voice. Her breath left in a soft exhalation, but he kept on speaking as if he hadn't heard. "I ought to know better than anyone that one must detach all feeling in order to make impossible decisions."

"Your anger was well-placed," she whispered. "I gambled with my sister's safety. I might have lost her." She wrapped her arms about herself and held still.

Win's touch at her lower back skittered along her senses. "I did not consider Daisy's nature or see the entire picture. You did. And your gamble paid out."

Poppy rubbed her arms. "Forget it." For all her neediness, his sudden praise made her want to run from herself, and she did not know why.

"I cannot," he said, but he dropped his hand as if he knew she was on the verge of bolting.

"The komtesse's house is just there," she said with a toss of her chin, desperate to bring the subject back to the task at hand. The grand, red brick town house jutted out from the rest of the buildings, elegant in design, with its Gothic arches and circular windows.

Poppy kept her stride quick, knowing he would keep up. Nevertheless, her limbs felt heavy, as though weighted down. "She is quite relaxed about societal manners."

Out of the corner of her eye, she saw his lip twitch. "Are you warning me to brace my delicate sensibilities, Poppy?"

She slid him a sidelong glance. "I suppose I needn't. I'm sure you've entered your fair share of bordellos and the like."

His mouth quirked further, and his blue-grey eyes twinkled. "All in the name of investigations, I assure you."

She sniffed. "I didn't think otherwise."

"Mmm."

A reluctant smile pulled at her lips. "The point being that one knows what to expect in such establishments, and thus one is prepared when the irregular occurs." She could almost feel his eyes rolling, and she gave him a repressive look. "It's another thing altogether to enter what you believe to be a respectable residence only to find a dwarf dressed as a cherub—or undressed as it were—or some such thing, now isn't it?"

Win stopped short, the scar on his left brow pulling tight as his eyes narrowed. "Is that what we're going to find? Naked dwarves?"

"Henri is often about, but he may be otherwise engaged." She shrugged and strode onward, lest he see her grin. "One never knows."

Poppy was having him on. Win was sure of it. He told himself this as they were led into Komtesse Krogstad's parlor. Even so, he kept his wits about him and his back to the wall. Not that he had anything against dwarves. Unclothed was another matter. Poppy, blast her, kept a serene expression but she was clearly reveling in his unease, the chit.

He leaned in, enjoying the way the skin prickled along her neck as he did. "If we do encounter a naked dwarf, I'm leaving him to you."

She raised a brow, her gaze studiously upon a gilded peacock statue that peered down at them from the green marble mantel. "Who said he enjoyed women?"

"All right, I'll sacrifice myself, but I detest displays of jealousy. So avert your eyes, will you?"

Win was rewarded with a bubble of laughter escaping her lips. On any other woman, he'd have called the sound a giggle, but he would never dare accuse Poppy of giggling. The sound went straight to his heart and turned it over. He found himself grinning wide as she turned her head.

"Cheeky," she said before glancing up. Their noses almost touched, they were so close. Poppy's smile faded on an indrawn breath, and his gaze fell to her mouth. Such a lovely mouth, wide yet feminine, the bottom lip a bit plumper than its bowed top. And so very soft. Heat rippled down his chest.

Her cheeks pinked as he stared. Struggling, he cleared his throat. "You started it." The heat within him grew, making him feel languid yet hard all at once. Her breath smelled of sugar and spice. *Everything nice.* He leaned closer, ready to take, when the door opened. Poppy jumped as though pricked with a pin, bumping his shoulder with her chin when she turned around. He took an awkward step back and turned as well.

Win had to give the komtesse credit; she obviously knew she'd walked in on something but she took no outward notice of their indiscretion. Though from Poppy's description of her, he gathered she'd seen worse, and often.

She paused at the threshold of the parlor to survey them, and Win took the moment to study her back. This was one of Isley's mistresses? Had she suspected she bedded a demon? Had it thrilled her to do so?

Though she was not what he'd expected, Win could see her appeal and why she'd been a favorite of dukes and the supernatural alike. She was tall, like Poppy, and lean as well. Her bone structure was strong, almost masculine, with high cheekbones, deep-set eyes, and a long, expressive nose. But her lips were full, puffed as if she'd just been kissed. Wheat blond hair rippled in twin waves down over her shoulders. The tresses glinted in the light as she came forward. She was a Botticelli, "La Primavera" gazing at them with quiet knowing. The effect was heightened by the white toga-style dress she wore.

Win took all this in like any other man who appreciated beauty. Yet he wanted to sigh in defeat. For all her grace, the woman did nothing for him. No, only the redheaded warrior woman at his side had ever stirred him. He was well and truly cursed. And wasn't that just splendid?

"Mrs. Hamon," said the komtesse, holding out a welcoming hand to Poppy, "it is good to see you once again." Her voice was dark honey. A fine trap for a man. And then Win realized what she'd called his wife, and his insides jumped. His gaze cut to Poppy, who sent him a warning with a mere flicker of her lashes.

Poppy took the komtesse's hand. "Komtesse. Thank you for seeing us."

The komtesse's laugh was light and airy. "Please call me Brit, as we are old friends, are we not?" She smiled at Poppy, but she made her awareness of Win known by the incline of her head and the way her gaze drifted over him.

Poppy straightened. "Brit. This is my associate, Mr. Belenus."

He caught himself just before he laughed out loud. The imp was using his middle names. Had she always done so? Associate, was he? Very well. He took the komtesse's outstretched hand and brushed a kiss over her knuckles. "Enchanted," he said, settling into his role.

"We came to talk to you about Lord Isley," Poppy said, her usual forthright manner a shade more brisk.

The komtesse's brows winged up, but her expression remained serene. "Let us use the studio." With a fluid swirl of her skirts, she turned from the room.

No one spoke as she led them down a wide hall whose walls had been papered in gold damask. The sound of laughter and the notes of a fiddle playing a mad tune as some fellow sang along, off key and rather badly, drifted through the house. Paintings covered the walls, although their subjects were not the usual staid compositions or classical portraits, but of life—little vignettes so real that Win felt he could reach into the frames and touch them. He was no true student of art, but he liked to keep educated and thus recognized the works of Whistler, Degas, and Renoir.

"You follow the Impressionists, Komtesse," he said.

"I prefer to say I follow what art pleases me, Mr. Belenus," the komtesse answered. "But you may make that assumption if you prefer to place art into neat categorizations."

He could almost feel Poppy struggle to hide her smile.

He kept his eyes on the paintings, appreciating them for the pleasure alone this time. His step slowed as a portrait of a lone young man sitting in languid repose by a glass of absinthe caught his eye.

The komtesse glanced over her shoulder. " 'The Absinthe Drinker' by Manet. One of my favorites." She stopped and came shoulder to shoulder with Winston and Poppy as they looked up at the painting. "The public hated it when Manet first presented it. They thought it vulgar, as if life should only be portrayed as tidy and perfect. It is the richness of color and the man's expression that draws me into this piece." Her voice turned soft. "What do you suppose he's thinking? Does he wonder if his life is slipping away?"

Win swallowed past the thickness in his throat. It was like looking at his younger self, that sad, hopeless wretch who'd bargained with the devil. A bead of sweat rolled down the valley of his back, so slow and steady that he could track its progress. "Perhaps he was thinking of what he could not have."

Poppy's voice, quiet with contemplation, touched his ear. "He looks a bit like you. When you were younger."

He could not breathe. His collar hugged him too tightly. Two sets of feminine eyes bore into him and another trickle of sweat rolled down his back. The moment pulled, vibrating like a plucked bow, then the komtesse stirred.

"There is another portrait I want to show you. Come." She opened a door, and they stepped into a room done up in vibrant shades of peacock blue. Four large, low slung couches of saffron and gold silk, covered with purple and red pillows, made up a sitting square in the center of the room. It hurt his eyes just looking at them so he glanced about at the paintings on the wall instead, lest he be overcome with indigestion.

"Have a seat," offered the komtesse.

Not bloody likely. Those horrid couches were meant to be lain upon, drink in one hand, a smoke in the other. Winston was damned if he'd put himself in a prone position in an unknown house. Poppy didn't seem to mind, though, and reclined with surprising finesse. The sight of her long, lean body uncoiled upon that harem couch, her booted feet tucked beneath her skirts and one hand at her nape to support her head, did strange things to his equilibrium. Winston shifted his stance with a surge of irritation. He supposed that was rather the point of the couches. The twinkle in the komtesse's eyes confirmed it, and that she knew all too well the effect Poppy had on him. But her voice was even and gentle as she pointed toward the far wall. "That is what I wanted to show you."

When he looked, his blood stilled. It was a large portrait, dominating the wall and encased in a heavy, gold frame. Done in tones of black and grey, the pale countenance of Lord Isley smiled down at them. It was a smug smile, full of knowing and trickery, as if even then, he was planning mischief. Isley wore the very same suit and scarlet cravat that he'd donned when meeting Winston, and Winston wondered for a moment if Isley ever changed, if the suit was even real but yet another illusion.

"Lord Isley as I knew him in eighteen sixty-five," said the komtesse.

By the pale tinge of Poppy's skin, Win realized that she recognized this man as well. Her eyes narrowed upon the painting with such hatred and determination that his skin prickled. The komtesse's gaze, however, was serene, perhaps a touch wistful.

Win walked closer. Nestled in the elaborate folds of Isley's cravat was a golden cartouche. Win did not know hieroglyphics but he made note of the symbols. "If I may, Komtesse," he asked, turning back to her, "how well did you know Lord Isley?"

Her lips curled a touch. "Given that I have his portrait hanging upon my wall, you mean? We were lovers as I gather you already suspected." She sighed, letting her chin fall into her cupped palm as she smiled up at the portrait. "He was lovely though. Always made me feel a queen even when I was close to rags." Deep-lidded eyes returned to study him and Poppy with equal measure. "I was on the verge of ruin before he came into my life. My protector had left me alone in Paris, and I'd not found another." She fiddled with the tasseled end of a vermilion pillow. "In truth, I was quite desperate, wishing for a quick death or a miracle, which at that point might have been one and the same. And, as if called, Isley found me. He brought me here to London." She grinned then, the act lighting up her face as if the sun suddenly shone upon her. "I've never had want of money again."

Ice swam through Win's gut. A miracle indeed. And just what had the komtesse given up to see her fortunes reversed? All the cold within him turned to burning bile, and he swallowed down the taste of acrid bitterness, for he knew she was as ignorant as the rest of Isley's victims.

Poppy glared up at the painted Isley before turning back to the komtesse with a neutral expression. "Forgive me for being blunt, Brit—"

"But you always are, Mrs. Hamon. It is one of your best traits," the komtesse answered with apparent fondness.

Poppy's severe brows lifted a touch but she forged on. "Well then. We are interested in one of Isley's possible paramours at that time. Moira Darling. Have you heard of her?"

The komtesse gave a little shocked laugh. "You certainly did not hold back that time, did you?" She sat up on the couch as if she could no longer bear to relax. "There was talk of other women. He was rather... voracious in his appetites, and there is no telling whether he visited certain houses on occasion. Though I would not be surprised if he did." Her shoulders lifted in a delicate shrug. "However, I've never heard of Moira Darling, I'm sorry to tell you."

"Have you the names of any women he might have visited?" Win asked.

"Often times, he consulted with a Mrs. Noble." Clear, direct eyes held his. "She is known to have an excellent eye for art. Isley was quite fond of her."

"Mrs. Amy Noble?" Winston asked. "The widow of Mr. Tobias Noble, the coal magnate?"

"The very one. She hosts a revolving house party at Farleigh, her estate in Richmond that runs from July to November. It is quite lively. One might meet the Prime Minister or some boy she brought in from the streets because she liked the sound of his singing."

Poppy glanced at Win. "Then it is to Farleigh we go." She turned to the komtesse. "Brit. Be careful, will you? No new visitors for a few weeks."

The komtesse's golden brows knitted. "Am I in danger, Mrs. Hamon?"

Poppy's skirts rustled as she stood. "At the moment, anyone who had been in contact with Isley is. I shall send word when it is safe. But for now, trust in me and do as I say."

"I always do."

Win stared at the clean, strong lines of his wife's face and form. Here was the leader, the woman who commanded an entire organization. People did as she asked. As always, it made him itch to get her alone and coax out that soft, sensual Poppy that only he had the privilege to see.

Her hand settled on the crook of his arm, and he tucked her close as he nodded to their hostess. "Komtesse."

She gave him a secretive smile. "It was a pleasure meeting you, Mr. Belenus. Do come back. At any time."

The devil in him couldn't help but feel a small sense of satisfaction when Poppy's hand tightened on his arm. If she only knew how little any other woman affected him.

He opened the door and ran directly into another man. Or rather, his crotch collided with a man's face. Win swallowed a silent curse as he took in the abundance of bare skin and a pair of pink-feathered wings shivering tremulously. They stared at each other, Win gaping down and the man blinking up in surprise. Then Win cleared his throat. "Henri, I presume?"

The man unfurled a slow, pleased smile while Win's face grew uncomfortably hot. "Why yes. Have we met?"

# *Chapter Seventeen*

~~~~~~~~~~~~

They made it out of the house and onto the embankment before Poppy burst out laughing. She did not laugh often, but when she did, she did so with her whole soul. Win watched, half bemused, half transfixed, as her laughter poured out in wave after wave, a gorgeous, husky sound that invited one to join in. Her shoulders shook with it, and tears streamed out of the corners of eyes that sparkled like topaz in the sunlight. Around them, a few strollers passed, and despite Poppy's unladylike manners, they could not help but be affected. Several smiled, and a chimney sweep just off the job laughed as well, sending bits of blacks and ash tumbling off his shoulders before he strolled away.

When she'd gotten herself reasonably under control, Win took her elbow lightly. "Yes, yes," he said, guiding them farther away from the komtesse's residence, for Poppy was still useless with her snorts and chuckles. "It was all very amusing. Have your laugh. I don't mind."

With a shaking hand, she wiped her eyes. "Your face,

Win." She snorted again. "For a moment, I thought you would turn and jump into my arms for safety."

His lips twitched. "It was a very near thing." And then he laughed too. Which meant they stood like two jack-puddings, making a racket while the sensible people of London scurried past, lest they be infected too.

Their gazes clashed, and his breath hitched, his laughter dying in a half-cough as he realized how close they stood, hunched over each other, her hand clutching his arm for support. Hers ended on a hiccup, and they stared at each other from across their small divide. No one saw him like this. Sheridan would likely faint on the spot should he hear Winston laughing. Only she truly saw him. Only with Poppy did he feel true joy. Just then, he missed her so much that he hurt, a physical pain that urged him to reach out and pull her near so that he could hold her.

She straightened, bringing herself closer, her expression suddenly as lost and as pained as his surely was. "Win…"

Win didn't know what had changed, perhaps the sound of a footstep that was too determined or the snick of a knife snapping open, but his attention shifted from Poppy's delectable mouth to their surroundings. She too seemed to have noticed the danger as well, for her eyes narrowed and her frame grew stiff.

"We've picked up an interested party," she said, as if conversing on the weather.

"Indeed we have." Taking her arm, he guided her down the path. They maintained a casual stroll, but his hand tightened on his walking stick. Win did not turn to see, but instinct told him there were at least three persons following. The foot traffic had thinned out, leaving them vulnerable to attack. Then again, it left him free to fight back without worry of hurting an innocent observer. His back tightened when, from the periphery, he saw four thugs fan out.

He leaned closer to Poppy and smiled as though he were paying her a compliment. "When we get to the overpass just ahead, move to the wall behind me and stay there."

Her brown eyes flashed in surprise. "And do what? Wait meekly until you have bested them?"

"That is the general idea, yes."

Her lips thinned in a parody of a smile. "How about this? You take two, and I take two." Her arm moved slightly, and she clutched her fan at the ready. A bloody fan? He almost laughed, only he wanted to strangle her more.

"Might I remind you," he said through his clenched teeth, "that you are with child."

"Which makes it imperative that we end this scuffle quickly."

Her logic appalled him. He was on the verge of pulling her to the side when she spun round to face their stalkers.

"Gentlemen," she said as the men halted. Four big brutes who looked spoiling for a fight. "I believe you have lost your way. I advise you to turn around before you regret it."

Win had to give her credit. She was as fearsome as the worst schoolmarm. Only these weren't boys. And he was certainly going to kill her when they got out of this. He stepped shoulder to shoulder with her, before easing her back. Or tried to; she wouldn't budge. Grunting in annoyance, he pulled his coat open enough to show the gun he wore beneath it. "You heard my lady. Go on and find easier sport."

Even as he spoke, the oddness of the men poked at his awareness. They hadn't said a word, but simply stood, weaving slightly on their feet as though foxed, their eyes unblinking. Beside him, Poppy appeared to notice the same, for she went pale.

"Shit," she said.

He risked a glance at her as he moved to pull his gun free. Her hand on his arm halted him. "No," she said. "Won't do any good. They're undead."

"What?" A breeze swept over them, and he caught the scent of rotting flesh.

Poppy backed them up, her hand like a vise on his forearm. "Undead. As in corpses called up from the grave to do their master's bidding."

Hell. One day, he'd wake up and it would all be a dream.

"Win, tell me that walking stick has a sword."

"Of course." He tensed, his hand going to the head of the swordstick. Now that they were closer, he could see the grey cast to their skin and the bluish rips where flesh had begun to cleave from bone.

"Saber or rapier?"

"Saber. Archer gave it to me."

Poppy gave a tight smile. "I think I love that man."

He'd have to address that remark later, for the thugs chose that moment to attack. He pulled his sword free with a ring of steel as Poppy shouted, "Aim for the throat. Decapitation is the only way to stop them." And then she was stepping in front of him to engage.

For a taut moment, he could only gape at his wife. She was poetry in motion, moving in a way he'd never before seen. One thug made a grab for her, and she struck the crook of his elbow with the blunt end of her fan. Two more moves, and his arm was broken. The fan snapped open, and Win realized that the slats were actually steel blades. With a whirl of red hair and blue skirts, the silver fan sliced through the thug's neck, and his head hit the ground with a *thunk*.

It happened in the blink of an eye, and then Win had his hands full. Bloody hell but these things were fast, and strong. One struck him on the side of the head, and he saw stars. Win reacted, his training setting in. Then it was a blur. His body moved through the macabre dance without forethought. Kick, swing, duck, step, swing. He decapitated an undead, and then there were two.

Poppy moved behind him, working in tandem with her back to his so that they were a singular force. A blow to his guts had Win tasting bile. He punched back, his fist connecting with cold, dead flesh. Behind him, Poppy staggered as one thug smashed his massive hand into her. She did not make a sound, but black rage took hold of Winston. With a roar, he swung around, moving Poppy out of the way as his sword cleaved the undead's head from its neck in one clean swipe.

He might have roared again in victory were it not for the shadow bearing down behind him. A knife headed straight for his heart. He had no time to move or block the blow. Win braced himself, but the hit never came. His wife snarled like an enraged cat and lashed out. Her slim arm deflected the hit. Another blow and she decapitated the thug with her clever fan.

And then it was over. Winston was battered. Every inch of him ached as he took in the carnage. Four undead lay sprawled on the ground. All were missing their heads.

His chest heaved as he straightened and looked at his wife. She was panting as well, her hair in a red tangle about her slim shoulders. A smear of blood marred her cheek, but the cut was shallow. She was glorious. He glanced about one more time, making certain they were well and truly alone. Nothing stirred.

"Are you harmed?" he asked. "Did they hit..."

"The child is fine." She smoothed hair back from her face. "You?"

"Not yet." His sword clattered to the ground. He took the two steps to close the distance between them and hauled her against him. Lust slammed into him at the touch of his lips to hers. Hard enough to make him stagger, taking her with him. He fell against the brick wall of the overpass as he cupped her cheeks with his hands and devoured her mouth, needing to touch her, taste her, more than he needed to breathe. This was what he'd been missing. This was what made him feel whole. Her fingers tangled in his hair and tugged hard as she kissed him back, biting his lower lip.

His head spun with want, and he took a shuddering breath to ease the tightness in his chest. He had to stop. He knew this. But for the moment, he closed his eyes and simply reveled in her. His tongue played with hers, a slow, torturous slip-slide, and he groaned. Then he let her go. And it was painful.

They panted for a moment, and her eyes were wide with surprise and wonder as he tenderly caressed her bloodied cheek.

"What was that for?" she said after a moment.

He rubbed his thumb along her bottom lip and told her the truth. "For being alive."

With the heat of battle still running riot through her veins, Poppy's hands were unsteady as she started to go through the undeads' pockets. Win had kissed her. She knew enough of combat to understand that the need for physical contact, or a sexual release, went hand in hand with the aftermath of getting one's blood up. She ought not make anything of it. Only her heart pounded, and she couldn't think straight.

He knelt next to her, his trousers straining against his powerful thigh muscles. How he had moved in the fight. She had never seen him like that, his body a lethal weapon, gliding and striking as though he owned the very air around him. It made her dizzy with lust.

"What are you looking for?" His smoky voice was low and even.

She reached into an inner coat pocket. "A guide. The undead cannot think for themselves. They'd need something to guide them to us. Something that identifies what victim they sought."

Beside her, Win began to do the same, his shoulder brushing hers as they worked. He sat back on his heels as he pulled out a folded piece of what looked like sheepskin paper. Poppy stopped and leaned into his shoulder to watch him unfold it. A coil of red hair fell out and onto his roughened palm.

"Well, that explains it," she said through her teeth. "They have my hair."

Win clutched the clump in his fist. "How?"

Poppy rested an elbow on her thigh. "Taken from my hairbrush? I do not know."

Win rose to his feet and held out a hand. Poppy did not need help, but she took it because she wanted to keep touching him. Foolish. She could not afford to be so weak. She let go as soon as she stood and then glanced down at the undead. "I would say it was Isley, but this is not his modus operandi."

"Do you believe someone else wants to hurt you?" His cool eyes grew hard and angry. "Have you an idea of who it could be?"

A short laugh escaped her. "The list is long, dear husband."

His jaw tightened. "You find this amusing?"

No. She found it wearying. Worse, she wanted to punch something, for he had been in danger too. By associating with her. Damn it all. She glanced up to find Win watching her. She'd seen the soft heat in his eyes just after he'd kissed her. The tenderness. He'd looked at her as he used to look at her. Before. This was her life now. Before discovery. After discovery. She wanted that look back.

"Why did you pull away?" She hadn't meant to ask, but now that she had, she would not flinch from it.

His expression closed down. "What is it that you want me to say, Poppy?" The scar on his lip was white as he searched her face. "That I am human? You know that all too well."

Her breasts lifted and fell as she fought for breath. "Perhaps that you wanted to kiss me?" *That you miss me the way I miss you. So much that it hurts.*

His expression was so stern that he might have been a marble carving. "I wanted to kiss you." He backed her up against the stone wall leading onto the Embankment. "I want you every thinking moment I have. I want you near. I want to hear your voice. Feel you." He leaned in, drowning her in his scent and his heat. "I want to take you hard, slow, every way in between. And the piss of it is, it's always been this way. From the moment I saw you."

She gaped up at him, and his scowl grew. "I want you always. In all things. I want...." He exhaled unsteadily. "It is pain, this wanting you. And I wish it were gone."

Her breath left in a sharp rasp. But he was past hearing. "Because it isn't about wanting, is it? A man gets to a point in his life when he realizes wanting isn't everything. There needs to be more."

"You will never forgive me, will you?"

His head snapped back, those deep eyes of his clouding for a moment. And then he sighed. "It is not a question of forgiveness. I lied, you lied, we both lied."

"Are you conjugating? Or is there a point? For I confess, I cannot understand what you are about."

His mouth twisted as he leaned in. "It isn't real. What we had was never real. It was an illusion. Our life. Our love."

"How dare you say that! How dare you belittle all that we had." He might as well have punched her in the chest.

"How can I not? Everything we are is a result of my folly and Isley's bloody machinations."

She hit his shoulder. Hard. "Fool! Your bargain reset your life's course. It did not make me want you afterward. It did not make us happy. It did not make me lo..." She swallowed. "It did not make me love you, Win. You did that, you ass." She shoved him again, hard enough to make him step back, which was good, for she could not stand another moment in his presence. "And if you cannot see that, cannot accept what we were, then our continued association is pointless."

He grabbed her upper arms. "It is you who cannot see!" When she tried to move, he held fast. "You kept turning me down when I first proposed. Do you remember that at least?"

Stiffly she nodded, not liking the hard, black feeling swelling within her chest.

His grip tightened, his eyes wild with pained frustration. "I thought you did so because of who I was. But it wasn't that, was it? I understand now. It was because of who you were."

The blackness turned to pain and pushed against her ribs, filling up her throat. "I did not want to love you. I did not want to risk you." She still did not want to face that risk.

Redness swarmed in his eyes as he looked at her. "I know, sweeting. I know it now. Can you not see it? I took away your choice." Softly, his thumbs caressed her. "Ask yourself this. Would Boadicea, Mother of the SOS, have given in and said yes to me?"

A garbled sound broke from her lips as all that black, raging pain became too much to hold in. She sucked in greedy pulls of air, but it was no use. The truth came whether she wanted to say it or not.

"No."

And then she was running. From him. From herself.

He watched her go. Every forceful stride she took drove a stab of pain into his heart. He bit his bottom lip to keep from calling her back. To keep from shouting out the truth. That he did not care if she wasn't truly his. He loved her. He always had. He'd die loving her. But she'd said her truth as well. She would not have chosen him. Absently, he rubbed his chest.

"You did the smart thing, Lane."

Hands fisting, he glanced down at the street urchin who had appeared by his side. A grubby little face blinked up at him, innocent, sweet with his button nose and too big eyes that flared with an inner fire. It took all Win had not to smash his fist into that face. "Did you do this?"

Jones looked down at the bodies littering the ground. "I thought this was your handiwork."

"You bloody well know what I mean."

"You've no sense of humor, Lane." Jones shrugged. "As she said, it is not my style. The woman has more enemies than the devil." His little face turned to watch Poppy go, and he grinned. "Ah, but she's glorious when she fights, isn't she?" Icy eyes settled on Winston. "She won't be talking to you for some time, though, will she?"

"I swear to God," Winston ground out, "I will find a way to destroy you, Jones. Even if I have to go to hell to do it."

The urchin adjusted his cap and spat on the ground. "Sweet words will get you nowhere." He shoved his small hands into the pockets of his short pants. "I'm doing you a service, really. Fate never meant for her to be yours."

"And what if I don't believe in your version of fate?" Each word was a razor dragged along Winston's throat.

"Then you wouldn't be here." A little foot kicked at a broken clump of paving, and the clump bounded away. "You'd be running after her." Hard eyes leveled on him. "Now, stop wasting time. You've got three days left. Then I come to collect."

# Chapter Eighteen

~~~~~~~~~

A man could make himself weak at the knees giving in to anticipation. Especially if gifted with a healthy imagination. He could watch the object of his desire and wonder. What would her lips taste like? Would they be tart and sweet like berries? Or warm and smooth like sherry? Would she willingly tickle her tongue along his? Or make him work for an entry? One glimpse of the shadow of her breasts and he could be hard, contemplating the shape of them once set free of their confinement. Pointed? Teardropped? Round? What color would her nipples be? Would they be big? Small? Pert? Or flat? It was an agony of delightful possibilities. A game of wondering how much torment a man could take before he acquired the knowledge.

Win had played that game before. He remembered the sharp sweetness of it. And he almost laughed now at the memory. For he now knew there was another far crueler sort of pain. That in knowing precisely, with vivid recollection, just what a man was missing out on. Imagination was a shadow of reality. Win knew what Poppy tasted like. That her breasts were small yet shapely little handfuls. He knew the exact shade and texture of her nipples. The very color her skin would flush when he pushed into her.

Ignorance was, as they say, bloody, buggering bliss. Knowledge, on the other hand, was an acute pain. A pain, to be precise, in his cock. Stuck as he was in a small coach with the object of his desire as they made their way to Farleigh, his cock was none too happy. Discreetly as he could, he adjusted himself and forced his gaze away from the cool length of her throat. He wanted to lick that expanse of skin, feel the throb of her pulse against him. He craved her flavor as a man imprisoned craves a juicy bite of meat.

He was an Englishman, for God's sake. He'd been raised on the denial of pleasure and control of one's wants. Only he'd never been able to master those things in regard to Poppy. Now, he'd cut himself off entirely. Like a bloody imbecile. At the very least, he ought to have joined Talent in the servants' coach and had Mary Chase ride with Poppy.

No words were spoken as they rode onward. Which was for the best. He couldn't think of what to say that would not draw himself closer into her orbit. And that was the problem: he wanted to be in her orbit. To be around her was the difference between going through the motions of the day and feeling every breath.

Poppy's stomach made a little growl, pulling him from his self-pity. Her lips flattened at the sound. He almost smiled, save her posture grew so rigid and the clench of her hands upon her lap so tight, that he knew she would not welcome it. Instead, he reached into his coat pocket and withdrew a small bag of chestnuts.

Her eyes went round as he handed them to her. But

she did not refuse. Her nimble fingers worked in a near greedy fashion as she stuffed a chestnut into her mouth. "I didn't know you to carry food around in your pocket." She munched industriously on another nut. As they hadn't spoken more than a few sentences since their argument, her words came out stilted and awkward.

"I don't, generally. Here..." He pulled a flask filled with cool apple cider out of his other pocket. She snatched it up and took a deep drink. "Save I've heard from some of the chaps that ladies in your condition are apt to need more sustenance." And if Poppy's appetite for the last few days was any indication, she needed a bit more than most.

Slowly she lowered the flask and peered at him. "These things are for me?"

"Of course."

It was clear that she did not expect him to look after her needs. Her hands fell to her lap, one hand clutching the chestnuts and the other the flask. She stared at him for a good moment, in which he had the irritating urge to look away, then she tucked the flask at her hip and ate another nut. "Thank you, Win."

"It is the least I can do. After all, I wouldn't want you to become irritable with hunger." He gave her a tight smile, for he didn't want her to see how much he enjoyed caring for her just now, not when she obviously believed it was no longer his duty, or his right. "A man learns to fear for his life when that occurs."

"Ha." She said it shortly, but good humor crinkled the corners of her eyes. The empty chestnut bag crumpled in her hand, and then she peered at him again, a thorough inspection that had him resting one arm casually over his lap to hide certain evidence.

"What else have you got for me, then?"

His breath hitched before he realized she was referring to food. Perfect. He gave her another smile. "A few meat pies in my satchel." *And that did not sound at all like a double entendre.* He cleared his throat. "Perhaps you ought to pace yourself? Not devour all and sundry in one sitting?"

Her warrior's brows snapped together, and her hand shot out. "Hand them over, Lane."

He laughed, because he could not hold it back, and then gave her the food, because he was not a complete fool. When she had settled back with her feast, he took hold of her legs and propped them on his lap. She squeaked in protest, and he gave her shin a light slap.

"Hush." His fingers went to the tight laces of her half-boots. "I've also been informed that a lady's feet may swell and become pained."

She shifted, finding a more comfortable position, and then regarded him with amusement. "I do not believe that occurs until I am a bit larger. However, I shall not complain." She took a bite of pie. "Wouldn't want to injure your tender feelings, after all."

"Gracious girl." He eased one boot off, noting her small noise of pleasure, before moving to take off the other boot. "Why did you not use your power on the undead we fought?" He had been wanting to ask, yet oddly had not been quite ready for the answer.

When she spoke, her words were measured. "The undead are magically manipulated, which means the rules of nature do not apply to them. At any rate, the degree of cold I would have needed to freeze bodies so large would have hurt you more than them." She shrugged and broke off a crumpling edge of the pastry. "Sometimes it is more practical to simply fight hand to hand."

*Indeed.* He kept his eyes upon his work as he dug his thumbs along the bottom of her foot. She sighed, the sound zinging through him, but the tension did not ease along her leg.

Poppy's voice was soft as it drifted across to him. "I knew it would bother you."

When he wrenched his head up, he found her blinking down at her clenched hands. A sad smile played about her lips. "I understand that a man wants to be the protector, to know that he can keep his wife from harm. What man in his right mind would want a woman who can freeze him solid with a thought?" She laughed weakly. "Who is versed in multiple weaponry and proficient in six forms of physical combat?"

Six forms? Hell, Archer and Ian had only taught him four. He looked down at his hands gripping Poppy's narrow foot. They were strong, capable hands. He'd just beheaded two undead thugs, though he took no pleasure from it. If he were honest with himself, he'd rather best a man with knowledge, not tear him apart. Still, as normal men went, he could easily hold his own on the physical field. Unfortunately, normal had long since left the station.

Poppy was silent. Then she swallowed audibly. "Part of me was happy to keep it all from you."

"Because you did not want to offend my manly pride?" He said it lightly, though the idea that she believed he was so small-minded bothered him.

Her dark eyes found him. "Because I didn't want you to stop looking at me as a woman. As a wife who needed you."

The carriage shuddered over a rut as he absorbed her words. Win cleared his throat, and it sounded overly loud in the space between them. "When we did battle against those undead, with your back to mine, each of us moving as one, I did not feel diminished. I felt alive." He stared at her, and his blood heated again. "I think you are magnificent, Poppy Lane."

"When I am in my twilight, and in a fit of ennui, I shall have a house party just like this," said Poppy. They strolled arm in arm, the picture of a content couple, along the stunning gardens of Farleigh. Hundreds of butterflies dotted the air, fluttering to and fro. Win did not know how Mrs. Noble's staff had managed to collect so many live specimens, but it made quite the picture. At present, he and Poppy wandered beneath an arbor hung with a profusion of blush pink roses that sweetened the air with their scent.

It had been fairly easy to pose as Mr. and Mrs. Snow, he a retired inspector turned prosperous wine merchant. Between the two of them, they knew enough about Hector Ellis's old business practices to speak proficiently on the subject. And Win wanted to keep his past as an inspector, as due to the oddness of human nature, people tended to open up to former inspectors more than they did actual inspectors.

"What is it about this party that appeals to you?" Despite their situation, relaxation softened his voice and made his gait slow. The gentle strains of Vivaldi drifted over the garden. Walking with Poppy was something he'd always loved to do. To hear her thoughts and to feel her arm pressed against him made his heart light. A butterfly alighted upon the intricate twist of her ginger locks and settled down like a golden ornament.

"None of them care," she said. "Have you noticed?

They aren't concerned with appearances or doing one better than the other."

A smile pulled at his lips. "If you are referring to the impromptu swim in the lake we witnessed upon arrival, then I could not agree more." A swim that did not include clothing.

Her cheeks went a charming shade of strawberry. "Yes, well that, and the general attitude of the party goers. There is such a carefree air. But genuine, which I can hardly comprehend in this day and age."

He stopped at the end of the arbor where a wood nymph water fountain made gentle music. "A bit too casual, I'm afraid." He glanced back toward the house, not visible from their vantage point, but there just the same. "We've been here three hours and have yet to see our hostess."

"I suspect we'll have to wait for this evening." Her red brows slanted down, highlighting her strong profile. "Do you suppose she'll keep to that horrid rule of separating the sexes after dinner?"

"Perhaps not," he said, not really paying attention. The butterfly had fluttered away, but a deep red strand of silken hair had slipped the knot and now coiled about Poppy's white throat. "Mrs. Noble does not appear to care for society strictures."

In her butter yellow gown, with her hair piled high, Poppy looked every inch the proper lady, yet he knew the steel core that hid just beneath the surface. But here, with the warm August sunlight dappling her white cheeks and glorious hair, she seemed almost at peace.

Unable to help himself, he stroked the smooth, alabaster curve of her cheek with his thumb, gliding it up a sunlit patch and along the downy tendrils of hair at her temple. She flinched at first contact, but did not step away. Her eyes studied him. They stood close. Close enough that he'd only have to lean forward and he'd be kissing her. He would start soft and mold her mouth with his, before gently opening hers.

His voice came out over-rough when he spoke. "I did not attend to you enough."

A little furrow deepened between her brows. "What do you mean? You always came home in a timely manner. You were always attentive."

He cupped her cheek, loving the cool feel of her against his skin. "No. I mean like this. We never just went away. Never spent time simply being. I lost track of appreciating *you*."

Her slender hand settled on his chest, and his heart thumped in return. "Win, you didn't have to take me away to make me happy. You just had to be with me." Her voice broke in a whisper. "And I was."

Quite suddenly, he hurt. His heart. Everywhere. He ached with a sweet, sharp pain that made him want to groan. "Poppy..."

His hands still cupped her cheeks, and he leaned in, needing to kiss her, but on a breath, she pulled back. "Win, what do you wish for?"

Wish for? What good was wishing? Hard truth stared him in the face, and the darkness there threatened to drag him down. The words were difficult to form. "I wish to be the father I never had." *I want my child to be born.* The lump in his throat grew until he could hardly speak. "I wish to see you safe."

Her nose wrinkled. "I'll never be safe. Not with the life I lead." She didn't flinch from it, but faced him head on when she spoke. Challenging him.

His fingers twined in the silken strands of her hair. She

wanted the truth? "And when you are also a mother?" She tried to edge away. He held her fast. "What of danger then?"

Her brows took on an aggressive slant. "It isn't—"

"Fair?"

"Yes, damn it!" Her cheeks flushed, and she took a deep breath.

His thumb stroked over the red wash of her guilt. "Little in life is."

Absently she nodded, and her scowl broke into something dark, more like despair. "I've wanted this child. So badly. Only now that it is real..." She bit her bottom lip.

"You want the SOS more." He tried not to feel the heavy weight of disappointment. She only wanted what most men he knew wanted as well. He couldn't fault her for not being like other women. He'd known that much about her when he met her. He'd loved her uniqueness then, so he'd have to accept it now. Only it was clear that she wanted the SOS more than she'd wanted anything. Including him.

Poppy, however, glared up at him as if he'd slapped her. "That isn't what I—"

"Is it the responsibility you fear losing or the danger?" He knew he was being a bastard, but he found himself unable to stop. Nor could he quell the tight ball of jealousy within him.

High color flagged her cheeks. "You are oversimplifying."

"Because it is simple. We all place a measure of importance on things in our life. I'm merely asking the order of yours."

"And what of you? As a homicide inspector, you risk your life every day. Would it be easy to walk away, then?"

"That choice has been made for me. I am no longer an inspector." And didn't it slash his soul to say it? It was akin to saying, "I am a failure."

Poppy blanched before her chin thrust up. "Bollocks. That is merely a title. But here," she slapped a hand upon his chest, "in your heart, you are a man who needs to fight for what is right."

"Yes," he said, despite himself.

Eyes the color of polished oak held him in place. "You sold your soul for it."

"And for you." For her most of all.

"And now?" Her voice shook with emotion as she gazed into his eyes. "Had you the chance to do it over again? What would you ask for? Knowing that I was a liar and a spy."

"You!" He grasped her slim arms as if he could keep her there, in this garden, forever. What was waiting for him at the end of this long journey weighed like an anvil upon his heart. "I choose my wife and my child."

The light in her eyes died, as swiftly as a candle being blown out. For the life of him, he couldn't understand why. Poppy was gentle as she removed herself from his grip. He tried to move, grab her back, tried to speak, to shout that he wanted her, needed her, but his body froze. Was his choice so very distasteful to her?

Poppy's voice was small and sad when she spoke again. "Only you did not choose me until you knew I was with child."

"No." No, no, no. She could not think...

Poppy shook her head. "When you look at me now, do you see only me? Or the child as well?"

How the hell could he answer that? To deny that Poppy and the child were the most important things in his life was illogical. His silence lasted too long. Poppy stepped back, straightening her spine as she did. "This talk gets us nowhere. Let us simply focus on the task at hand." She walked backward, fading into the shadows beneath the trellis. Leaving him. "I shall see you at dinner."

# Chapter Nineteen

───≈≈───

*Paris, 1869—A Bargain*

Winston sat in the crowded Parisian cafe and felt no pain. The little green fairy was taking care of that grandly. He slumped back in his seat, heedless of those around him, and simply stared. Faces swirled about him like a kaleidoscope gone mad. Eyes grew larger, rows of gleaming teeth flashing behind stretched lips. Too much laughter here. He needed to find another cafe. One where the somber chaps congregated as they drank their way toward death.

Death. He did not fear it. Why should he? He was already dead inside. No dreams left, no hope, no Poppy.

Ah, there it was, the pain. Like a marriage-minded mama with daughter in tow, pain pushed with insistent hands through the layers of alcohol-induced numbness and put itself front and center, demanding attention. He rubbed his tender chest. She'd ripped his heart out. And had been messy about it. Gaping wounds remained. He took another deep drink, and as the viscous anise flavor slid down his throat, he grimaced and looked down at himself, wondering how it was that there wasn't a bloody hole in him. No. Simply a slightly soiled waistcoat and rumpled evening kit.

Was it evening? Or morning? When had he arrived?

Gas lamps burned in this murky place. Heavy velvet curtains lined the windows. One could never see the passing of time here. He hunched over his glass and wished for... what?

He thought of his dream to become a detective and realized that he no longer cared. Without Poppy, and the joy she brought into his life, any happiness he might find as an inspector would be a shadow of the real thing.

"It's hopeless," he muttered into his glass.

Foxed as he was, it took him a while to realize that the sounds around him had stopped. Completely, as though a thick blanket had been thrown over everything. His head heavy, Win had a bit of a time getting it to lift. When he did, he gawked. The cafe had gone still. Still as in every soul inside of it had simply frozen, as if they'd turned to marble. Now that was a trick. He looked about, blinking to clear his eyes. But the woman at the table beside his remained bent forward, her mouth stretched in a silent laugh, her bosom nearly falling out of her low, green velvet bodice. The waiter's eyes remained glued upon those white mounds as his hand hovered an inch above the tabletop, the coffee cup in his hand steaming.

Footsteps echoed in the ringing silence, and Win wrenched his gaze toward the sound.

A man strolled toward him, his gait easy as he wove between the frozen patrons. Wearing a black walking suit and a waistcoat of scarlet satin, he appeared neither young nor old. His form was trim, his features almost indistinct. Dark hair hung unfashionably long from beneath a top hat that hid his eyes. And while Win stared, the man's thin lips curled in a smile. The man's chin lifted, and Win caught sight of his eyes. White. White irises that looked anything but human.

Win inhaled sharply. But the man blinked, and the eyes turned a normal hazel brown. The strange smile he wore, however, remained. The click of his boot heels stopped as he stood before Winston.

"Mr. Lane." The man inclined his head. "So sorry to keep you waiting."

Waiting? Perhaps absinthe wasn't the way to go. Perhaps opium would be better. Winston tried to reply and found his voice did not quite work. Decidedly, he'd imbibed too much.

Not waiting for an invitation, the man pulled out the chair opposite Win and sat. A slim, pale hand extended toward Win. "You may call me Mr. Jones."

Win stared at the hand, and then at the man. He could not make himself move to shake hands. Mr. Jones let his hand fall and smiled again as though Win's rudeness amused him. "Your glass is empty, Mr. Lane."

Was it? Win hadn't noticed.

"Let me get you another." Jones's fingers snapped, and like that, the cafe buzzed with life once more.

A waiter appeared at their table as if he'd been there all along. Win tried to think but found himself unable as the waiter set down a fresh glass of absinthe. Jones tapped the marble tabletop with one long fingernail. "Nothing is hopeless, Lane. Drink up." His hand dipped into his coat pocket, and he pulled free a rolled length of foolscap. "Then we can discuss terms."

Win touched his throbbing head. "Pardon, sir...I am a bit...muddled." He took a deep, clearing breath. "Do I know you?"

Again came that smile, curling and dark with promise. Again the eerie flash of white in his eyes. "No. But you will."

# *Chapter Twenty*

"Come with me." Winston waited impatiently at his dressing room door as Jack Talent put aside a pair of boots he'd been polishing.

"Where are we going?" Talent asked as they traversed the long, wide upper hall.

"As Mrs. Noble proves elusive for the moment, we are going to question one of the other guests."

"Wouldn't you rather question the servants?" Talent asked.

Most guests were preparing for dinner, and the light of the day was fading fast. Around them, maids were lighting the lower gas lamps as tall footmen attended the upper sconces. A golden glow began to rise through the house. Drinks were being served in an hour, but Poppy refused to dress with Win in the room—another change that chafed his nerves—so he had dressed first.

"Not now. No servant likes to be questioned during the busiest hour of the day." He'd track them down mid-morning, in that slim hour between breakfast and luncheon. "Besides, I've heard tell that a Colonel Alden has just arrived." Five bob to the lower footman had done the job.

"Don't see what an old colonel can do for us."

"Ah," Win stepped lightly down the center stairs, "but he is reputed to be an art collector. As was the demon Isley."

Talent's nostrils pinched as though scenting something foul. "Bloody demons. I hate dealing with them."

"You can always go back to your room." Win fought a smile as he glanced at the library door where the footman had told him Colonel Alden was taking a solitary drink. Winston tapped a finger against his walking stick and considered how best to approach the man. He looked Talent over. "How good a dog can you be?"

The corners of Talent's eyes creased. "You're attempting to flush a supernatural out, Inspector?"

"I gather most supernaturals would detect a shifter in their midst as opposed to a mere dog?"

Something dark flickered over Talent's eyes then was gone. "Not all. But a demon ought to."

"Then we'll be sure to pay close attention to the colonel's reaction."

Winston expected Talent to find some privacy to change, but the man merely glanced about and, finding the corridor they'd stopped in empty, turned back to Winston with a devilish grin. The air about Talent suddenly shimmered, or perhaps it was Talent himself that shimmered. Whatever the case, it happened in the blink of an eye, too quickly for Winston to study. One moment Talent stood before him, the next an enormous dog looked up at him, panting as if it were laughing. By its side lay a pile of clothes and Talent's boots.

Winston eyed the grey, shaggy beast with appreciation.

"A wolfhound, eh? Cheeky." He gathered up the clothes and stuffed them behind a potted palm. "Come along then, Felix."

A low growl had him glancing down. "Too bad," he said. "I'm keeping the name. Always wanted a dog named Felix."

Winston entered a large library that looked much like any other manor library, filled with the ubiquitous leather couches and imposing portraits of ancestors past. It smelled of books and wood polish.

A man sat, half hidden by the wings of the red leather armchair he occupied. Blue coils of smoke drifted in lazy tendrils just above the chair. When the scent of tobacco hit Winston, he tensed. Jones's cigarettes. Was it Jones?

The occupant of the chair stirred, and the firelight caught the reflection of one polished steel arm. Curious.

"Good evening, sir," Win said as he came farther into the room.

The man gave a small start then leaned forward. Alert eyes watched Winston from beneath a set of white brows.

"Evening." The man tapped out a line of ash in the crystal tray by his side. The action brought Win's attention back to his false arm, which started at the elbow. From there, a true work of metal art was attached in the form of a forearm and hand, currently resting upon the leather arm of the chair. "Impressive beast you have there."

Winston had almost forgotten about Talent. "He is my most loyal companion."

Talent thumped rather hard against his leg on the way to find a patch of warm sunlight on the gleaming oak floor. He settled down with a grunt and promptly lowered his head.

"Lovely breed," said the man. "Rare, though. I know of a Captain Graham who is attempting to revive it."

"Admirable work," Winston said.

The man's keen gaze raked over Win's face. "Hell of a set of scars." The man said it with appreciation rather than disgust. "Didn't think there were many wolves left to hunt. Seems you found one, though."

Winston blinked. Strangely enough, most people did not ascribe his scars to a wolf attack. Most assumed they were the work of knives. "In this instance, it was a case of the wolf hunting me."

"Good thing you had the dog."

Winston ignored Talent's amused huff and took a seat on the couch perpendicular to the man. "Are you Colonel Alden, sir?"

The man's massive frame twitched just a bit. "Yes. And you are?" Not defensive, but cautious.

"Mr. Snow of London. In my earlier days, I was an Inspector First Class of the Criminal Investigation Division." The lie flowed from his lips like wine from a bottle.

Colonel Alden made a sound of amusement. "Mouthful of a title, young man." He sat impossibly straighter, his legs braced before him. "How can I help you?"

Winston had expected to ease into his interrogation. If only all the people he questioned were so accommodating. However, he would not mistake accommodation for truthfulness.

"I've been working on a case, by way of helping out a friend. I have heard that you are a collector of art, as is the man in question."

"'Tis true. I admire art. Save, I am but a dilettante." Alden's remaining hand lay relaxed against his thigh. "Nor can I think of how I might be of service to you, but ask your questions."

"Do you know of a Lord Isley? I believe he is old friends with Mrs. Noble."

Alden's hard gaze turned inward, a slow rotation that spoke of shock one tried to process quietly. "Well, well," he said at last, "I've not heard that name in a while." His stiff shoulders eased a touch as he looked down at his artificial limb. "Look here." He lifted the limb and pushed back his coat sleeve. "Have you ever seen its like?"

Winston inspected the limb. Made of stainless steel and forged in the exact replica of the human skeleton, it actually appeared quite delicate. The only deviation from anatomical correctness was found in the palm of the hand. There, a flat surface made up a palm, upon which a long, undulating snake had been carved out. Thin wires ran from each finger joint, up past the wooden cap that attached the limb to flesh and under the colonel's coat.

"Never."

Alden grunted. "Nor will you, I gather. Observe." His biceps bunched and, to Winston's shock, the steel fingers curled inward. "The wires," Alden explained, "are attached to a brace at the muscle." He lifted his sleeve higher to reveal a rather large and intricate brace made of leather and webbed with wires. "When I flex, the hand reacts."

"It is brilliant." Winston wasn't sure where the colonel was going with this demonstration but trusted that he'd get there eventually. People either answered questions directly, avoided them with belligerence and counter questions, or told him stories.

The colonel let his sleeve drop. "My father was the Marquis of Danville. He wanted me to become a soldier. Go to war like all other good third sons did. After all, the heir had produced his fair brood, and the spare had done the same, leaving our line stocked with plenty of fallbacks.

Thus for what use was I if not to fight for England? And if there wasn't a war, why, we've plenty of colonies to keep in line." He sat back in his seat. "I might have defied him but he held the purse strings."

How well Winston knew that predicament.

"So a soldier I became, even though I detested the thought. I wanted to be alone with my books, truth be told. Didn't give a fig for following orders or barking them out, as the case may be."

Alden extracted a cigarette from the slim gold case on the side table. "Have one?"

The image of a serpent was etched upon the fine gold case. Winston tore his gaze from the case and peered into Alden's eyes. Nothing stirred, save mild curiosity as to why Winston was staring. Upon the floor, Talent noticed his querying look. His dog brows twitched as he too glanced at Alden then he grunted, not bothering to lift his head from the floor. Presumably, not threatened by the colonel in the least. So not Jones then. Or another demon. Winston centered his attention back on Alden, who waited for an answer. "Thank you, no."

Alden paused to fiddle with his matches and lit the cigarette, a rather neat trick for a man with an artificial hand. The familiar perfume of fine Turkish tobacco filled the space, a blue cloud of it floating past a rather fine Leighton portrait of a girl. "Do you know what happened upon gaining my commission?"

Winston gave him a small smile. "I could not begin to fathom."

"I fell in love with the army." He took a deep draw and let out a trail of smoke. "Loved the order of it. The simplicity. Found it soothed my mind." He laughed, a rather rattling sound deep within his chest. "Took to it like a duck to water. And then this happened." He lifted his artificial limb. "Ridiculous thing. A paper cut, if you can believe it. A deuced paper cut that turned gangrenous and had to be chopped off."

The colonel frowned down at his limb as if remembering the indignity of it.

"Bad luck," Winston said.

"Cursed luck is what it was!" The steel fingers curled slightly as the colonel rested his arm upon his bent knee. "They sent me home. Where I was useless. Away from my men." He cleared his throat. "You were an officer of sorts, an inspector at least. You know what it is to be among your comrades. They understand your life. Not like those at home."

Winston ducked his head in agreement. He was as cast off as the colonel had been. It left one unmoored and aimless.

Alden did not seem to notice Win's disquiet. He took another draw at his cigarette before peering thoughtfully at Winston. "That's when Isley came in. Met him at some party given by Mrs. Noble. An art exhibit for that painter who died this spring... Manet. Heard of him?"

"Yes," Winston said, shifting uncomfortably. "Quite talented, I believe."

The colonel waved his cigarette in a lazy fashion. "It was Isley who found me this hand. He took me round the next day to a tinker, of all things, although I suppose it's about right. Who else could fashion such a thing?"

"Did you ever meet a woman named Moira Darling?" Winston asked.

The colonel shook his grey head. "Never heard of her." He stared at his steel hand again, as if discovering it anew. "Clever thing. Saved my life, really."

Winston was losing the colonel. Soon he'd be on a different track, and it would be impossible to get any further information about Isley out of him.

Idly, Alden tapped a finger against his gold case again but did not open it. His long, weathered fingers stroked the thing with a sort of meditative reverence. An action, Winston suspected, that was habit.

"Did Isley give you that case, sir?"

The colonel stopped. "This? No. I bought it.... That is to say someone..." The colonel's expression went blank as if he were trying to catch a memory or perhaps one had tickled the corners of his mind, but then he harrumphed and his intense focus returned. "Tell you the truth, I am not sure where I picked this up. But it wasn't from Isley. Couldn't have been..."

"Merely curious," Winston said.

"Isley was the one responsible for my returning to the army, you know." Alden's big body seemed somehow frail in the setting sunlight as he squinted at him. "I mentioned my distress at being sent home and the man made a few inquiries. The next week, they called me back in." Alden frowned, looking off into the distance. "I'd forgotten that. Can't imagine how I could..." He shook his head slowly.

"Must have simply slipped your mind," Winston said. Or someone put the thought back into it. The question was why? And what was another of Jones's victims doing here?

"Might I ask, sir, what it was that brought you to this party this weekend?"

The colonel's bushy brows lifted. "Damnedest thing, really. I hadn't thought of Amy Noble in years, then my butler brought in the mail and an invitation was there. Figured, why not?"

Indeed. Win studied the colonel anew. There was obviously something about this man that Jones wanted Winston to discover. Usually, Win enjoyed games of wit. But today, he barely stifled the urge to curse. Or perhaps try to shake the truth out of the colonel.

But the colonel's attention had drifted to the window, his keen eyes tracking a lady as she strolled along the terrace with the other female guests. Winston's muscles clenched. He was staring at Poppy. Poppy, who looked utterly breathtaking in a gown of deep silver satin.

"Do you know her?" he asked the colonel without taking his gaze from his wife.

Alden shook his head. "She simply caught my eye. The way a fine piece of art might, you gather?"

Win nodded. He did not imagine the colonel's interest to be more than abstract.

The colonel's attention wandered back to Poppy as she strolled along the terrace. "It is strange. Just then, it felt as though I've seen that very picture before. Perhaps in a painting. Note the evening light, the way it glows on the soft curve of her cheekbone, how it gleams along the edge of her jaw and the small shadows beneath the pillow of her lower lip. Chiaroscuro, they call that effect."

"Yes." Win watched his wife, the sunlight kissing her skin and setting the red in her hair aflame. He gathered he would never see a more beautiful woman in the world. Because she was his. Win lowered his voice confidentially. "The lady happens to be my wife."

The colonel colored. "Really, man, you ought to have said something. I do apologize for speaking out of turn."

"Think nothing of it, sir. I found no offense in your admiration, certainly."

"Good of you," the colonel grumbled before giving

Win a light slap on the shoulder. "Go collect your lovely wife then, my boy. Before someone younger and wilder than I sets his eye upon her."

It was strange, but when Poppy pictured the sort of woman Isley would be attracted to, she thought of the typical English rose. That paragon of femininity and grace who men fought wars to protect and who never spoke her mind when she could be making a man feel that his opinion was the only one that mattered. Poppy knew of such women in an academic sense, but had never befriended any of them. The closest thing she had to female friends were her sisters, and they were hardly model ladies, thank God. It appeared that Isley had little interest in proper English ladies either. Not if Mrs. Amy Noble was anything to go by.

Surrounded by young men who seemed to hang on her every movement, she held court from a large red velvet divan, her elbow on the arm of it, and her feet propped up on one end in a pose of utter relaxation. That she lounged about as if she were in her boudoir instead of entertaining guests was not so extraordinary. That she dressed as a man was. Her fine black dinner suit did not hide her femininity, but rather was cut to accentuate her curves. Her hair was raven black, save for a swath of white that started at her left temple and was swept back with the rest to fall in a sleek river down her back. She looked utterly foreign and utterly lovely.

Resting her hand upon Win's forearm, Poppy walked across the room. Smoke grey satin rustled with each step she took, the heavy slide of those yards of fabric against her legs. How would it feel to always walk unfettered, not just when playing the role of spy? More to the point, why did she persist in wearing corsets and proper gowns? It irked her to realize that she had more in common with those English roses than she'd thought. Despite believing herself to be independent, she had tried to please everyone, take care of them all. As a result, she'd lost a bit of herself in the process.

Mrs. Noble looked up as they came before her. She had to be at least fifty but did not look a day past thirty-five with her skin as smooth and unlined as a peach. Her eyes flashed ebony in the candlelight, and Poppy thought for a moment that Mrs. Noble recognized her. But they'd never met before, and the strange look was gone, replaced by one of mild interest.

"Mr. and Mrs. Snow," she said with a young maiden's voice, "how delightful to meet you." She took in Win's scarred profile with interest. "Now there's a story waiting to be told. Sit down and perhaps I can manage to entice it out of you."

Win's mouth quirked but he accepted the light chair a footman had pulled up, just as Poppy accepted hers. "Madam," he said, "perhaps we can trade stories. One of mine for one of yours."

Mrs. Noble leaned in, and the drop crystal beads on her black velvet diadem caught the light. "A barter?" Her trilling laugh had more than a few men smiling. "I like that."

Win settled more comfortably on his chair, crossing one foot over the other. "Mind you, it's quite a story. I'll expect something similar in return."

Mrs. Noble cut a glance toward Poppy, giving away the fact that she had been constantly aware of Poppy's presence. The woman appeared to feed off of it, taking a base feminine pleasure in having Poppy watch while Win flirted with her.

Though Poppy detested to admit it, part of her had never understood why Win had pursued her on that long ago day at Victoria Station, nor why he'd immediately begun courting her. She was not beautiful, or charming, and was in possession of rude, red hair. Her manner could at best be described as abrupt, but was often called mannish. And while she rather liked the person she was inside, she did not suffer fools lightly. In a society that revolved around shallow, false behavior, this was not a beneficial tactic. That this handsome, intelligent man, a duke's son for pity's sake, seemed to see no other woman than her... At times, she'd wondered if it had all been some grand mistake.

That had not, however, stopped her from claiming him. She was not a fool, and if he wanted to make her his, she would make him hers in return. He'd spoken of choices, and how hers had been taken from her, not understanding that there was a difference between choosing what was best and wanting something with one's entire soul. She'd always wanted Win. Had she the ability to slap a sign upon him proclaiming "mine!" she would have done so.

With that firmly in mind, she maintained a neutral deportment as Mrs. Noble's sweet voice addressed her. "What say you, Mrs. Snow? Is his tale worth it?"

"It depends," Poppy said. "How good a trade do you offer?"

Mrs. Noble threw back her head and laughed. "Oh, I do like you two." With a languid lift of her hand, another footman came over. "Our guests require refreshment," she said to him, then turned her eyes back on Winston. "There are stories to be told."

Win planted his feet and rested an elbow on his thigh, moving in that way of his that was at once precise and yet languid. A trick of movement that made one feel comfortable, beguiled into spilling secrets to a man who they were certain would not let them down. She hadn't fully appreciated it until now. Pride shot through her, and with it, the nearly overwhelming desire to touch him, caress the silky locks of his hair, anything that would proclaim him hers.

Mrs. Noble was no less affected. Her eyes tracked Win's movement as her bosom swelled on an indrawn breath. As if drawn by a string, she leaned into him, her lips parting in anticipation. His blue-grey eyes twinkled, a shared amusement, another ruse. Win's smoky voice lowered intimately, and he spoke as if they were the only two in the room. "But you see, madam, I am quite...shall we say, shy about revealing this story to just anyone." The widow's lids fluttered at the near purr of Win's voice. "I would much rather discuss such things in private."

Their eyes held a beat, and then hers reluctantly slid over to Poppy. About bloody time, too. Poppy returned her look with what she hoped was a secretive smile. Win caught her eye, and he smiled too. "My wife prefers these little intimacies as well." A cloying shade of wickedness tinted his words, and Mrs. Noble licked her lips.

Poppy valiantly held back from rolling her eyes. Really, who was this man? What had he done with her proper husband?

"Well then," Mrs. Noble said, "shall we?" However, she paused and affected a moue of disappointment. "But I almost forgot, there is someone I believe would love to hear your tale. I'm sure you will not mind. He is most discreet." She raised a hand, and a man moved away from his place by the mantel at the far side of the room and headed their way. The handsome younger man stopped by her side and took her hand, placing a light kiss on it.

"You summoned, my dear?" His voice was deep and smooth with the ease of a lover's.

Mrs. Noble smiled a Cheshire cat's smile, all teeth and malicious intent. "I did indeed." She gave the man's hand a squeeze. "Mr. Snow here claims to have the most interesting story to tell."

All eyes fell on Win, and a twinge of alarm hit Poppy, for her husband had gone completely white. A fine sweat peppered his brow, and his throat worked as if he'd soon be ill. His gaze was not upon Mrs. Noble but on her companion.

# *Chapter Twenty-one*

❦

Poppy did not know what it was about the man that upset Winston so, but she was going to find out. She turned to Win, and his glazed eyes locked onto hers, wild and confused, as if he could not focus. "Darling," she said, "come with me to retrieve my shawl? I find myself chilled." It was hot as Hades.

With a little flicker of her power, an icy draft swirled through the room, causing more than one woman to shiver.

She did not wait for Win to answer but rather tugged him out of the room, down the hall, and onto the terrace where he could get some much needed air. He was shaking, his breath coming out in raw pants. The dark thing had him. She'd seen it before in others. Strong men and women who had faced death and terror and come away with a bit of it still clinging to their minds. Sometimes it never left them, that ugly residue of death. It would catch them unawares and torment them. And each and every one of them believed they were weak because of it. Poppy rather thought the opposite. That they were the brave ones who had been chased by death and escaped to forge onward.

She did not stop until they were beneath the arbor, now dark with shadows and thick with the scent of roses in the warm, moonlit night. Win sat with a thud upon the stone bench, and she followed him down, placing a hand on his fevered brow. Her touch grew chilled, cooling him. "Win," she whispered, looking into his unseeing eyes, "come back to me."

He struggled for breath and she pulled him close, stroking his ravaged cheek. "Win, who was that man?"

His hands clutched her upper arms hard. "My brother."

Her heart stilled. Win's family had always been rather a closed subject. Which Poppy hadn't fought, as she was likely to work herself into an indignant state when she thought of their treatment of him, of how they had abandoned him without a backward glance, solely because he had chosen to become a detective. She cringed now. All of that had been a lie. A bloody trick.

She thought of the man they'd just encountered. He was younger than Mrs. Noble but perhaps a bit older than them. He didn't look anything like Winston but had raven hair and coal black eyes. His features were more Gallic than Anglo-Saxon. "He looked right at you. How could he not recognize you?"

Win's head jerked up. "Why should he? He's been led to think his brother is dead. It's Isley's bloody bargain at play, after all." His features twisted. "Never mind that I hardly look as I did before."

Her stomach dipped. "But to not have even experienced a glimmer of recognition? To not even feel... something?"

Win laughed, a dark, unhinged sound. "You of all people ought to understand with whom we are dealing. He altered our lives, Poppy. He can twist things until up is down. How are we to know what is real and what is not?"

In her heart of hearts, she did not like to give Isley credit for the power he wielded. Certainly not now. Not when it was her life he'd toyed with, violated. She lurched up and began to pace, needing to feel her limbs move over solid ground. "Why is your brother here? And with Mrs. Noble? It cannot be a coincidence. She knew you would be affected. Her little grin was downright nasty." The bitch. "She knows who we are, Win. She must."

Win rose as well and scrubbed a hand over his face. "Isley is playing with us. Enjoying our pain and frantic searching. I do not want to believe that Osmond too is ensnared by Isley, but he may well be."

"Osmond?"

"My brother." He lowered his hand. "I'm sure I told you his name."

"I would have remembered that. You always referred to him simply as your brother." Poppy's lips twitched. "Your parents certainly were creative with their name giving."

Winston leveled a glare at her, but she could tell he was trying not to smile. He had never liked his name and had grumbled about it when they'd first met. "Father fancied old English names. Undoubtedly he sought to shout to the world our Englishness through and through. My brother goes by Oz, or Marchland now, I suppose. Jesus."

He rounded on her. "I believe you are correct, however. Mrs. Noble looked at you as though she knew you."

"You noticed that as well? I did not like that look. It was as if she was seeing straight into me." She rolled her shoulders as if the movement could dispel the sticky feeling that crept along her skin.

"Damn it." He started to pace along the path she'd beaten down. "None of Isley's victims ought to remember him, and yet they do. I have to believe it is because Isley has allowed it, that he wants us to find Moira Darling."

"Well of course, he wants us to find her. Why else would he make the bargain with you?"

"No," he stopped. "You misunderstand. I think he knows exactly where Moira Darling is. If you remember, he asked me to find what Moira Darling stole from him. Not necessarily to find *her*."

Poppy's blasted corset held her too tight to draw a proper breath. "He would hardly need you for that. If he knew where she was, he could easily force her to give whatever it is back to him."

Standing half in shadow, the ruined side of Win's face glowed in the moonlight. "Something is not right."

"I'd say, presently, just about everything is 'not right.' "

Win waved this off, his countenance fierce with concentration. "It is Isley." He halted and pinned Poppy with the intensity of his gaze. "He needed us to be together."

"I'm sorry?"

"We weren't speaking. I gather Isley did not plan on that all those years ago. Do you not see? We took the wind from his sails. He had no idea how we might respond once he placed his cards on the table."

"Surely he would figure that we'd protect our child."

"No, he needed that extra incentive. Whatever Moira Darling stole must be something that requires both of us working together to find. Isley is a gambler, but not a foolish one."

"Let us drop this search and go and kill the bastard."

Win's mouth canted on a smile, but his voice grew soft yet resolute. "No, sweet. First off, the bargain is still in play. Kill him and he still gets our child. No, we are going to find this Moira Darling, because when we do, I'm going to discover just what it is he truly expects to get out of this game, and I'm going to beat him at it."

By the time Winston and Poppy had returned, guests were wandering in to dinner. Thus they were forced to do so as well. Those around Winston appeared to be enjoying themselves, drinking wine, eating their food with appreciation. As for Win, he might as well have been eating mud. Food stuck to the roof of his mouth and clung at his throat when he tried to swallow. He could do little more than ignore his dinner companions and steal pain-inducing glances at his brother.

Dear God, how could he have forgotten Oz? Certainly, the knowledge that he had a brother hadn't gone, but Win simply had forgotten to think about him. The very notion now shamed and saddened him. Though they were only two years apart in age, they'd never been close brothers. Oz had been forever at Father's side, learning all things ducal, while Win had been his mother's pet, chafing under her clinging nature. Oz had chosen Cambridge and Win Oxford. After that, there had been only Poppy, the CID, and his deuced bargain. Had Oz a wife? Was this a weekend fling? Had he too bargained away his soul like a fool? Somehow, Win thought not. Or perhaps he simply hoped.

"I've heard to expect the unconventional here, but that man is a sight to destroy one's appetite." The man across the way made no attempt to lower his voice. Winston wasn't surprised; not really. He had received enough remarks by now to expect it. His years as an inspector had taught him how deep the capacity for human cruelty could go. He told himself this as he placed his linen in his lap and accepted the second course brought in by the waiters in liveried white. However, it did not stop him from feeling multiple eyes upon him or from biting back the urge to snarl at the people gaping at him. Perhaps if Poppy weren't visibly bristling on his behalf, or the fact that the boorish man's remark had caught Oz's attention as well, humiliation wouldn't be filling his throat this very moment.

"So Snow," said Colonel Alden next to him, "I suspect you worked on some interesting cases in your time." He deliberately raised his steel hand into the air to wave over the waiter pouring out the wine. "Any you are able to discuss?"

As attempts to divert attention went, it wasn't all bad. It might have even been welcome if it wasn't so bloody obvious. Winston took a sip of wine, forcing it past the lump in his throat. "I cannot name names, Colonel. However, no detective is without a good anecdote to share."

Again came the loud man's voice, more forceful this time. "Looks like a butcher's been at him. What did he say was his work?"

Winston set his wineglass down with care. The ruined side of his face burned, which made his hands ache to curl into fists. Archer once said he'd made up songs and sung them in his head to get him past the fury.

"Songs?" Winston had repeated, incredulous. "Such as 'Row Your Boat' and the like?"

Archer had given him a tight smile that acknowledged Winston's goading for the easy shot that it had been. "More like, 'Fuck you, fuck you, and your miserable mother too.'"

"I'm impressed," Winston had said. "It is at once utterly vulgar and completely puerile."

Archer had flashed a rare grin then. "But quite effective."

Winston glanced up at the man who'd done his best to annoy him, and Archer's song played in his head. Surprisingly it did help. Enough to allow the corners of his eyes to crinkle with evil glee. "I didn't."

The man blinked, actually shocked to be addressed by Winston. "Didn't what?"

"I did not give my profession, Mr . . . ?" The man was a new arrival, and Win wondered offhand what the bastard would have made of the nude swim party.

"*Lord* Butherwell," the man corrected with a sniff.

At the word "profession", Butherwell's long nose had wrinkled in disgust. Win returned his look with one of bland disinterest. He made it his business to know the names and station of London's *ton*. Butherwell was a second generation baron with little money and even less influence. Exactly the sort insecure enough to throw stones at glass houses. "However, *Butherwell*, I am happy to assuage your rampant curiosity."

He did not have a chance to, for Poppy suddenly leaned forward, her brown eyes promising bedlam beneath those slanted brows of hers. "He is an Inspector First Class with the Criminal Investigation Division of Scotland Yard. It is men like my husband who keep your soft hide protected from London's criminal element."

A pinch of pain took him in the gut upon hearing his old title. He was finished as an inspector. But damned if he was going to rectify Poppy's error here and now. Not that it mattered. Butherwell's disgust grew into a sneer.

"A tradesman, in our midst," he said to the populace of the table, most of whom were looking on in avid interest. It wasn't every day a squabble broke out over dinner.

"This is what so called 'progress' has brought us, being forced to share a meal with a man who—" he gave Poppy a condescending look—"consorts with London's criminal element." He turned to Winston and raised his voice as if he feared Winston had trouble hearing. "I say, oughtn't you be slumming in some back alley down in London?"

Winston neatly sliced his roast. "Do I give the impression of being lost, sir?"

Butherwell's grey mustache quivered with a snort. "You give the impression of a man who does not know his place."

"Come now, my lord," tittered Mrs. Noble. "We are all friends here, are we not?"

God, but Oz's gaze was a palpable weight on Win's neck. They shared the same blood, bluer than any person sitting at the table, or in the district, for that matter. Even if he could admit the truth of his birth, Win would rather be hung by his balls than admit it to this lot. Tossing out pedigree was not the way he wanted to earn respect, nor did he need theirs.

"My dear Mrs. Noble," said Butherwell, "I merely fear for your reputation. There are curiosities, and there are riffraff. It is best you know the difference."

Win's hand clenched his knife. He did not look up. Should he do so, he'd be planting Butherwell a facer. Past the buzzing in his ears came Oz's deep voice. "I do not believe our hostess needs assistance in discerning the difference, Butherwell."

Poppy's voice followed shortly after Oz's. "A true gentleman does not feel the need to make his station known."

"And a true lady does not voice her opinion in the presence of a man," snapped Butherwell. "However, as you are not a lady, I shall forgive your blunder."

A tremor went through Winston's arm. "Enough." The entire table hushed as Winston set his silver down and let his gaze lift to Butherwell. "I remind you that there are ladies present. *Including* my wife."

Butherwell's complexion ran to florid. It became magenta now and again his overlong mustache moved as he snapped, "I do not believe I understand your point, man."

Winston held his gaze and spoke in measured tones so as not to further confuse the buffoon. "It is simple. I shall strive to keep that fact in mind in order to refrain from exercising my brute, working class strength upon your flaccid, gentleman's face." He let his lip curl enough to highlight the sneer of his scar. "But it shall be a very near thing. Pray you remember likewise before you utter another word."

There was a gasp, and Butherwell went pale. His nostrils flared, his hand holding the knife clenching. Winston stared back, waiting. It would take two seconds to disarm the man, one more to shove his face into the pudding. Beneath the table, a slim hand fell to his thigh and gave him a squeeze, not in warning, but in solidarity.

Winston lifted one brow, and Butherwell's mouth snapped shut. The man promptly turned his attention to the waiter hovering just beyond the table. "The beef is dry. Take this back and bring me another. Bloody."

By Winston's side, Poppy leaned in a touch, and her clean scent tickled his nose. "Do you know," she murmured, low enough that no one else could hear, "I could make him disappear with one missive."

His lips twitched, but he kept his eyes on his dinner. He could not face her. Not yet. "It is a very good thing I'm no longer with CID or I'd have to do something about that information."

From the corner of his eye, he could see her wicked grin. It was that grin, conspiratorial in nature and one of thousands that they'd exchanged over the years, that made him forget where he was, who he was, and grin right back.

Thankfully, the dinner ended. Win was one of the first to rise. He needed fresh air, Poppy, a drink—and Poppy. Her dark gaze collided with his, and he wondered if he'd have to sell his soul again to bed her without regret. For right now, it felt essential that he get her alone and sink into her tight embrace. Perhaps he wouldn't feel as if he were flying apart if those endless, smooth legs of hers were wrapped around him and held him close.

Shouldering past slower, carefree guests, he was following her out when a man stepped into his path. Deep-set eyes of near black bore into him, and Win's heart slammed against his ribs. That face, that blade of a nose that was almost aquiline, that slightly put-out expression, was so like his father's that Win could almost believe he faced a ghost instead of his brother.

Oz's intense gaze eased first. "Marchland," he said by way of introduction. "Mr. Snow, was it?"

"Yes, Your Grace." Years of training held him back from brushing his brother aside and getting the hell out of there. But he was unable to say anything more. If he were lucky, Oz might think him overwhelmed by standing face to face with a duke. One could hope. Oz nodded. He was too well-bred to mention Butherwell's remarks, but speaking to Winston showed a mark of his favor. Were Win simply an inspector, and not his brother, he might feel gratitude. As it was, however, an old tightness banded about his chest. This was the world he'd been desperate to get away from, where rank and title superseded character. Oz might keep a dozen mistresses, beat his children until their bones broke, destroy lives on a whim, and if he did, not one soul would lift a finger to stop him, much less utter a word of reproach. Win did not want to go back to that. And he most certainly needed to get away from Oz. Now.

Unfortunately Oz's study of him returned. This time, his brother's lips turned down at one corner. Yet another painfully familiar gesture. "Do I know you?"

*Shit.*

Oz's dark brows met in the center. "I do not know why, but I cannot shake the feeling that we've met before..."

It was on the tip of Win's tongue to deny it and flee, save his brother was here and he could not believe it a coincidence. "Perhaps at an earlier party? Are you old friends with Mrs. Noble?"

"Mrs. Noble was a very dear friend to the former duke." His expression tightened. "She was a great comfort to him when my younger brother died unexpectedly."

Oz's words slammed into Winston, hard and brutal, and it was all he could do not to react. Oz nodded to a man who passed by before turning his attention back to Win. "My father was a great lover of art, as is Mrs. Noble."

*Yes.* He almost said it aloud and cleared his throat to cover the gaffe. "Did they perchance meet through a Lord Isley?"

"You know him as well?"

He was going to be ill all over Oz's polished leather shoes. "In passing. You?"

Thank Christ, Oz shook his head. "Never met the man. Only know the story of how my father and Amy met. Father became one of her greatest financial backers, and Amy has always been grateful."

Win forced a bland smile. "Well then, sir, I am uncertain

how or where we might have met. A face such as mine is hard to forget."

Making mention of his maimed appearance had the reaction Win expected. Oz very deliberately did not look at his scars. "Likely you are correct. Pardon my mistake." He began to ease back as most people did upon being forced to address his maiming.

"No pardon necessary, Your Grace." Win gave him a tight nod and then slipped away. He did not give a damn if it wasn't done. Or if the room fell in a dead faint because he'd left before a duke. Isley had found consolation for his father, had he? Forget being ill; Win was going to punch something in a moment.

Poppy caught up to him, her lemon-linen scent soothing him even as she searched his eyes in gentle concern.

"He thought he knew me," he said. "But he couldn't make the connection." With terse words, he told her the rest of the conversation.

"Jesus, Win." Her lips went pale, and she angled her body as if to block out the rest of the room. That she still sought to protect him made his chest go tight. He did not need it, but the better part of him wanted to be worthy of her devotion.

"I'm all right." He was. Now that he could touch her and hear the steady cadence of her voice.

"Good." She leaned closer, her silken cheek near his. "Shall we track down Mrs. Noble? She was headed toward the library when dinner let out."

It was a strange destination, as most of her guests were going to either the smoking room or the grand parlor. "Let us go then. God help me if Oz shows up there as well."

The pale arc of Poppy's neck gleamed in the candle-light as she looked back over her shoulder. "He appears to be heading off to the smoking room with the other gentlemen. I believe we are safe from that fiasco."

He laughed without humor. " 'Fiasco' is an understatement."

However, when they reached the library, they found it empty. Poppy's keen gaze caught his. "Now where do you suppose Mrs. Noble has got off to?"

The answer came by way of a footman, who headed toward them. "Sir, Mrs. Noble has retired for the evening," he murmured. "She would like to receive you tomorrow for tea." He bowed neatly and left them standing in the hall.

"Botheration," Poppy muttered. "I do not want to be here for tea tomorrow. This place feels wrong to me." Around them, ladies and gentlemen wandered to and fro, laughing and pairing off. A quartet softly played Beethoven in the parlor, and the golden light from hundreds of candles gave the house a muted glow. Music, beauty, laughter. It ought to be soothing and yet Poppy was correct; there was something off about the whole thing this night. What once felt like true gaiety now shone false and brittle, as though Winston was watching a play.

Poppy made a furtive gesture. "Blast it, I could almost believe that woman is toying with us."

Win frowned in the direction of the stairs. "Mmm. As if she is aware that we are ruled by a time limit, perhaps?"

"Could she be under Isley's control?"

Still watching the stairs, Win clasped Poppy's hand in his. "Come. Let us see what we can see."

Poppy's voluminous silk train rustled and swayed as they made their way to the second floor where Mrs. Noble's room lay. Flickering lamplight guided their path. Below, *Moonlight Sonata* began playing in steady, ponderous notes that spoke of amateur piano lessons.

"Someone's been practicing," Poppy murmured as they plodded along to the tune. The notes followed them, rising and crashing. It was almost enough to drown out the rhythmic sound coming from the end of the upper hall. But not quite.

Perched at the top of the stairs, Winston and Poppy exchanged looks. Color crept over Poppy's high cheeks. "You must be joking."

Win glanced toward the dim corridor where the unmistakable sounds of sexual congress rang out. "I rather wish it were a joke."

Cautiously, they moved closer and the sound increased, both in tempo and in fervor.

"Well," Poppy cleared her throat, her nose wrinkling in a charming manner, "surely they cannot go on for long."

Knowing that one of the participants was likely Mrs. Noble only served to irritate Win. He scowled at the door from which the sound emerged. "I do not know, sweet. But if *Ode to Joy* begins to play, I am going to be most thoroughly put out."

With surprising speed, Poppy pressed her face into his neck and burst out laughing. Her warm breath seeped into him, and he wrapped his arms about her to keep her there. He smiled against her temple. He wanted to vent his frustration, but holding her as she laughed made his heart light just the same.

A huff of irritation escaped her, and then Poppy's muffled voice rose up from the crook of his neck. "Bloody woman, going off to tup. I swear to God, Win, I could kill her."

His fingers toyed with the loose strand of silken hair at her nape. "That is one way to shut them up." When she choked out a weak laugh, he leaned back a little until she raised her head and faced him. As expected, she wore her warrior's expression, one that promised mayhem and retribution, but fear lived there too, so guarded that he might have missed it did he not know her so well. "I could force my way in there, but we won't get anything from her like that." Softly, he brushed his thumb across her cheek. "I'm afraid we're done for the night, sweet Boadicea."

"Damn it, Win. What if she doesn't know Moira Darling either? What if Isley's led us astray?"

His hand slid to her neck and clasped it. When he spoke, his voice was far calmer than he felt. "Hear me, wife, we will find Moira Darling, and we will win. On my life, I swear it." Cold foreboding touched his spine at the vow, for he feared it might come to that.

# *Chapter Twenty-two*

———————⟡∼∼∼⟡∼∼∼⟡———————

*London, 1869—The Wedding Night*

Win?"

Sweat slicked and replete, Win had a hard time opening his eyes to focus on his new wife. Wife. Now there
was a word he adored. Lying on the bed next to him, she
wore nothing more than a gilding of candlelight and a
soft, contented smile. He adored that too.

"What is it, sweet?" He threw an arm around her and
pulled her closer, loving the feel of her sleek body against his.
They'd known each other for such a short time, and it still felt
as if he'd waited an eternity to hold her like this. "Stop jostling
and let a poor man sleep. You've exhausted me completely."

"Ha. Are you complaining?" That stern gaze did
things to his insides. Made him feel illicit.

"Yes." He smoothed his hand over her pert bottom
before smacking it. "Exhaust me some more, will you?
There's a good girl."

"Ack! Stop, you beast." She laughed as he rolled over onto her, but her brown eyes were serious. He knew already that Poppy, once on a subject, would never veer off of it until satisfied—quite like him in that manner, actually. Not one to let him down, she put the question to him directly. "Do you have a nightshirt?"

He settled more comfortably, sliding his cock along her slickness just to tease. "Why, yes." God, she was wet again. And her neck. It smelled of lemons and sex. He nuzzled it. "I don't want to put it on if that is what you are asking." Not now, not ever again. Though this was their wedding night, he planned to repeat their performance every night hereafter.

She wriggled again, making his breath quicken. Her endless legs tangled with his. He was going to lick his way down them later. But first, her breasts. Those sweet little plums that he'd yet to become thoroughly acquainted with.

"Can I wear it? Ah…ah…when we sleep…oh…"

Curiosity had always been his weakness. He released her nipple with a pop. "Of course, but why?" He'd hazy notions of sleeping skin to skin.

Almost idly, she traced the line of his brow before touching his lower lip. "I don't like sleeping undressed. I hate the way the skin of my arm sticks to my side." She kissed his neck and then his jaw. He blinked, nonplussed, and fairly distracted by the way she suckled his earlobe as she talked. "You should probably know, I also like to sleep on the left-hand side of the bed and hate floppy pillows."

Her scarlet hair, now loose and free, spread out in a starburst on the pillow and ran in silk ribbons over his forearms where he braced himself on either side of her slim shoulders. Only he would see her like this. Only he would know her strange quirks. His heart clenched, and his breath caught. Slowly, he smiled. "You're going to be difficult to manage, aren't you?"

Her grin unfurled like a cat in the sun. "Extremely. Afraid, Win?"

He shifted, nudging her thighs farther apart with his own. "Afraid? I can hardly wait." And with that, he plunged home, making her gasp, before he made her moan.

Just before they finally fell asleep, she slipped out of bed and found the nightshirt.

# *Chapter Twenty-three*

～～～～～

In the quiet confines of the guest room, Poppy stared at the door, knowing that *he* would soon walk through it. He would lie with her and share their bed for the night. And she wanted him so badly that her teeth ached as she clenched them.

The sounds she had heard coming from Mrs. Noble's bedroom haunted her. At the time, it was all she could do not to barge in on the woman and pull her out of the bed by the roots of her hair. Now, she could only think of being in bed with Win and losing herself in his arms. She wanted to forget this night, forget what they faced. And she wanted to forget with him. Only him.

It did not matter that their last union had been a disaster. Her body remembered not his ultimate rejection but the feel of him sliding home and the look in his eyes when he took her. Her fingers still shook with need for him. Were other women like this? Did they quiver with want? Did they grow tetchy and achy from imagining stripping their husbands down and servicing them with their mouths before begging to be mounted?

Poppy blushed hotly as though someone might hear her thoughts. No one but Win knew how illicit her desires ran or that she—who was dominant in her work—liked to be dominated in bed because it made her feel feminine, wanted, needed. Oh, but Win knew. He could wind her up so tight that she all but snapped before he gave her release. Even when they were so very young and had no idea what they were doing, he'd made her want with a ferocity that blurred the lines between pleasure and pain. Just from touching him, from being touched by him. And he was going to enter the room at any moment.

Well then, he was to share a room with Poppy. That was easy enough. They had shared one for the past fourteen years. It was rote. Like old friends, they had a pattern, a way of moving in tandem when getting ready for bed. Poppy at the washbasin, brushing her teeth with quintessential vigor. Him following suit as she drifted to the dressing table to apply her face cream and then give her hair its hundred strokes. He'd put away his clothes and tell her an anecdote about the day. Simple. Easy.

He would not think on the times he took the brush from her and stroked the glorious silk of her hair until her neck bent just so in relaxation. Or how he'd quietly set the brush aside and let his hands slide along her cool skin, under her chemise, to cup those firm breasts, knead them until she bit her bottom lip and whimpered.

Hell.

Win stopped dithering in the corridor and slammed into their shared room with undue force. And found Poppy staring at him in question. He stared back. She'd already gotten ready for bed. A thick, lumpy dressing gown hugged her lithe frame, from just under her chin down to her white and narrow feet. Hardly tempting. He scowled all the same.

"I thought you'd be brushing your teeth or some such preparation."

She flipped her long, demure braid over her shoulder. "No. You gave me more than ample time. The bathing room is all yours."

Fine. He was glad of it. Half the time, she left tooth powder all over the sink, and he had to clean up after her.

His ablutions were quick and thankfully peaceful. Just as they'd been these past three months without her. He stopped and stared in the hanging mirror. Butherwell had been correct; the reflection was not pretty. Half a face belonged to a man with a stern countenance, the other half was a monster's. Two-faced. In every sense.

"You, sir," he muttered to his reflection, "are a lying nodcock who wants to shag his wife senseless." He threw down his toothbrush, and it clattered around in the basin. "Only you are not going to ask for that. Are you?" The reflection's scowl of discontent grew. "No, you are not. You haven't yet sunk that low." They'd already gone down that path, and look how well that turned out.

He raked his fingers through his hair, and keeping on his repressive yet extremely necessary smalls, went out to face Poppy. She looked him over in that cool way of hers, and he resisted the urge to shift his feet. Bloody woman always saw more than she ought to.

"Were you talking to yourself in the mirror?"

His lips pressed together. "If you have to ask, you must have heard me." Christ, please say she did not hear the specifics. "So I'm going to assume the question is rhetorical."

She rolled her eyes and began to unbutton her dressing

gown. "Fine. I won't ask you what you were muttering about."

*You could. It might be interesting. Say, Pop, fancy a quick shag for old time's sake?*

"I simply was trying to make conversation to ease this awkwardness," she said.

"Commendable but futile." He fluffed a pillow, and then another, punched it actually. "I don't think there is any good way to ease—" His voice strangled to a halt as she shrugged out of the dressing gown. "You must be jesting."

Her head lifted. "What?" She tossed the gown upon a chair back and frowned at him from across the bed. "Good lord, Win, don't look at me like that. I'm perfectly respectable."

"Respectable," he repeated as if every muscle in his body weren't quivering. As if right this moment his cock wasn't rising. Shit. He sat at the edge of the bed before he betrayed the proof of his interest. Damn her eyes, but she was wearing his nightshirt. The very one she'd stolen from him so many years before.

For a moment, all he could see was Poppy, naked and wriggling against him in bed on their wedding night. Win took a bracing breath. That damned nightshirt. She'd worn it almost every night of their marriage. But he didn't think she'd be so heartless as to wear it now. It was *his* shirt.

"That thing is so old and worn it has holes in it," he said through his teeth. Inconvenient holes that showed glimpses of things he could not have.

Her hands went to her hips. "It's comfortable."

"It's a rag." A nearly transparent one at that. Sweet mother of... What was a negligee compared to seeing one's wife draped in one's own, very thin and very revealing, nightshirt? Hells bells, it would almost be better if she were naked. He fisted the sheet. Maybe he ought to ask for a comparison just to be sure.

"You're being ridiculous." She tossed the covers back and flopped onto her side of the bed. "And hurtful."

Her slim arm whipped out from under the covers to lower the lamp, and the room plunged into darkness. He sighed and got under the covers, gritting his teeth at the stiffness in his lower extremity and the way his body hummed with awareness of her. But the tight way in which she huddled on the far side of the bed cut through his skin. Damn it; how was it that her pain affected him so much more than his own? It was like a hand pressing on his chest, making his flesh crawl with shame. Because he had caused it.

He drew a deep breath through his nose as he lay like a lump of coal on his side of the bed. "I did not mean to be hurtful."

Silence greeted him. Then her small voice broke it. "I love this shirt."

Hell. Win squeezed his eyes closed, even though it was dark as pitch. "I know."

Her response was a decidedly feminine sniff that communicated both a grudging acknowledgment and made it clear that his effort wasn't enough. Well, he rather doubted she'd appreciate his other method of apology. Win closed his eyes and prayed for sleep, for his cock to go to sleep, rather. But no, it lay, a heavy, nagging weight against his belly, pushing against the strings of his smalls in a valiant attempt to get free. *Architecture*. That was soothing. Sleep often took him when he made a mental tour of London's architectural wonders.

*Westminster Palace, The Clock Tower, Tower of London, Cleopatra's Needle. Christ, stop thinking of erect monuments.*

Poppy made an abrupt, irritated move, disrupting his musings and unfortunately aggravating his current situation when her bottom hit his hip. Gritting his teeth, he risked a glance. The hunched shape of her shoulders were outlined in the darkness. Her head lay significantly lower than his. Again she shifted. A covert sort of move she employed when she did not want him to notice. Ridiculous, as he was always aware of her. He wondered how long she would go on pretending she wasn't vastly uncomfortable. Forever, it would seem. So very Poppy.

Wanting to smile and wanting even more to roll over and push himself into her until they were both exhausted, he gave in and did the safe, less pleasurable thing. He smiled and lifted the pillow from under his head.

"Here." He handed it to her. She stared at the thing as if it were a rat, and he sighed. "Take it. I know you don't like the pillow you have."

"It's too flat," she said after a moment.

"Yes, I know." She preferred a plump pillow. Always had.

His throat closed, and he turned away, pounding the flatter pillow he took in exchange into a reasonable lump. "Now will you stop wiggling about and go to sleep?"

He felt her settle and then heard a little sigh of relief. Well good. At least one of them was comfortable.

Body aching and head resting upon a woeful pillow, he chased sleep once more.

*St. Paul's, London Bridge, Buckingham Palace, Kensington Palace—*

"Win?"

He cracked open one eye. "Yes?"

A faint touch landed on the sheet at his back. And then it was gone. Her whisper drifted over him. "Are you sorry you did it?"

Again came that tender ache within the region of his bruised and battered heart. He gripped the pillow as he willed himself not to turn. "Sorry?" But he knew what she meant. Only it hurt too much to answer.

The sheets moved as she shifted. "Sorry that you gave up so much. For me?"

Ah gods, he couldn't... White spots danced before his eyes. He squeezed his eyes shut. "No." Winston cleared his throat. "I am only sorry that I did not know the whole of you."

The desire to let her secrets spill forth rushed through Poppy, but the familiar tug of repression caught her. *Never speak. You lead a double life. Remember this always.* She'd followed the instructions to the letter, even when it tore at her soul. Even when her sisters suffered and her husband turned away from her. The SOS was her other half, sometimes the greater part of her. To what end? If she let it, the SOS would take her happiness away and leave her empty.

"I was eighteen when I took over my mother's position."

Win's voice came at her through the dark. "The year we met."

She sighed. "Yes. The day we met, actually."

He was silent, as if he too were remembering that day upon the platform. She wondered what the memory held for him. For her, it had been both the best and worst day of her life. Every step down the long, cold train platform had been a struggle to pull herself together, to remind herself who and what she was. And then he was there, as if forming from the mist. It had been such a shock to see the handsome young man walking beside her, looking at her as if she had just become his whole world. She'd thought she was dreaming.

"What were you doing at the station?" He laughed shortly, as if disgusted with himself. "Do you know, I never even thought to ask you." Another choppy laugh filled the air. "I was too stunned with lust to think on anything more than keeping you with me."

Her breath hitched, and she struggled to find another. "And I thought you were the most handsome madman I'd ever seen."

His voice rolled over her like fog. "Mad for you."

God, the things he could do to her. Just a few words and it was all she could do not to fling herself at him. She cleared her throat. "I'd just been appointed Mother. Lena fulfilled the duty while I completed my training. Actually, I thought she might keep the position, but she's never liked the role." Lena had always been strange in that regard, preferring to be a guardian of the SOS, rather than the leader of it. Poppy settled further into her pillow and continued her story. "There is an SOS tunnel exit at the station, and I'd used it to leave the ceremony."

"You were eighteen years old." The shock in his voice was strong. "And they appointed you head of an entire organization?"

"I'd been training for the position since I was six." Pride prickled along her skin and she fought to tamp it down. "I am the seventh generation of first daughters to carry out the duty. My family, along with another, founded the SOS."

Letting out her secrets filled her with utter weariness, but it felt easier to say them in the dark. "In the early days, we were simply called the Regulators. It was actually when we began to work in conjunction with the King and the Prime Minister that we became more formally organized and called ourselves the Society for the Suppression of Supernaturals."

She shifted a bit, sinking further into the plump pillow. "That was in my great-grandmother's time, though I can honestly say I've no fondness for the newer name as it stirred up trouble with certain supernatural factions."

"Because it made them sound like a problem to suppress," Win said with a decisive clip to his voice.

"Yes. At any rate," she said, "the SOS has always been my life. You do not understand the will of Mary Margaret Ellis. Every day was a new lesson. Every day a reminder." Poppy adopted the implacable tone of her mother. "Do not let the world know. Do not reveal your true purpose to anyone. Not even to family. Especially not to family."

"She had to suspect that your sisters had talents of their own."

"Oh, she knew. And she did not like it. Daisy was her little lamb, her sunshine. And Miranda was her rose, a delicate flower to be protected. She was adamant that neither of them be tainted by her dark world."

"And you?" Win's voice was tight.

A wobbly smile pulled at her lips as she blinked up at the dark ceiling. "I was the competent one. I never cried, nor fussed."

"Which meant that you should live a life in darkness?" He made a noise of annoyance. "I never thought I would say this, but I think I prefer your father."

Poppy could not help but smile a little. Even so, she needed him to understand. "She believed in me." Poppy sighed. "And yes, at times it hurt that she did not seek to protect me as she did my sisters. But Win…" She licked her lips. Inside, she trembled. "I liked being useful. I liked what I was doing. I still do."

The bed creaked when he rolled onto his back, their shoulders touching as he did. "He beat me. My father."

She grew still. Enough to hear the roaring of her blood in her ears. How could it be? He never cowered, always stood so tall and proud. And yet shadows had always dwelled within his eyes at odd times. "Win—"

"I never told you," he said over her, his voice strong yet brittle, as if he were forcing himself to speak, "because I was ashamed of the way…" His arm brushed over hers as he shrugged, "Well, you can guess. I was weak when I ought to have been strong."

She tried to swallow and failed. "For how long, Win?"

"As long as I have memory." In the dark, she could make out the lines of his profile as he stared up at the ceiling. "Too long."

She wanted to kill his father. Her hand shook as she rested it on his forearm. He did not shrug her off, nor did he turn to her. "That is why I made the bargain with Jones." His smoky voice was a living thing between them, making her heart bleed for him. "When I met you, I woke to life. You saw me for who I was. And in return, I wanted to live again. You gave my life flavor, color, texture, and I found myself willing to do anything to keep that."

She moved to embrace him, and he sucked in a sharp breath. "Don't." His body was rigid. "Not now. Not because of what I said."

"But—"

His voice grew emphatic, stern in that way of his that brooked no argument. "When I take you to bed, Poppy Ann, it will not be under the auspices of sentimentality."

He turned his head and, in the dark, she could see his eyes looking at her with clear, direct heat. "It will be because you're wound up so tight with need that you fear you will break if you don't have me." He moved an inch closer, and his warm breath gusted over her neck. "And then we will be in perfect accord, sweeting."

# *Chapter Twenty-four*

————————❧⫷❧————————

Winston lay in the slumberous warmth of the bed he shared with his wife and contemplated her. Bright morning light gilded her sleeping form, highlighting the paleness of her arms and the dusting of copper freckles upon them. Those freckles had been one of many delights he'd uncovered when he'd first undressed her on their wedding night, for she hadn't a one on her face. Stardust, he'd called them, those glorious freckles that were sprinkled over her arms and shoulders. He'd made it his mission to kiss every one of them. It'd had taken him an hour, and she'd quivered beneath him, her voice husky with need as she pled for him to take her now.

He'd meant what he'd said to her last night; he did not want her back from pity. And he knew she feared he wanted her solely because of the child—a ridiculous notion—but if he could acknowledge his fears, he'd acknowledge hers too.

It seemed such an easy solution to simply call pax, to say *I am sorry, now let's be done with this.* Yet when

Win tried to do just that, a wall reared up within, holding him back. He suspected the same wall rose within Poppy too, for shadows inevitably crept into her eyes when they shared unguarded moments. The ugly truth was that, deep down, they still distrusted each other, and he could not figure out how to fix this.

It wasn't as if he did not want his wife. Sweet Christ he did. Lying next to her now, with the scent of her sleep-warmed body filling the air, and the sight of her long length spilled out before him, was the veriest of tortures. Every nerve ending along his body thrummed with an impatient need to thrust into that snug, wet cove whose embrace he knew so well. He shifted slightly, his hips rocking his cock a little farther into the mattress. A sweet pain bolted through his lower gut at the action.

Poppy was a deep sleeper, which went directly against the alert way in which she conducted her waking hours. Right now, he didn't know if that was a blessing or a curse, because he could look his fill without her noticing.

She appeared younger in sleep, lying on her side with one arm tucked beneath her pillow and the other resting before her, her hand curled into a loose fist. Her pink lips parted just enough to let a soft breath out. Red rivers of her hair streamed over her shoulders and ran along the small slopes of her breasts.

Breasts that moved with the steady cadence of her breath. Up. Down. And his blasted nightshirt she insisted on wearing hid nothing. The shabby shirt was gossamer thin now. Holes grew along the seam where it buttoned down the front. Those holes held his attention, for each breath she took revealed a tantalizing glimpse of the curve of her breast.

His body grew hard and heavy, a languid sort of ache

that had him both wanting to move and to remain utterly still. She moved on a sigh, the sheets rustling as her body canted back just a touch. His breath stilled. The wretched nightshirt had moved too, one of those damnable holes slipping just over the tip of her nipple. For one tight, hot moment, the pink nub was revealed, then a thick lock of copper hair slid over it and clung, hiding his prize.

Win gritted his teeth. His fists curled into his pillow as he willed that tendril of hair to slip away. But it was stubborn, clinging lovingly to the pert tip. In, out, she breathed, her breast moving beneath the thin gown. A strand of hair fell, revealing just a touch of pink. He was going to lose his mind. His cock throbbed against the mattress, and the sunlight burned hot against his bare back. But he remained transfixed. Like a randy schoolboy, he stared. It became essential that the nipple be revealed to him.

Another few strands drifted down. A quarter moon of rosy areola winked at him. He licked his lips, his breath growing ragged. From a nipple. He might have laughed if he wasn't fighting a groan. Bloody hell, it was only a nipple. He'd seen it a thousand times before. He knew its taste, how it would stiffen against his tongue. Which was the entirely wrong thing to think. His blood thrummed through his veins. He could not stand it any longer.

Heart pounding in his ears and his body wound like a coil, he reached out. His fingers shook. Just one more inch. Her breath remained even, the coy little nipple still hiding from him. The tip of his finger grazed the tenacious tresses, careful not to get too close to his target, lest he be tempted to touch.

The red locks slithered away. Triumph surged though him, base yet undeniably glorious. The sweet pink bud, perfectly framed by the hole in the nightshirt, was his at last. The thought coalesced then froze like slush in his veins as he realized she'd gone still. Every muscle in his body tensed. *Caught.* Her gaze was a living thing that burned his skin. Slowly, he lifted his eyes.

Their gazes collided, hers so very dark and wondering, and waiting. They stared at each other. Never before had he been so aware of his body, of the tense quiver of his muscles, of the tendons in his outstretched hand, holding him there, just above her warm breast.

Something flickered in her eyes. A dare. One that sent rivers of heat through him with each sharp breath he took. Christ, she infuriated him. Making him want, making him regret and yearn. The ropey network of muscles along his arms were iron hard. Then he moved, slowly, deliberatively, not looking away from her. Her lips parted, her breath growing uneven. Her soft, pink nipple pointed upward, straining to meet him, yet she did not move. He felt the heat of her skin before he touched her. So close. His cods pulled tight and sore, his cock an aching thing pressed against the bed. The tip of his forefinger brushed over her budding nipple, and his gut clenched.

Her breath caught, her mouth opening further. He held her dark gaze, swimming in it, even as he watched his own finger skim across that sweet little nipple. It stiffened, rising up to his touch, and he made a sound close to pain. The areola was darker now, almost raspberry in color. Larger too. He traced the circumference. Was it because she was expecting? His throat closed. His child. In her. So still she was as he stroked her, only the gentle pants of her breath giving witness to her agitation. Feeling fiendish, he lightly flicked the tip. A whimper sounded deep within her throat, and her lashes fluttered as if she were fighting not to close her eyes. It sent a wash of want through him, so dark and hot that it was all he could do not to fall on her and suck that succulent breast until she screamed his name.

His hand began to shake as he fondled her, reveling in that one small point of contact. A flush worked over her ivory skin as she fought to keep still, and his breath sawed in and out. His cock pulsed, and his heart slammed against his ribs. Jesus, but he was on the verge of spilling like a lad who'd just discovered his pizzle and what it could do. He had to move, do something. He could no longer stand it. He held her gaze, and then very deliberately, yet very gently, pinched her nipple. A helpless cry tore from her lips, and she arched her back, thrusting into his touch. And then he was moving over her, his mouth latching onto the poor, tormented bud.

"Shh," he whispered around her flesh, "I'll make it better. I'll make it better..." Words were lost to the luscious nipple filling his mouth, the ragged edges of the nightshirt growing wet against the lave of his tongue. Her cool palms framed his face, holding him there as he sucked her in deep and pressed against her soft body. They moved against each other, her murmuring words of encouragement, pleas. He would give it to her. Anything she needed.

Her thigh was endless, so smooth and strong. His fingers traversed its length as his mouth travelled down her body, lost in the billowing softness of her gown and the subtle flesh hiding beneath. The linen whispered against her skin as he slid it high. Sweet honey greeted him, glistening in the morning light. He nipped her hip, loving the way she squirmed, how her legs glided apart for his touch.

"That's it, sweet." His mouth wandered along the hot crease of her upper thigh. "Let me give it a kiss."

The sweet taste of Poppy. Poppy writhing against the

flat of his tongue. Heaven. Another kiss. *I'll make it better.* He would make it better.

It was his last thought before a terrorized scream from somewhere down the hall rent through the air.

Lost in the fevered mists of need, Win had almost missed the scream. Whoever the lady was with her inconvenient fit of vapors, she could go to the devil. Only his core maintained a policeman's soul. It did not matter if he no longer carried a badge, he could not ignore a cry for help. And so he'd untangled himself from his luscious wife, grabbed some clothes as she struggled to find hers, and was now striding down the hall, which was rapidly filling with other guests, most of whom wore dressing gowns and frightened expressions.

"Pardon." He slipped through the crowd. Oddly, people stepped aside as they always had, never once questioning his right to take charge. Christ, what was he to do without the CID?

The commotion stemmed from a guest room at the end of the hall. Win's blood chilled when he caught a familiar scent in the air. Death. It was going to be bad.

A gaggle of lords clogged the doorway, but they too parted ranks as he edged closer. He caught the eye of Osmond, who stood guard next to the door. Bloody perfect. "Your Grace, what has happened?"

His brother nodded grimly. "Chambermaid found the body. Looks like strangulation. I've called for the local magistrate. However, the butler tells me the man is away on holiday."

Yes, and where was the lovely Amy Noble, now that her house had fallen into disorder and a guest murdered? One thing at a time.

Win eyed the door again. He itched to get inside. "As my wife said last night, I am an inspector. Let me have a look."

Oz frowned. He obviously did not like superseding his ducal authority to a mere tradesman, inspector or not. It was all Win could do not to say, *get your knickers out of a twist, Oz, and shove off*. It might have worked when they were twelve and fourteen, and still brothers, but he rather thought it'd earn him a punch to the nose now.

"We need a guard for the door," Winston added. Nothing mucked up a crime scene better than well-intentioned "helpers", be they houseguests or the bobbies who often found the corpses in London. "Mrs. Noble's guests ought not see this." He tossed a worried look over his shoulder at the crowd. A look that invited camaraderie between conspirators. "I think they would be more inclined to listen to you, sir."

Thankfully, Oz took Win's bait. He straightened in a move that reminded Win of their father. "I will take care of them."

Oz's ensuing orders to go back to bed and the shuffle in the hall faded to the background as Win fully entered the room and took in the scene. A man lay in a slump on the floor by the foot of the bed. Colonel Alden. A bluish tinge colored his broad face, growing darker about the eyes and his mouth, from which his tongue hung out blue and thick. His fine linen nightshirt had a rent along the collar and was ruched up about his waist as if he'd been kicking about in a struggle. Win glanced away from his pale, spindly legs and the flaccid fall of his penis. Damned undignified, death was.

He stepped around the drying puddle of urine and offal that had spread about the colonel. He was used to the stench of death, but suddenly that smell and the strange, almost sweet odor of a dying body hit him hard. His pulse raced, and a fine sheen of sweat broke out over his skin. Blackness dotted before his eyes. He saw not the room, but *that* alleyway, with that scent. The thing coming for him, and the sharp bite of pain on his face. He couldn't breathe. *Run. Run away.* Shaking, he lifted an ice-cold hand to his brow. *No, not now. Do not fall into it.* He forced himself to stare at the body and drew in a lungful of the foul smell. He was here, in a manor house. Not there, in hell.

"Was he strangled?"

Win jumped at the sound of Poppy's voice. She stood just inside, no longer his panting, blushing temptress, but covered up by sensible brown worsted, respectable attire, unlike his dinner trousers and mismatched day shirt he'd snatched from the chair arm. Her gaze fell on the body with clinical detachment. How many bodies had she seen? He swallowed several times, trying to find his voice. He didn't want her to see this, didn't want her to see *him* like this. She drifted closer and, not really looking at him, handed over a thin flask. Win didn't ask what was in it but took a deep drink. Fine, warm scotch smoothed down his throat.

"I don't think I'll ever become used to you Ellis sisters' penchant for whisky."

She waved an idle hand as she surveyed the room. "We're half Scottish. I think there might be a law against us not liking it."

He laughed shortly, and the pain in his chest eased enough for him to move again. "Strangulation appears to be the cause." He didn't ask how she'd got past Oz—a duke was no match for her—but knelt down to inspect the body. The fingers were soft. "Rigor mortis has passed. Death most likely occurred last night."

"After dinner?"

"I'd say a few hours later. Decay hasn't set in very far. I ought to have . . ." Unable to say more, he met Poppy's eyes and saw the worry in them. And the anger.

"This is not your fault, Win."

"Mmm." It felt very much like it was.

Poppy stood a bit closer to him, as though she were somehow shielding him. "Isley's doing?"

"Mmm." Win wasn't ready to formulate a theory. He bent closer to the swollen neck. Five puncture wounds were evenly spaced in the shape of a hand.

Poppy inspected them too and sucked in a sharp breath. "Colonel Alden's false arm is missing."

A quick search found the steel limb on the floor beneath the tangle of sheets. Squatting by the bed, Win studied the artificial limb. It was a solid, cold weight in Win's palm. A small smear of blood marred the index finger.

"Well, he couldn't very well have been strangled by his own arm, now could he?" Poppy said. Win glanced up, and her brows snapped together. "I do not mean he choked himself to death. I mean the thing cannot be manipulated in such a manner as to strangulate a grown and fighting male."

Win stroked the scar at the corner of his mouth. It was no mustache, but it helped him settle. "Perhaps it could." He turned the hand over, and gravity pulled the loose fingers back a fraction, making it appear as if the hand was opening up to him. "If the colonel was another victim of Isley, perhaps the bloody thing possessed a will of its own." Given the things he'd seen lately, what was one murderous arm in the scheme of things? "Perhaps Alden too had signed a contract, and his time was up."

"If this is part of Isley's machinations, why kill Alden with his own arm? Such a thing is bound to raise questions."

He sighed and rose to his feet. "I don't know." Needing to think more clearly, he paced, tapping the artificial arm against his thigh as he walked. Poppy noted the movement and lifted a brow. With a noise of irritation, Winston passed her the arm and kept pacing. "Damn, but you are correct. Why kill him now? Isley clearly lured him here…"

He stopped before the bed to glare out of the window, and something crinkled beneath his toe. Win stepped back. Just under the bed lay a crumpled piece of vellum. "What do we have here?" Win frowned as he smoothed the paper out and read its contents. "It's a note from Colonel Alden to me." His frown grew. "He says he remembered something about Moira Darling. Something I might find enlightening."

"Whatever that means." Frustration pulled Poppy's voice taut.

"Mmm, the script cuts off in a violent slash of ink." Win glanced down at the sad specter of the colonel. "I gather he was interrupted and killed for his efforts."

"Typical of Isley. His puppet cut himself free of his strings, and so Isley destroys him." Her brown eyes darkened. "That is what he does, Win. He makes promises, makes you believe that he is a gentleman. But he is a killer, through and through. And I fear…" her jaw trembled for one moment before tensing, "I fear that regardless of whether we find this Moira Darling or not, he will do the same to you."

"We've no proof that it was Isley." Win's gut reaction was that it did not fit with his behavior. "Regardless, we cannot become emotional. Stay on task, sweet. That is all we can do now."

"How can you be so calm?"

"How can I not? Our child's life is at stake. I will not muck it up by falling victim to rash behavior." No matter how badly he wanted to pound on Jones's face until his hands gave out.

Poppy looked at him for one agonizing moment, then nodded sharply before lowering her gaze. Her brow furrowed as she peered closely at the scrollwork upon the limb. All at once, she flinched as if slapped, and he moved to take it from her, fearful for one moment that it had come alive or hurt her in some manner, but she held up a staying hand. "Bloody hell," she murmured, glaring at the inner wrist.

"What is it?"

Cold anger rested in her eyes. "I've found the maker's mark." She pointed to a tiny crescent moon with a star nestled in its curve.

"I gather you recognize it?"

"I do." Her long fingers curled around the steel wrist, hard enough to whiten her knuckles. "The Evernight family has worked with the SOS for generations."

"Isley is the one who provided Alden with his arm. Which means that—"

Poppy's lips flattened. "We may have a double agent on our hands."

# Chapter Twenty-five

Mary hurried down the hall that led from her small room. Mrs. Lane had alerted her about the murder.

"Find Mr. Talent," she'd snapped in that brusque manner of hers. "Then both of you scout the house. If Isley is not here, one of his minions likely is." And then she'd strode off to join the inspector.

Like hers, Talent's room was below stairs, in a small corridor cordoned off for guest servants. As much as she'd like to turn around and not speak to Talent altogether, Mary's steps did not slow as she went to him.

She had not seen much of Mr. Talent since being on board the *Ignitus*. He had chosen to ride a horse alongside their servant's carriage on the trip to Farleigh. Upon arrival, he'd kept mostly to his room, and she was glad for it.

Drawing herself up, she knocked on the door, ignoring the way her heart clicked away beneath her ribs and the coldness in her fingers. A noise from within told her he was coming. She willed herself to be civil.

The door opened, and Jack Talent surveyed her. Hair mussed and shirt gaping at the collar, he'd evidently just risen and hadn't the decency to fully dress before receiving her.

She pressed her lips together. "Mr. Talent."

"Miss Chase." His voice rumbled along her skin, followed shortly by a hot gaze that had her pausing.

"I..." She cocked her head and glared at him when the gaze lingered on her breasts. "There's been a murder, Mr. Talent. Mrs. Lane requests that you search the grounds."

Slowly his head lifted. "Is that so?" Smiling faintly, he leaned a shoulder against the doorframe. "Are you certain this isn't simply a way to pay me a visit?"

"Do not be absurd." What game was the bastard playing now? "Stop acting the idiot and get dressed."

She moved to go when he was suddenly in front of her. He smiled again, not his usual one but a stretched and strange smile.

"Not so fast." His voice lowered to a whisper. "Why don't we take our time? Perhaps start our search in here?"

She gaped at him. Jack Talent propositioning her? Hot fingertips brushed her jaw, and she stilled. His eyes were glazed over with heat and dark promises. She searched that lusty gaze and found nothing more. No anger, no resentment. No Jack.

Her mouth went dry as dirt. But she made herself cup his hand to her cheek. Such a hot hand. "Say my name again," she said. "I want to hear it fall from your lips."

Again he smiled. But he did not light up. "Mary. The lovely Mary Chase."

His voice was flat, wrong. She forced a smile. "Right you are." She patted his hand. "Now, behave yourself and get dressed." She glided away, keeping a sedate pace as if all was right with the world. When she knew it bloody well wasn't.

Taking Poppy's hand, Win went directly to Tully, the butler of Farleigh. Like most butlers, the man was impeccably dressed, groomed, and mannered. He gave them a small bow as they approached. "Mr. Snow, I understand you are acting as investigator in this bit of unpleasantness. Is there anything I can do to assist you?"

"You can take us to your mistress directly." Win was prepared to hunt her down if Tully proved uncooperative. However, the man simply gave another small bow.

"Your timing is exemplary, sir. Mrs. Noble has asked that you meet her in her private parlor."

Win did not know exactly why the information that Mrs. Noble had sent for them bothered him, only that he grew weary of being batted around like a mouse trapped between a lazy cat's paws.

When they reached the hall leading to Mrs. Noble's personal parlor, Poppy halted him. "I think you ought to go in alone, Win."

He glanced at the paneled walnut door a few feet off then back to her. "Why? She is expecting both of us."

"Yes, but she wants you to tell the story. Not me. And there is the matter of questioning her in regard to Colonel Alden."

He did not know if he liked the sound of that, nor the way she was offering him up like a shank of beef. But as Poppy never proposed anything without good reason, he did not outright protest. Not yet. "You think she will be more amiable in speaking directly with me, do you?"

The way her lips flattened in distaste gratified him

somewhat. "I do. Never mind that I can then skulk about while you two talk."

" 'Skulk', eh?" He grinned. "How un-apologetically blunt of you."

She looked at him askance. "I thought you would approve." She nudged him with her elbow. "Go on, then."

"Very well." He gave her a short nod before muttering, "The things I do."

He had almost got to the door when she grabbed his arm and yanked him back. Her face scrunched up in a manner he knew to mean that she was struggling with some internal conflict. When she finally found her words, they came out clipped and efficient. "Mrs. Noble might have certain expectations should you go in there alone."

Winston bit back his laugh, but he could tell by the way her lips compressed again that his effort to hide his amusement failed. So he let it show as he leaned in close enough to feel her soft breath against his cheek. "Yet into the lion's den you send me." When her scowl formed, he grinned, suddenly enjoying himself. "Do you know, Poppy Ann," he said against her smooth cheek, "I do believe you are worried."

Her straight, strong teeth closed over his earlobe and the muscles along his abdomen tightened in response. "And I believe that you like me worrying over you." Her warm breath against his ear sent shivers along his skin. She nipped him then, hard enough to make him jump. "Behave, Winston Lane."

His hand found its way to her neck, holding her there. His mouth touched her ear. "Then it would be wise not to give me a cockstand while I am working, wife."

# *Chapter Twenty-six*

❧~~~~~~~~~~~~~

**A**s Win entered Mrs. Noble's parlor and closed the door, Poppy cursed roundly. What had she done? She shook her head lightly as if to clear it. She trusted Win in this. Of course she did. He wanted her. The evidence was clearly outlined in the quite impressive bulge of his trousers and the heated gleam in his eyes. It was the same look he'd worn earlier when he'd touched her. Touched her nipple to be exact, before he'd done other things. Her cheeks warmed. She'd thought she'd been dreaming at first. And then that look in his eyes. So very hot and needy. She'd wanted to scream herself when they'd heard the chambermaid cry out.

Thwarted desire was an emotion Poppy was ill-equipped to deal with. She preferred simple feelings. Anger, sadness, joy; they could run their course through her system. She could shout, cry, laugh, and it'd be done. She'd been spoiled. Desire, the want of a man, had come hand in hand with meeting Win. And Win had never denied her. The want of him still burned inside her, swirling and pushing against flesh until it became a physical irritant.

Bloody man. He thought their former life an illusion. Wasn't everything? She knew what she felt for Win right now. Did it matter what happened before or what would happen next? Now was what mattered. Of course, now she was walking away. After leaving him in an aroused state. Before tossing him over to another woman.

"Buggering…" She bit her lip, stopped because the action was too telling, then bit it again. Striding away from the parlor, she concentrated on the task at hand, not on Win and that…cow having a quiet tête-à-tête. "I'll freeze her bloody fingers off if she touches him."

Poppy took a deep breath. She was muttering when she ought to be quiet. Mrs. Noble's bedroom was near. Poppy simply needed to find it. Creeping along now, she put an ear to a door a few feet down from the parlor. Nothing stirred from within but that did not mean a maid couldn't be lurking inside. From out of her pocket, Poppy pulled a small mirror attached to the end of a length of thin steel. Kneeling, Poppy slowly slipped the mirror beneath the door and rotated it. The mirror sat on an angle so that, when Poppy adjusted her grip, the room within came into view. Keeping half her attention on the corridor and the other half on the mirror, she moved the mirror about and searched the room. Nobody there.

It was an easy thing to slip inside. Despite the flash attire Mrs. Noble favored, her inner sanctum was rather plain. Cozy even. A light maple wood paneled the walls, and cornflower blue drapes of sensible cotton graced the windows. A matched pair of well-worn armchairs flanked the hearth. Poppy's fingers trailed over the back of one chair. On the floor lay a knitting basket with half a stocking still attached to the needles. The room was well-dusted, but something about the way the knitting had settled into the basket led Poppy to believe that Mrs. Noble had not picked up the needles for quite some time. Poppy tried to imagine the woman knitting and failed.

A wrought iron bed, painted a pleasing shade of creamy white, sat on the far side of the room. Given the furnishing, Poppy expected fine linen bedding, but instead found expensive and rather gaudy silk sheets of a deep and rather incongruous shade of black. Lena furnished some rooms within her club Hell with such things.

Frowning down at the rumpled and glossy sheets, for the maid had yet to make the bed, Poppy fingered the fabric. It slid over her skin and sent a ripple of disquiet along her spine. The Mrs. Noble she was familiar with would certainly admire sheets such as these. But not this room. One did not fit. Mrs. Noble was said to have lived here for many years. A woman who selected silk sheets would not decorate her room in such a quaint style.

Poppy slid a hand into one of her pockets and found the gun resting there. She preferred a knife for most situations, but this gun had the happy feature of being both a gun and a switchblade—one that hid alongside the steel barrel until needed. As Poppy did not know what she might encounter, it seemed a fitting choice. The grip was a comfort in her hands as she made her way on cat feet to the dressing room. Here dwelled the Mrs. Noble she knew. Thick crimson carpet covered the floor, and matching drapes of fine velvet hung from the windows. Silk and satin gowns in bold colors hung like butterflies against the deep mahogany walls. A copper tub big enough for two sat in the center of the room. The thought of Win alone with the woman who enjoyed this room had Poppy's teeth gnashing. *She lets just one finger stray…Focus, Pop. Focus.*

Muscles tight with the thrill of the hunt, Poppy surveyed the room. The cloying scent of bath salts clogged the air. Too much. It stabbed at her nostrils and pierced her skull. Horrid smell, violets. She'd always hated it. A quick look at the glass shelves lining one wall confirmed that there were not enough salts to cause such a stench. Poppy held her gun secure as she crept toward the wall, the perfume of violets growing headier. Carefully, she ran her fingers along the edges of the wood paneling. It appeared solid. *Look for the wear. Finger oils will eventually wear down a varnish.* Win had taught her that, a lesson gleaned from listening to him wax on about his work. At the time, she felt guilty about learning tricks of the trade from him without telling her own, but now, as her eye caught the slight fading of varnish along the second panel, gratitude filled her instead.

Whipping her knife open, Poppy held it at the ready. Now that she knew what to look for, the hidden thumb notch in the panel gave easily under her hand. With a small clink and a smooth glide, the panel slid open. Poppy braced herself against the cloud of perfume that assaulted her nose. Vile as the scent was, the large, rough wooden box resting within the shadows of the small closet had her complete attention. Quickly, quietly, she exchanged her knife for a small stake tucked along the back ribbing of her bodice. True to her word, Miss Chase had outfitted all of Poppy's clothes with the essentials. Blessed girl.

Every sense snapped to full alert as she approached the box. She had the upper hand, for whatever might lurk within would have to spring up, while Poppy need only strike down. Even so, sweat trickled along her neck, and her breath grew short. There was always fear on the job. One simply had to respect it and keep going. The lid gave easily. She paused, not yet lifting, adjusted her grip on the lid and the stake, and then wrenched it open. Nothing moved.

Past the eye-watering smell of the bath salts that partially covered the body, Poppy made out the shape of the former Mrs. Noble, her eyes open and her mouth wide in supplication. Her soul had departed, but there was still enough blood in her to sustain a host demon.

"Fucking hell." The lid banged shut as Poppy turned and raced from the room, toward Win and whatever demon was cozying up to him.

Win stepped into Mrs. Noble's parlor and found the room was inordinately dark. Heavy brocade curtains barred the morning sun, leaving only the light from the fire snapping in the hearth and one silver candelabra for illumination.

Mrs. Noble sat in repose along the length of a scarlet satin fainting couch. No longer attired in men's clothing, she now wore a provocative black silk dress that was not at all proper day wear. Cinched tight and thrusting her breasts up high, the bodice did not have sleeves but was held up by a webbing of sparkling strands composed of diamonds.

"Mr. Snow." She undulated in a forward move, and a coil of black hair fell over her shoulder. "But where is Mrs. Snow? I thought I was to be entertained by both of you this morning."

Innocently put words that managed to sound illicit. He walked into the room. "She has developed a migraine, I'm afraid."

"Wives are known to do so. We simply shall have to forge on without her." She curled her legs under her. "Sit, Mr. Snow, and let us get better acquainted."

She patted the space next to her, and basic manners demanded that he comply. As an inspector, he'd had his fair share of dealing with forward women. Most of his colleagues did as well. Lonely widows, bored wives, the guilty, the curious—there were many reasons to find an inspector fair game. Some men took advantage. Win found those situations to be a lit fuse of danger. Pull away too quickly and the insulted lady wouldn't tell you a thing. Let it go too far and you had an unwanted tongue down your throat, and the lady wouldn't tell you a thing either.

On reluctant limbs he moved to sit, inwardly cursing Poppy as he did. Despite their discussion, he had no intention of seducing answers out of Mrs. Noble.

Satisfied, Mrs. Noble smiled prettily as her fingers danced along the wood filigree just behind his neck. "Now then, Mr. Snow, you promised me a story." The tip of her finger touched his collar. "How did you acquire such magnificent scars?"

He eased away. "First, we must discuss the murder that has occurred under your roof, madam."

She appeared remarkably unconcerned about the fact, but composed herself accordingly, lacing her hands in her lap and looking at him with wide, almost solemn eyes. A façade that might have worked had he not spied the mockery beneath it all.

"Tell me what you know of Colonel Alden," he said.

"Ah, Charles." With a sigh, she rested against the couch, arching her back just so. "The poor dear. I shall miss him. Though he'd always been a bit of a disappointment to me." The diamond webbing on her shoulders glittered as she shrugged. "He was a bit of a bore." She traced the scar closest to his jaw, and he managed not to flinch. "Such lovely wounds. They intrigue me."

"If the colonel was a disappointment, why invite him here?"

Her finger moved to his neck. "I did not invite him. He showed up unexpectedly."

Gods, but he itched to smack that finger away. "I was under the impression that you had invited him." Someone was lying, and he did not think it had been the colonel.

She laughed, but the sound came off as affronted. "Really, Mr. Snow, you are beginning to sound accusatory."

"Merely curious." He turned toward her, sliding his thigh a bit onto the couch. Her eyes went to the movement. Damn him, he should have sent Poppy to question this viper. "The magistrate will likely ask you the same questions."

Her lids lifted slowly. "You know, Mr. Snow, I really cannot recall the specific reason why I invited Colonel Alden. It was a simple, sudden urge." She eased over an inch closer. "You know urges, Mr. Snow. They cannot be denied."

He refrained from snorting. Subtlety was not her forte. "Have you met a woman named Moira Darling?"

As he hoped, the question threw her off balance. It was a moment before she answered. "I am beginning to suspect that your only interest in me is to ask questions."

"The asking of questions implies interest, does it not, Mrs. Noble?"

"Do not think that fetching smile will deter me, Mr. Snow." Unfailingly, she found the one white coil of her hair and toyed with it. "Now then, by your logic, you would not object to a question or two yourself?"

Win objected to many things about this interview, and

this place, but he kept his benign social smile in place. "I can hardly do so."

Her teeth flashed in the candlelight, not white but an unnerving grey color, as if she was decaying from the inside. "Excellent." Her bosom swelled as she leaned close. "Do you regret the choices you've made in your life, Mr. Snow?"

He sat back against the settee, away from her. "Pardon?"

Round and round the white coil twisted, her finger nearly swallowed up by the act. "Do you regret having not lived a fuller life?" Ebony eyes held his. "Bedded more women? Taken more risks?"

"Moira Darling," he snapped back. "Do you know her?"

"Yes. A sad woman who never lived life to the fullest. And all she was left with were pain and loneliness."

He nearly jumped in his excitement, but she slid closer, placing a pale hand upon his arm. Blood rubies glittered on her fingers. "The risks, Mr. Snow."

"Where is she?" He wasn't going to play this game. He'd already given up his soul. He would not give anything more.

She ignored his question as neatly as he'd ignored hers. Her fingers tiptoed along his sleeve. "I've quite a number of most excellent talents, Mr. Snow. And one of them is reading a man." The tip of her finger touched the thick scar on his cheek. He steeled himself not to retreat, and she smiled as if she knew exactly what he was thinking. "You, sir, have played your hand entirely too safe."

Had he? Had he wasted his opportunity to live a larger life? The edge of the armrest bit into his side with each breath he took. Lord Winston Hamon Belenus Lane might have had numerous women lined up to bed him, simply because he was a duke's son. He might have lived in utter opulence, traveled the world over, gone to a different party every night. Inspector Winston Lane had bedded only one woman, put numerous criminals in jail, and been slashed within an inch of his life for his efforts.

The smile upon Mrs. Noble's face grew, stretching and coiling at the ends. He looked back at her and what she so blatantly offered, but in her place another woman sprang up in his mind, her vermilion hair spread out like a satin banner upon his pillow and her brown eyes alight with keen intelligence.

Mrs. Noble's simpering voice brought him back. "You see it now, don't you? How you might have lived in glory."

Win detached Mrs. Noble's creeping hand from his arm. "Risk doesn't signify a life well lived. It is what you risk your life for."

In the wavering light, her eyes appeared to go pure black, but she blinked, and the illusion was gone. "Then let us risk some more."

Before he could question, she moved onto him, her arm sliding around his neck. His hand shot to her shoulder, staying her progress. "I believe you have misunderstood the situation, Mrs. Noble. I am not interested in bedsport."

Her breath gusted over his cheek, bringing forth a strange scent of smoke and iron. "Come now, Lane. All men are interested."

"That depends on the partner." He leaned in, giving her a smile with bite. "I prefer my wife."

A mistake to get closer. Her palm cupped him warmly. "That is because you haven't yet tasted the meal I offer."

He locked his hand about her wrist, wrenched her hand away, and pushed her against the arm of the settee. "You called me Lane. Which means you know why I am here."

The simpering look did not leave her face. "Did you

enjoy meeting your brother?" Her hips lifted against his. "I'm desperate to see how you two compare."

He growled low and shoved back, hard. "Did you kill the colonel?"

Her grey teeth glinted in the lamplight, the points of her canines appearing sharp. "That canary was not invited to the party. I'm afraid he had to go."

Bloody hell, but he hated coyness. Past all patience, he pressed his forearm across her chest. "Who is Moira Darling? Where is she?"

Like a snake, she coiled her leg around his. "Closer than you think."

He gave her a rough shake. "Where?"

She laughed then. Laughed and laughed. "I would not try to find her, Winston Lane. The knowledge will only bring you misery." The whites of her eyes disappeared with a wash of inky black. And then she disintegrated. Winston blinked, his mind not catching up with his eyes as she literally fell to pieces before him, her body crumpling, turning to black lumps. Lumps that moved. Spiders.

With a shout, he jumped up. Hundreds of spiders swarmed, crawling over his arm, up his boot. The door slammed open with a bang. Poppy stood in the doorway, her gaze fierce as she took in the scene.

"Get back!" He ripped off his coat and flung it. Spiders scurried and surged as he stamped at them.

She did not heed. A shiver lit over the room, a swirl of air. The arctic blast of cold hit hard and fast, sucking the air from his lungs, biting into his skin. More forceful than what he'd felt on the ship, this air tore through the room with the strength of a gale, tossing spiders about, freezing them where they lay. He trudged toward Poppy, his teeth chattering, his body hurting from the cold. When he got to her side, she cut the power loose.

"C-c-cold..." His teeth rattled.

"I know," she said, grimacing. "I'm sorry."

"Cold b-blooded." He glanced at the piles of little black spiders littering the room. "Spiders are."

# Chapter Twenty-seven

Horrid little beasts." Poppy fought a violent shiver as Win shoveled the last pile of frozen spiders into the roaring hearth to assure that they were destroyed. The spiders popped and crackled in the flames, and she swore she could hear tiny screams. She shuddered again, her stomach turning sickly.

Win caught her eye, and though a touch of humor lit his gaze, he spoke with solemnity. "You were very brave to face them." He knew how much she detested spiders. She'd rather face a horde of undead than those little creatures.

They'd been all over him, swarming and scurrying. She rubbed her arms. "Are you injured? Did one of them bite you?"

Win set the coal scuttle back on its stand. "No." Shadows rippled along his face as he stared into the fire. "That wasn't Mrs. Noble, I gather?"

"No." Now that the spiders were gone, Poppy dared to come farther into the room. The gilded little sitting room appeared too lovely, too proper to have witnessed such horrors. In fact, it was almost peaceful now, cozy and quiet. She stopped beside Win and let the heat of the flames seep into her freezing skin. Cold did not bother her, but this cold was in her bones. "Mrs. Noble's body is currently stuffed in a vat of bath salts."

"Jesus."

"The demon you were tangling with used her blood to take on her form. Although from the condition I found Mrs. Noble in, the demon got a bit carried away. Most demons have better control when stealing blood."

Poppy glanced at Win, noting that despite the casual way he stood, his muscles bunched with tension. His look of fierce concentration worked away the coldness better than the fire had. Frowning, Win massaged the back of his neck with one hand. "She killed the colonel."

His fingers tightened on his neck until his knuckles stood out white, the skin around them too red. "The colonel said he was invited here. But Mrs. Noble—or whatever that was—claimed he was an unwanted visitor who needed to be silenced." He flung his arm down. "I think Jones brought the colonel here because he wants us to find Moira Darling, but someone else does not. Mrs. Noble was most unhelpful before she turned into a mountain of spiders..." He ran a hand over his face. "Hell, I can barely bring myself to say that aloud."

Yes, that had been most... She gave his arm a light nudge, lest she think too hard about spiders and be tempted to faint. "I gather the lady found you intriguing, Mr. Lane."

Cool blue eyes pinned her with a glare. "You knew perfectly well what she would be about, did you not?" When she pursed her lips, he leaned in, and his breath caressed her cheek. "You never truly answered me before, sweeting. Were you curious to see if I'd rise to the occasion?" He moved closer, his hard chest pushing against her shoulder, his lips tickling her ear. "Or did you simply long to see my cock manhandled?"

Futile and hot jealous anger surged. The bloody woman had touched *Win*.

Win read her emotions well, for his eyes lit with satisfaction. He pressed into her, and the length of him was hot at her hip. It was all she could do not to grind back or beg for release like a wanton thing. His lids lowered a fraction, hiding his thoughts from her. "Let me assure you, wife. I've only one master—"

"Yes, I know. *You*." She rolled her eyes and pushed away from him, her skirts sliding about her legs as she strode to the door. "You've made your point. Now may we return to London before I expire from another lecture? We've a false limb to investigate."

He caught up to her easily with his long legs and determined gait. His hand closed over her upper arm, halting her retreat. "If that is what you think the answer was, Boadicea, then you've missed the point of this morning entirely." His grip grew possessive. "It is *you*. No matter how much both of us wish to ignore the fact, I have always been entirely yours."

Winston and Poppy kept a brisk pace as they headed for their rooms.

"Mary," Poppy called as they entered, "start packing. We are to leave posthaste." She turned to Winston, who was busy gathering his own things. "What of your brother?"

His back tensed. "What of him?" A shirt landed in an

open portmanteau, and he just kept himself from rubbing at the hollow spot that formed in his chest. "He was lost to me long ago."

Her efforts stilled. "I am sorry, Win."

He did not turn but lifted his shoulders. "What is done is done. It was my doing, in any event. No use crying over it now."

Mary glided into the room, and Poppy turned to her. "We found the demon. Posing as Mrs. Noble, I'm afraid. What of you and Talent?"

"Mum." Mary Chase lowered her voice as she approached. "About Mr. Talent."

Poppy tossed a pair of throwing knives into her valise. "If you are about to tell me that you do not trust him, Miss Chase, that has already been duly noted."

Mary's small nose wrinkled. "I trust him well enough, mum. At least in the capacity not to betray you or the inspector. It is he who does not trust me." Her rosebud mouth twitched. "I simply do not like him." The scent of cinnamon and ambergris drifted up as she leaned forward. "In point, mum, I am worried."

Winston paused in the act of unloading the revolver Poppy handed him. "Why?"

Mary's expression did not lose its serenity. "I do not think it is Talent in that body."

That got Poppy's attention. Her brows snapped together. "Explain."

"I believe he is either hosting, or that is not him at all."

"You base all of this on what, precisely?" Winston wasn't about to confront Talent on something so flimsy.

Mary straightened with the offended dignity of a duchess. "He is not himself, sir. He is being ... kind to me."

Winston had to laugh. "And this is cause for alarm?"

Her brown eyes turned a shimmering gold. "Mr. Talent is nothing if not consistent in his behavior. Then overnight he is, well, let us simply say solicitous toward me. His voice is off as well."

"He sounded right enough to me." Win knew he was being argumentative, but one must consider all possibilities before making a judgment.

However, Mary Chase did not appear offended. She simply considered him with the same implacable expression. "Humans never give proper appreciation to the voice. If the eyes are the windows to the soul, the voice is its song. You can tell a great deal about a man by listening to him." Her mouth pursed. "A demon may mimic another's voice, but the shade and tone of a voice is colored by one's life experience. Talent's is hard like flint and dark grey with a core anger. It now lacks that driving force of inner rage."

He'd underestimated this woman entirely. Win vowed not to do so again. Mary appeared to see the acknowledgment in his eyes for some of the stiffness in her shoulders eased. She turned to Poppy. "And there is his body temperature to consider. He touched me just a moment ago."

Poppy's fierce scowl remained. "Hot?"

"Feverishly so," confirmed Mary.

Anger brightened Poppy's eyes. "Given that poor Mrs. Noble was drained of her blood to host a demon, I'd say it's highly likely they have done so to Talent as well."

"Damn it." Win paced. "Talent was with me when I questioned the colonel. If it is a demon, then it knew the colonel or suspected he might eventually help us with the case." It rather made Win's skin crawl to think of a demon being that close to Poppy all of this time. And that he'd exposed the colonel to the devil.

Poppy's fingers drummed on her skirt. "Where is Talent now?"

"I do not know." Mary said. "He was in his room about twenty minutes ago."

"Well then," Winston said, "let us have a word with Mr. Talent."

He moved to go when Poppy's hand touched his elbow. "Take him to the lake. I shall meet him there."

"We shall both talk to him," he countered.

Her touch stilled. "You must leave him to me."

He frowned, and her grip tightened. "Win, if this is a demon, he is guilty of breaking the laws set down by the SOS. Which makes it my duty to destroy him. This is what I do."

When he stared into her eyes, he saw not just his wife, but the warrior goddess that so beguiled him from the start. "Be that as it may, Boadicea. But from now on, this is what I do too." He smiled with just enough teeth to show his determination. "Consider me your new partner."

Poppy waited by the lake. As much as it was her duty to dispatch any rogue demons, she did not want to do so in the middle of a house filled with innocent bystanders. She knew in her heart Win would not fail her. He'd claimed himself her partner, growling the words as if she might protest. In truth, he'd unknowingly granted her deepest wish.

A breeze slid over the wide lawn, rippling the grass before it toyed with the edges of her skirt. She hadn't dared to waste time changing and instead gathered her weapons, but now she regretted it. The chocolate wool day-gown, while elegant and slender, was also cumbersome. Damned if she could figure out why she stuck with wearing women's clothes when she could just as well be done with all society and don lighter and more practical men's clothing as the demon Mrs. Noble had done. She kept her eyes on the distant house terrace and cleared her mind. In her hand, the crossbow was a comfortable weight, smooth and cool against her skin.

She did not have to wait long. Two silhouettes appeared on the horizon, their shapes outlined in the morning sun. It struck her how similar Winston and Talent's forms appeared, both broad of shoulder and lean of waist. The similarity ended there, however. Win's walk was even, sedate, as if no one or nothing would rush him. Talent's stride held impatience; it always had, so she could not be sure if it was truly him or an impostor. Besides, any proper demon would mimic Talent's movements with precision.

They came abreast of each other, and their heights aligned. A few months ago, Talent had been perhaps an inch shorter than Win. Now he was the same height. A year from now, she knew Talent would be taller. He was entering his prime, and as a shifter, he'd bulk up and grow a few inches more, most likely ending up on par with her brute of a brother-in-law Archer. Sadness filled her breast at the thought. If this was not Talent coming toward her, then he might truly be lost, never to become the man nature had planned to make him.

Her grip tightened on the crossbow. With her other hand, she slipped the gold throwing knife from her pocket and held it close.

"Poppy," Win said as they walked up to her, "you have news?"

"Yes." She flew into motion. The knife hissed through the air just as she raised the crossbow and shot. Talent barely had time to blink before both projectiles slammed into his shoulders, taking him down to the grass and pinning him there. Win's start of surprise was lost as Talent roared. Not at all the roar of a shifter.

"Poppy," Win shouted, "you haven't given him a chance to defend himself."

She did not take her eyes off the thing writhing on the grass, trying to free itself from the gold weapons holding it down. "It won't do permanent damage," she said to Win before addressing the demon. "Rise then, Jack Talent, if you can." A shifter could be held fast by iron, but not gold. A demon, on the other hand, detested gold. What she did not know was whether this was Talent's body or an illusion of it.

Talent's eyes flashed with an inner fire before turning deep yellow. Demon eyes. She advanced on him, snapping another golden arrow into place. It whizzed and thumped into his thigh, and he screamed. Win stepped closer, horror etched on his face. Talent's body arched, straining against the shafts.

Poppy stood over him. "Who are you and where is Jack Talent?"

Caught, the demon let his glamour go. Human in appearance except for his pale grey skin, he glared up at her with his yellow eyes. "Fetch my mettle, you bunter bitch."

Win snarled at the foul words, and his foot slammed into the demon's side. "Address the lady properly or I'll have your tongue."

The demon sneered as blood streamed down his lip. The gold was affecting his system now, turning the network of veins a deep black against his grey skin. "Get me out of these bonds, and I'll make a capon out of you. Stuff your lobcock down your gullet, I will."

Win moved to strike him again, and Poppy placed a staying hand upon his arm. "Do not bother. He's merely a weak and pathetic raptor demon. They feed off the pain and misery of others and are notoriously foul-mouthed." She glanced down at the demon. "And quite stupid."

The demon on the ground showed his sharp teeth. "Go bugger yourself, you bleeding three-penny upright."

Win looked capable of murder. Poppy tightened her grip on him, and giving the demon a pleasant smile, aimed her last arrow at its crotch. "If anyone is in danger of being a capon, it is you. Now talk before you spend the rest of your short, miserable life as a eunuch."

A bloody grin worked over the demon's face. "Can't." He craned his neck to reveal the image of a chain tattooed upon his skin. "Am bound by Master."

"Which means he is physically incapable of divulging any information," Poppy explained to Winston. "No matter what we do to him. That tattoo will literally choke the life out of him if he says anything against his master's wishes."

"Aye," said the demon with a gurgling laugh. "But can tell you Mr. Jack is having good fun with my mates." His dark tongue ran over his teeth. "Tasty is Mr. Jack. Been having fun with him since the boat." At that, the demon shifted his appearance to the murdered ship's officer, then to Mary Chase, before going back to his ugly, demonic self.

Something cold and dark passed over Winston's eyes as he looked down at the demon. "If you have nothing to tell us, then you are of little use." Tight-lipped, Win turned his attention back to Poppy. "Decapitation works with this one, yes?"

Below them, the demon began to writhe against

his bonds, snarling and spitting like an enraged dog. "Shanker covered, whore pipe, pig-fucking—"

"Are you sure you want to do the deed?" Poppy asked. SOS law gave her the right to execute any demon guilty of body theft and torture, which this demon clearly had done to poor Jack Talent. However foul the criminal may be, executing one still ate at the soul. She felt the weight of every life she took and did not like to think of Winston carrying that same burden.

But Win's expression was set as he pulled his sword free from his walking stick. "Quite." Dispassion etched his expression in harsh lines as he stared down at the demon, who still cursed a blue streak. Win raised his sword. "For Jack." He struck true and clean.

# *Chapter Twenty-eight*

❦

They searched the Noble house from the dank cellars to the roof rafters, but found no sign of Jack Talent. And so they headed for London and Ranulf House to let Mary off there. She would alert Ian Ranulf to the problem, and the lycans would begin the search for Talent.

"It will soothe The Ranulf to search," Mary said. "But they will not find him before I do." Though she and Talent had never got along, fierce determination heated her voice and shone in her eyes. But her fervor quickly died.

Mary's lids lowered as she grimaced. "I ought to have realized that one stole my blood aboard the *Ignitus*."

Poppy rested a hand upon Mary's. "None of this is your fault."

No, it was *his*. Winston ought to have at least noticed Talent was not himself. He clutched the handle of his walking stick harder so that he would not smash something. "What is to say that Talent is still alive? Do you not suppose that he might have been dispatched when we discovered the demon? Or perhaps drained dry like poor Mrs. Noble?"

"Mr. Talent is a shifter." Poppy glared out the window as if she too were overcome with distaste. "His blood is extremely valuable, as it allows a demon to change appearance with the ease of a shifter. As Mr. Talent is one of only five known shifters in Europe, he is very rare."

"Gods. I had no idea. I simply assumed he was one of many."

Poppy's eyes went cold with anger. "Talent took risks flaunting his nature. There are always those who would hunt down a shifter and use them. Which is why there are so few left alive."

"No one deserves to be used against their will," said Mary with sudden anger. She ducked her head, and the brim of her bonnet hid her expression but her gloves stretched tight against the knuckles of her clenched fist. "There are no better trackers than a GIM, Inspector Lane. I will not fail."

After leaving Mary and their baggage at Ranulf House, Poppy gave the coachman directions to Fleet Street market, of all places. "One of the entrances to the SOS headquarters is there," she explained to Winston. "There are others close by, but this one will garner less attention."

The coach let them off at the market. A light breeze caught the pervasive stench of moldering water, garbage, and cooking and carried it off. People crowded the sidewalks, creating a general din of laughter and conversation. St. Paul's dome shone against the grey sky. He hefted the satchel they'd brought along more securely over his shoulder and then offered Poppy his arm.

Daylight dimmed as they turned a corner and came alongside the Fleet river canal bridge. There the River Fleet slipped beneath London on its subterranean course.

Poppy stopped by a service door and, blocking the door with her body, quickly pushed a series of numbers into the punch lock. Despite the worn and rusted appearance of the door, the lock clicked with well-oiled ease. She glanced over her shoulder as she pushed the door open. "This way."

The scent of mildew and fetid air washed over them as they stepped inside the dark space. Winston blinked, waiting for his sight to adjust to the dimness, since the only light came from behind them and the small pinholes from the sewer grates. Foul didn't begin to describe the smell. The rumble of street traffic and the dripping of water echoed in the underground tunnel. Without further ado, Poppy nudged him inside.

"It isn't the most pleasant of entrances, I'll grant you." She pulled a slim cylinder from one of her many hidden pockets, and with the flick of a knob, yellow light shot from its end. It was an electric torch. He'd heard of them; hell, he'd even seen a rendering of one, but nothing as elegant as the model she held.

"Hold a moment." He took the torch from her and studied it. The thing was heavy, an effective weapon if need be. The light it exuded was strong enough. Certainly better than nothing. "It's brilliant."

Poppy allowed a quick smile. "The SOS is privy to technological advancement that the public doesn't see. We have a team of inventors who are quite clever. Our top inventor built several prototypes this year. I've been testing this one." She moved them forward, and Win duly pointed the torch toward the ground before them to light the way. "It doesn't last long, unfortunately, so we'll have to be quick."

She guided them along a narrow walkway that hugged

the underground section of the river. Now that they had a bit of light, he could see that the tunnel was about twenty feet in diameter and lined with bricks. It extended in both directions, allowing the river to flow beneath London proper. A small craft was moored at a bend in the tunnel. "We are going on that, I presume?"

"Yes." Her steps were quicker now, her countenance an eerie green in the weak light. "This tunnel leads directly to our headquarters."

They were silent as she stepped into the craft and lit the lantern hanging off the prow, and he untied the mooring rope. The boat rocked precipitously as he stepped in, and she pushed off, using the long pole provided. Win widened his stance and, taking the pole from her, acted the part of gondolier.

"Something about that encounter with the demon bothered you. What was it?" He had questions on top of questions but he knew peppering her with them now wouldn't get him answers. Tension held reign over her slim shoulders and long neck. Her fists gleamed white among the dark folds of her skirt.

Beneath the straight slash of her brows, her eyes were pained and withdrawn. "It is nonsensical, really."

"Emotions often are. But tell me anyway."

They were silent for a moment, with only the trickle of water and the distant clatter of the life above making noise.

"Knowing that a demon hid among us, seeing you slay it…" Her fists clenched tighter. "I don't know, Win." Dark eyes lifted to find his. "I am used to danger following me. I am not used to it following *us*."

"Do you think it different for me?" He put his back into the next push, and they surged forward. "The lot I usually deal with might not be undead or, Christ, turn into spiders"—That still had his nerves dancing—"but the danger of being gutted is still there."

Her gaze steadied on his scars and went darker still. Win did not let her comment but continued. "I rather liked that danger, if we are telling truths. But it is another thing entirely to see you in the thick of it. Especially now."

Ducking her head, Poppy's voice grew unusually soft. "We've already lost too much in Talent."

Win's fingers tightened on the pole. "You believe Miss Chase will succeed?"

She smiled thinly. "Do you know it took Daisy one day of being a GIM to weed out the fact that I was Mother? The little brat followed me to work, and not once did I notice. GIMs find what others cannot. They are the best spies we have. Which is why goodwill between them and the SOS is so important."

Her good humor faded, and the air grew chillier still as she glared pure murder into the dark, foul waters. "Regardless of whether or not we find Talent, the ones who took him will pay."

Apprehension tightened Win's gut. "Poppy Ann," he said, "do not even consider haring off on your own." Which he was certain she was.

The eloquent lift of her red brow confirmed it. "I'm not going to sit in a bunker and twiddle my thumbs while you and our child are in danger."

Win gritted his teeth as he shoved the boat farther along. "I swear to all that is holy, if you do not stop mollycoddling me, Poppy, I shall take you over my knee."

Her brow rose higher. "I should like to see you try."

"Shall we have a go later?" The notion inflamed him in more ways than one.

"I'd freeze your arse before you got started."

"Play dirty, do you?"

"Always."

True anger rose to the surface. It ought to be bloody degrading to know his wife could take him down without mussing her hair, but what really bothered him were the risks she took. How close had death been to her over the years? And he hadn't even known to comfort her.

# Chapter Twenty-nine

Mary settled herself upon the worn armchair in Jack Talent's bedroom. The door was locked. Even so, Ian Ranulf had given orders that this section of the house not be disturbed while she was here. Which was good, as a GIM's method of tracking a soul was one of their closest kept secrets. Relaxing, she stared up at the dark, coffered ceiling. All was in order here—quiet, still, waiting. It smelled of him, that faint, almost illusive combination of sandalwood soap, fine linen, and the earthy scent of shifter.

Talent liked quality; that was clear. His was a small room, a little jewel box tucked away in a quiet corridor of Ranulf House. Everything in his room was expensive, yet understated, as if he did not want to acknowledge his lust for luxury. But it was obvious in the soft leather chairs, the thick nap of the velvet throw lying upon the ottoman, and the smooth indigo silk counterpane covering the bed. Plump, down-filled pillows were piled high against the impressive mahogany headboard and practically invited a person to lie down. The man lived like a pasha behind closed doors. And a monk in the public eye. Which was the real him?

The rosewood Vulliamy clock on the mantel ticked away, no doubt keeping perfect time. She stirred with the unnerving need to look over her shoulder.

As a professional voyeur, she was accustomed to invading the private places of others. It never truly affected her. And yet distinct edginess plucked at her skin here in Talent's inner sanctum, as if he would barge in at any moment, brassed off and shouting about her shady ways. The thought almost had her rising up and walking out of the room. She resisted the urge. Whatever he was to her, he deserved to be found. The others were fond of him, though lord knew why; the man was a braggart and a hypocrite.

Even so, she settled back and let her fingers stroke the smooth leather. Such a comfortable chair. One could drift off to sleep in its arms without even realizing. His essence lingered here—a dark, complex mix, like aged Scotch, smoky and rich yet with a sharp bite. It disturbed, pulling one down into a confused mire. Mary took a quick breath and willed herself to sink deep. Deeper into the unwelcoming feel of Jack Talent.

"You will owe me," she muttered, not liking the task one bit. But it was working. Some essential part of Jack Talent grabbed hold of her neck as if he'd like to shake it. Most certainly this was Talent. She let it pull her along, and on the next breath, she was drifting. The heavy shroud of her body fell away, and she was lightness and air. A spirit, free to go where she pleased. Only at the moment, Talent had a hold of her. The connection was thin, no more than a thread of light. She concentrated on it. Talent's light was a base mix of blue and grey, a survivor of life yet conflicted and one of dark thoughts. What concerned her more was the muddy, mustard fog that coated his light. It spoke of pain. Great pain, if one considered how very weak his light glowed.

Up she went, over the smoking chimneys, pitched roofs, and sharp spires of London. Skimming over crowded avenues and the heads of strolling pedestrians. Life teemed, swelled, and extinguished before her. It was, as always, beautiful, mesmerizing, and haunting.

She focused on Jack Talent. She thought of his voice, always hard and unforgiving, thought of his eyes, bottle green and full of distrust. Gods, but it was an exercise in tolerance and a test of her will to keep going. When she reached Victoria Docks, the thread of light flickered, then failed. Below her, a large iron boat was docked. Iron, to keep a shifter contained. Iron, to keep a spirit out. Jack Talent was there.

The tunnel opened up into a massive underground cistern. Win counted at least forty columns, lined with yellowed bricks and topped with Egyptian-style lotus blossom carvings, laid out in a grid pattern and holding up the vaulted ceiling. Torches flickered on either side of each column, providing enough light to turn the dank, fetid water into a golden sea. The place appeared empty, but when they reached the end of the stone dock, Win spied a man sitting upon an ebony chair beside a large door. The bloke appeared to be reading.

The reader did not look up, nor move, as they docked their craft. Poppy's heels echoed in the hollow place as she led them toward the man, a brute whose burly hands dwarfed the thick book he read.

"Mum," he said as he turned a page. Win glanced down at the book. *Candide*. Well then.

"Clive." Poppy nodded just as the massive door unlocked with apparently no help from anyone. Gears and levers along the front of the door groaned as they released, and the door slowly swung open.

"Who is the fellow reading Voltaire?" Win asked as they went through the door and it creaked shut behind them.

"Clive is our guard."

"He did not so much as look up."

"He doesn't need to. He can read your thoughts from about fifty yards off. He knew we were approaching and who we were long before he saw us. We would not have reached the cistern were we unwanted. The outer doors would have closed on us."

"A little warning in that regard would not have been remiss, Poppy." He tried to remember what he'd been thinking of fifty yards off. None of it was anything he wanted old Clive to know about.

Poppy's lips curled. "You sound quite guilty, you realize."

"My thoughts are the purest snow."

As neither of them could quite swallow that, they remained silent as they walked down a white-tiled corridor.

"It looks like the London Underground," he said after a moment.

"Yes." She turned a corner. They did not encounter a soul as they went. "We've our own train system as well. There are stops beneath a few palaces and Westminster." She paused before a pair of massive coffered doors. Each panel featured a frieze depicting the burning of a witch. "To remember," Poppy said, "what happens when the people start to believe in the supernatural."

It wasn't a comforting memory to have. "Were any of those women truly witches?"

"Some. Most were simply women caught up in the tide of fear. Fear of the unknown is a deadly thing."

The dark, burled wood of the door highlighted the clean lines of her pale profile and the red flame of her hair. His voice was jagged as he spoke. "This is what you truly do, isn't it? Keep things like this from happening again?"

"It is what we try to do."

"Where is everyone?"

Her long finger punched in another code. "Around. Most regulators are out in the field, and this sector is fairly high level." Beyond the door, a series of rooms opened up. Unlike the sterile feel of the halls, this new place had a domestic look about it. Each room led into the other. One was rather formal, the other looked more like a gentleman's retreat, and another a small library. Here and there, men and women sat in chairs, reading, smoking, or paired off in small groups for conversation. None of them looked up as Win and Poppy passed, and he rather thought that it was an unwritten rule in regards to privacy. But they were all aware of Win's presence. Never before had he felt more of an interloper. While not outright watched, Winston felt their surreptitious looks with every step he took.

This was Poppy's world.

Poppy read his expression well. Her voice dropped to a murmur. "Here, I am known as the director of this sector. Seven sectors, seven directors, Mother and Father overseeing all."

"And who is this Father?"

"Augustus." Lamplight flashed in her eyes as they walked along. "The man who saved you."

"The…er…man with wings?" He refused to say angel, but he had his suspicions.

The corners of her mouth curled. "He is a demon. A special sort. I would introduce you but he went away on personal business." A faint frown marred her brow but she let it go and ascended a long spiral staircase with steady proficiency. "There are certain activities for which we require above-ground rooms. We've taken over a few warehouses as cover."

Poppy led him into a large, light-filled room, walled on one side with a grid of floor-to-ceiling windows. An ebony lake of marble spread out before them, and her reflection rippled along its surface as she strode forward between one of the rows of black-topped worktables that held various mechanical devices in stages of completion. Young men and women stood before many of them. The workers gave them an idle glance as they passed but it was clear Poppy was a regular visitor. Above their heads, the ceiling soared twenty feet up and crested in the center with opaque glass window panels. Poppy's red hair shone like a beacon among the drab color and the pale-faced workers.

When she reached the center of the room, she turned and headed toward one of the two massive fireplaces at the side of the room. Neither was lit at the moment, for it was summer. A tall, shining steel worktable had been placed a few feet in front of the fireplace on the left. There a woman stood, her head bent as she fiddled with some apparatus too small for Win to discern its function.

"Miss Evernight." Poppy's crisp voice caught the lady's attention, and she set down her tools.

A small jolt hit Win. She was young. Very. Perhaps eighteen or nineteen. She still had a touch of childhood roundness in her cheeks, but her dark eyes snapped with quick intelligence.

"Mrs. Amon." She gave a small curtsey. "If you've come about the gun, I am to commence testing this afternoon."

Hamon, Amon, Belenus, Lane, Poppy, Mother... The woman had more names than the Queen. Win could only guess at what insane name she'd call him now.

Win stepped closer, and Poppy acknowledged him. "This is Mr. Amon."

He tried not to let his surprise show. Miss Evernight was less successful. Her eyes widened, and her winged brows disappeared beneath the shining black fringe that she wore.

"Mr. Amon." She made an awkward attempt to extend her hand, but noticing that her fingertips were covered with oil, lowered it and nodded instead. "It is indeed a pleasure to meet you, sir."

It was clear that she hadn't expected Poppy to actually possess a husband. Perhaps they all had aliases.

"Mr. Amon," Poppy said, "may I present Miss Holly Evernight, our chief firearms master."

Miss Evernight flushed with pleasure, but she did not try to downplay her title. Instead she stood tall and at the ready as if to answer any question he might have.

"Miss." He turned his gaze to the table beside her and was finally able to see what she worked on. "Is that what I think it is?"

With a delicate touch, Miss Evernight handed the ring to him. "A pistol ring, sir."

The thing was exquisite. About an inch wide, the steel ring held on its top a tiny, six-chamber wheel.

Miss Evernight took the ring from him and slipped it

on. It hung loosely on her slim finger. She turned it so that the chamber fell toward her palm. Intricate scrollwork adorned the sides, aiding in concealing the true purpose of the ring. "It relies on the element of surprise."

"I should say so." Win smiled as she handed it back to him and urged him to try. The fit was snug on his finger.

"Fires a 5-millimeter shot. Close range for true efficiency. A flip of the wrist to aim it..." She pointed to the ornately carved metal panel resting at the side of the firing chamber. "Push the panel to shoot."

Poppy took the ring next and held it up to study it. "Marvelous, Evernight." She peered into the empty chambers. "A 5-millimeter shot does not pack much of a punch. I assume you have taken that into account."

Miss Evernight's cheeks dimpled, and she appeared a schoolgirl. "Each silver bullet contains a small dose of oil of vitriol."

"Which will do quite a bit of damage to many a beast's insides," Win said with admiration.

Poppy's severe brow quirked, and he repressed the urge to tweak her ear. "I am not entirely ignorant, you know," he said instead.

"I would never presume to call you ignorant, Mr. Amon." Lips pursed, she handed the gun back to Miss Evernight. "Excellent work. When will it be ready for the field?"

"If testing goes well, next week."

Poppy dug into the parcel bag she had slung over her shoulder and pulled out Colonel Alden's artificial arm.

The reaction in Miss Evernight was immediate and stunning. The young woman held her hand out for it with a look of near reverence. "I remember this." Her fingers skimmed over the steel hand before pausing on the tiny star mark.

"The Evernight mark, yes?" Poppy said.

Miss Evernight's dark eyes lifted. "My grandfather's."

"Mr. Eamon Evernight," Poppy said. "He passed away two summers ago."

"Yes." Miss Evernight's slim fingers did not stop their exploration of the piece, even as she gave her attention to them. "I was a girl at the time, but I remember him working on it. He was quite proud of this hand."

"Do you know anything more about it?" Win asked.

"It was a special commission. It had made his name within the SOS."

Win exchanged a glance with Poppy.

"Do you know who placed the order?" Poppy asked.

Miss Evernight finally took her hand from the steel limb. "They were Regulators. A man and a woman."

"How can you be sure?"

"The pin upon the woman's cloak." A small grimace twisted her mouth. "I wasn't supposed to watch."

"But children will be children," Win said, drawing her in. "Did you see their faces?"

"The man I saw. He was about your height, Mr. Amon. Dark hair, strangely pale eyes."

"And the woman?" he prompted.

"Never got a good look at her, I'm afraid. She wore a hooded cloak that covered her hair. However, I remember thinking that they were more than simply partners, for the man called her 'darling'."

Poppy's mouth thinned. "Moira Darling?"

Miss Evernight's dark eyes lit up. "Yes, that's it."

They had moved to go when Mary Chase burst into the room. Her footsteps were oddly soundless as she hurried past the workbenches to get to them. "I've found Mr. Talent," she said without preamble. "I'll need your help."

# *Chapter Thirty*

━━━◄━►━━━

Deep in the bowels of the ship, Mary Chase searched. Sound echoed here; the Thames slapped against the outside of the iron hull and made the air a damp blanket. The stench of rot and dank water grew stronger. A sick fug that clogged her nostrils.

The inspector and Mrs. Lane had fanned off in other directions, each of them taking a section of the ship. Now she was alone, and she did not like it. So many places she'd been, so many things she'd seen, and still her heart whirred and clicked with quick fear. She yearned to break free of her heavier body and drift away. But an iron door loomed before her, calling her forth. Whatever lay behind it was wrong. So wrong. She felt it to her very core.

Even so, she kept going, her feet nothing more than a whisper over the floor. The lock proved intricate and advanced, but she'd dealt with worse. She crouched before it, her knees aching. The puff of her breath obscured her view, and she willed herself calm, willed her numb fingers to work.

The tiny snick of the lock turning sent her whirring heart into high speed. Slowly she rose and lifted the hatch lever. Damp, hot air escaped the door in an audible gasp, and the fetid scent of iron, blood, and human waste assaulted her. Opening all of her senses, she slid the spiked baton out of its hiding place within her sleeve and grasped the handle tight. And then she crept into the dark maw of the room.

Steam curled her hair and filled her lungs. All was quiet. She eased into the room, keeping her back to the wall, and glanced about as her blood pounded in her ears. It was dark, but that was all right; she could see well enough. A table, iron and crusted over with dried blood, sat dead center. Blood coated the floor, creating sticky pools that pulled at her boots and released them with a sick, squelching sound as she moved on. Despite the unbearable heat of the room, her hands turned to ice. An orange glow came from the far corner, the source of the heat. The small furnace burned at full power, hissing and cackling as it ate up its fuel. Her mouth went dry. Another step and she was almost next to the furnace, and the whole of her left side burned, her skin going tight and too hot. Her body shook as she scanned the rest of the room and stopped. A scream surged up her throat and came out in a helpless gasp.

She stumbled forward, her gaze darting around. She was alone. Save for him. And then she let herself really look, and bile burned her throat. She'd found him.

Jack Talent hung on the wall, naked and crucified. Thick iron spikes drove through his hands, shoulders, thighs, feet, and heart. Iron to keep him from shifting. His blood ran in thick rivulets to be collected in iron pails beneath him. Hair shorn off, his head hung forward, resting against one pike.

"Jack," she whispered, shaking so hard it came out as a sob. Whatever she felt for him, he did not deserve this. No one did. He did not move. The scent of death was too thick for her to determine if it was his or another's. Oh, but he was pale. So pale. Her baton clattered to the floor as she reached him. His skin was clammy yet hot and covered with symbols carved directly into his skin. A grunt, so low and weak she might have missed it, broke from his cracked lips.

"Help!" She hadn't realized she'd shouted the words until footsteps pounded along the iron floor. She glanced back and saw the familiar outlines of Mr. and Mrs. Lane.

Mary pressed her palm against Talent's quivering side, and his pain screamed in her ears. "Help him."

The inspector swore as he rushed forward, his strong arms lifting Talent's weight off the spikes as he began to wrench them out. But it was Mum's face that captured Mary's attention, for it promised vengeance and death.

Jack lay within the womb of his bedding. If he kept perfectly still, barely drawing a breath, he could almost remain numb and think of nothing more than how good the weight of the quilt felt on top of him and the softness of the mattress beneath him. But it was impossible to keep himself in that state of nothingness forever. A sound would break out from somewhere in the house, a laugh or the creak of a floorboard, or perhaps the rattle of a passing conveyance outside, and he'd flinch, his entire body seizing with terror and pain, and then the panic would claw at him. He was safe. Safe in Ranulf House. His true home. The thought held as much weight as smoke. It drifted away too soon, leaving him with the memories. Pain, degradation, the sick slide of it that had him shivering like a babe and burrowing down further into the bed.

When the terror had him, those once soft and secure blankets meant nothing. They could not protect him. Not from the memory of those hands on him, pinning him down, holding him tight as the knife scored through his flesh, or worse, when they'd stroked him, gently, manipulating a response that rose his gorge. And then the horrid, churning humiliation as they pinned him in a different manner, and their laughter as they enjoyed him.

Jack curled in on himself, gagging even as he held himself as tightly coiled as he could manage, his arms wrapped about his drawn up-knees. The position hurt and tore into his wounds. But he'd fly into pieces if he didn't hold on.

The door opened, and he tensed. He was safe. Safe. It wasn't them. Couldn't be. He shivered hard and held on.

"Jack." Ian's voice. Ian's scent, as familiar as his own. He swallowed convulsively. He'd never admit it to anyone, but Ian's scent struck a chord deep within him, at the childlike part of him that immediately thought, "father." His own father meant nothing compared to this man. Humiliation writhed inside of him that Ian should see him like this. That he should know what had happened— for Jack was certain he did—he could not bear it.

"Get out." His voice was no more than a dry whisper.

Footsteps sounded, bringing Ian closer, not away. Jack tucked his chin into his chest. Ian stopped next to the bed. Jack could feel him there, hovering.

"Lad." Ian sighed, and Jack shivered until his teeth rattled. His eyes burned, a hot, wet pressure building behind them. *Oh, hell, just leave. Do not see this too.*

But the edge of the bed dipped as Ian sat. In the periphery of his vision, Jack saw Ian's broad hand and his golden wolfhead ring wink in the light. Jack squeezed his eyes shut.

Ian's voice came just the same, blunt and unemotional. "It's a bolloxed shite thing that happened to you."

Jack stilled, his heart in his throat and his stomach twisting. Ian made a sound of anger. "I do not know what to say to you, *mo mhac*. Other than if you think yourself unmanned because of...of what they did, then I'll personally rip yer cods off and feed them to ye."

Irritation made Jack snort. It wasn't bloody Ian's body being tortured in that bloody room. Bastard lycan.

"Brassed you off, did I?" Ian retorted. "Good. You deserve your rage."

He moved, and the edge of his thigh came close enough to touch. Or punch. It was tempting, but the shaking had started again.

"You'll heal," Ian said. "You're too strong to do anything less."

The shaking grew until Jack couldn't control it, and his world grew watery. A blur as the rage and pain tore out of him in a sob. He wasn't aware of moving; perhaps he hadn't, but in a blink, his face was crushed against Ian's chest, his fists slamming into Ian's sides as if he could pound him to dust. But the man who'd called him his son, the man he called father in his heart, simply held him fast and took the punishment as Jack raged against the irrevocable tear in his soul.

# *Chapter Thirty-one*

———— ❧❧ ————

*London, 1869—Love Requited*

Well, I think you are wrong."

Winston stopped and gently turned Poppy away from the foot traffic that flowed along the busy sidewalk on Oxford Street, tucking her between his body and the large glass window of an empty storefront to let. Most couples took their strolls around Hyde Park or some such landscaped area. Not Poppy. She preferred to roam the city proper. And as Winston would follow her anywhere, he simply let her take them wherever her whim demanded. "Explain."

Her stubborn chin rose a touch. "Ophelia absolutely did not go mad because of Hamlet's defection. It is utterly absurd to presume that unrequited love can drive a person to madness. Clearly that poor woman contained a fractured mind well before Hamlet waltzed onto her stage."

His cheeks ached in an effort not to grin. He braced

an arm on the window frame, which gave him an excellent excuse to lean in close and lose himself in her lemony scent and feel the subtle warmth of her body. The ever present ache in his gut—one that she'd put there—tightened a bit more. They had been married a week. A strange time, for whenever Winston thought of events before their marriage, his mind went a bit fuzzy. They'd fought. She'd been afraid to marry... and that was when his memory became muddled. He'd gone to Paris, drunk too much absinthe—a beverage he resolved never to touch again—and he'd come home, only to be cut off by his father. Win hardly remembered the words they'd exchanged. But Poppy had married him. That joy he knew to be true.

Now, however, he needed to find work, preferably with the Metropolitan Police, needed to find a home for them, for they were staying with her father, and still his want of her stayed foremost in his mind.

"You do not think it romantic that her love for Hamlet was so great that she fell into unending despair when he left?" he asked.

Sharp red brows snapped together, and he wanted to kiss the little furrow between them. His hand curled into a fist as she, oblivious of his lust, proceeded to lecture him. "Romantic? Bah. Such is a man's idea of how a woman ought to love. By all means, let us poor, emotionally weak females fall into utter helplessness for the want of a man. Especially a man who couldn't be bothered to treat her with any sort of—"

He kissed her. Because he couldn't stop himself and didn't have to. Her lips were soft, her tongue tart and slick. He slid an arm about her slim waist and suckled her lower lip before breaking away. "You'll soon have me in despair," he whispered, smiling against her mouth, "if you don't believe in all-consuming love."

Her arm snaked around his neck, her cool fingers slipping into his hair to toy with it. Had he the ability to purr, he would.

"That isn't love," she said.

"No?"

"No."

He nuzzled closer, brushing his mouth against hers. "Kiss me again."

"We are in public." But she sipped at his upper lip as though she liked the taste of it.

Winston chuckled and reluctantly stepped back a pace. His gaze landed again on the storefront window beside them, and he looked back at a wonderfully flushed and mussed Poppy. "Do you realize you take us past this empty shop with every walk we take?"

Her cheeks darkened more. "Do I?" She moved to go, but he blocked her way with his shoulder.

"Yes." He nudged her chin with his knuckle. "And you won't get me to believe it's by chance, either. Confess, Boadicea. Why this shop?"

Standing straight and smoothing her hair back into place, she attempted to look past him, her sweet lips pressed into an annoyed line. But then a noise of defeat sounded in her throat, and she glanced at the shop before meeting his eyes. "I want to let it."

When his brows rose in surprise, she pushed on. "It is a bookshop. Or was." Her nose wrinkled as she made herself speak. "I would like to see it reopened. I-I have always wanted... It is a silly dream, I know."

Her words cut into him. He hadn't expected her to have dreams. Why? Why hadn't he thought of her wants? It shamed him that he'd been so oblivious. Putting a staying hand around her waist when she squirmed to get away, he looked over her shoulder and studied the shop. "Have you any experience in running a bookshop?"

Poppy's expression closed. Tension tightened the muscles along her back. But she did not drop her gaze from his. "No."

He looked into her dark eyes, his hand firm upon her. "Then you shall learn."

She flinched. "What?"

He smiled then, tucking a stray lock of fire-bright hair behind her ear. "We have need of funds and a place to live. There is a flat attached to the shop, I see. You want this shop. So you will have it."

Her breath left in a gust. "Win... How can you..." She drew herself up. "What if I fail?"

Slowly he shook his head. "My love, I have no doubt that if running a bookstore is what you want to do, then you will do it. And do it well. You are too strong-willed to fail at anything."

She gaped at him, and he cupped her cheek. "I believe in you, Pop. I always will."

A startled cry broke from her before she flung herself at him, the force of it making him stumble back a pace. Laughing, he caught her up and held her tight. Then she was kissing him, tender yet fierce. And all was right in his world.

"I love you. I love you so much, Win." It was the first time she'd ever said the words.

# Chapter Thirty-two

~~~~~

Usually the SOS library brought Poppy a good measure of peace. A cavernous space, two stories high and the length of two city blocks. Rows and rows of golden wood shelves flanked the walls and ran down the sides like soldiers in formation. The second story was open to the first and mirrored it with perfect symmetry, cresting with a Moorish arch ceiling, tiled in golden glass. The library was always cool and quiet. A refuge. Today, however, Poppy restlessly toyed with her quill pen and ended up getting ink on the tips of her fingers for her efforts.

They were at a dead end. Miss Evernight could not direct them to anyone else who might know Moira Darling, and Jack Talent was in a bad way, unable to divulge who or what took him. Poppy swallowed thickly. Talent's torture had shaken them all. Ranulf House was in an uproar, with Ian demanding blood. But whose? Isley's? Winston doggedly maintained that they were missing the whole picture. His solution? Investigative research.

Poppy could not fault his methods, but while Win was

a man of planning and precision, she was a woman of action. Like two parts of the same weapon, she thought bemusedly. He was the cutting edge of the blade and she the thrust behind it. Suppressing a sigh, she shifted in her chair, easing the tension in her lower back. Research was all very well and good, but after going through about two hundred old newspapers, she had nothing to show for her efforts. Not one bloody mention of Moira Darling, or Isley, for that matter.

Tossing her pen aside, Poppy watched Winston while he read. Really, she ought to be reading as well. Only he did the job so much more thoroughly. The whole of his concentration went into the task of discovery. And he sat, spine straight yet shoulders hunched over the desk, his gaze firmly upon the book in his hands. With his attention diverted, she could study the clean lines of his profile and the way his lashes swept down in a thick, gold-tipped fan. It wasn't fair, really, that a man should have thick, curling lashes while she was cursed with ones that were straight and red. Indeed, his lashes ought to make him appear feminine. Yet paired with the square arc of his jaw and the determined slash of his mouth, those thick lashes tempered him somehow, giving him a bit of vulnerability among all that masculine hardness.

He smelled of wool, books, and man. An intoxicating concoction that made her want to lean closer and inhale. Warmth radiated from his lean body. Delicious warmth that she, who always ran slightly cold, craved with every breath. His lips parted a touch as he read on, and a flush of heat rose up her breast. How many times had they sat just so? With him reading as she'd torment him, bringing her body against his, knowing he would feel the press of her breasts on his upper arm. He'd remain unmoved, a smile working about his lips as if daring her to try harder. And she would. First by threading her fingers through his hair the way he liked, gentle touches that made him relax. And then, when that smile grew, she'd lean in, lick that sensitive corner of his mouth, and wait for his breath to catch. There were days when he'd be stronger, when he'd keep himself utterly still until she had mounted his lap and tossed his papers aside, then she would shriek when he'd catch her up and—

"Find anything?"

She sucked in a breath at his sudden query and glanced down at the papers in front of her. "Ah…no."

He was too silent. The heat of his body too unnerving. She risked a look. Blue-grey eyes stared back with steady focus. There was a question in them, as well as recognition. He'd noticed her attention. And remembered. The warmth in her skin flared white-hot. Surely her face was scarlet. His gaze flicked to her cheeks, and his color grew as well. Yes, she was assuredly red. His lids lowered a fraction, his attention settling on her lips, and his own lips quirked.

On a breath, he was closer. Or perhaps she was. The hard swell of his biceps pushed against her breast, and she tensed. Damn it, but she was tired of this separation. She wanted him. So much she couldn't breathe.

"Win…" The silk of his hair slid over her fingers. When had she moved?

His nostrils flared as his attention intensified. "Boadicea."

Carefully, she cupped the rough terrain of his ravaged cheek. He swallowed audibly yet offered no resistance as she turned him toward her, closer, and her back arched with the almost decadent need to press her breasts harder against him. His pulse thrummed where she held him. The sound of crumpling paper filled the air, and vaguely she realized it was Win's hand clutching at pages. His breath brushed over her lips, and everything within her went tight. A helpless sound escaped her as her lips parted. She could almost feel him there. Almost. Her lids grew heavy, yet she could not close her eyes. She needed to watch. Needed to see that mouth of his part for her, come to her.

The first brush was so soft it almost didn't register. Yet every nerve along her skin leapt to life, and she trembled. Her fingers twined in his hair as he pulled back a fraction. An unsteady breath left him, and his mouth returned. Another brush, a bit deeper. An exploration, the warm, wet glide of his tongue into her mouth. His fingers touched her cheek. She trembled and leaned closer, ready to crawl onto his lap and slip her hand into his trousers to grasp that cock she knew would be so very hot.

"Ahem!"

The voice was loud enough to make them freeze. Anger and frustration stabbed her breast as Win pulled away. But she blinked in surprise as a puff of frosty air left his mouth. Had she done that? She stayed where she was as Win looked up at whoever stood behind her.

"Yes?" Win sounded far less irritated than she.

The man—it was a man—made a sound of reproach. Poppy did not turn around. The voice belonged to Grevis, the old fusspot librarian who always gave her the gimlet eye. And though she was in fact his superior, she did not favor the idea of having him catch her in the act of kissing. Likely the man had an idea who she was—her red hair being unique—however, as long as she did not turn, they both could maintain the illusion of anonymity.

Grevis's sonorous tones rippled over her. "The Reading

Room is for study and reflection, sir. Not for...loose behavior with one's..."

"Wife?" Winston supplied softly.

The mere word had Poppy's heart skipping a beat. It had been so long since he'd openly used that tone, as if he did so to not only protect her honor but to lay a claim. A pulse beat at his neck, and then a warning flashed in his eyes. His hand still cradled her cheek, not letting go.

"Yes, well, kindly finish what you are doing here and attend to your wife," Grevis paused and Poppy felt his censorious stare upon her shoulders, "elsewhere."

Win held Grevis's gaze for a beat and then he eased. "We are nearly finished here." With that, he turned his attention back to the papers, dismissing the man with nothing more than a shift in posture, and Poppy could see the son of a duke shine through. Did he even realize it?

Winston glared down at the papers in his hands but could not focus. "And to think, I used to like librarians." Everything in him shouted to finish what he and Poppy had started, to take her now. Had the librarian not caught him, he just might have done so. "Bloody busybodies."

Poppy laughed, but her voice held a huskiness that danced along his spine. "You're merely sore because he had impeccably bad timing."

" 'Sore' is an appalling understatement," he muttered, shifting uncomfortably in his seat.

He cut her a quelling glance, and her grin widened. "Why, Winston Lane," she said, "I do believe you are in a snit because you got your fingers caught in the biscuit bin."

"Lovely metaphor." His lips pinched as he tried to read. Really, the words ought to make sense now. But they merely swam before him. "Are you going to crow or concentrate upon the task at hand?"

"I thought I'd crow a bit more. After all, it's always a bit of a triumph to see even the smallest of cracks occur in the great Winston Lane's polished veneer."

He set his papers down then. "Ah, Poppy love, all you have to do is touch me, and you'd feel the cracks in my veneer well enough."

His reward was her deep blush and the way she nibbled her lip.

"Cheeky," she said, and then met his gaze. "Kiss me again."

His breath left him in a rush. *Need. Want. Take.* Primitive lust had his hands shaking and his heart slamming against his ribs. Her soft lips were so close, plumped up from his earlier ministrations. He could lose himself in her mouth, kiss her until he no longer thought about failure or what he'd done to put them in this predicament. And if what he'd just sussed out about this case was correct, things were going to get a lot uglier before they got any better.

With shaking hands, he gathered his papers. "It is not a good idea." His eyes stayed on his movements as he further ordered his things, then left the neat stack on the desk for the librarian to shelve. Not waiting for her, he stood and walked away.

"Damn it, Win." Her footsteps clattered behind him. He did not even know where he was headed, but he didn't want to face her. Not when the feel of her lips was still upon him. "I know what we said before about choices but... Blast it, will you stop?"

He kept going. Down the bloody endless rows of bookshelves.

"I did not love you when we married!"

Win halted, the soles of his boots scuffing along the marble. Her confession robbed him of air and sent a spasm of pain through his chest. Slowly, he turned on his heel to face her, his heart going in slow, aching thuds. "What?"

Her expression was almost serene, as if she hadn't just made him bleed internally. "I did not love you." Her slim shoulders lifted. "I lusted after you, to be sure. Cared for you very much. But it wasn't love."

Cold comfort that. He swallowed and tried to think of a reply that did not involve shouting or cursing the world to bloody hell. Did she ever love him? No, he could not ask it. He knew he wouldn't recover from that blow.

Perhaps aware of his turmoil, she looked about and then tugged him down a shadowed aisle between the shelves. Her voice, smooth as cream, surrounded him. "Do you remember that day when I told you about the bookstore?"

For a moment he couldn't think, but merely searched her face and wondered if pregnancy left her slightly touched in the head. But she was watching him earnestly so he managed to nod.

Her eyes turned the color of fine cherry wood. "You believed in me," she whispered, taking a step closer to him, "without proof of my ability, without question of my motives."

He swallowed hard, his hand fisting at his side in an effort to keep still, for he needed to see this conversation through, not tug her into his arms. "I will always believe in you." It was the truth. She was the strongest person he knew.

Her sweet mouth trembled as she smiled, a small,

secretive smile. "I fell in love with you in that moment, Win. Utterly, irrevocably."

Understanding washed over him, and it had his heart flipping over in his chest. "It had nothing to do with my bargain."

"No. It never did. I hadn't wanted to fall in love with you. It was too dangerous. But I fell despite myself."

He reached out for her. The soft press of her breasts against his chest was the sweetest sort of pain. Her smooth cheeks were cool under his palms. "Poppy." He leaned his forehead against hers and gave a helpless laugh. "Why do you tell me this now? When we are here?" When he couldn't pull her to the floor and touch her the way he needed to?

"I've always had bad timing."

Her lower lip pouted, and he gave in, suckling it between his lips for one gorgeous moment before letting go. "Yes, I know."

Her breath turned unsteady. "But I wanted you to know." Searching his face, she wrapped her hands around his wrists, holding him steady just as he held her. "I needed you to know. Isley is not responsible for our life."

"To hell with it." He was done resisting. He kissed her then. A gentle sip that shaped her lips against his like warm wax. He lapped at her wide bottom lip, nipped her shapely upper lip, and his body swayed, and only her hand upon his heart could keep him steady. He brushed his lips over her cheek and she sighed. The smooth column of her neck was cool against his mouth. Cool and fragrant. The scent and feel of her blindsided him, and he found himself simply holding her as he pressed his lips against her skin and inhaled. God she smelled good, like no perfume man could devise. It was simply *her,* unique and irreplaceable. She trembled and he gathered her closer, only to realize that it was he who shook. How could he have let her go?

"Win," she placed a soft kiss upon the scar near his eye, "give me more. I need more."

The desperation in her touch, so similar to his own, had him hauling her closer. They fell back against the shelves. Her hands were at his jaw, holding him still as she went at him with hot, luscious little bites that had him groaning. He fisted the coiled mass of her glorious hair and kissed her back, all lust and need, no finesse.

"God, I've missed you," he said against her lips. "Missed this." She tasted of Poppy, dark spice and cool water. It was a taste that haunted his dreams. So utterly familiar and so long denied that he drank her in like a man stumbling out of a desert. His body seared with need, and his hold upon her turned greedy. He wound his fingers further into her silky hair and opened her mouth with his, thrusting his tongue into her warm recesses. It was nearly anger, this feeling that coursed through him and made his movements too rough, too clumsy. His hands fisted her skirts as he stepped between her thighs. Desperate, he grabbed onto the bookshelf for leverage, ready to haul her up and take her there.

"Poppy..."

A book slammed to the floor beside them and they both jumped. Jesus, but Winston had forgotten where he was. For a moment, they both panted, then Poppy's arms slid from his neck. He leaned in, wanting to snatch up that maddening mouth of hers once more, but she held him fast and he blinked, trying to pull himself out of the haze of lust. He laughed but it came out as a choking sound. "Right. Not here."

Her smile was wry yet wobbly. "Not unless we really want to scandalize old Grevis."

Win took her hand in his and held fast. "Come along then. I think I've figured out the last piece to the puzzle."

She was half-smiling, half irate. "And you didn't say so!"

Laughing a bit despite it all, he nipped her bottom lip. "A certain glorious redhead distracted me."

WINTERBLAZE

# *Chapter Thirty-three*

❧

I am assuming you have a weapons room," Win asked Poppy as they left the library.

"Of course." She found herself grinning widely. "A ridiculously large one."

His chest rumbled against her side as he chuckled. "Bloodthirsty girl."

The weapons room was in another sector, so they returned to the Fleet River craft. Win took over punting once again.

"Tell me we are going demon hunting," she said as they glided down the dank tunnel.

Shadows slid over his features and along his trim length. "I fear we are, sweeting."

"You need not sound so dour." She leaned back a bit in the seat so that she could look up at him properly. "I, for one, am itching to lay into that bastard." Her jaw ached where she clenched it. "After what he did to Talent."

"Mmm."

Aware that he wasn't truly listening to her, Poppy

raised her voice. "Darling, you are aware that your 'mmm's' can drive a person to distraction."

He grinned. "And here I thought it was part of my charm." He plunged the pole into the murky waters and stared off into the distance, where the tunnel disappeared into a wall of black. "I was reading about demons, how there are different types."

"Yes." Impatience colored her tone. He ignored it.

"Let us go back to the beginning." He guided the craft around a bend. "The first demon I saw aboard the ship was in the process of procuring blood from the ship's officer."

"Yes." Poppy knew better than to hurry Win once he was on an exposition, but she wanted to.

The corner of his mouth quirked as if he knew her thinking as well. "And then it used Mary's blood to assume her appearance and get close to Talent. Not to mention that Mrs. Noble was drained of her blood as well. And yet Isley does not need blood to assume a new appearance."

"All correct. So he had help. We know this." Unease tickled along her spine. Win had a theory, one he was reluctant to share. She could tell by his even gaze and the way he made her think the process out.

"Isley's eyes are white or crimson when he reveals them," Win went on. "The eyes of the demon I beheaded turned yellow. And Archer's eyes, when he was changed, went silver. I remember thinking how remarkably different his eyes were back then." He smiled a little. "Only I hadn't any idea the extent of it."

"What is your point, Win?"

"I assume that the color of a demon's eyes gives away what type of demon it is?"

"Yes." Her voice was cautious now, the heavy dread increasing within.

He ran a finger along the edge of the pole. "Mrs. Noble's eyes flickered to unnatural black."

Poppy plunked her chin into her palm. The ugly sensation within her grew but she could not quite acknowledge what was knocking about in her mind. Not yet. "There is a sort of demon whose eyes go black," she said with reluctance. "The sort who feeds off of sexual congress and blood."

The pole stilled in his hand. "Do not say it. Do not..."

Her smile was grim. "You might have heard of them referred to as vampires, or nosferatu."

"You said it." He sighed, leaning slightly on the pole.

Despite herself, she laughed. "It is simply a name, you know. They are pure demon. Only they favor blood for nourishment. It is because they yearn for human contact, usually in the form of sexual contact, that the human world has developed stories and myths about them. Too much interaction has led to leaks in information."

Slowly he nodded, but his focus was on the oily water beneath them. "Here is what bothers me." He softened his tone, which made Poppy's skin tighten and her fingers grow cold. "Your lieutenant Lena has such eyes. She knew we were onboard the *Ignitus*, did she not? And she knew we'd interviewed the komtesse as well."

The temperature dropped so quickly that Win's next breath came out in a puff of white steam. Cold pervaded Poppy's insides. No, it could not be. But it was there, dangling before her like a signpost.

"Is Lena a demon?" But he knew the answer. It was written in his sad eyes.

"Yes." Her voice lowered. "She was the one who

brought me Isley's threat. The undead followed us to the komtesse's house, and she knew we were going to Farleigh…" Her fist struck the side of the boat. "I should have seen it."

"Why? You trusted her."

A sharp laugh rang out. "Hell, Win, you know as well as I that trust is merely an illusion."

An awkward silence fell over them, but he broke it with a softly spoken, "I know, sweet."

Queasy in the rocking craft, Poppy drew in a breath of dank river air. Lena was more than a lieutenant. She was her mentor, a surrogate mother—albeit a rather cold one. "But why?" Poppy hated that the question came out in a pathetic warble.

Win's scarred countenance hardened like mortar, and Poppy shivered at the sight of him standing tall and glowering, yet she felt at once protected and glad to have him on her side. "That, sweeting, is what we shall find out."

Poppy frowned at the smoldering wreckage that used to be the gaming club and brothel known as Heaven and Hell on dilapidated West Street. Thick smoke billowed up into a pale grey sky, and the facade of the burnt-out building appeared like a leering, blackened skull. The street was abandoned, thieves having long since scavenged anything of value. It felt odd, though, to stand in the middle of London's East End and not see a soul. A timber groaned as she and Win made their way down the blackened steps to the entrance of Lena's Hell.

Water dripped from above, landing in hard plops upon Poppy's shoulders. A trickle of it ran down her neck and under her collar. The smell of smoke was so pervasive that it coated her tongue with its acrid flavor. The heavy iron gate that served as the doors to the underground night-club was jammed shut, and she stepped aside to let Win wrench it open. He did so with surprising ease, and a little base feminine thrill shot through her.

"You're certain about this?" he asked, his hand on the knob of the inner door.

"Lena started this fire." Poppy lifted her skirt away from the diamond-bright shards of window glass that had fallen from above. "Sanguis demons might be known for their feeding habits, but they also have the ability to manipulate fire much like Miranda does."

"Sanguis demons?" Win's mouth turned down at a corner. "Is that what you call vampires?"

"I told you, they are not vampires. That would imply that they are reanimated human corpses, when they have never been human, or dead, for that matter."

"Of course," he murmured dryly.

From one of the deep pockets sewn into her skirt, she pulled the foot-long stake made of Christ's thorn wood she had procured from the weapons room. "For you."

Win held the thing loosely in his hand. A slight frown marred his features as he studied it. "Not vampire, eh?"

She ignored the irony in his voice and focused on practical matters.

"Gold will cut through a demon's skin quite well," Poppy explained. "And it will adversely affect them. But each type of demon has a particular weakness that will kill them instantly. The trick is to know it beforehand and be prepared. The sanguis demon's weakness is Christ's thorn wood. Hit straight under the chin and into the brain, or through the heart."

"If all demons have weaknesses, what is Isley's? How can we kill him?"

"I don't know. He is pure Primus and older than any other I've encountered. Perhaps he has evolved into a true immortal state." Poppy looked at the stake in Win's hand. The unpolished point was as sharp as a blade. "Now, as to method of attack. I prefer the chin. The torso is too well-fortified with ribs and cartilage, and one might miss with the first hit."

Heat and humor lit Win's stormy eyes. "Would now be the wrong time to tell you that I get as hard as this stake when you talk shop?"

Warmth suffused her cheeks, but she refused to look down. "Your timing is worse than mine, Mr. Lane."

Grinning, he tucked the stake into his inner coat pocket. "Tit for tat, Mrs. Lane." His expression slid back to seriousness. "You do not think that she has left town? Given that she torched her own home?"

"Lena would not run. She knows I am coming. She must have known the moment Mrs. Noble scattered into tiny spiders. Masters can mentally communicate with their acolytes." She brushed an errant flake of soot off of Win's shoulder. "Now, may we proceed? I can feel her down there, waiting for me."

That did not appear to please him, for his shoulders tensed and he held his walking stick more securely. However, he opened the door without argument. "So you know," he said as he took her hand and guided her through the threshold, "I will not hesitate to destroy this woman should she try to hurt you."

Poppy thought of Jack Talent hanging from iron spikes, and her blood heated. "I am tempted to do so even without any outward threat. But let us speak to her first."

The door opened, releasing dank air and the scent of smoke. The air grew cooler as they descended. Water damage stained the crimson silk walls with dark patches, and the rug underfoot was rumpled as if kicked up by a stampede of feet. The emptiness of the place was pervasive, a living thing that had Poppy's senses heightening. Gaslights hissed and threw off shadows that seemed to move as she went by. Side by side, she and Win walked along the abandoned corridor, passing quiet rooms where expensive furniture lay tipped on its side or knocked askew.

Down another flight of stairs they went, the acrid tang of smoke giving way to a headier perfume of incense and blood. Win visibly tensed, his hand staying close to his coat where he'd tucked the stake.

"Her parlor is there," Poppy said in a low voice as she gestured toward the red lacquered door at the end of the corridor. A white slipper lay abandoned and forlorn in the hallway. She stepped over it, her gaze set upon the door.

Win's hand touched her elbow. "I enter first." The look in his eye gave little room for argument.

She didn't. She knew Lena would not hurt them. Not yet. Poppy's hands clenched her skirts as she strode forward.

Just as she remembered it, the little parlor where Lena held court was cozy, the furniture comfortable and worn, and a fire crackled in the grate. Lena sat in her favored place by the hearth. Her pale hands rested upon the arms of a black leather chair, and her legs were tucked up upon the seat. The position was almost feline. And like a cat, she affected a lazy but alert repose. So very alert.

"Mother." Lena inclined her head. "Inspector."

Poppy took a seat in the armchair facing Lena. "Was it necessary to burn your place down?"

"I do not expect to be here much longer," Lena answered as Winston moved to stand next to Poppy.

As she stared at Lena, Poppy's anger swelled within her breast. "Bloody hell, you sent the undead after us!"

"Having trained you," said Lena smoothly, "I knew you could dispatch them. The intent was to slow you down and hopefully take Lane out of the game." Her dark gaze flicked to Winston. "Apologies, Lane, but you have been a bit of a bastard to Poppy these past months, which rather dampened any feelings of sentimentality toward you."

Win's expression was bland as he stared her down. "I'd say your current actions outshine any of mine."

Lena glared at him, then gave a dismissive shrug.

Poppy, however, was not about to be shrugged off. "Why?"

Lena's dark hair swung forward as she reached for the silver cup resting on the table at her side. She took a deep drink. "You were not to know about Moira Darling."

Poppy's back teeth met. "Who is she?"

Lena's pale finger ran along the rim of her cup. "I have sworn not to tell you."

"Even though it threatens Poppy's child?" Win snapped. Shadows danced over his features, and his eyes flashed with bright anger.

The corners of Lena's eyes tightened. A flinch for her. "It is an uncomfortable situation."

Poppy leaned in, the chair creaking beneath her. "And was it worth it?" she hissed. "To torture Jack Talent?" Bitterness coated her tongue, and she swallowed against it.

Lena looked away, into the fire. "I was most displeased with my acolytes." The delicate curve of her jaw bunched as she lifted her eyes to Poppy. "They were to use his blood, not get...carried away."

Win's hand curled into a fist. " 'Carried away?' That is

what you would call it?" He sneered. "Your control over your staff is severely lacking, madam."

"They have been destroyed," she said. "Painfully."

"Not good enough," Poppy said. "He would not have been under their control had you not ordered it."

Obsidian eyes bore into her. "I know. Which is why I have waited for you to mete out a punishment."

Poppy shot to her feet. "I don't want to mete out a bloody punishment! I want you to tell me who the hell Moira Darling is and why you feel the need to protect her."

Lena's head tilted back. "I made a vow. You know all about those, Poppy Ann."

Poppy's body jerked as if struck. "You would have Isley take my child?" She leaned over Lena then. "My *child*, Lena."

Neither of them spoke as they held each other's gaze. Lena's red mouth quivered once, but then went still. "I will tell you if you promise not to give Isley what he wants from her."

A red haze washed over Poppy's sight. Behind her, she could almost feel Win quivering with rage as well. Poppy looked down at her lieutenant. "I could make you talk. You know we have ways that would leave you begging."

Lena merely blinked. "You would not get your answers, and you know it." She sighed then, and her voice grew uncharacteristically soft. "You will want to agree, Poppy. Trust me on this one last thing."

Poppy's throat worked as she looked at her old friend. Lena had to be at least one hundred years old, and though she could have done anything she wanted with her life, she'd chosen to stay with the SOS, training others and keeping their secrets safe.

A sense of dull foreboding crept up Poppy's back.

Lena was loyal. To a fault. Why had she betrayed Poppy? Poppy's heart pounded against her ribs. The unease grew until it was all she could do not to turn and run from the room. But the heaviness within her womb and the feel of Win at her back made her stay. "Fine," she said. "I will not give it to him."

"Poppy!"

She turned at Win's protest. "She's right. We won't know any other way."

Win appeared mutinous. His lean body vibrated with fury, but he did not protest. Poppy stepped back a pace, not wanting to be close to Lena. "Tell me," she said. "Who is Moira Darling?"

As if gathering herself, Lena sat straighter. "She was Isley's lover. It was doomed from the beginning."

Poppy sank back into her seat. "She was SOS."

"Yes," said Lena. "Isley was… You only know to hate him. You have no idea how charismatic he could be. How passionate." Her gaze turned inward, and she stared off into the fire. "She loved him, you see. Without meaning to, she did."

"How long did it go on?" Poppy asked softly, not wanting to break the spell.

"Years."

Poppy's breath caught, and Lena looked back with a wry smile. "Many years. I think… I think he loved her too." She leaned her head back against the chair. "But he detested that immortals hid from weak humans as if they ought to be ashamed. It was he who started the Nex, you know."

Poppy gave a short nod. She knew that much.

Lena continued. "She pled with Isley to understand that for humans to know the truth would bring about pain and chaos. It was a long-standing argument." Lena's chest lifted and fell on a soft sigh. "He kept playing his tricks, and she kept ignoring them, because she could not let him go. He was like a disease within her. And then the inevitable happened."

Lena sat up and rested an elbow on her crossed leg. "She ended it. For you see, she finally realized that passion without trust, without compromise, was a useless thing that only served to burn her out."

"Isley did not take it well?" Win asked, his voice as soft and rough as Poppy's had been.

"No. There were . . . complications." Lena's black gaze flicked to Poppy. "She was with child."

The air in the room vanished. On stiff limbs, Poppy rose and paced away. "A child." Her tone was brittle, disbelieving. But she did believe, and it made her ill. His child for hers. She braced a hand upon the back of the chair she'd vacated.

Lena did not move. "He promised not to interfere with her children," she whispered. "But he wanted this one. Because this one turned out to be male. He believed the boy would inherit his legacy, be made into what he was."

"Children?" An ocean roared in Poppy's ears. Somehow she made her numb lips move. "I thought . . ."

Lena rose with subtle grace. "No, not me."

Poppy swallowed hard. Dimly she felt Win's hand slipping into her ice cold one. "Moira Darling?"

"A nickname for Mary," Lena said. "His Mary Margaret darling."

Poppy broke free from Win's grasp. "Oh Jesus."

Win looked wildly between the two of them. "Mary as in Mary Margaret Ellis?" He paled.

"Yes," said Lena. "As in Poppy's mother."

Poppy sucked in a breath and then another. "Is he . . . Is he my father?"

The distaste and regret in Lena's expression spoke before she did. "Yes."

"My sisters." Fear for their safety had her surging toward the door.

"He cannot get to them. Nor the boy." Lena's fists pressed against her thighs as she looked up at Poppy. "It was a bargain Isley and Mary Margaret made from the beginning. A safeguard laid down by your mother. Isley cannot know his children unless someone presents them to him."

"What do you mean 'cannot know'?"

"Just that. He literally cannot see his own children, even if they are right in front of him. The agreement won't allow it. Unless another person presents his children to him, they are invisible to his eyes. She did so with you." Lena's gaze slid away. "He lost interest after that. Until he knew he was to have a son. They fought over it. And he killed her. I think it was an accident, for his rage knew no bounds afterward."

Poppy paced again, ending up at the wall and slumping against it. "A brother."

Lena did not blink. "When the baby was born, Margaret told everyone that he had died. I took a blood oath to hide the babe away where Isley could not get him and to do everything in my power to keep the babe's existence secret."

Poppy uttered a vicious inward curse. To a sanguis demon, nothing was as sacred as a blood vow. Its bond was stronger than friendship or kin. To break it would fracture a sanguis's soul. And Poppy's mother knew this well.

As if reading Poppy's mind, Lena gave a slow nod.

"When I heard of the bargain Isley had made with the Inspector, I knew I would ultimately fail. But I had to try."

Lena had made her vow, but Poppy could not condone the actions she took to keep it. "Where is my brother?"

Lena's lips flattened.

"Where, Lena?" She pushed off the wall and stalked closer. "He is my brother! My sisters' brother too."

"He is more his father's child than his mother's. If you expose him to Isley, he may turn for ill. You cannot taint him with this life."

"Do not... I will not keep another one of my mother's secrets in the name of protection! No more."

"Then I will not tell you where he is."

Poppy did not think. The back of her hand met Lena's cheek with a blow that made her bones burn and sent Lena's head snapping to the side. Momentum still carried her arm forward when Lena reared, her fangs out, her nails extended. She could take Poppy's head with one swipe. But a blur of movement and a looming dark form came between them.

A loud thud sounded on the wall as Win slammed Lena into it, setting the crystals in the sconces tinkling. In a blink, he had her pinned, the long stake in his hand jammed up under her chin with enough force to tilt Lena's head back. Freezing, she eyed the stake and then Win.

His face, twisted with rage, was an inch from Lena's white fangs. "Tell me, have I the way of it?" He tightened his grip on the stake, and Lena sucked in a breath. A trickle of garnet blood ran down her neck. "I wouldn't want to get it wrong now."

"That should do," she said through her teeth. Her dark gaze slid to Poppy. "You owed me that hit. I should not have tried to strike back. Now call your dog to heel."

Win bared his teeth. "You do not give orders to her." Slashed of face and murder in his eyes, he appeared the monster in the room. But it was simply his strength unfettered by civilization. He'd been torn apart and reformed into something more. Strange as it was, Poppy could not shake the feeling that part of him had been found rather than lost. That Winston Lane had finally become wholly what he was meant to be.

Beyond the crackle of fire in the grate and the sound of the mantel clock ticking came an unmistakable cry, a long, almost mournful sound that ended on a sharp, rising note that spoke of rage. Win paled, but his concentration did not ebb. Lena too paled. As if answering the first howl, another, and another cry rang out. The call of wolves.

"They call for you, Lena." Poppy took a step toward her, speaking as if her heart was not broken. "Jack Talent is Ian Ranulf's kin. He thinks of him as a son. He calls for blood."

Lena's eyes narrowed. "I do not fear The Ranulf."

Poppy glanced at Win. "Let her go." When Win tensed, she said, "Ian has the greater claim. Let him have it."

Another howl broke out. Stronger. It was The Ranulf's call.

"For what we were," Poppy said, "I will delay them, give you a head start." Sadness filled her breast and made it throb. It would enrage Ian, but despite what Lena had done, she would do this small thing for her.

Win stepped back, a swift move that gave him space to defend himself should Lena retaliate. But she did not. With dignity, she straightened her gown and smoothed her hair. "I will not run from him."

"Go then," Poppy said to Lena. "Face your fate, and maybe you shall come out alive."

Cool and implacable as always, Lena nodded sharply. Standing next to Win, she appeared little more than a girl just out of the schoolroom. An illusion if ever there was one. "I trust you to make the proper decision, Poppy Ann Ellis Lane." Her dark eyes drifted over Poppy's face, and her tone softened. "You are a better leader than your mother was. Stronger of heart."

Later Poppy would feel this. *Later.* She held her breath as she nodded back.

Lena blinked once. "He's with Cornelius Evernight in County Clare, being raised as an Evernight. Margaret named him St. John."

Poppy's throat convulsed. She could not speak.

"Be careful, child." Her black eyes stared, unblinking. "The Nex infiltrated my brood and turned them against me. Even now, most of the Onus are converting to their side, lured by promises of greater power and free rein to prey on humans. Dark times lie ahead, I fear."

In the next breath, Lena was gone, moving from the room with such speed that it made a mockery of their efforts to threaten her earlier. Had Lena wanted to kill either of them, she would have done so.

Beyond the room, the howls came again, and then snarls and the gnashing of teeth. When her mother had died, it was Lena who had filled that role, Lena that she placed her trust in. Hearing her die cut through Poppy's soul. Poppy cried out and turned toward Win. His arms came around her tight and strong. He was shaking, his flesh cold where she pressed her face against his neck. But he held her, leaning heavily against the wall. The sounds of wolves fighting grew louder. It was his nightmare, she knew. Just as she knew that he fought now to govern that terror.

"Win." She clung more tightly.

They clutched each other, cheeks pressed together, breathing the same deep breaths as the sounds of violence ran their course.

Win's hand upon her head was a grounding weight. His smoky voice whispered at her ear. "I would take your pain into me if I could."

Her lips brushed the lobe of his ear as she answered. "I know."

The pain would only grow worse, for she now had to decide if she would give up her innocent brother to save her child. And she would have to tell her sisters. Everything.

# Chapter Thirty-four

Poppy and Winston stayed inside of Hell until the sounds of fighting had died down and Ian walked into the room. Bathed in sweat and blood, he'd wrapped a kilt about his lean frame but wore nothing else. Proof that he'd fully turned to face Lena. He was the only lycan with the skill, and it gave him a tremendous advantage.

"Is it done?" Win asked for Poppy.

Ian's chest lifted and fell in a light rhythm. "No." He cursed roundly. "She got away."

Poppy stiffened in Win's arms and turned around to fully face Ian. "What do you mean?"

"She pulled some bloody spider trick and fell apart on me just before the killing blow." He wrenched a hand through his hair. "Turned into spiders and scattered to the four bloody winds." He scowled as if still picturing the act. "Haven't seen her do that before."

"We are familiar with the trick," said Win.

Poppy's heart raced. Lena alive. She did not know how to feel about it. Ian's blue gaze burned into her. "I should be after her soon. But I wanted to know what she said. Anything that might help Jack."

Poppy sighed. "She hadn't meant for things to go that way with Talent." She held up a staying hand. "It does not condone it, nor did she try to. Only that what happened to Talent wasn't her intention. The Nex had the greater hand in this."

Ian said a few harsh words in Gaelic before giving Poppy a terse nod. "Regardless, I'll be hunting her down soon enough. I'll have my own answers from the wee bitch."

"I will not stop you, Ian," Poppy said. "I only ask that you wait until later. There are things I must discuss with my sisters." She leaned against Win, unable to stop from doing so. "Daisy will need you."

Ian grunted. "Aye, well, let's get on with it." He hesitated and looked at Win. "The rest of the clan has gone."

Win laughed shortly. "Lovely of you to worry about my tender feelings, but I live in your bloody house, Ian." His expression darkened. "And there are far worse things to haunt me than wolves."

Winston sat quietly in Poppy's office at the SOS. Ian had gone to collect the family, and Poppy was off readying herself to confront her sisters with the truth. Before she had gone, she had shown him this little section of her life. Even though his initial reaction had been one of hurt, the same hurt that invaded him whenever he thought of the other life she'd hidden away from him, her tidy yet comfortable office carried her scent and was imbued with the feel of her in a way that had him growing still and thoughtful. She'd asked him before if he'd ever forgive her. Sitting in her chair, he touched her files, stroked the smooth polish of her desk, and followed the path of a crack along the ceiling plaster with his eyes. She was more like him than he'd ever imagined.

Before, he'd felt a connection to her on a level that was instinctual and had appreciated her quick mind and strong opinions. Now he knew with every fiber of his being that she was his. Not as a possession, but his in a way that made him who he was. Take Poppy out of the equation, and he was all wrong, an uncompleted work. He'd thought he'd known his wife all these years. Now? Now he understood his wife.

Needing to see her, he rose from the chair, but the door opened. Mr. Smythe, Poppy's secretary—which might have been one of Win's biggest shocks—walked in. The older man was stiff, pale, and proper.

"Mr. Smythe," Win said as the man simply stood in the entrance, his collar sharp and his suit unwrinkled. "How may I be of service?"

Mr. Smythe closed the door behind him before leaning against it in a lazy manner. A smile eased over his sharp features, and Win's blood ran cold.

"You," Win said.

"Me? Mr. Lane?" Smythe came away from the door with elegant grace. "You do sound rather accusatory."

Win's hands curled into fists. "Good. I am accusing. What the bloody hell do you want now, Jones?"

Jones chuckled and then sat in the chair placed in front of Poppy's desk. "I suppose there is no fooling you."

"I do not believe you've really tried." Win did not want to sit. Nor did he want to stand like a ninny while Jones stared up at him through the eyes of Mr. Smythe. So he sat, planting his feet and keeping his arms loose at his sides so that he might move quickly should the need arise. "What now?"

Jones ignored the question and looked about Poppy's office with idle ease. It made Win's skin prickle. Jones did not belong here. Unfortunately, Win did not have a way to get him the hell out. When Jones had finished his perusal, he turned back to Winston. "Did you kill my colonel?"

"Your colonel?" Win's pulse thudded dully against his neck.

"His soul was mine, thus *he* was mine."

The look in Jones's eyes was telling. By logic, Winston was also his. Win swallowed down his nausea. "I rather thought that you killed the colonel." Of course, they now knew it had been Lena's doing. Win had to be careful, and so he glared at Jones with hard accusation. A little deflection could not hurt his cause.

"Kill him?" Jones scoffed. "He was a gift for you. A nice little breadcrumb to help you along the trail."

Win leaned forward and laced his fingers together. "You know, you could simply tell me what you want. It is an easy thing, really."

Jones snorted then went back to glancing about Poppy's office. "Do you know I am one of the SOS's top criminals, so to speak? They've been trying to be rid of me since their inception." His smile grew tighter. "Which is really rather tedious. They ought to revere me. Gods have tried to destroy me and failed. And yet this ragtag band of do-gooders thinks they can do better."

"Is that what bothers you about Poppy?" Win settled further into his chair, as if he wasn't twitching with the need to strike Jones down at that moment. "That she managed to imprison you?" Poppy was the key to this. The thought both gave Win a chill of terror and left him with a small window of hope.

A small flame appeared to flare in each of Jones's

irises. "You know, that is precisely what bothers me about Poppy Ann Ellis Lane."

"Mmm." Winston ran his thumb along the edge of his chair arm before looking up. "You give her too much power by seeking this revenge."

In an instant, the room grew several degrees hotter as Jones growled low in his chest.

Win watched him as one watches a mad dog, waiting for the inevitable strike. "Who are you? Really?"

"Nothing your small human mind could comprehend." Pale, veiny hands slammed onto the desk top and trembled. "When did you plan to tell me you found Moira Darling?"

*Bugger.* Win's pocket watch ticked overloud as they stared each other down. "But you don't want Moira Darling," he said finally. "You want what she stole."

"Come now, Lane, you asked for directness. You know very well that he is my son."

Winston paused and studied the demon. "You've been watching us this whole time." He didn't know how Jones managed to be everywhere, but it left Win with a foul taste in his mouth.

"Some things I'd rather not witness," Jones said with a noise of disgust. "You are a fool to believe that by satisfying your wife's needs you will make her compliant." His nostrils flared, and another burst of hot air filled the room. "Elemental witches fuck because they enjoy it, not out of loyalty."

Win's hands stayed heavy upon the cold arms of his chair. "Poppy is not Mary Margaret."

"No," said Jones, "she's not." Without warning, he shot forward and got into Win's face. "Now tell me, where is my son?"

Win wouldn't tell him even if Jones were to conjure up a werewolf here and now. "If you've been watching, then you ought to know where the boy is."

Jones bared his teeth in a snarl. His reply was halting and forced. "And you should know that I cannot comprehend his location until a human being willingly presents him to me."

"How unfortunate," Win murmured.

Like a snake, Jones struck, catching Winston by the neck. Win scrambled for purchase, his throat locked tight in an agonizing grip. Crimson flooded Jones's irises. "It appears that you do not take my threat seriously."

Though Win's vision had gone spotty and his brain screamed for air, he refused to cower. He glared back at the demon.

Jones hauled Win close enough to feel the heat of his breath and smell the sulfur in it. "I gave you a way out, and now you throw it in my face. For that, I am taking your soul with me as well as your child's."

"Bullshit," Winston ground out. "You cannot—"

"Cannot what? I never said your soul was yours to keep." He laughed lightly. "Now did I?"

No, he hadn't. Win had just assumed. His guts rolled as the realization sank in.

Jones's eyes gleamed, obviously seeing the horror dawn over Winston's features. "You think to play with the devil and win? Be assured, you are mine, whether you give me my child or not. Taking your soul is child's play to me. Would you like to see?" The tip of Jones's finger burned against his forehead, and everything went dark.

Ice cold, then raging heat, flared through him in an instant. Every fiber of his being screamed at once, yet he knew he hadn't made a sound. Jones's finger seemed to burrow into his skull, and sharp, blinding pain shot down his center. The touch tugged at his soul, pulling it out of his body and into Jones's finger. Win lost himself, lost all sense of what he was. Screams and the sharp tang of pure, unending terror surrounded him, growing larger and more violent, until he feared he might shatter. He sobbed, but he had no body, no way of escape. Utter hopelessness filled him. *Please. Please.*

And then it was gone, and he found himself huddled on the ground. Shaking and covered in sweat, he looked up at the demon standing over him, still wearing the appearance of Mr. Smythe.

"Have I made myself clear?" the demon said.

Win's teeth chattered, and his heart threatened to beat out of his chest. "Fuck you, Jones."

Jones grinned, revealing a row of brown and jagged teeth "If you ask again nicely when I take you to Hell, you just might get your wish." There was a pause in which the air in the room grew thin. Jones's expression turned almost serene, his voice soft. "You and I both know Poppy will never agree to give me what I want. I need an heir. If I cannot have the boy, then give me Poppy. Do it and you can keep your child, once it's born, and your life. I'll allow you that much."

His child. Win hadn't expected to have a child. Not after years of Poppy being barren. Her disappointment was his, but he'd been resigned to the notion. Now that he knew that a child grew within her womb, he loved the unknown babe with a fierceness that almost frightened him.

He forced his mouth to work. "Why Poppy?"

"Come now, Lane. You are no fool." Jones paused, looking, for once, distinctly uncomfortable. "'Tis a fair trade, after all. She does not even want the child."

"Shut up!" Win wouldn't believe that of Poppy, wouldn't let Jones drive a wedge between them.

But Jones merely shook his head as if pitying him. "I am her blood. When she is away from me, I can see through her eyes, know her fears. She doubts her ability to rear this child. But you don't, do you, Lane? Take it, and leave my firstborn to me."

And all this time, Win had thought Jones followed him. The bloody bastard. Win struggled to rise, but whatever Jones had done to him had left him weak as a babe. "Get out."

With a shrug, Jones stepped away from the desk and headed again for the door. "You have one more day. The choice is yours, Lane."

"I will never give her up. Never." He said it with all the conviction in his heart, but bloody, bloody hell, Jones had him by the cods, and they both knew it.

Jones's smile was tired, but the gleam in his eyes spoke of victory. "Then you are, as you say, buggered, mate."

# Chapter Thirty-five

Someone made a sound. Ian, perhaps; he had the least patience. Poppy stirred, realizing she'd simply been sitting there as her family sat around the SOS conference table waiting for her to speak. Best to get it over with quickly.

Her voice was modulated and smooth in the quiet. "What I must tell you cannot go further than this room."

"We rather thought that a given, dearest," said Daisy with a small smile. She was trying, Poppy knew, to ease the way. Poppy appreciated it, especially given that Miranda would be the angriest. She still had not forgiven Poppy for withholding information about her own powers. Poppy did not blame her one whit.

Miranda would truly hate her now. Daisy too. All those expectant gazes, all of them knowing they wouldn't like what they were going to hear, but waiting for it anyway. For one horrid moment, Poppy feared she might jump up and flee. Then her gaze collided with Win's. He'd entered quietly and stayed in the back of the room, reclining against the corner wall, his hands thrust deep in his pockets. The pose might have been construed as relaxed; he was anything but. Tension tightened the line of his shoulders and flattened his mouth. But his eyes softened, and she could all but read the message there: *Out with it, old girl. It won't get better with the waiting.*

In this, they were together. She spoke again.

"There is a demon that is after Win and me.... If we do not give him what he wants, he will take our child's soul."

"What!" Miranda slammed forward. "You are expecting?"

Poppy managed a small smile. "I'm afraid so."

Archer and Ian exchanged a look that made Poppy think they'd already figured as much.

"It isn't a prison sentence, you know," said Daisy, rather heatedly, and Poppy winced. As a GIM, Daisy would never have a child of her own.

"I only meant..." Poppy couldn't say more without breaking down so she looked away.

"Well then," said Archer, "we shall give him what he wants."

We. The simple word warmed her heart, and broke it all the same. "As much as I'd love to," she said, "I cannot." Poppy touched her brow and then let her hand drop. Christ, she needed to get the words out. "He wants his son."

Archer's dark brows rose. "Why is it that you refuse to give this demon his son?"

"For God's sake, Poppy," Daisy said, "if you know where the spawn is, give it to this thing and be done with it."

"She cannot do it." Win's smoky voice held surprising strength as he bit out the truth.

"Why?"

That from all of them.

"Because," said Poppy, "the demon's son is our brother." And with that, chaos descended.

It was all Winston could do to be heard. Miranda's chair had gone up in flames, which Poppy almost absently doused with a blast of ice. The room shook with Daisy's deep tremors, and Winston rather feared for the foundations. And all of them shouted at once. Win took a long look at the chaos, and at his wife, who sat stiffly in her seat.

"Enough!" He slammed his walking stick down on the scorched wood table. The resounding bang made them all flinch, but it shut them up as well. He leveled a gaze around the room. "Sit."

On the inside, Win felt sick, but he simply looked around to see if they were all settled before glancing back at Poppy. "Explain it to them."

Poppy's white hands fell to her lap, and her dark gaze turned inward as she stared at the tabletop before her. The red fan of her lashes blocked her eyes as she recounted what Lena had told them about Margaret and Jones's affair. When she finished, Miranda blanched. "Bloody hell. Are we his as well?"

Poppy flinched. "Yes. I did not know until today," she snapped before her sisters could protest again.

"Hell." Miranda pinched the bridge of her nose.

"You all remember Mother as this benevolent protector," Poppy said. "You have no idea what she really was. The lies she could tell. Or how iron her will could be."

"I'm beginning to get an idea," Daisy muttered.

Poppy's face flushed red but she forged onward. "He killed our mother over this."

"Mother died due to childbirth," Miranda said woodenly.

"No. It was..." Poppy nibbled her bottom lip. "It was a lie."

"God damn it, Pop!" Daisy banged a fist on the table. "Of all the low, disgusting—"

"I cannot make amends." Poppy rested a hand on the table. "We need to discuss our brother. His name is St. John. He's being raised in Ireland by the Evernights, one of the oldest SOS families."

"He ought to be around sixteen," murmured Daisy. She smiled a little. "My God, a brother."

"Hell." Miranda plopped her head into her hands and groaned. "We can't give him up." She lifted her head. "But I'll be damned if we give up your child."

Winston had to smile at that. "My sentiments exactly."

Archer leaned back in his chair and regarded them all. "What do you propose to do? Is there a way to get out of the bargain? Kill the demon perhaps?"

From the gleam in Ian's eye, Win gathered he thought this was a perfect idea. Poppy, however, braced her arms upon the table, her mouth set in a grim line. "I have not been able to destroy him, only to send him back to hell."

"How did you do it?" Win asked. He'd never gotten the specifics, and he needed them now more than ever.

"With one of these." She pulled a small object from her skirt pocket and set it on the table.

"A scarab?" Archer sounded as dubious as Win felt. The basalt carving of the Egyptian dung beetle was flat and roughly the size of his palm.

"It might look innocuous, but this little fellow becomes quite active when in the presence of demons. It is a tool of Ammit, the Eater of Souls."

Archer shifted uncomfortably. When he'd married

Miranda, Archer had been turning into a soul eater, one of Ammit's children. He eyed the scarab askance. "What does it do?"

"Rest it on the heart of a demon of Egyptian origin, and the scarab will judge it. If the demon is unworthy, the scarab will deliver the demon's soul to Duat, the underworld, and then on to a place we'd call Hell."

"I wish we'd had use of one of those before," Miranda muttered, and Poppy gave her a tired smile.

"Had I known what Archer was becoming," she said, "I would have given you one. However, it isn't as easy as it looks. One has to get near enough to the demon to place it against the demon's chest." Her expression grew hard and remote. "One is more likely to lose one's head than succeed."

But Poppy had done so before. Cold blew through Win's gut at the thought. His wife rested her thin hand upon her belly, low where no one would likely notice. But he did, and his heart twisted. She would not face Isley again. For he could not face the idea of her being hurt, nor their child. It was all he could do to keep himself together. He would not see his child born or grow. Would it be a boy, as Isley thought? Or a girl? With shining red hair like her mother's? Clenching his jaw, he looked away from Poppy rather than risk falling to his knees and burrowing his head into her lap.

"It works on Isley," she was saying. "Trial and error have taught me that. However, while he might be dragged back to Hell, he does not die." Her long finger touched the back of the scarab.

Archer's brow drew into a scowl as he looked down at the scarab. "The Egyptians believe that to know a person's name is to have dominion over them. Were Isley's true name inscribed on the scarab, it might have the power to hold Isley in Hell forever."

"It is a good thought," Poppy said wanly. "Only we've just one more day, and I've no idea where to begin to search." With a sigh, she leaned back in her seat. "The real problem is that regardless of whether we kill him, all bargains in play would stand. Any souls belonging to Isley would be his to take with him to hell."

Perfect. Win ran a hand over the back of his neck and paced. "In short, we are buggered."

They gaped at him, and he scowled. "I am capable of uttering the word 'bugger', you know."

Ian laughed, shortly but without much vigor. "Do not break my illusions, old boy."

Win tried to smile but failed. "Look. Poppy and I will have to find a way."

"Bollocks to that," Archer said with heat. "Let us help you."

"You can." Win moved to the table and braced his fists on top of it. "You take care of Talent," he said to Ian and Daisy before looking at Miranda and Archer. "We need to protect the boy."

"Of course," said Miranda.

Poppy's gaze turned to her youngest sister. "Lena said he was more his father's son. Isley, aside from trickery and bargains, shares a similar talent with you, dearest. Fire."

Miranda blanched. "Hell." She slipped her hand into Archer's. "We'll go to the boy. I don't know what we'll say..." She shook her head. "But we'll go."

"Simply tell him the truth," Poppy said.

The transformation of Miranda's features was chilling. "The truth," she said faintly. "By all means." She took a breath and rose. "I'm sorry, Pop, I know this predicament is hard for you, that you've had a rough go of it, but to lie to us about Mother. Even after she was gone. I just can't... I need to be away from you for a while."

Poppy nodded shortly. "Yes." It was a ghost of sound.

Daisy rose as well. "You would never have stood for such treatment, sister mine." Golden curls trembled as she shook her head. "And yet you did so to us. Badly done." Daisy left the room with Miranda and Archer. Ian hesitated for a moment, looking pained, but he gave Poppy a short nod and followed his wife.

Winston moved to call her sisters back and got all the way to the door when he stopped. He had no right to interfere. When he turned back to give Poppy some bit of consolation, she was gone.

# Chapter Thirty-six

Winston walked through the house he had shared with Poppy for the past fourteen years. Standing within its walls flooded him with both comfort and pain. He did not know what made him search up rather than down. He'd never gone onto his roof before. Really, why would one? Even so, his steps took him there, steady and sure as he climbed the risers to the attic. The temperature did not rise as he expected but grew distinctly cooler, prickling his skin.

His breath came out in frosty puffs as he reached the top. An icy breeze, unnatural in the late summer evening, blew through the open window at the top of the landing. He crouched down and glanced through it, only to shiver when soft snowfall landed upon his neck. White billows of snow covered the wide ledge that ran along the front of the house and melted just as quickly as it competed against the surrounding summer heat.

Cursing beneath his breath, he eased out of the window and picked his way along. She sat in a small, flat space between windows. Poppy was a tall, strong woman, but seeing her huddled down, she appeared diminished, almost fragile. And it made his heart hurt. Big, feathery flakes of snow fell, covering her bright hair and slim shoulders in a mantle of pure white. He glanced up, fascinated to see where it began, but the murky sky held its secrets.

Obviously sensing him, her shoulders hunched in closer, and her head bent down as if, by avoiding eye contact, he'd somehow not see her. He eased his coat off and sat next to her, ignoring the ice that seeped into his trousers. She did not move as he gently brushed the snow from her shoulders and then put his coat over her. "You'll freeze out here."

Poppy shrugged. "I don't really feel it." She glanced in his direction, not meeting his eyes. "You ought to take this back before you catch a cold."

"My gentleman's sense of honor insists that you wear it. Even if I am the one freezing my arse off."

A small smile played about the corners of her mouth, as he had hoped, but it did not remain. "I don't know why I can't control it anymore." She scowled down at her hands. "It is irksome in the extreme."

"Perhaps the baby affects you?" he offered with due caution. Women, he'd heard, were notoriously sensitive about such matters.

But her scowl waned in favor of a short nod. "Perhaps so." She sighed and then took a deep breath, and with it, the snowfall stopped. "Better?" she asked as she gathered the ends of the coat sleeves into her lap.

He drew his knees up and let his forearms dangle over them. "I don't know. Are you better?"

The elegant column of her neck moved on a swallow

as she glared at sights unseen. "I deserve this," she said at last. "Every bit of their censure. Of yours." Her lip wobbled but she bit down on it. "Even so, it wears on me, Win."

He drew her against his chest, where it was warmer, where she could rest against his heart. He held her tightly as she started to cry, silently at first and then in choking sobs. His Poppy crying. He'd never seen her do it. And it made him angry, made him want to slay dragons for her. Only he'd been one of the fiends who had made her cry.

"Let it out, sweet." He pressed a fierce kiss to her temple. "Let it out. I've got you."

She wrapped herself around him as a child might. Gently he rocked her, stroking the smooth crown of her head. A sound from the windows had him stiffening. Miranda and Daisy stood at the edge of the roof. Twin looks of disbelief held their expressions as they watched their sister sob. A part of him wanted to snarl at her sisters and drive them away. He wouldn't see Poppy hurt further. But it was not his place, and they deserved to have their say.

Sensing his tension, Poppy stilled and lifted her head. Tears gleamed on her reddened cheeks. She flinched, her hands tightening on his shoulders. Win leaned in close. "I will send them away if you want me to."

"No. Thank you. I should talk to them."

"As you wish."

Miranda and Daisy waited for him to approach. They were beautiful women. Stunning, really. Yet he remembered them as girls. Miranda started when he reached out, but she let his hand rest on her cheek.

"We ought to have insisted on bringing you into our house when we left," he said. "I've always regretted that."

Her green eyes widened. "No, brother. My life had to be as it was. Or I would never have found Archer."

He found himself smiling. "I still view you as the little girl who taught me to polka, and yet you are far wiser than me." When her hand clasped his, he leaned closer. "You know, I do not think I'd change a thing either. As you said, one change and the whole story alters."

Miranda's shrewd eyes lit with amusement. "Well played, Winston."

"I've no idea what you mean."

Daisy peered at him, her blue eyes glittering in the way of the GIMs. "Don't you?"

He leaned over and kissed her cheek. "None whatsoever."

Her sisters were here. Horribly, she could not stop sobbing. Her emotions were out of the gate now, stampeding with impunity. Now she clung to Daisy like a child. "I'm so sorry," she whispered against the plump smoothness of Daisy's cheek. "I-I did not mean to hurt you two."

"We know that. You've always tried to balance the world's troubles on your shoulders. You are so strong, sister mine." Daisy's blond curls trembled as she shook her head. "Rock of Gibraltar and all that. I have always been in awe of your strength."

Poppy made a noise of irritation. "It isn't strength. It's tenacity. It simply isn't in me to let go of an endeavor once I start." A lump formed in her throat and made her words thick. "But it is not strength. Each day I feel weaker. So very weary." She clenched her fist, and snow began to fall again, landing in icy flakes upon her skin. "I'd like nothing more than to lay my head down and forget the world, truth be told."

Miranda's voice was soft. "And yet how can a person keep holding on without strength?" Her green eyes assessed Poppy from beneath dark lashes. "You simply have to learn how to lean on one of us now and then."

Poppy stared down at her workworn hand with its short clipped nails. Her wedding ring gleamed on her finger. It was a glorious ring, a delicate gold band that held a fiery orange cabochon carnelian surrounded by diamonds. She'd been speechless when Win had slipped it on her finger, for it spoke of beauty, grace, and strength. His eyes had been dark when he looked at her, and in that moment, she felt as though she was his whole world, that no one existed for him but her, just as he was the only thing right and perfect in her life. *"It is only a ring," he whispered, his fingers warm upon hers. "Not nearly enough to encompass my love for you. But wear it and know that I am yours. Always."*

She'd lost that because she hadn't opened herself up fully. Was it as simple as saying what one felt? Her lips twisted in distaste, but she had to try.

"We always end up bickering," she said to her sisters as she stared at her hand. "But I..." She gathered herself and met her sisters' wary gazes. "I have always wished I could be more like the two of you, able to find light in the darkness." Daisy's eyes widened, and Poppy forged on. "If I pushed you two, it was because I never wanted anything to snuff out your light. I wanted you to be strong and be more than I ever could. And... well, now you both are."

Daisy's lips parted, shock apparently rendering her silent for once. Poppy's face heated, and then Daisy smiled. "Good Lord, but you'll have me watering like a pot in a moment."

Miranda's hands stroked her hair. "Oh, hell, Pop, it isn't as if I've a right to cast stones. I burned down Father's warehouse and ruined the family. And you... You never once shamed me for it." And then she was sobbing too.

Poppy turned into her embrace, trying to quiet her even though she couldn't quiet herself.

Beside them, Daisy began to sniffle. "That's old news. If you really want a confession, I must admit...I was the one who ate those cream caramels Winston sent you when you were courting!" With a pathetic pout, she held her arms out for a hug.

Miranda and Poppy glared at her, and then Miranda snorted. "And you talk of old news."

"You had a caramel smudge on your chin when you denied your sins and did not even notice," Poppy added in disgust.

Daisy scowled. "I felt terribly guilty! For hours!"

"Bah," Miranda said as Poppy wiped at her face. "You merely had a sour stomach to lament."

There was a small silence in which someone sniffled. And then they were laughing.

# Chapter Thirty-seven

*London, 1869—At Home*

**W**inston awoke in the dead of night, knowing immediately that something was wrong. Lying on the big bed he and Poppy had recently purchased for their new home, he focused on the plaster and wood-beamed ceiling above him before taking stock of his surroundings. All was quiet, the room warm from the late spring weather. Why then did his heart race? And then it hit him—Poppy was not beside him. He lurched up and looked around for her. The ghostly blue light of the moon reduced the bedroom to an array of sharp angles and shapeless lumps. Still no Poppy.

Finding his smalls, he slid them on and left the room. Years of avoiding his father's notice gave him the ability to negotiate the narrow stairs that led from the bedroom down to the main flat without a sound. His skin was too tight, twitchy with anxiety that he could not name, and as he descended, so did the temperature. The slight chill that first greeted his feet, then his bare torso gave him pause, but he supposed it was to be expected—the bedroom was always warmer than the rest of the house. Even so, the cool air rushing through his lungs as he breathed felt odd.

Ahead of him, past the dark hall, toward the kitchen, a soft light glowed. For reasons he couldn't name, Win held his tongue and did not call out for Poppy. His heartbeat was a hard rhythm against his throat as he crept toward the door and moved into the kitchen.

There, hunched over the table, was Poppy, her vibrant hair gleaming copper in the light of a single taper. The air here was cooler still, and sharp with silence and tension. She hadn't heard him and he couldn't make himself speak. Inexplicably, he felt as if he were trespassing on her privacy. She appeared to be fiddling with something, the line of her shoulders drawn tight even as she moved. But then she stopped, and her shoulders began to shake. The movement snapped Win out of whatever spell that had hold of him, and he stepped farther into the room.

"Poppy?"

She whipped around, her eyes wide in her pale face. "Win."

He smiled. "Were you expecting someone else?" he teased. His smile faltered when she merely gaped at him, and again came the odd feeling that danger lurked. "What are you doing up, love?"

"I…" She said nothing more, but he'd stopped listening at any rate, for he spied the blood-covered rag that lay in her lap.

"You're hurt!" His bare feet slapped over the icy floor, and he was kneeling before her in the next breath.

"Win." Her voice was a rasp. And her hands were so

very cold when he closed his own over hers. She winced, and he looked down. A deep gash marred her inner forearm. Cursing softly, he picked up the rag and pressed it back over the wound.

"What happened?" he whispered as gently as he could, for the sight of her bleeding left him inexplicably angry. "And why didn't you wake me?"

Poppy was silent for a moment, then she leaned into him. Fell into him, rather, which alarmed him more than anything. Instantly he wrapped his arms around her and held on tight.

"Poppy," he said against her hair. "Tell me what makes you tremble."

Her broken voice was half-lost against his skin. "I..." She took a breath and calmed a bit. "I had a nightmare."

"Sweeting." He stroked her hair. "About what?"

Her slender throat moved with a swallow. "A monster was hunting me." So quietly she spoke that he had to strain to hear her. "He almost had me, but then I...I defeated him, Win." She shook violently, and her good arm slung around his neck. "I defeated him. I did it."

The relief and joy in her voice was so strong that it almost sounded as though she thought the dream real. He knew of such dreams. They lingered in the flesh and shook one's soul.

"Of course you did, my brave love," he said. "I never doubted you for a moment."

She made a sound somewhere between a laugh and a sob and squeezed him tighter. Cooing under his breath, he rose and then, with a bit of shifting, settled on the kitchen bench and settled her upon his lap. Gently, he brushed a long lock of scarlet hair away from her face. "Why did you not wake me?"

Her lids lowered as if she couldn't quite face him. "I did not want to bother you."

Win cupped her cheek and made her look at him. "You will never be a bother to me, Boadicea." His thumb stroked her skin. "You can tell me anything. You know that, don't you?"

She grimaced, and he understood; his Poppy had always been self-sufficient. To the point of stubbornness. Letting her have a moment, he lifted her wounded arm and tended to it. "How did you hurt yourself?"

She tensed again and cleared her throat. "I came down for some tea and grew hungry." A small sound of derision left her. "I suppose the dream still had me, for in my clumsiness, I let the bread knife get the upper hand."

"Poor girl," he murmured, and they shared a smile. Poppy was grace in motion yet oddly clumsy. From time to time, she'd appear with the worst bruises, the result of walking into table corners or some similar accident.

Winston held her close and cleaned her up, quietly talking nonsense until she settled. Then he took her up to bed and tucked her in. It wasn't until much later that he realized there hadn't been any food on the table, nor a bread knife.

# *Chapter Thirty-eight*

❧❧❧

**P**oppy wanted to sleep. She wanted it so badly her eyelids drooped. Yet in the same breath she wanted to act. Crying things out with her sisters had drained her, but it had also strengthened her resolve to see this thing with Isley finished. A bath had not helped her relax. Only one thing would, and Win had not returned to their rooms so she stood alone before the rain-streaked window and stared out at the desolate street. The night was thin, and even the most exuberant of revelers were now in bed. All in bed, save her and Win.

While Poppy might have stayed at her own home, she'd returned to Ranulf House. Call it stubbornness, call it pride, but she wouldn't, couldn't return home with Win until things were settled between them. Besides, Win's things were still here at Ranulf House. So here she would wait.

Perhaps he wouldn't return at all. He'd comforted her well, but some small, childish part of her feared that he'd done so out of pity. A humorless snort left her as she rested an arm on the window sash. Why shouldn't he pity her? She'd cocked up her life by hurting everyone she'd ever cared for.

A small click of the door handle had her stiffening. A sliver of light traveled over her shoulders and made the window shine as the door opened. In the reflection of the glass, Win was a tall shadow against a patch of yellow. He stood for a moment, watching her watch him in the window. Then he closed the door behind him with a muted thud. She lost sight of him as the room grew dim once more.

His steps were almost undetectable as he moved farther into the room. "Are you well?"

"As I can be." Still she did not turn. Everything in her screamed for her to go to him, beg him to hold her until she felt whole once more. But she couldn't. She was too raw, an open wound, and he was her salt.

The rustling sounds of him removing his coat and hat filled the void. Domestic sounds. She knew them well. Poppy swallowed convulsively. The moment was almost normal, a peaceful close to the end of a long day. Save nothing would ever be normal again. Sacrifices had to be made. Someone had to die.

She could feel Win getting closer, as if he were a magnetic force and she a length of steel. He stopped behind her, close enough for her to feel his energy and smell his scent. He did not touch her. Not yet, but it was coming, and her whole body tensed with anticipation.

"Why aren't you asleep?" he asked in the quiet.

Poppy blinked down at her hands, so white and clenched upon the sash. When her voice came it was a whisper. "Because you weren't here."

His breath caught on the inhale, then slowly left

him. Win shifted his weight, and the specter of his face appeared at the window, hovering over her shoulder. Poppy closed her eyes against the pain in his expression.

"When you were gone, I never slept," she said. "Not really."

Win's voice cracked between them. "Every night I ached for you." He stepped closer, his heat and his strength bracketing her. Soft lips touched the outer shell of her ear. "Every night I counted myself a fool for leaving." Slowly, so very slowly she might have imagined it, his hands skimmed her arms, setting off little tremors of want in their wake. "You asked me once for forgiveness." He leaned in, his lips just touching the tender point of her neck. "Will you grant it to me?" Wide palms traced her waist, barely touching, just enough to make her tremble with the need to press against him. She stayed her course, her fists pushing against the cold window glass.

Gently, he swept her hair away from her neck, then pressed a lingering kiss there. Poppy's knees went weak.

"I am tired of pretending," he said. "Of spending another agonizing night lying next to you and trying to think of anything else but shagging you until my cock gives out."

"Win." Her voice croaked. She wanted to turn around, to tell him how much she needed him. And yet she was frozen.

"No more, Poppy." His tongue traced a heated path along her neck, back to that spot just below her ear that made her shiver and flush. She did not move, barely breathed. Win's attention was a fragile thing, a dream that she might wake from and find herself alone again. As if sensing her thoughts, his touch grew stronger as he ran his palm up to her throat.

His smoky voice was at her ear. "No more acting as

though I am not so utterly in love with my wife that it tears my heart out not to hold her. Not another night, Poppy. It makes a mockery of what I feel for you."

With agonizing deliberation, his fingers went to the buttons of her dressing gown. Her breath caught just as he slipped the first button free. "From the very first moment I saw you, you were all I thought about."

Cool air crept beneath the widening gap in her dressing gown. She stood before the open window, facing the night, her pulse racing and her breath unsteady.

"All I wanted." He paused, and then his hand slipped underneath her open gown. His palm met with her bare breast, and he groaned low and deep. "All I want."

Gently he played with her, brushing over her areola, lightly cupping the small swell of her breast until it grew heavy and tender, her nipple aching to be pinched. Poppy gritted her teeth. Lust had her lower belly coiling tight and hot.

"Win..." Her breath caught as he worried the very tip of her nipple with his finger. "Don't play."

A low, seductive chuckle rumbled in his chest. His mouth closed over her earlobe, and she gasped when he bit it. "You like it when I play."

Oh, but she did. Her lids fluttered closed when, as if opening a delicate tome, he parted her gown.

Her fists unfurled, and her palms pressed against the glass, foggy now from the heat of her breath. "Win." Their room was dark, but not as dark as the street. Anyone passing by might see her. See them. The knowledge sent fire and ice through her sensitized flesh. Her breath grew to panting. He was exposing her, and he knew it. He knew what it did to her, how it made her heart race and her sex grow white-hot with need.

Win stood quiet, his warm breath stealing over her

neck and down her bare skin. "Just look at you," he whispered. "So lovely and strong."

The dark street opened up before them. The sight of her own breasts jutting out, her nipples hard and dark, sent a thrill of base excitement through her. Every breath she took sent a shiver over her skin. Decadent heat licked over her as she arched, thrusting her breasts toward the window. Win's hard weight pressed into her back. He grunted as his thick erection nudged between her buttocks. "What you do to me, Poppy."

He touched her hair, tilting her head just slightly to get at her neck, and his words vibrated through her as he murmured against her skin, " 'Through the dancing poppies stole, a breeze, most softly lulling to my soul.' " His teeth grazed her. "You are the spark that lights my soul, Boadicea."

Then his hands . . . those big, rough hands glided along her tender skin, touching her aching nipples in brief acknowledgment before sliding down. An inarticulate sound left her as his fingers delved between her thighs.

Her legs trembled as she parted them further. For him. The feel of him teasing, and the window like a big eye upon her, not letting her hide. His broad chest rocked against her shoulder blades with each breath he took as he explored her with slow, gentle strokes.

"Softly," he whispered. "Always so softly, until the moment I take you hard."

Gods, but she wanted it. Fast and hard. From behind, until she couldn't stand, couldn't think of anything other than him and how she felt when she was under his control. He set her free. Undone, her forehead thunked against the glass, her eyes tightly shut. But his arm snaked around her, his free hand coming up to cup just beneath her chin. He forced her head up, made her pay attention. His reflection was a blur in the glass, all but his eyes that gleamed in the dark.

"Do you want me, Poppy?" The long length of his cock ground into her. "Here?"

Her knees buckled. Only his arm about her kept her from falling. "Yes," she managed. "Yes."

He pushed a finger into her. A brief invasion to make her quake. His hand slipped away, leaving her wanting. His lips touched her cheek. "Show me." He stepped back, far enough so that she might turn.

Her legs wobbled, and the dressing gown slithered to the floor as she faced him. He stood before her, tall and proud, his scars white in the shadows of his face. She traced the one that led to his mouth. Back and forth, she rubbed the small knot of scar tissue that bisected his upper lip. Win's deep-set gaze was a living thing, burning her skin. His lips parted for her, and her thumb slipped inside him. Heat and wetness. He sucked her with firm pulls, and she swayed. Her thumb slipped free when he spoke.

"Undress me, wife."

He'd taken off his waistcoat, but still remained in shirt-sleeves and trousers. His braces emphasized the width of his shoulders and the length of his lean torso. No words were spoken as her hands slipped beneath the suspenders and slid one then the other off. Crisp linen met her palm, and beneath it his heart pounded. Poppy rested there and shivered, not from cold but for the want of him.

Poppy cupped his cheeks. One smooth cheek, the other bumpy with scars. Slowly, she kissed his ravaged cheek, and his eyes fluttered closed. His lips hovered near hers, close enough to touch, but he did not let her kiss him.

"Finish what you started." His voice was low, nearly stern, but a glint of tender amusement lit his eyes. A dare.

Holding his gaze, she went to work on his shirt. His body canted the slightest bit as she tugged his buttons free. Countless times she had undressed him and still it felt new, slightly forbidden. The heat in his gaze and the sound of his unsteady breath, ratcheting up with each button she eased free, sent her own need rising. And all the time, she was conscious of the window at her back and the humid air kissing her hot skin.

With efficiency born of experience, she pulled his shirt over his head and then simply looked at him. He'd called her lovely. He had no idea what he was to her. His strength, the hatch-work of his scars, the dark golden chest hair that gilded a path down to the bulge beneath his low-lying trousers—all of it made her dizzy with need.

Her mouth found the thick slash along his neck. He swallowed hard as she licked it. She placed a kiss on the hollow of his throat, loving the way his flesh jumped and his breath hitched.

"I forget about them when I am with you."

"Don't," she whispered. "They are testament that you lived." Her soft kisses followed the lines of his scars. He was utterly edible. And so she bit him, her teeth sinking into his hard muscle. Win grunted, his hips thrusting against hers as if he'd been jerked.

"Cheeky girl," he murmured.

Grinning, Poppy nuzzled the spot. Win's heavy hand grasped her nape. His serious eyes bore into her as, exacting gentle but firm pressure, he guided her to her knees. "Now show me."

Kneeling before him, Poppy looked up at him. Only he could command her like this. Only he thought to try, as if he knew how much she needed to let go and be in someone's keeping. The tips of his fingers touched her lower lip. "Give me that lovely mouth, sweeting."

Suppressing a shudder of hot lust, she reached for his trousers. His erection strained against the fabric, pulling the buttons tight. With shaking fingers, she worked him free. Her hands flowed along his skin, smoothing over the rough, long muscles of his thighs as she eased his trousers and smalls down.

Against her cheek, the hard shaft of his cock twitched, nudging up to get her attention. He had it. His heavy cods drew up tight, and the glorious shaft pulsed with life, the head shining and ruddy with impatience.

Her mouth watered. The need to take him set her skin on fire. But she wanted Win as undone as she was. Holding his gaze, she leaned forward. A tender kiss upon his navel had muscles there moving up and down in an unsteady cadence. The skin along his lower abdomen grew tauter, silken. Her teeth grazed the sharp edge of his hip bone, playing there.

He did not let her get away with it. Strong fingers threaded through her hair, gripping her. His scarred hand wrapped around the root of his cock, holding it for her as he pushed her head forward. "Take it, wife. Take me."

It was all she had ever wanted to do. Poppy opened for him. He filled her mouth, and a groan tore from the depths of his chest. She suckled him, a light tease.

"Ah...God, Poppy." The muscles in his forearm stood out as he held the back of her head. "Suck it hard, sweeting." His hips canted as if to make his point. But she held him fast, pressing her hands upon his hips as she paid homage to the very tip of him, loving the smoothness, the taste of him. Loving the way his breath grew ragged and his big body bowed against her.

"Poppy Ann Lane," he ground out, between her light licks, "if you don't..." His breath left in a rush as she drew him in as deep as she could. "Oh, yes." His hand drifted to cup her cheek. "There's a good wife."

She smiled around him. Then her eyes closed as she concentrated on filling her mouth with him. Her tongue drew along his thick ridge, her hands stroking him. His thighs trembled, and she knew he was close to his peak. Win's fingers twined in her hair. He was taking over, holding her head as he worked himself in and out of her mouth. And she shuddered. She was purely feminine, and he was purely male.

The sound of his grunts and the feel of him sliding in and out of her mouth made her whimper. White heat licked over her skin and set her body shaking. Poppy pressed her hand between her thighs, touching herself as she loved him. Her climax hit, unexpected and hard. She shuddered through it, and, as she did, she tried something she'd been aching to do for years—she let her power go. Cold filled her mouth, licking over his length.

"Hell," he rasped. He arched against her, his fingers digging into her hair, the hard muscles of his torso straining and glorious. There was power in that too, making him come undone and helpless. The essence of him filled her mouth, and she swallowed it down, taking that small part of him into her. She attended him until he grew limp and fell back against a chair with a jagged sigh that spoke of satisfaction. Before she could speak, he was pulling her up and gathering her close.

His chest trembled, and she rested her palm on him. When he spoke, his voice was like rust. "That bit at the end..." He swallowed.

Poppy rested her forehead against his as he traced her

jaw and cheek with a shaking hand. She smiled against his skin. "You liked it." It wasn't a question; she knew him too well to wonder.

"Exceedingly." He nuzzled her neck as he held her. "I missed you."

Poppy's hand fell against his damp chest. "Of that I have no doubt."

They both stilled, and then as if by some agreement, they laughed. He shook with it as he kissed the tip of her nose. His gaze, when he caught hers, danced with a light she had missed so much. He grinned wide, boyish and free. "Now then, let us see how else we can utilize that talent of yours."

Loose limbed with slumberous warmth, Poppy drifted on a cloud of contentment. Dawn was here, and the very idea of it threatened to pull her down into a sea of terror. An unfamiliar sensation that she struggled to avoid for the moment in favor of just being. If only for a little longer. Heavy male legs twined with hers. A strong arm held her close against a wall of muscle and hot skin. The warm cup of Win's palm was against her breast. For years she had awoken in this manner, surrounded by Win. For months she had awoken alone. And though her body was quite used to the sensation of Win, her heart felt fragile as thin ice over deep water.

When he stirred, she turned to meet his gaze. Nearly nose to nose, they studied each other. He'd come to her again and again. Stopping only when they were both too weak to move. And she ached now, in places that had been too long ignored. Even so, the unwelcome morning light lay full upon them now, making her squint as she studied his deep set eyes.

Win's wide mouth quirked. "Shall I speak first then?" His damaged voice was husky and uneven.

Poppy's hand, resting on the small of his tight back, pressed against him. "If you insist." Flutters ran through her belly but she did not lower her gaze.

The cool blue of his eyes turned warm. "I love you."

Her breath caught, and he said it again, against her mouth. "I love you." Moving in that assured, greedy way only a man intent on tupping could, he rolled on to her, making himself at home between her thighs. His lips ghosted over her neck and down to the pendant resting in the hollow of her throat. His teeth clinked on the gold as he took it in his mouth and gave it a light tug just as he used to do. Poppy smiled up at him, and he let it go. "I love you." *All of her.*

The hot crown of his cock found her opening, and he shuddered. She was wet already.

A lazy grin slid over his lips as he eased into her. And in, and in. Until he was fully seated. "I love you, Poppy Lane." His hand glided along her skin, over her arm, and their fingers threaded. He held her hand as he made love to her, in an undulating movement that never paused. She wanted it to last forever.

"Win..." She wrapped her legs around his hips, holding him there.

Win's response fell short as someone pounded on the door. "Bloody—" He bit his bottom lip as if to keep from shouting, then turned his head. "Whoever it is, we are not receiving callers."

Laughter burst from Poppy. "Good lord, Win."

He gave her a repressive look. "Ought I have said we were shagging instead?"

"It might work better."

The insistent knocking returned, followed shortly by Ian's deep voice. "It's rather important, Lane."

"Buggering hell." Win wrenched round, and his voice boomed as he responded. "If you do not leave this instant, I will tear your cods off."

Poppy covered her face with hot hands as she pictured Ian Ranulf standing on the other side of the door. "Just go see what he wants," she said through her fingers.

Inside her, Win's cock twitched in protest. "Not likely." He moved his hips, a delicious glide that had her attention.

"It's about Talent," said Ian through the door.

"Oh, God." Poppy shoved at Win's shoulders, rather like trying to budge a barge for the way he resisted. "Just go." When he frowned down at her, she tucked a lock of his hair behind his ear. "The moment is over, love. I can't do this now. Not with him," she jerked her head toward the door, "out there."

Several raw and rather creative curses left Win's mouth as he slipped free. Poppy felt the loss acutely, but had to smile at his ire. Win pointed a long finger at her. "It is *not* over. Stay there."

Still cursing, he grabbed his trousers and shoved them on before stalking to the door.

Winston wrenched the door open and caught Ian mid-knock. "What is it?" Win wanted nothing more than to slam the door in Ranulf's face and return to Poppy, but he had to ask. "Is Talent ill?"

"No." Ian grimaced. "Not more than he was. Here is the thing—"

Win's hand tightened on the door. "Tell me about it later." He had only so much time before he had to face the day and figure out his bloody fate, and he was going to revel in it.

Ian's brows snapped together. "Look here, Lane—"

"Not right now," Win ground out through his teeth.

They glared at each other for a wild moment in which Win struggled to keep from shouting like a madman. Something in his expression must have registered with Ian, for the man's scowl dissolved, and he finally took in the fact that Win was half dressed. "Ah, I see."

"Just—give me an hour." Win halted and winced. "Two."

He could have sworn Ian's cheeks colored. "I'll go."

"I say," came a feminine voice from the direction of the hall. "Is Poppy in there?"

Win groaned and let his head thunk against the door-frame as Daisy came up behind Ian. He could only thank God that Ian spun around and caught Daisy by the arm. "Later," he said to his wife.

"I only wanted to check if she was truly all right," Daisy protested as he led her back down the corridor.

Ian leaned close and murmured something in her ear. Before Win could see her response, he closed the door on them both. If he got out of this mess with Jones, he was taking Poppy back to their home in short order. He missed their cozy house. With its utter privacy.

A sense of foreboding crept along the back of his neck as he walked back into the bedroom.

Poppy listened to the exchange in the hall and bit her lip to keep from laughing. Ordinarily, she'd have gone and shooed Ian away. But Win had it in hand, leaving her to do as she pleased. Content to do just that, Poppy flopped over on her stomach and hugged the bed. But a thud from below caught her attention. She bent over the side. A small, slim leather notebook lay upon the floor. Win's notebook. He had many of them. The last one she'd seen had been battered and bloody, a ravaged survivor pulled from his pocket after the werewolf had attacked him. Poppy had found a way to get that notebook into Ian Ranulf's hands so that he might have the facts needed to defeat those who'd hurt Win.

The leather was smooth against her palm as she reached down to pick up the notebook. It appeared to have fallen from the little side table by the bed. So then, not hidden away.

This was what she told herself as she opened it. She was outright prying, yes. She did not care. She'd long gone past the point of respectable behavior in regard to him at any rate.

His familiar slanted scrawl across the page made her throat tighten. She'd read his notes before. Win committed every fact to memory, but he liked to write them down as well for, as he'd say, sometimes seeing the story written down cast it in a different light. Those notes were often disjointed, little facts written here and there, interspersed with his musings. But this was different. These words were orderly, a narrative. Her frown grew as she began to read... *From the moment he'd stepped off that train, his life changed completely. And it had been because of a woman...* By the end of the first page, her heart thudded against her breast.

"I wanted you to find it."

The notebook landed on the ground with a slap as she jumped.

Bathed in the morning light, Win stood just inside the room. Anger did not lurk in his gaze, but sorrow, deep and pained. "Just not at this moment."

"You're writing about when we first met." Her cold fingers wound themselves into the sheets. "But it is different. I don't remember events quite in that way."

His lashes lowered, hiding his soul away from her. "It is what really happened. Before."

Before bloody Isley.

"Why write it down, Win?" Bile crept up her throat.

"I wanted you to know."

She went to him, close enough to smell the scent of their lovemaking against his hot skin. Close enough to see the muscle tick at his jaw.

"Why not simply tell me?" Pain and ugliness would come with his answer. Even so, she pressed on. "Why write it all down?"

His shoulders hunched, and in the silence, the sounds of the household drifted up from below.

"Win."

An eternity passed before he lifted his gaze to hers. His voice was ice crunching beneath a boot. "Because I won't be here. And I wanted you to have something to... to remember me by."

She could not breathe, could not move past the numbness taking hold of her limbs. She tried to speak, shuddered, then tried again. "W-what do you mean?"

Still he did not move, as if he too were frozen. His eyes filled, highlighting their winter-blue color, before a single tear spilled over, bumping its way down his ravaged cheek. "Boadicea."

Her breath left in a gust. "The bargain. He's taking your soul regardless of whether we succeed or not."

He didn't need to say a thing. It was written on his skin, in his eyes.

"Why didn't you tell me?" Dimly she heard something crack, the shattering of the lamp glass. Ice cold swirled about her.

He moved then, gathering her in his arms and pressing

her against his warmth. "Stop." He held her tighter. But she could not stop the cold that invaded her soul, nor stop it from slipping out to freeze the room.

"Why, Win?"

His lips brushed her temple. "Saying it aloud would make it real." Then his fingers were in her hair, his cheek pressed hard against hers. "I did not want it to be true."

She couldn't stand it. She needed to move, but he wouldn't let her go. "I will kill him." She pushed against Win's chest to little effect. "Let me go."

"No."

"We are going to meet him, and then I am going to destroy him, Win. I swear to God, I will."

He pulled back far enough to look into her eyes. "You will not." His fingers gripped her tighter. "You will not put yourself in harm's way."

"This is why you did not tell me."

His expression grew implacable. "In part." He leaned closer until they were nose to nose. "I will not have you risk your safety over me."

Seething, Poppy pressed her palms against his chest. "Why is my life so much more valuable than yours?"

"Because of this." His hand slid down to rest gently upon her abdomen. And her heart stopped. Win saw her understanding, and he nodded weakly. "You are my joy, and my purpose. I came alive when I met you." His hand smoothed over her in a whisper of a caress. "But this babe inside of you. That is my legacy. You will protect him. See him grow and bloom."

"Not alone…" She shivered, and he kissed her. Softly. So softly, as though he were cherishing it, memorizing the feel of it. Poppy tore her mouth away. "You will be here. With me. With us."

His eyes traveled over her face, his touch upon her cheek tender. "I will never leave you. Not really."

She squeezed his hands, uncaring if she crushed his fingers. "No! Not in spirit! You will be here. I cannot..." Blood coated her tongue, and she realized she'd bitten her lip. "I cannot do this without you, Win. *I will not*."

His smile was tired, as if he'd already given up. She squeezed him harder, but he did not seem to notice. "Boadicea, not even your force of will can stop everything."

"I can stop this!"

Win gave her a measured look. "Whatever you are thinking, don't."

But she most certainly would. Knowing he wouldn't expect it, she shoved him hard, causing him to stumble back, then she fled into the dressing room.

# *Chapter Thirty-nine*

————— ✿◦✿ —————

**W**in stared at the space Poppy had vacated. That had gone well. "Shit."

The look upon her face had reflected his misery. He ought to let her have her privacy. Only Poppy did not retreat as other ladies might. She fought. That she had closed herself up in the dressing room had his instincts clamoring to go after her. As instinct had kept him alive for years, he followed it now and went to the dressing room door.

"Poppy?"

Not a sound. He tried the handle, unsurprised to find it locked.

"Poppy Lane, open this door and talk to me."

Nothing. Win raked his hands through his hair before slamming them on the door. "Open it, Poppy!"

When she did not answer, fury licked over him. "Right, then," he shouted. "I'm coming in, whether you like it or not." Win smashed against the door, putting his weight into it. Over and over, until the heavy wood creaked. This wasn't the way to do it. Cursing, he stepped back and kicked the thing in.

The scent of Poppy filled the air, subtle, almost ineffable, and yet so familiar it hurt his heart. Something was off here. His heart kicked furiously in his chest. Glints of deep red against the white porcelain sink caught his eye. He was across the room in two strides.

"Jesus Christ!" Red was everywhere. Long, thick strands of red hair, scattered like discarded ribbons, filled the bowl of the sink. His shaking hands grasped at them as if he could turn back time, put them back where they belonged. The silken locks slipped through his fingers. "Jesus!"

"Come now, it isn't that bad, surely."

He spun at the sound of Poppy's voice, and his blood rushed to his toes. The shout he wanted to utter stuck in his throat as he gaped at her. In return, she merely smiled, a small curl of her pink lips, as she leaned against the door frame in the perfect parody of a young man, one leg crossed over the other, her slim hands tucked in loose trouser pockets.

He wanted to smash something. Her hair—all her lovely, long hair—was gone, hacked off until it lay in a short, bright crown against her well-formed skull. Christ, it was shorter than his. "Why?"

She shrugged, her thin shoulders moving beneath the coat of a brown sack suit, an old one of his from when he'd joined the MP. "Last time I faced Isley, it got caught in his claws." She lifted off from the doorjamb in a graceful move. "It was a liability. So I cut it off."

He gnashed his teeth against the helpless tide of anger. He lifted a handful of hair in accusation.

"Have you gone completely mad? To maim yourself

for..." He couldn't speak. Her hair. Hours of burrowing his face into cool and fragrant tresses. Spreading the mass of carnelian, bronze, and copper over her pillow. He might have wept.

Poppy's straight brows snapped together in annoyance. Her face, no longer framed by that mass of red, appeared stronger now, the clean lines of her jaw and nose highlighted, and yet she also looked strangely delicate and exposed.

"Maim myself?" she said. "It is only hair, Win. It will grow back." Again she shrugged. "Though speaking practically, it feels rather nice to be free of it. Lighter."

"Bollocks!" His fist, still clutching her shorn hair, slammed into the sink and a satisfying jolt of pain went up his arm. "Bollocks to this, Poppy!"

"Really, Win, there is no need to shout."

He raked back his own hair for fear of hitting something. "Why the suit?" It was an inane question in the scheme of things but he could not move past the sight.

"I can move better in trousers. Besides," her full lower lip thrust out, "I hate corsets. Especially now."

Befuddled by the act of violence she'd committed to her hair, it took him a bit longer to catch up on her intent. It fully dawned on him then, what she was trying to say. "You think to fight Isley?" He blinked. "When you are with child."

Poppy scowled. "Have you a better plan? For I am not giving him my child. Nor my brother, nor you."

"Have you—" Blood rushed to his head, making his ears ring. "You've lost your bloody mind if you think I'm going along with this."

Poppy crossed her arms over her chest and huffed. "You act as if I am offering a choice."

"And you act as if I'm offering you one! You have a duty to protect our child."

A blast of cold hit him so hard that the looking glass behind him shattered.

"My life is rot!" Poppy shouted. "Utter rot, because of duty." Tears filled her eyes, and she dashed them away. "I almost lost my sisters, lost you, because of bloody, fucking duty."

He tried to touch her, but she swatted at him. "I will not lose you, Win. I cannot see you dragged to hell when I can do something about it."

"You can, sweet," he said, softly now because her pain lanced him through the heart. "You can let me fight him."

Through her tears, she laughed. "Win, you know it won't matter if you destroy him. He will bring you to hell regardless."

"And were you thinking clearly, you'd realize that he'll do the same whether it is you who delivers the blow or me."

She recoiled as if struck. The words he'd thrown back at her hovered between them, taking her hope, and his heart broke for her. Her gaze darted away as if she couldn't bear the sight of him.

"Poppy," he said softly.

But she drew herself up and faced him. The resolve in her expression chilled his blood. "I'll offer myself in your stead."

"No!" He grabbed her. "Do not even think it." *Give me Poppy...*

"Why? He wants me. You know it." Her dark eyes searched his face. "You've known it for some time, haven't you?"

"I know nothing of the sort." But it was a lie, and they

both knew it. His fingers dug into her flesh as if the action could somehow stay time. "And what of our child?"

The warrior look he knew so well stole over her features. "I will make a deal with him to keep the child safe."

He gave her a small shake. "No." It was all slipping away from him, his control, his choices. They were playing right into Jones's hand as if he'd planned it from the start. And perhaps he had. Win ground his teeth. "No, Poppy, no."

Glaring, Poppy pushed him back. "Yes, Win."

He didn't remember moving, but in the space of a breath, her back met with the wall. "Christ, you never listen!"

"It is you who does not listen," she shouted back.

On a curse, he dropped his head to her shoulder and punched the wall. The plaster rattled as he leaned against her and silently raged, his chest lifting and falling in rapid fire.

"I will not let him divide us in anger," he said into her shirt. Her hands grasped his shoulders then, and he snaked an arm about her waist to hold her.

Her lithe body bowed with tension for the space of a heartbeat and then she sagged against him, her hands holding his collar. "Win." She sobbed his name, a plea, a prayer, and a curse. "God, you're right. I don't want that. I don't . . ."

For a long moment, they stood, panting in the resounding silence, then he sank to the floor, pulled her onto his lap and simply held her. His throat ached when he finally spoke. "I didn't know what I had in you. Not truly." Admitting it hurt, but he wondered if anyone really appreciated their life until they faced the end of it. "I loved you. So much. But we drifted apart, didn't we?" And that hurt too.

Her gaze lowered, yet her tight nod confirmed it.

He held her closer, needing to say this, to explain. "You hid what you were—" Poppy stiffened, but he stopped her protest with a brush of his lips to hers. "I'm not laying blame anymore, sweet."

He kissed her again, with reverence, and though she eased, her eyes were glossy with regret as they searched his face. "I was always waiting for the other shoe to drop," she admitted in a ravaged voice. "Waiting for you to find out and never relaxing because of it."

"I know." He sighed and let his forehead rest against hers. "I think I was too, deep down. I never felt everything was completely safe. I think part of me knew I'd gained you through false means."

Her arms came around his neck then, her fingers threading through his hair with such gentleness that he shivered. "Win," she whispered against his mouth, "my heart was always yours, never think otherwise."

They sat, breathing each other in. The feel of her in his arms was a precious thing, and his heart ached at the idea that he could ever let her go. Slowly he opened his eyes and looked at her. God, she was everything to him. His morning, his day, the dreams in which he dwelled at night. His voice threatened to break when he spoke. "Are we in this together, Boadicea?"

A harsh breath left her. The rustle of her coat sounded in the silence as she moved to touch his face. "Always, Win."

He cupped her cheeks and held her fast. "Then be my partner in all things, Poppy. Now, until however long we have." Her skin was silk against his thumbs as he stroked her. "Trust me to find a solution." When she moved to speak, he leaned in, coming nose to nose with her. "Just as I will trust you to look into that Machiavellian mind of yours and make the proper choice between bad and worse."

Her expression was implacable as she looked back at him, and he thought she might protest, but then she reached up and unfastened the chain around her neck. The tiny Isis pendant winked in the light as she moved to wrap it around his neck.

"Poppy," he protested. "I cannot take this."

"Isley cannot stand the symbol," she said, putting it on him despite his objections. "I don't know why, nor will I question it now."

"All the more reason for you to wear it," Winston countered, trying to take it off.

She stayed his hand with a touch. "Please, Win. You ask that we work together. Well, this will make me rest easy."

Damn if he could object to that. Though he tried one last time. "It is a woman's necklace, Pop."

But she only smiled. "And it looks well around your manly neck." He grinned back but her smile suddenly fell. On a ragged sigh, she burrowed against the crook of his neck. "I'm afraid, Win."

He knew what it cost her to admit it. And so he held her secure and let his cheek rest on the silken crown of her head. "I am too, sweeting. But if we can survive this, we can survive anything."

She kissed him then, a tender touch on his neck that cut into his heart with the precision of a sword. "I love you, Winston Hamon Belenus Lane."

A simple declaration. And enough to make the whole of his life worth it. Should he die today, should everything fall apart, he had Poppy's love. A better gift he did not know.

* * *

As soon as Poppy slipped into her bath, Win left her. The fragments of a plan had begun to take shape in his mind. But he needed help.

"I assume you've come up with a solution?" Archer said twenty minutes later, after he'd let both Winston and Ian into his personal library.

Winston looked up from the rolls of papyrus he'd laid out on the high examining table. His insides were in knots, and his muscles bunched with tension. It took all he had to focus on the present and not give in to the rage rolling within. Win gripped the back of his neck, and his aching muscles cried out in protest. "Not quite. Let us call it a start."

He pulled out the item he'd hidden in his pocket and set it before the men.

"Poppy's scarab." Archer looked at the thing as if it might bite him.

Ian, however, laughed. "You nicked it from your wife? And here I thought you were a lawman."

"That was your first mistake, Ranulf," Win replied, "you *thought*."

Archer snorted.

"Hilarious." Ian folded his arms over his chest.

Win let his tight smile slip. "The truth is, I had to steal it. Isley watches Poppy. He's admitted to it."

"Christ." Archer shook his head.

Win eyed them both. "Poppy cannot know my plans because he'll know them. Which means whatever it is I do, I'll have to keep her in the dark." Knowing his wife as he did, the aftermath would not be pretty. By the looks on his friends' faces, they understood that just as well. "Look," he said to Archer, "you are the best reader of hieroglyphics I know. The only one, actually."

"Which puts me in a prime position to help you." Archer stopped alongside Winston and bent his head to survey the scrolls.

Ian strolled over to the table as well. "Good thinking, Lane. Archer adores compliments."

Archer ignored them both in favor of the scroll. "Let us see . . ." His brow furrowed as he read. "This text refers to Apep."

"Yes." Winston moved closer. "He is said to be a demon of darkness and chaos."

"Not a god, precisely," said Archer, "as none worship him. He is more the thing to be feared, the great evil that good must smite."

Win moved to stroke his mustache, only to remember that it was gone. Instead he ran a finger along the scar at his jawbone. It was smooth now, thanks to Archer's neat stitching. "According to this text, Apep can hypnotize a person with his gaze. He is associated with serpents, thunderstorms, and earthquakes and is also known as the soul—"

Archer's head snapped up, and his gaze narrowed on Win. "The eater of souls."

The air grew still between them. Win leaned his hip against the table and watched Archer. "I know you are thinking of what you were becoming." He glanced back at Archer and found him staring back. "Not all soul eaters are evil. I believe you know that too."

With a scowl that said he'd rather not comment, Archer straightened and tapped a finger on the scrolls. "What is all this leading to, Lane?"

God, Win wanted his pipe. If only to have something to do with the restless energy that came over him when he was on the chase. "It's like this. Jones can hypnotize a person with his eyes in some capacity. If his jewelry is anything to go on, he is fond of serpents. And he escaped his prison during an earthquake. All of which are in keeping with Apep's talents."

He pushed his hands into his pockets, excitement making him edgy. "He has the arrogance of a god, not a demon. Jones said the SOS ought to revere him. That gods have tried to defeat him and have failed. I think he yearns to announce who and what he is, but he fears it as well. Because he believes in the power of his name. And I wonder..."

"If he is Apep?" Archer's mouth twisted. "It is rather far-fetched."

"It is. He could be any number of demons." But he *knew* he was correct; the knowledge hummed in his bones. More so, he knew there was a way to prove it if only he could figure out *how.* He turned and studied the drawing of Ra and Apep, depicted as a cat and a snake doing battle.

He glanced down at the scrolls once more as a memory hit him. "Is Apep's name here?" Quickly he scanned the symbols, his heart racing ahead of him. "There." He pointed to a familiar grouping. "Is that it?"

Archer peered down. "Yes. How did you know?"

"Son of a bitch." Win grasped the back of his neck with both hands. "He wore his bloody name on his lapel. In the painting." He pictured Jones's smug grin immortalized in oils and laughed.

Archer grinned too. "I'll put the name on the scarab."

"I'm grasping at straws, and we all know it," Win said. "There is still the matter of the bargain. But any small thing can help."

"Since you have that under control, Lane," Ian interrupted, "I've a favor to ask of you."

"Is this what you came to talk to me about before?" Irritation at the interruption still rode high and colored Win's tone.

Ian coughed, not meeting Win's eyes. "Yes. It's about Talent." Ian's voice was only moderately under control when he spoke again. "Put him to use on this case again. As soon as you can."

"You think he's ready?"

"He has to be." Ian raked a hand through his overlong hair. "If he does not find a way to vent his rage, he will be lost."

Just as Win had been lost before coming back to Poppy. Wincing, he squeezed the bridge of his nose. "I wish I could be of better help to him, but I don't know—" His hand fell to his side, and he stared at the papyrus before him. "They all have a weakness."

"Bloody hell, Lane," said Ian. "What are you going on about now?"

Something surged within Win's chest. He did not want to examine the emotion for fear of chasing the fragile feeling away, but it felt much like hope. Fighting a grin, he turned to Ian. "Where is Talent now?"

Ian's eyes narrowed as he searched Winston's face. "In his room at Ranulf House. Why?"

Win could not answer. Instead he clasped Ian in a hard hug, pounding the lycan's back with one fist. "You're bloody brilliant, Ranulf."

"Well, yes," Ian said as Win let him go and headed toward the door. "But would you mind telling me what brilliance I imparted this go round?"

# *Chapter Forty*

❦

Talent sat in a worn-down leather armchair the color of dried tobacco. He did not greet Winston as he walked into the room, nor did he appear to even notice. Winston knew better. Shoving his hands in his pockets, he strolled near. Talent stared out of the tall window, and the grey London light fell hard on his face, highlighting the lines of fatigue, and the tributaries of pain recently wrought upon him. The only movement in him at all was the quick motion of his hand as he flipped an object over and under each finger before repeating the action.

Win stepped closer. The object was a cross. A crude thing made of iron, it was no more than three inches long. Whether Talent noted Win's study of the cross, or he'd simply grown tired of fiddling with it, was unclear, but he stopped and covered the thing with his hand.

"I might wonder if you've come to gape." Talent turned then, and the coldness in his gaze chilled. "Only I suspect you've been on the other side of that coin too long to do so."

Win leaned against the footboard of the bed. Being

a shifter, the external damage Talent had sustained had healed without scars, but emotional trauma was far crueler. "I've a job for you."

A flicker of interest entered Talent's eyes. "Go on."

"I have to ask it. Are you able?"

In the blink of an eye, Winston found himself staring at himself. The sensation was off-putting, to say the least, but he nodded in satisfaction as Talent shifted back. "It will be dangerous. You may not come out of it."

"Wouldn't be interested if it wasn't."

"Mmm. And are you, then, willing to perform the lowest sort of skullduggery?"

Talent's gaze narrowed, his body growing taut and poised to act. "I'm listening."

Poppy emerged from a bath clean yet worn out. The warm water had soothed her tired muscles and made her crave sleep. But she was hungry. Again. Glancing about, she tentatively settled a hand on her belly. "You are turning me into a glutton."

Tender feeling fluttered across her heart. She hadn't spoken to the little barnacle before now. A smile tugged at her lips. Barnacle. That's what he was, attached to her insides and attached to her. And she would not let him go.

Her hand hovered before drifting down. Later, she could feel this. Later, she could say it, when Isley was captured, and Win...Her vision wavered. He'd asked her to trust in him. She did, but giving up control ate at her. As did the fear. The idea of losing him or her child made her insides heave. A knock on her room door cut through her racing thoughts, and she moved to answer it.

To her surprise, Jack Talent stood at her threshold.

"Mr. Talent. It is good to see you."

He looked well. Healed at least and dressed in a fine linen suit very similar to Winston's. His eyes, however, held shadows and pain. But he offered a tight smile. "Mrs. Lane. I've brought tea."

It was then she noticed the tray he carried.

"I saw the inspector," Talent said as she stepped aside to let him in. "He's downstairs sparring with Ian and Archer."

No doubt to alleviate his tension. Had she any energy, she would be inclined to join them. As it was, however, the sweet, yeasty scent of bread held the greater allure.

"However, he thought that you might be hungry and asked me to look in on you."

She followed Talent to the small sitting area by the hearth and sat as he set out a meal for two.

He caught her looking and hesitated. "May I take tea with you?" The corners of his eyes tensed. "If you'd rather—"

Poppy touched his arm, then drew away when he flinched. "I would enjoy the company, Mr. Talent."

He did not wait for her to pour but did the honors himself, his movements precise and assured. "How do you take it?"

"Right now? With milk and lots of sugar."

"The babe?" he asked with gentle amusement.

"I believe so." Poppy accepted her tea but looked around him. "Are those cream buns?"

Thankfully, Talent did not say a word as he filled her plate with not one but two buns. Bless the man. Poppy gave the offered treats the attention they deserved. Bliss. Utter bliss. She did not care what Talent thought of her; she was going to eat every bun that he did not.

Talent sat on the chair next to hers and quietly sipped his tea as she devoured her food. The silence between them, while not quite awkward, was not entirely peaceful either. They both were too aware of what had happened to Talent.

Licking a bit of cream from the corner of her mouth, Poppy finally spoke. "Mr. Lane tells me you want to be a regulator." It was one of the many things she and Win had discussed before he had slipped out to consult with Archer and Ian, about what he wouldn't yet tell her. But she had to trust him.

Talent's gaze slid away. "I thought to be, yes."

Poppy set down her plate. It was empty anyway. "I think you shall make an excellent Regulator, Mr. Talent."

When he lifted his head in quiet surprise, she spoke on. "Accept the offer and you shall start training Monday morning."

Ye gods but his concealed joy made her flush. She did not know why that would be so, but the room grew decidedly hot. Or perhaps consuming four cream buns in three minutes was not advisable. Her stomach turned, the room swaying a bit.

Oblivious, Talent leaned forward, bracing his forearms on his knees. "You honor me, ma'am." His visage blurred before her eyes, the words he spoke a buzz in her ears. "I can only hope," he said with strangely drawn-out diction, "that you will feel the same come Monday morning."

Ice ran along her skin, and she gripped the arm of her chair. "What have you done?"

He stood, looming, his eyes holding regret. "Nothing I'm proud of." Then he guided her heavy body down to lie upon the couch and slipped a small square of paper into her limp hand. "Do not worry, Mrs. Lane. The chemist assures this won't hurt the baby."

The baby. Their baby. Win. She needed to save them. But her world went black and she could think no more.

# *Chapter Forty-one*

❦

Late as it was, the Victoria Embankment appeared abandoned, peaceful even. Winston's footfall was little more than scuffs along the wide, flat pavers. A warm breeze rustled the leaves of the trees so carefully planted along the path. Before him, the many spires and towers of Westminster Palace pierced the grey sky, and the glowing face of Big Ben stared back like a yellowed, unblinking eye.

He walked past the electric lampposts that ran along the curved wall of the embankment. Their strange, unwavering white light made him see the world clearly. The rippling waters of the Thames reflected those harsh lights and the ones coming from the gaslights upon the distant Westminster Bridge. Above the bridge, the moon hung bright in the mottled sky, the edges of it indistinct beneath the moving clouds.

Though he had many things to worry over, Win took it all in. This was his city, and he loved it well. Dark and strangely beautiful, London was his home. And he might never see it again. He shoved his shaking hands into his pockets and took a deep breath of acrid air. One last and proper taste of the city before he fought for his child's soul, and for his.

The air stirred again, a swirling gust that did not appear to come from any one direction, and then Jones was simply there, standing beneath the garish light of an electric lamp. "I almost wondered if I'd have to hunt you down," he said.

Winston took a step closer. Tonight, Jones wore his own skin, or rather the skin Winston knew him in. His white eyes followed Win's movements in a twitchy sort of way, and Win fought the urge to laugh. Jones was nervous.

"I gave my word that I would be here," Win said. "I do not go back on my word."

Jones leaned one elbow on the high embankment wall. "And yet you have not brought me my son."

"We shall get to that in a moment."

Jones bared his teeth on a growl. "We get to it now!" Before Win's eyes, he seemed to grow taller, broader, less human. "Mary Margaret Ellis kept him from me, and I'll be damned if my daughter continues to do the same."

Winston returned the stare, ignoring the sweat trickling down his collar and the tremor in his back. Part of him wanted to look over his shoulder for fear of seeing Poppy appear before he could get this business done. Instead, he leaned against the embankment wall as Jones had done. "All right," he said. "I'll tell you where he is."

"You most certainly will not!" Poppy said.

They both stood at attention upon hearing Poppy's irate shout. She walked out of the shadows, her dark eyes snapping with fury, her long legs eating up the ground as she advanced. And still dressed as a man.

Win watched her, not daring to look at Jones.

"What on earth have you done to yourself, Poppy Ann?" Jones said with a shocked laugh. Oddly, Jones almost sounded affectionate.

Her straight brows nearly touched. "None of your bloody business." Her gaze swung around to Winston and went ice cold. "You unmitigated bastard. That you would drug me and betray my trust—"

"For our child!" Win snapped. Inside his heart raced with nervous fear, but he could not let it show. "Did you honestly expect me to give up our child for anything on this earth?"

She winced, her face crumbling. "I cannot... I promised not to let my brother come to harm."

Win threw up his hands and made a noise of disgust.

"Be reasonable, Poppy." Jones took a step in her direction. "He is my son."

"So say you."

Jones took another abrupt step closer, and she stiffened, her hand drifting to her side, where no doubt several weapons were stored. Jones paused. "Moira said so too. Do not doubt that."

Winston heard the sorrow in Jones's voice and, for a brief moment, he felt sympathy for the devil. Poppy, however, seemed to suffer no such sentimentality.

"Tragic for you," she snapped.

Flames erupted over Jones's face as he growled. "Then it shall be your child and husband, and I will gladly take them to see you suffer."

"No!" Winston shouted. "I will tell you."

Poppy pulled a blade free. "Another word and I will kill you."

Win's fists bunched, but he didn't move. He dared not overplay his hand now.

Poppy looked away first, her white skin glowing in the moonlight as she studied Jones. "Let us get to the heart of this. Do not pretend that you did not hunt down Win that night fourteen years ago in order to arrange this very moment."

"Of course I did." Jones sneered. "You and yours stole from me, hunted me down as if I were at fault." He stabbed his thumb against his chest. "You imprisoned me."

"Yes." Poppy did not so much as blink, yet she appeared to look down her nose at the demon. Such a perfect Poppy gesture. "And you hate me for it."

Jones flinched as if slapped, but then stood taller. "I want you to suffer."

"Then take me."

"Poppy, no." In two steps, Win was at her side. "Do not do this." He had to make a good show of it, make it appear that he did not want her to suggest this very offer. He grabbed her arm and gave it a small, imploring squeeze.

"You no longer have a say." She shook him off, her strength almost too much. He shot her a look but let go, stepping back. Poppy lifted her brow as she looked at Jones. "Well? Take me and leave Win and my child alone. They aren't what you really want at any rate."

Jones cocked his head. "And my son? I will see him."

She crossed her arms in front of her. "When he is of age, I will give him the option of being introduced to you."

Seconds ticked past. Time in which Winston felt as though his life was ebbing out of him. Everything ached; his muscles were tight with fear and helpless rage. Almost finished now.

"It is a good bargain," Poppy said in a low voice.

Jones's smile was smug. "Yes. It is." His eyes turned white as snow. "Terms."

"My child will not be snuffed out of existence. Win's

soul goes free. In return, you get what you see." She spread her arms wide and willing, before cocking a brow. "I'll need that in writing."

Fire and ice flared in Jones's eyes but he simply drew out another rolled foolscap. "Here. Does that meet with your approval?"

Poppy hesitated, and it seemed that Jones leered over her. Thoughtfully, she rested her knuckles against her chin. "One contract should be to free Win and the child. The other should be for me."

Everything stilled as Jones studied her. Poppy stared back. "I do not trust you."

Jones's teeth flashed in the light. "Nor I you." Watching her, he reached into his pocket and pulled free another contract. "Winston Lane's blood will be needed for this."

Poppy's eyes narrowed. "As I thought." She glanced at Win, and he steeled himself not to react. "Sign it."

"And if I don't?" His voice nearly broke.

"Then our child will be destroyed."

Not looking at either of them, he pricked himself and signed in blood. His eyes burned as he watched the crimson stain of his name spread across the paper. Jones's pale hand came into view. With an elaborate flourish, he pricked his finger and made a sign in black blood. Hieroglyphics. Win glanced at the demon but Jones was already stepping away, his attention on Poppy.

"Now yours."

Poppy accepted the next scroll. With Jones's glare burning into her, Poppy read the contract over. "Quill?"

Jones's nostrils flared as he took another breath and then handed Poppy the same black feather quill that he'd presented to Winston. Poppy took the quill in hand, and Win's heart nearly slammed out of his ribs, his anticipation was so thick. On a sharp curse, he paced away, feeling the weight of Jones's mocking stare with every step. *Steady on. Almost there.*

Poppy pricked her finger, then leaned forward to sign.

"Poppy."

She looked up at Winston's call. Their eyes met, and he swallowed hard. "I . . ."

"Get on with it," snapped Jones.

The red fan of her lashes lowered, and with the selfsame flourish as Jones, she signed. Win sagged against the stone wall as Jones repeated the action. It was done.

"Most excellent," said Jones.

Poppy glared at him, refusing to move closer to Jones's outstretched hand. "Why me?" she asked. "You owe me that much."

"Now that I have you, it is an easy request to make." Jones grinned then, a self-satisfied gesture that had Win aching to smash his face. "My kind does not fear fire, nor earth, but ice?" He chuckled low and malevolently. "Oh how my enemies fear that. With you at my side, there is no one I cannot defeat."

Cool, calculating eyes of deep brown studied Jones. "And if I decide to turn my powers against you?"

A short laugh punctuated the air. "You are bound to me now, daughter. To do as I say." Grinning with glee, Jones held out a hand once more. "Now, my dear, if you'd come with me."

It was Poppy's turn to grin. "I do believe you have been tricked."

It took a moment for Jones to comprehend that the voice coming from Poppy's mouth was that of a man. Jones's white glare went to Win, his lips curling back in a feral grimace before he slowly turned back to Poppy.

The air about her stirred, and then Jack Talent stood smiling before them. "Isn't that correct, Inspector?"

"I believe so, Mr. Talent." Win spoke lightly, but the battle had only just begun.

Jones's thin body swelled and grew. "Then I shall take you to hell with me, Jack Talent."

Talent peered up at him. "Already been, thanks. Besides, you might have my blood but the name on the contract says Poppy Ellis Lane."

"In short,"—Win gave Jones a pleasant smile—"the contract has been forged, and thus is null and void. This one, however,"—he held up the contract absolving Jones from touching him or his child—"is quite valid."

Sharp teeth flashed before a roar of utter outrage tore from Jones's lips. It shook the night and rattled his bones. Then Jones broke free of his mortal body in a burst of fire and smoke, knocking Win and Talent back. Talent hit the pavement hard, his head bouncing against it. He did not get back up. Smoke swirled then coalesced into the form of something that froze Win with terror. It rose to full height, all seven feet of it, as it snarled at them.

*Werewolf.* Win's mind screamed the word as he scrambled back, his body instantly in full-flight mode. It was an illusion. An illusion. The *were's* roar and his hot, fetid breath had Win's body thinking otherwise. Bile rushed up his throat. Win held it down and whipped out the short swords he had strapped beneath the back of his coat. Clutching them in his hands, he rose to face his nightmare.

The *were* pounced. Win leapt to the side, his sword slashing down as he moved. It met with bone, and blood sprayed his face. *Hot, wet. Get away. Run away!* He ignored the command. The *were* howled in pain and rage.

Win hadn't time to move again before the thing lashed out, catching him on the chest. Win flew back several feet, smashing into a lamppost. Stars sparkled before his eyes and he tasted blood.

*Move!*

Win rolled, knife-sharp claws raking the cobbles where he'd lain. Again, Win struck, cutting and swiping with his swords. Teeth snapped before his face, claws gouged his flesh. Oh, how he remembered. His body shook, threatening to break down against his will. Grunting, he kicked the beast in the stomach, flinging it away with all his strength.

The *were* tumbled back then righted with blinding speed. "A fighter now, are you?" Jones's voice was garbled under the guise of the *were*.

Sword hilts held tight in his sweating hands, Win crouched low and ready. "Damn right. Now fight me in your true form." The scarab lay heavy and waiting within his trouser pocket. He only needed the chance to use it. "Or are you afraid, Apep?"

"You dare?" Jones snarled. "You dare speak my sacred name!"

But even as he shouted, the *were* form faltered, becoming grey and wavering until Jones once more stood before him. No longer thin, but bulky with muscle and skin of deep crimson.

Win gripped his weapons. "We are children of Isis, no longer under your spell."

Jones's eyes went to Poppy's charm dangling about Win's neck, exposed now that his shirt was in tatters. "You think Isis will protect you? Stupid Winston Lane."

He flew at Win, a blur of red skin and flashing eyes. The impact jolted through Win and took his breath. Fists pummeled his face, quick, hard explosions of pain. He held onto consciousness by a thread as his shaking hand reached for the scarab in his pocket.

Above him, Apep's eyes burned with crimson fire. "You will beg for relief, Lane, beg to be my slave." And then he stabbed into Win with claws that had grown long and shining black.

Win bellowed, his body bowing against the pain. The claws sank deeper into his flesh, down into his chest. Convulsions hit him, blood filling his mouth as he writhed. Blinding flecks of white burst before his eyes, but not enough to block out the sight of Apep's sharp grin. "This is only the beginning."

No, it was the end. With a shaking hand, Win pushed the scarab toward Apep's bare chest. The scarab vibrated against Win's palm as if it yearned to be free. So close. Win's vision went dim, the pain wrenching through his bones. But the moment before the stone touched Apep's skin, the demon snarled and knocked it away.

A sob of defeat broke from Win's lips, and then the demon twisted his claws deep. White lightning ripped through Win as he bellowed, loud enough that he almost missed the sound of his wife's scream.

Poppy raced along the embankment, the sight of Isley's claws stabbing into Win's thrashing body making her scream and sending a lash of sheer rage through her drug-weakened limbs.

She didn't think, didn't speak. She acted, throwing the full force of her power at Isley. From behind her, the water of the Thames launched up and around her in a wave of freezing water. It knocked into Isley and Win, sending the demon tumbling and Win flopping like a fish upon the ground.

Shit. She pulled the power back as she raced forward, and without pausing, kicked Isley in the head. He skidded farther away from Win, his red limbs flying akimbo. Again, Poppy struck Isley's torso, then his head, taking advantage of the demon's stunned state, moving him away from Win.

She'd got him ten feet away when Isley surged upward on a roar. A meaty fist hit Poppy square upon the cheek. Black pain exploded in her skull. Ducking another hit, she fled to Win as she threw out another punch of power. A wall of thick ice barely formed around her and Win before the blast of the demon's fire struck. The burning heat of the attack melted the wall. Wrenching her hand around, she grabbed a chakram blade from her pocket and threw it. The demon deflected the round, spinning blade with a swipe of his claws, so she sent another wave at him, encasing his upper body in thick, blue ice.

His roar blew back her hair, but she did not flinch. More and more ice surrounded him. She was lowering the Thames in an effort to keep him contained, and he was melting it just as fast. He was almost free. She reached for another blade when Win's voice croaked. "The scarab. His name." Blood trickled from Win's split lip. "He is Apep."

Apep? Understanding lit through her. Apep's name was on the scarab. It could destroy him. She scrambled, slipping on slush, banging her knees as she rose and stumbled toward the small, stone beetle that lay a few feet from the lamppost.

Apep screamed, the sound of crackling ice filling the air. Poppy's hand closed around the scarab. She ran toward Apep and his snarling rage. She snarled too, running at full speed with her breath burning in her throat.

Apep's arm broke free of its icy bonds. He swung his claws as she neared, knowing that one hit would take her head.

"Poppy!" Win's voice, strong with desperation. "Drop!"

So she did, not knowing why, but only that she trusted him. She fell back, hearing the high-pitched whine of a blade flying over the space she had just occupied. Poppy glanced up to see the gold blur of her chakram as it sliced through the trapped demon's arm like a greedy spoon through warm pudding. The severed arm fell to the ground with a thud. Apep screeched as he thrashed, trying to free his remaining arm. Cracks grew, and the ice crumbled from the force.

Heart in her mouth, Poppy called on her remaining strength and leapt up. Apep's arm was nearly free. On a cry borne of desperation, Poppy slammed the scarab against Apep's red chest.

With a flash of light, the scarab came to life, burrowing into his flesh as the demon writhed and shouted. Light filled Apep's eyes and shot from his nostrils and mouth with golden fire. He stared at Poppy, anguish etched in his face. "You were mine too. You could have been like me."

A strange sensation of loss filled her, and then the demon exploded in a burst of smoke and fire.

The explosion sent thick chunks of ice through the air and knocked her and Win down along with it. Apep's final roar rippled through the night. And then he was gone, so abruptly that it almost felt as though Poppy had dreamed the whole thing. Exhaustion hit her in the same instant, and she sank back with a sigh. Her heart beat a steady but hard rhythm in her chest, the strain of using her power weakening her as always.

For a moment, she simply breathed, then Win's boots

came into view. Her eyes traveled up the long length of his lean form until she met his gaze. A greenish tint colored his skin, and beads of perspiration dotted his brow. His hands shook, though she could see his effort to keep them still.

"How did you know who he was?" Her voice was even, despite the shiver of fear that ran through her. Win could have been killed. She hadn't allowed herself to think about that before. The knowledge ran in cold spirals down her back now.

He turned his head, giving her his scarred profile as he examined the small mountain of melting ice before them. A soft breeze lifted the ends of his hair and tossed them around his strong profile. "A little research never hurts one's case."

A flicker of amusement lurked in his eyes when he turned back to her. But she could see how very pale he was and the way he swayed on his feet. "Have you an entire arsenal tucked beneath your shirt, then?"

"Not an entire one," she said, matching his light tone. "I've a few things in my pockets as well."

His lips curled, but the smile was tremulous and hard won. "You're late."

Laughter burst from her, choked and abrupt. "I ought to be. You drugged me, you bastard."

The very notion of his high-handedness had her seeing red. Only the greater part of her could not help but think *bravo, and well done.* For she would have done the same to him, had she thought of it. Win was a shrewd bastard when he wanted to be. That he'd thought to put the drug inside the cream buns had been particularly devious.

She'd been livid when she'd awakened. But, true to his promise not to keep anything from her again, he'd left her a note explaining where he was and how he had to trick Isley. Like a consummate gambler, Win had left so much to chance, but he'd done it with such finesse that her heart swelled with pride.

His breath gurgled. "I thought you might...appreciate...that." Then he fell to his knees.

"Win?" She pushed up, scrambling toward him. Her arms caught him before he hit the ground. She'd forgotten about his wounds. A crimson stain spread out across his ravaged white shirt. "Win!" She ripped the shirt farther open. Holes punctured his flesh and a thick chunk of melting ice was embedded in his right shoulder. "Oh hell."

His lashes fluttered. "It appears that I might need a bit of assistance."

Shaking, she leaned close, resting her hand on the wound and chilling it down. "If you die on me, Winston Lane, I shall kill you."

His lips tilted. "Don't worry, sweeting. I live to thwart you." Then his eyes slid closed.

# *Chapter Forty-two*

❦

One would think after months of convalescing from a werewolf attack, one would at least be accustomed to something so trivial as being impaled by a shard of ice. Well, "one" was not. Win lay on his side and tried not to breathe as he dozed. Despite his haze, a sound at the door brought him to instant attention, every sore and battered muscle screaming in protest.

Someone entered the room. He hoped it was Poppy, but the step was too heavy, and the atmosphere in the room felt off, foreign. Beneath his pillow, his hand curled around the gun he kept there. Heart pounding and his body throbbing with pain, Win remained still. He was too weak to whip about and attack so he had to rely on the element of surprise. The slow footsteps came closer. A buzzing sound filled his ears. His clammy hand held the gun firm.

From beneath lowered lids he watched as a pair of long, trouser-clad legs came into view. It might have been Archer or Ranulf, but they would have announced themselves. Win waited for the man to come a step closer. Gritting his teeth against the pain, he opened his eyes, thrust his gun out, and aimed.

His brother froze, his dark eyes wide and staring.

Win relaxed a fraction. The shock of seeing his brother before him made his chest burn. For the life of him, he couldn't think of a word to say. So he waited, unable to lower his gun before he knew what the man wanted.

"I know you." Oz swallowed, his raised hands shaking as badly as Win's. "You're my . . . Good God, Win. It is you, isn't it?"

Slowly, Win let his arm fall. He did not want to answer, did not want to see his old life collide with this one. But that had already occurred, and Oz was not his father. Win's throat closed tight against the emotion welling up from within. He hadn't allowed himself to think of his brother, the man he'd left behind.

"Oz." His voice came out in a croak.

Oz's jaw worked as he lowered his hands and peered into Win's face. "I thought you were dead. I remember..." He shook his head. "I don't know. I remember you dying. Your name is on the family crypt." It was an accusation full of pain and bewilderment. "And then..." He ran a hand along the back of his neck. "I woke up this morning and knew. Knew you were not dead. Knew where to find you as well." Coal black eyes bored into Win. "How? How is that, Win?"

It took several tries for Winston to find his voice. "I don't know."

Oz drew himself up, his tone becoming stronger, more ducal. "You were here, in London, all this time. Working as a detective. How could you not—" He pressed his lips together. "How could you not come to me? You let me believe you were dead. Why?"

Win took a deep breath and regretted it. "Father disowned me when I married Poppy."

"The merchant's daughter."

Win did not know nor care what Oz thought about Poppy. She was his, and he'd be damned if another Duke of Marchland stood in his way. "I thought you knew. And that you disowned me as well." It was as close to the truth as Win could devise.

Oz sneered, his head snapping back as though Win had spit in his face. "You think so little of me?"

God forgive him. "It was what Father led me to believe." Poppy had been correct; lying to one's family was not nearly as easy as it would seem.

Oz gave a terse nod, then lowered his eyes before raising them once again, cold accusation still there. "We met. At Amy's party. You acted as though you did not know me."

Bloody hell. "I was ashamed." Hell and damnation. "And you did not appear to know me, either."

"Damn it all, Win. You are my brother. But you do not look as you once did. Had I recognized you, I would have…" His mouth snapped shut. "What happened to you?" he said after a moment.

Win sighed. He hadn't the energy to make up a lie for his scars. "My life is different now, Oz."

Silence answered him, and then his brother took another step closer to the bed. "It will be better now. I don't care what Father did or said. You have an estate, funds that I will readily—"

"No."

Oz blinked. "What do you mean? I give these things to you freely. With joy."

Win held his brother's gaze. "I don't want any of it. I

never did. When I said that my life was different, I meant that it was apart from your world. This is the life I want to live." He laughed abruptly, the action sending spears of hot pain through him. "Aside from my current predicament, that is."

Oz tilted his head to frown down at Win. For a moment, he appeared so much like the boy who had taught Win to climb trees and shoot a gun that Win's breath hitched. But the illusion vanished in the face of a duke thoroughly put out. "I will not let this go, Win."

"I beg of you," Win rasped back, "please do."

The dark frown grew. "I don't understand you at all." Oz's gaze slid away, focusing on some spot above Win's shoulders. "Do you not want to know me then?"

Win gripped the bed sheets tightly. "I would be honored to know you again, my brother." He swallowed hard. "I simply ask that you do not bring me back into that world. Winston Lane is not the brother of a duke. He is a detective."

Oz's hand closed over his. "Lord Winston Hamon Belenus Lane can be both."

Win cleared his throat. "We shall see."

"Yes, we shall." Oz's thin lips slanted in a gesture that was disturbingly like Win's own. "You haven't changed, you know."

"Nor you." By God, Win hadn't realized how much he'd missed him.

After Poppy saw Osmond out, she crept back up the stairs and slipped into their bedroom. This time it had been Ian who'd tended Winston. Now with his wounds stitched, treated with ointment, and bandaged, Win lay in the center of the bed they had shared for so many years asleep and peaceful. Sunlight painted his hair in shades of gold and bronze. A morning beard shadowed the hard line of his jaw and made his lips appear softer. He shifted in sleep, and a lock of hair fell over his brow.

Poppy's hands curled around the door handle. She itched to lie next to him and brush back that hair, cup his cheek with her hand, and soothe him. Her gaze settled on the white swath of wrappings that covered one shoulder and coiled around his upper torso. Her ice had done that. In some way, every scar upon his body had been because of her. What would Winston Hamon Belenus Lane have been had he not met Poppy Ellis? A lord. Safe.

Her life would not change. There was always danger. And she could not give it up. She did not want to. On sluggish limbs, she turned to go.

"Poppy Ann Lane." His voice, though rough with exhaustion, commanded capitulation.

She turned back, resting her shoulder against the wall. "Yes, Mr. Lane?"

Purple smudges ran beneath his eyes, exaggerating their winter blue color. His mouth kicked up in a half smile, but it was not an amused smile. "You've never run from anything in your life. Do not tell me you mean to do so now."

But she wanted to. Her body ached as she made herself speak. "When we first met, I thought I knew everything. I thought self-sacrifice, playing the martyr, would somehow ennoble me. Foolish. What is the point of living a life if it is spent in the shadows? And if fate had turned the other way, and I had said no to you, to our life together, then I would have been the worst of fools." The very idea caused her to shiver. "You asked me about choices. Well, I choose you now, Win. I will always choose you." Her fingers tightened on the doorframe. "I will always love you."

His mouth opened as he strove to speak. Poppy held up a hand. "But this is not about my choice. It is about yours." Poppy took a harsh breath, and it hurt. "What if you had your life back the way it was before?" She grimaced. "What if there is someone out there better for you? Safer. *You* could be safe."

Win's eyes narrowed, but he did not move as he studied her. And though her heart threatened to thunder right out of her chest, she held his gaze. After an endless moment, he blinked. His voice was clear when he spoke. "Winston Lane was born when he met Poppy Ellis." His raspy voice grew stronger. "My *life* began with you. And it will end with you. That much I know."

Her breath hitched, his words lancing her heart and making it bleed. "I'm afraid. I-I don't like seeing you in danger."

"Nor I you." Again came that tilting smile of his. "But we shall have to get used to it."

"Will we?" Her insides jumped and twitched. She rubbed her arms as if the motion would calm her.

Win's gaze went to the action. His staid expression did not alter but he held out a hand. "Come here." When she hesitated, he gave her one of his reproachful looks. "If you don't, then I'll have to come to you. And my chest hurts like a bugger."

She had to smile at that. Her skirts whispered in the quiet as she walked forward and stopped by his bed. Win cocked a brow as he looked up at her. "Sit." That imperious voice of his grew emphatic. "On me."

A shocked laugh left her lips. *"Win."*

*"Poppy,"* he answered in the same tone. A smile hovered about his lips.

"Bossy," she muttered. But she loved it when he was,

and he knew it, the canny bastard. Lightness bubbled up within her breast.

His grin became outright when she hauled up her skirts and climbed on to the bed to carefully straddle him. The moment her weight settled on his upper thighs, he groaned and his hands came to her knees. "I needed that."

She laughed again, a breathless sound, for his rough palms trailed up her thighs, catching her attention. "You needed to be crushed on your sickbed?"

His eyes gleamed, no longer winter cold but blazing with heat. "I needed to feel you against me."

How well she understood that need. Something within her had settled the moment she touched him. She sucked in a breath as his thumbs came to rest upon the crease of her hips. Lightly he stroked there as he looked up at her. "Certain events in the past few months have taken years off my life, I'm quite sure."

"Win, don't even joke about that."

"*Years.*" The imperious look came back. "Undo my trousers."

His trousers tented over the rippled expanse of his abdomen. She'd been ignoring it, as he was injured. But Win in a mood could not be ignored. Her fingers shook a little as she obeyed. The first button set the crown of his cock free, and her gut tightened in response. Dark, smooth, and hot. Her knuckles grazed the head as she set about her work. With each give of a button, a bit of her tension released as well. Soon, he was free.

Win sighed in response, and his hands slid up to cup her bottom.

Laid out beneath her, he was a banquet of male beauty, golden skin, and taut muscles. The expanse of his chest lifted and fell with each light breath he took. He'd have a scar there, to match the hash marks covering the left side. A warrior's body, hiding beneath a gentleman's veneer. His ruddy cock lay thick and heavy against his skin.

"Touch me," he whispered.

Heat swirled and nipped her skin as their gazes clashed, and she filled her hand with him. Win twitched within her grasp. He licked his lips quickly. "Stroke me."

"Like this?" she whispered, gliding her palm lightly along his silken length.

He shivered. "Harder. Ah... Now there's a good wife."

Biting her lip to keep from laughing, Poppy stroked him. With a grunt, he wrenched her closer so that she rested on his hips, the tight sac of his cods nestling against her heat. Poppy stifled the need to rub against him. Later. Now was his turn. She worked her hand up and down the length of him, and his eyes closed.

He lay like that for a moment, panting and prone from her attentions, then his eyes opened and settled on her with slumberous contentment. "Not once have I truly regretted the danger, Boadicea." His fingers clenched her bottom. "Never have I felt so alive as when I have faced death and known that you would be there waiting for me should I defeat it."

Poppy searched his face, taking in the ragged scars, and the wild heat and the joy in his eyes. Her heart leapt within her breast as she smiled. "It is always going to be like this, isn't it?"

His grin was slow to unfurl, but when it did, it was wicked. "What is?"

He knew perfectly well, but she told him anyway.

"You craving danger, seeking it out." Gently, she kissed his mouth before pulling back to look at him. "Somehow, I fear you are going to be difficult to manage, Mr. Lane."

"Oh, extremely—" He chuffed out a breath when she gave him a decadent squeeze, "difficult." He rallied and met her eyes once again. His voice turned to smoke and sand. "Afraid, Mrs. Lane?"

"Afraid?" She swirled her thumb around his crown, eliciting a gasp. "I can hardly wait."

# *Epilogue*

---

Jack preferred darkness now. It soothed. Muted the harsh angles of reality. In darkness, he did not have to fear talking to others or trying to pretend that he was not broken. In darkness, he could sit. And watch.

Crouched on the edge of a roof, the whole of London lay out before him. The round dome of St. Peter's and the endless chimneys tucked between the roof peaks. Smoke drifted up from those chimneys, black even against the night sky. Thousands of funnels of smoke lifting to the heavens, like souls leaving the earth. Yet his attention was focused on the window below him. A rectangle of golden light, a small patch of room—a table before the window, the thick rug upon the floor...and *her*. Light flickered as she walked by. Graceful limbs, flowing hair and swaying skirts. His gut clenched with pain. And yet, like the dark, the fluid way in which she moved soothed him.

So he watched. And she never knew that he was there. Every night, watching for just one brief glimpse before slipping away into the darkness. And she would never know.

# THE DISH

*Where authors give you the inside scoop!*

*From the desk of Kristen Callihan*

Dear Reader,

I write books set in the Victorian era. Usually we don't see women with careers in historical romance, but one of the best things about exploring this "other" London in my Darkest London series is that my heroines can lead atypical lives.

In WINTERBLAZE, Poppy Ellis Lane is not only a quiet bookseller and loving wife, she's also part of an organization dedicated to keeping the populace of London in the dark about supernatural beasts that roam the streets—a discovery that comes as quite a shock to her husband, Police Inspector Winston Lane.

Now pregnant, Poppy Lane develops a craving for all things baked, but most especially fresh breads. Being hard-working, however, Poppy has little time or patience for complicated baking—an inclination I share! Popovers are a great compromise, as they are ridiculously easy to make and ridiculously good.

## Poppy's Popovers (yields about 6 popovers)

**You'll need:**

- 1 cup all-purpose flour
- 2 eggs

- 1 cup milk
- 1/2 teaspoon salt

Topping (optional)

- 1/2 cup sugar
- 1 teaspoon ground cinnamon
- a dash of cayenne pepper (to taste)
- 4 tablespoons melted butter

### Directions

1. Preheat oven to 450 degrees F. Spray muffin tin with nonstick spray or butter and sprinkle with flour. (I like the spray for the easy factor.)
2. In a bowl, begin to whisk eggs; add in flour, milk, and salt, and beat until it just turns smooth. Do not over-beat; your popovers will be resentful and tough if you do! Fill up each muffin cup until halfway full–the popovers are going to rise. (Like, a *lot*.)
3. Bake for 20 minutes at 450 degrees F, then lower oven temperature to 350 degrees F and bake 20 minutes more, until golden brown and puffy.
4. Meanwhile, for topping, mix the sugar, cinnamon, and dash of cayenne pepper—this is hot stuff and you only want a hint of it—in a shallow bowl and stir until combined. Melt butter in another bowl and set aside.
5. Remove popovers from the muffin pan, being careful not to puncture them. Then brush with melted butter and roll them in the sugar mix, shaking off the excess. Serve immediately.

Inspector Lane likes to add a dollop of raspberry jam and feed them to his wife in the comfort of their bed.

He claims they make Poppy quite agreeable…*Ahem.* You, however, might like to enjoy them with a cup of tea and a good book!

# FIRELIGHT

### *London, 1881*

### Once the flames are ignited . . .

Miranda Ellis is a woman tormented. Plagued since birth by a strange and powerful gift, she has spent her entire life struggling to control her exceptional abilities. Yet one innocent but irreversible mistake has left her family's fortune decimated and forced her to wed London's most nefarious nobleman.

### They will burn for eternity . . .

Lord Benjamin Archer is no ordinary man. Doomed to hide his disfigured face behind masks, Archer knows it's selfish to take Miranda as his bride. Yet he can't help being drawn to the flame-haired beauty whose touch sparks a passion he hasn't felt in a lifetime. When Archer is accused of a series of gruesome murders, he gives in to the beastly nature he has fought so hard to hide from the world. But the curse that haunts him cannot be denied. Now, to save his soul, Miranda will enter a world of dark magic and darker intrigue. For only she can see the man hiding behind the mask.

'Debut author Callihan pens a compelling Victorian paranormal with heart and soul'
*Publishers Weekly*

# MOONGLOW

**Once the seeds of desire are sown . . .**

Finally free of her suffocating marriage, widow Daisy Ellis
Craigmore is ready to embrace the pleasures of life that
have long been denied her. Yet her newfound freedom is
short lived. A string of unexplained murders has brought
danger to Daisy's door, forcing her to turn to the most
unlikely of saviours . . .

**Their growing passion knows no bounds . . .**

Ian Ranulf, the Marquis of Northrup, has spent lifetimes
hiding his primal nature from London society. But now a
vicious killer threatens to expose his secrets. Ian must step
out of the shadows and protect the beautiful, fearless Daisy,
who awakens in him desires he thought long dead. As their
quest to unmask the villain draws them closer together,
Daisy has no choice but to reveal her own startling secret,
and Ian must face the undeniable truth: Losing his heart to
Daisy may be the only way to save his soul.

'A sizzling paranormal with dark history and explosive
magic! Callihan is an impressive new talent'
Larissa Ione

# SHADOWDANCE

Jack Talent is tormented by the demons of his past. Though Jack loves his position in the SOS, he cannot forget what was done to him. And so he hunts down the remaining demons that tortured him and metes out his own brand of justice as the Bishop of Charing Cross. The only thing that soothes him is his secret visits to fellow agent Mary Chase. But while something about Mary calms him, she is also his greatest torment, for she is a reminder of his worst crime – the night he lost his soul by taking her human life.

Mary Chase is now free. After years of service to the Ghosts in the Machine, she now assists the head of the SOS and is finally enjoying life – except for the one thorn in her side: Jack Talent. The temperamental shifter unsettles her and awakens a need she's never felt before. But when a copycat killer begins to mimic the Bishop's signature and Jack is assigned to the case, Mary volunteers to join him, eager to unravel Jack's mysterious façade. Can Jack protect his secret – and his heart – from the one woman who could be his ultimate ruin?

Do you love fiction with a supernatural twist?

Want the chance to hear news about your favourite authors (and the chance to win free books)?

Keri Arthur
S. G. Browne
P.C. Cast
Christine Feehan
Jacquelyn Frank
Larissa Ione
Darynda Jones
Sherrilyn Kenyon
Jackie Kessler
Jayne Ann Krentz and Jayne Castle
Martin Millar
Kat Richardson
J.R. Ward
David Wellington
Laura Wright

**Then visit the Piatkus website and blog**
www.piatkus.co.uk | www.piatkusbooks.net

**And follow us on Facebook and Twitter**
www.facebook.com/piatkusfiction | www.twitter.com/piatkusbooks

piatkus